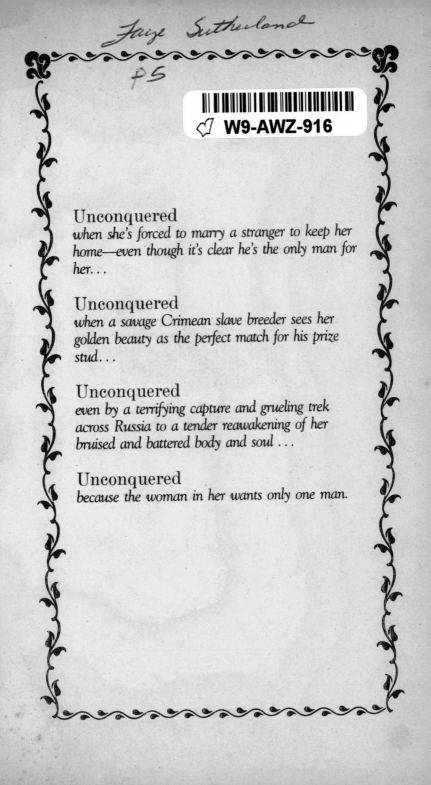

Unconquered
when she's forced to marry a stranger to keep her home—even though it's clear he's the only man for her...

Unconquered
when a savage Crimean slave breeder sees her golden beauty as the perfect match for his prize stud...

Unconquered
even by a terrifying capture and grueling trek across Russia to a tender reawakening of her bruised and battered body and soul ...

Unconquered
because the woman in her wants only one man.

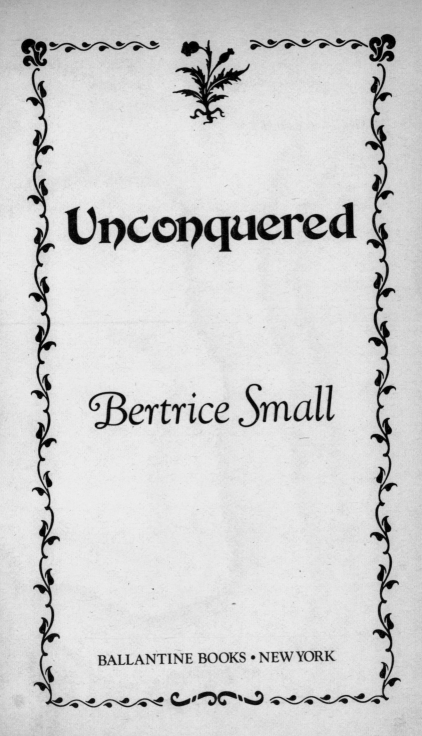

Unconquered

Bertrice Small

BALLANTINE BOOKS • NEW YORK

Library of Congress Catalog Card Number: 81-66654

ISBN 0-345-28712-6

Manufactured in the United States of America

First Ballantine Books Edition: January 1982

1 2 3 4 5 6 7 8 9 10

For all those people
for whom
there is but one love...

Contents

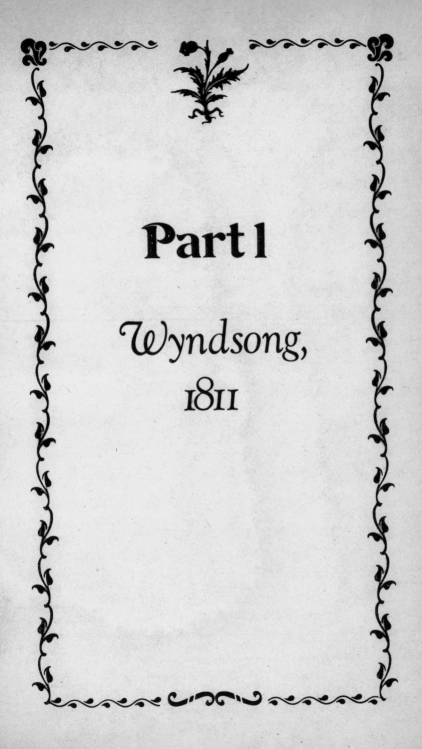

Part 1

Wyndsong,
1811

❧ Chapter 1 ❧

"Y ou do realize," said Lord Palmerston slowly, "that what you and I are doing could be considered treason by both of our governments? I am, you know, considered somewhat of a maverick because I prefer direct action to all the talk that goes on in Parliament and His Majesty's cabinet." He paused for a moment to contemplate the deep red claret in his glass. The etched Waterford crystal sparkled bloody crimson with firelight and wine reflecting onto Lord Palmerston's handsome face. Outside, the midnight silence was broken by the soft hiss of the rising wind, bringing in streamers of fog from the coast. "Nevertheless," continued Henry Temple, Lord Palmerston, "I believe, Captain Dunham, as do the interests you represent, that our real enemy in this situation is Napoleon, not each other. *Napoleon must be destroyed!*"

Jared Dunham turned away from the window, and walked back to the fireplace. The young man was lean, dark and very tall. He was considerably taller than the other man, and Henry Temple was six feet tall. Jared's eyes were an odd dark green color and his eyelids were heavy, giving the impression of always being half-closed, weighed down by their thick, dark lashes. His long, thin nose and

3

narrow lips helped give an impression of sardonic amusement. He had big, elegant hands with well-pared, rounded nails. They were strong hands.

Seating himself in one of the two tapestried wing chairs set before the cheerful blaze, Jared leaned forward to face Lord Palmerston, the English secretary for war. "And if you would successfully attack the enemy at your throat, m'lord, you would prefer not to have another enemy at your back. Am I correct?"

"Absolutely!" Lord Palmerston stated with complete candor.

A chill smile lifted the corners of the American's mouth, not quite reaching his bottle-green eyes. "By God, sir, you are honest!"

"We need each other, Captain," was the frank reply. "Your country may be independent of England these last twenty years, but you cannot deny your roots. Your names are English, your styles of furniture and clothing, your very government is much like ours without, of course, King George. You cannot deny the bond between us. Even you, if my information is correct, are due to inherit an original English land grant and title one day."

"It will be quite some time before I inherit, m'lord. My cousin, Thomas Dunham, eighth lord of Wyndsong Island, is in excellent health, God be praised! I have no desire to be settled at this point in my life." He paused a moment, and then continued: "America must have a market for her goods, and England gives us that market, as well as the necessities and luxuries our society requires.

"We have already rid ourselves of the French by purchasing the vast Louisiana Territory, but in doing so we New Englanders have allowed ourselves to be outnumbered by a group of enthusiastic young hotheads who, having grown up on exaggerated tales of how we whupped the English in '76, are now spoiling for a fight.

"As a man of business, I disapprove of war. Oh, I can make a great deal of money running your blockade, but in the end we both lose for we cannot get enough ships through the blockades to satisfy the demands on either side. Right now there is cotton rotting on the docks of Savannah and Charleston that your factories desperately need. Your weavers are working only three days each week, and you have riots by the unemployed. The situation in both our countries is appalling."

Henry Temple nodded agreement, but Jared Dunham had not finished.

"Yes, Lord Palmerston," he went on, "America and England need each other very much, and those of us who see it clearly will work with you—secretly—to help destroy our common enemy, Bonaparte! We want no foreigners in our government, and you English cannot fight a war on two continents right now."

"However, I am instructed by Mr. John Quincy Adams to tell you that your Orders in Council forbidding America's trade with other countries unless we first stop in England or another British port must be canceled. It is a supreme piece of arrogance! We are a free nation, sir!"

Henry Temple, Lord Palmerston, sighed. The Orders in Council had been an extremely high-handed and desperate move by the English Parliament. "I am doing what I can," he replied, "but we also have our share of hotheads in both Commons and Lords. Most of them have never held a sword or a pistol or seen battle, but all are more knowledgeable than either you or I. They *still* think of your victory over us as cheeky colonial luck. Until these gentlemen can be convinced that our fortunes are bound together, I, too, will have a rough road to travel."

The American nodded. "I am off to Prussia and then St. Petersburg in a few days. Neither Frederick Wilhelm nor Tzar Alexander is an enthusiastic ally of Napoleon's. I will see if my message of possible Anglo-American cooperation can undermine those alliances further. You have to admire the Corsican though. He's whipped all of Europe into almost one piece."

"Yes, an arrow aimed at England's heart," replied Lord Palmerston with savage hatred in his voice. "If he overcomes us, Yankee, he'll quickly be across the seas and after you."

Jared Dunham laughed, but the sound was more harsh than mirthful. "I am more well-aware than you, sir, that Napoleon sold us his Louisiana territories because he very much needed the gold America paid him in order to pay his troops. He could also not afford to garrison such a vast area peopled mostly with English-speaking Americans, and wild red Indians. Even the French-speaking Creoles of New Orleans are more American than French. They are, after all, the relatives of the *Ancient Regime* wiped out by the revolution that helped to bring Napoleon to power. I know that if the emperor thought he could have both American gold and American territory he would take them. He cannot though, and he would do well to remember the outcome of America's war with England."

"Damn me, if you're not direct and to the point, sir!"

"A distinctly American trait, m'lord."

"By God, Yankee, I like you!" replied Lord Palmerston. "I suspect we will do quite well together. You have already done quite well for a colonial," he chuckled, leaning forward and refilling his guest's glass from the decanter at his elbow. "I must congratulate you on your election to White's. It is quite a first for them. Not only an American, but one who earns his own keep! I am surprised the walls didn't come crashing down."

"Yes," Jared smiled now. He liked Lord Palmerston's sense of humor. "I understand that I am one of the very few Americans ever admitted to that sacred grove."

Palmerston laughed. "True, Yankee, but you realize, of course, that a true gentleman's riches are supposed to just be there. No matter that too many of our *gentlemen* are badly debt-ridden, and quite to let in the pockets, they remain nonetheless unsullied by work. You must have powerful friends, Yankee."

"If I am now a member of White's it is because you wanted it so, m'lord, so let us not fence with one another, and my name is Jared, not 'Yankee.'"

"And I am Henry, Jared. If our mission is to succeed you must associate with the right people here in London. It would be odd indeed if we were seen together without some obvious, harmless connection. Your cousin, Sir Richard of Dunham Hall, was a good starting point, and then there is your eventual inheritance from the current lord of Wyndsong Manor."

"And, of course," remarked Jared wryly, "my very full purse."

"Noted reverently by the mamas of every fledgling making her debut this season," chuckled Lord Palmerston.

"Good God, no! I am afraid I shall be a great disappointment to the mamas, Henry. I enjoy the bachelor life too much to settle down yet. A skillful divertissement, yes, but a wife? No, thank you!"

"I understand your cousin, Lord Thomas, is lately arrived from America with his wife and two daughters. Have you called on them yet? I hear one of his girls is pure perfection, and already settling the gentlemen of the ton to poetry."

"I only know Thomas Dunham," replied Jared. "I have never even been to Wyndsong Manor Island, nor have I met his family. I believe he has twin daughters, but I know nothing of them, and I have no time right now for giggling debutantes." He drained his glass, and abruptly changed the subject. "I'm after timbermasts in the Baltic. I assume England can use some."

"Lord, yes! Napoleon may be superior to us on the land right now, but England still controls the seas. Unfortunately the only decent timbermasts in quantity come from the Baltic area."

"I'll see what I can do, Henry."

"Will you be back in England afterwards?"

"No. I'll go directly home from Russia. You see I am expected to be a visible patriot also, and so as soon as I get home I must take my Baltimore clipper out on patrol. I remove impressed American seamen from English ships."

"Do you indeed?" drawled Lord Palmerston.

"I do," and Jared Dunham laughed. "Sometimes I wonder if the whole world has not gone mad, Henry. Here I am working as an undercover agent for my government in cooperation with your government, and then upon finishing my mission here in Europe I shall hurry home to do battle with the British navy. You don't think that slightly mad?"

Henry Temple was forced to join his American guest in genuine laughter. "You certainly have a more unique viewpoint than I do, Jared. It is all madness, but that is due to Napoleon, and his insatiable desire to be emperor of the world. Once we have destroyed him all will be well again between us. You wait and see, my Yankee friend. Wait and see!"

The two men soon took leave of one another. Lord Palmerston slipped first from the private room in White's Club where they had been meeting, and Jared Dunham departed minutes later.

As he rode in his carriage, Jared felt along the velvet seat for the flat jeweler's case he had tossed inside earlier that evening. It contained a diamond bracelet of the first quality, his going-away present to Gillian. He knew she would be disappointed, for she was expecting a great deal more than a bracelet. She was expecting something he could not give her.

Gillian expected a declaration of his intentions once she was widowed, an event that seemed imminent, but he had no intention of marrying—at least not yet and certainly not Gillian. Gillian Abbott had slept with half the fashionable and unfashionable bucks in London, and she assumed he didn't know it. He would enjoy her favors this one last time, proffer his gift, and bid her farewell, explaining that he must return to America. The diamond bracelet should soothe her. He had no illusions about why Gillian Abbott wanted to marry him. Jared Dunham was a wealthy man.

He might never have been, had it not been for the foresight of his maternal grandmother. Sarah Lightbody loved all her grandchildren, but realized objectively that only one of them, Jared, had the need for her wealth.

Her daughter Elizabeth had three children, and although she loved them equally, her stern husband, John Dunham—a pious hypocrite if Sarah Lightbody had ever seen one—was always singling out his younger son, Jared, for abuse.

At first Sarah Lightbody had not understood the reasons for her son-in-law's behavior. It bordered on the cruel. Jared was a handsome boy. Indeed, he and Jonathan, his elder brother, were identical in looks. Jared was well mannered, and highly intelligent, yet if the two boys were caught misbehaving it was always Jared who was blamed and beaten, Jonathan let off with a warning. Jared was criticized for the very things Jonathan was praised for. And then one day, Sarah Lightbody suddenly realized the reason. There could be only one Dunham heir, and John thought that if he could break Jared's spirit he would protect Jonathan's inheritance and position. Then, when Jonathan took over the Dunham shipyards, he would have an obedient and underpaid clerk in Jared.

Fortunately, the brothers' ambitions were not similar. Jonathan had the Dunhams' love of shipbuilding, and was a skillful, inventive ship designer. Jared, however, was a merchant-adventurer like his Lightbody relations. He found that making money was the supreme game. He enjoyed pitting his wily mind against odds and winning. His instincts were excellent and he never seemed to lose.

Because Sarah Lightbody's home and heart were always available to Jared, she was the one to whom he turned. The one who was always honored with his confidences and his dreams. In his youth he had never complained of his father's unfair treatment, bearing all stoically, even when his grandmother was tempted to take a poker to her coldhearted son-in-law's head. Sarah had never understood her daughter's love for the man.

When Sarah Lightbody was close to death she made a will. Then she called Jared to her side, and told him what she had done. He had been astounded, then grateful, and had made no foolish protestations. She could see his subtle mind already working on his inheritance.

"Invest and reinvest, as I've taught you," she said to him. "Keep an ace or two up your sleeve, boy, and remember to always have a rainy-day fund."

He nodded. "I'll never leave myself short, Gram. You know, of course, that *he'll* try and get his hands on your money. I'm not yet twenty-one."

"You will be in a few months, boy, and until then your uncle and my lawyers will help you keep him at bay. Hold your ground, Jared. He'll cry disaster, but I know for a fact that the Dunham shipyards have never been in better shape. Don't let him fool you. My fortune is meant to free you from him."

"He wants me to marry Chastity Brewster," said Jared.

"She's not right for you, boy! You'll need a creature of fire to hold your interest. Tell me, what do you want to do right now?"

"Travel. Study. I want to go to Europe. I want to see what they want in the way of American goods, and what they have to offer us in return. I want to learn something about the Far East. I think there's a helluva trade to be had from China, and you can bet that the English will be there first if there is."

"Aye," the old woman said, her eyes misting with dreams there was no time to fulfill. "There's a great age coming for this country, and damnation! I wish I were going to be here for it!"

She had died peacefully in her sleep several weeks later, and when the news of his inheritance was made known, Jared's father tried to claim the fortune for his shipyards.

"You're underage," he said coldly, ignoring the fact that his son's coming of age was but a few weeks away. "Therefore it is up to me to administer your money. What could you possibly know of investment? You would squander it."

"And just how do you plan to administer my money?" demanded Jared just as coldly.

Jonathan stood back, seeing the clash coming.

"I don't have to answer the questions of a stripling," was John Dunham's icy reply.

"Not one penny, Father," pronounced his son. "I will not give you so much as a pennypiece for your yards. It's mine, *all* mine. Besides, you don't need it."

"You are a Dunham!" thundered John. "The shipyards are our life!"

"*Not mine!* My ambitions lie elsewhere, and thanks to Grandmother Lightbody's generosity I can now be my own man—free of your damned shipyards, and free of you! Touch one cent of my inheritance and I'll burn your shipyards down around your ears!"

"And I'll help him," Jonathan spoke up, astonishing his father.

John Dunham's face puffed up like a blowfish, and he grew beet-red.

"We don't need Jared's money, Father," said Jonathan, soothing the older man. "Look at it from my point of view. If you invest his money in the family business then we are beholden to him, and I do not want that. You have my baby son John, after me, as heir. Let Jared go his own way."

Jared won, and immediately following his twenty-first birthday, he sailed for Europe.

He stayed several years, first studying at Cambridge, and then

getting polish in London. He was never idle. He made discreet
investments, reaped his profits, and then reinvested. He had an
uncanny knack, and his London friends nicknamed him the Golden
Yankee. It was a sport among the bon ton to try and find out where
Jared Dunham was placing his next investment so they might place
their money where he did. He traveled in the best circles, and though
pursued at every turn, enjoyed his freedom and remained single. He
bought himself an elegant townhouse on a small, fashionable square
near Greene Park which was furnished in excellent taste and staffed
with a core of well-trained servants. For the next several years Jared
Dunham then traveled back and forth between America and England,
despite the problems involved between the two countries, and
France. When he was not in residence in London the house was
managed by his very competent secretary, Roger Bramwell, a former
American naval officer.

Jared's first return to Plymouth, Massachusetts, found the peoples
of New England in an uproar over the Louisiana Purchase. Though a
Federalist like his father and brother, Jared Dunham didn't believe as
they did that expansion west would subordinate New England's
commercial interests to the agricultural South. Rather he saw a
greater market for his goods. What bothered the politicians and
bankers, he believed, was the definite possibility of losing their
political superiority, and clout; and this was, of course, a serious
consideration.

The peoples of the East were different from their southern and
western counterparts. The owner of a vast plantation scarcely held
the same views or had the same interests as a Massachusetts
merchant prince; but then *his* views were also quite different from
those of a fur trapping mountain man. Jared saw no serious conflict,
although other Federalists did.

In Europe war had again broken out. England constantly agitated
in St. Petersburg, Vienna, and Berlin against the French emperor,
trying to persuade Tzar Alexander, Emperor Francis, and King
Frederick Wilhelm to join in a common alliance against Bonaparte.
None of these leaders would listen, hoping perhaps that if they

remained neutral, the French would not deign to notice them, and go away. Besides the French army seemed unbeatable although Britain still dominated the seas, a fact that rankled Bonaparte. Still, mid-Europe was controlled mostly from the land and not the seas, so the English were of little help.

When England successfully withstood the combined French and Spanish navies at the Battle of Trafalgar, Napoleon next resorted to an economic war against his greatest enemy. From Berlin he issued a decree ordering the seizure of all British goods in his and his allies' territory and forbidding English ships entry from his and all allied ports. Napoleon believed that France could produce all the goods previously supplied by England; and the continent's supplies of non-European articles would be delivered by neutral nations, primarily the United States.

England was quick to act in response to the Berlin Decree with their own Orders in Council. Neutral vessels were forbidden from stopping at ports from which the British were excluded unless they first stopped at British ports to take on consignments of British goods.

Napoleon's next move was to declare that any neutral ship obeying the Orders in Council would be subject to confiscation, and, indeed, many American ships were seized. Enough of them, however, got through the various blockades, and on the whole American merchant interests prospered extremely well, Jared Dunham among them.

By the beginning of the year 1807 he owned five trading vessels. One was off in the Far East seeking spices, teas, ivory, and jewels. The other four he kept plying the Atlantic, and the Caribbean. Fat bribes usually silenced any overzealous French officials, for the French were no longer as strong in the Caribbean area.

Jared Dunham saw the handwriting on the wall, however. War was coming as sure as spring, and he had no desire to lose his ships to anyone else. So far he had managed to keep the good will of the English, evade the French, and, by running his Baltimore clipper at his own personal expense, to rescue enough impressed seamen to appear an obvious patriot and mask his far more dangerous missions.

If governments were run, he thought irritably, more like businesses, there would be fewer problems; but alas, egos and personalities were always taking over governments.

Jared Dunham's carriage pulled up before the Abbott town house. Telling his driver to wait, he entered the mansion. His cloak taken, he was escorted upstairs by Gillian's maid.

"Darling!" Gillian greeted him from her bed with outstretched arms. "I didn't think you were coming tonight."

He kissed her hand, wondering why she seemed so nervous, and noted the artful way in which she clutched the silken sheets to her naked breasts. "I came to say good-bye, my dear."

"Why are you joking, Jared?"

"I am returning to America shortly."

She pouted adorably, and shook her dark red curls at him. "You can't! I won't let you go, my darling!" He let her pull him onto her bed, inhaling the musky perfume she always wore. "Oh, Jared!" she whispered huskily. "Abbott cannot last much longer, and when he is gone ... Oh, darling, we are so good together!"

He untangled her from his neck, and said in an amused tone, "If we are so good together, Gillian, then why do you find it necessary to take other lovers? I really do insist on fidelity from my mistresses, at least while I keep them. And I have kept you very well indeed, Gillian."

"Jared!" She tried looking hurt, but as she realized that she was having no effect on him, her topaz eyes narrowed dangerously and she hissed at him. "How dare you accuse me of such a thing!"

His mouth twitched. "Gillian, my dear, your rooms stink of bay rum. It is certainly not your scent, nor is it mine. Therefore I conclude that you have been entertaining another gentleman. Since I came only to bring you this token of my admiration, and to bid you farewell, you are quite free to continue as before." He casually flipped the jeweler's case at her, stood up, and turned toward the door.

"*Jared!*" Her voice held a pleading note.

He turned back, and saw that she had lowered the silk sheet to expose her magnificent breasts. He remembered the pleasure they had given him. Seeing him hesitate, she murmured, "There really is no one but you, my darling."

Vanity urged him to believe, but then he caught sight of a rumpled gentleman's cravat lying on the arm of her chaise longue. "Goodbye, Gillian," he said coldly.

Striding purposefully down the stairs, he called for his cape, and left the Abbott town house.

❧ Chapter 2 ❧

O
h, Papa!'' Amanda Dunham's cornflower-blue eyes filled with tears, and her blond ringlets quivered. "Must we really leave London now?''

Thomas Dunham regarded his younger daughter with amusement. Amanda was so predictably like her mother. As he had been dealing successfully with Dorothea for the past twenty years he felt little challenge in dealing with Amanda now. "I'm afraid so, puss," he said firmly. "If we don't leave now we will be forced to either stay the winter in England at a time when things are not good between our countries, or else make an uncomfortable, very likely stormy crossing.''

"Oh, let us stay for the winter! Please! Please! Please!'' Amanda danced around her father, childlike. "Adrian says there are wonderful skating parties at Swynford Hall on the lake, and at Christmas the mummers and carolers go from door to door. There is a huge Yule log, wonderful wassail, plum puddings, and roast goose! Oh, Papa, let us stay! *Please!*''

"Oh, Mandy! Don't be such a spoiled little fool!'' came a sharp voice, and the voice's owner emerged from the shadows where she

15

had been sitting on the window seat. "Papa must return to Wyndsong. His obligations are there, and on the chance that your social
rounds have kept you from noticing, things are not particularly
cordial between England and America at the moment. Papa brought
us to London as a treat, but we are better off going home now."

"Miranda!" wailed Amanda Dunham. "How can you be so cruel?
You know the depth of my feelings for Adrian!"

"Fiddlesticks!" said Miranda Dunham sharply. "You are always
in love with one man or another, and you have been since we were
twelve. You didn't want to leave Wyndsong several months ago
because you believed yourself in love with Robert Gardiner—or was
it Peter Sylvester? In the time we've been in England you've had a
tendresse for at least six young men. Lord Swynford is only your
current beau."

Amanda Dunham burst into tears and flung herself into her
mother's lap, sobbing. "Miranda, Miranda," scolded Dorothea
Dunham gently. "You must not be so impatient with your twin."

Miranda made a derisive sound and clamped her lips together, a
gesture that made her father chuckle. Twin daughters, he thought, as
he had so often. My only legitimate descendants, and they don't
appear even to be related, let alone twins. Amanda was petite,
dimpled, and round, like her Dutch-American mother, a pink-and-
white feminine confection with large blue eyes and daffodil yellow
hair. She was gentle, and fairly simple, a fluffy creature who would
make a charming wife, a loving mother. He understood Amanda, as
he had always understood her mother.

He was not so sure about Miranda, the elder twin. She was a far
more complex creature, a quicksilver girl of fire. Born two hours
before her younger sister, at five-feet-eight, four inches taller than
Amanda. A coltish girl, Miranda was more angles than curves. The
curves, he suspected, would come later on.

Amanda's face was round, but Miranda's was heart-shaped with
high cheekbones, a straight, elegant nose, a wide, lush mouth, and a
small, determined chin with a little cleft. Her blue-green eyes were
oval and fringed with thick, dark lashes. Where had she gotten those
sea-green eyes? Both he and Dorothea had blue eyes. Miranda's hair
was another mystery, the color of moonlight.

The twins were as different in temperament as they were in appearance. Miranda was bold and confident and brave. Her mind was quick and her tongue sharp. She lacked patience, but she was kind. He suspected that her wicked temper came from his having spoiled her.

But Miranda had a deep sense of justice. She disliked cruelty and ignorance, and was quick to defend the helpless. If only, he thought sadly, if *only* she'd been the son he wanted. He loved her greatly, but he despaired of finding a husband for her. She would need a man who would understand her fierce streak of Dunham independence. A man who would handle her firmly, yet gently and with love.

He had told young Lord Adrian Swynford, Baron Swynford, that his formal engagement to Amanda must wait until Miranda, the elder, was betrothed. Thomas Dunham had met no one in England he felt right for his oldest child. He did have an idea on that subject, but first there was a matter to be changed in his will.

He smiled. Dear little Amanda! She was so sweet and gentle. She would grace the Swynford family table, and the Swynford family jewels. She would never be a particularly interesting conversationalist, but she played the pianoforte nicely, and she painted pretty watercolors. She would be an excellent breeder, a dutiful wife who would never complain if her husband amused himself occasionally with a bit o' muslin. In Amanda, he and Dorothea had produced a perfect daughter, Thomas thought smugly.

In the elder of the twins he had produced a self-willed, independent vixen, and had he not seen her slip from her mother's straining body himself he would have sworn that she was someone else's child.

As the girls had grown it was Miranda who was the obvious leader of the pair. She walked a full five months before her twin, and spoke clearly by the end of her first year. Amanda babbled nonsense for over two years before she became intelligible. Only Miranda completely understood her, sometimes translating the childish prattle and other times anticipating her twin's desires in a wordless form of communication that amazed everyone. Amanda was uncomplicated, Miranda complex—yet they loved one another dearly. Miranda might storm and rage at Mandy, but no one else was allowed, and woe betide anyone foolish enough, to offend the gentler of the two girls, for Miranda protected her twin like a tigress her cub.

Now, though, Miranda Dunham was impatient. "For pity's sake, Mandy, stop wailing!" Miranda could not contain her irritation. "If Adrian Swynford really loves you he'll offer for you before we return to America."

"He has already offered for her," said Thomas Dunham quietly.

"Oh, Papa!" Amanda scrambled to her little feet, her eyes shining with delight.

"There, you see? I told you so!" said Miranda as if the matter were finished.

"Come, my girls," said their father. "Sit down with your mama and me, and I will tell you everything." He settled his daughters between their mother and himself on a long silk settee. "Lord Swynford," he began, "has asked for Amanda's hand in marriage. I have tentatively given my consent provided that no formal announcement be made or sent to the *Gazette* until I have also made a suitable match for Miranda. She is the elder, and her betrothal must come first."

"*What?*" the twins exclaimed in one voice.

"I don't want to get married!" shouted Miranda. "I will not leave Wyndsong, or be chattel to some damned pompous fool of a man!"

"And I don't want to wait to wed Adrian!" cried Amanda in a rare show of spirit. "If she doesn't care if I'm the first to marry, then why should you?"

"Amanda!" cried her mother, surprised. "It is a family tradition that the eldest weds first. It has always been so, and it is only fair." She turned to Miranda. "Of course you will marry, child. What else would you do?"

"I am the elder," said Miranda proudly. "Am I not to inherit Wyndsong? Am I not to be the next lady of the manor? I need nothing else, and I certainly need no man! I have never met one besides Papa that I truly liked!"

"A respectable woman always needs either a husband or a father, Miranda. I will not always be here to protect you." Thomas Dunham was uncomfortable with what he had to say next, but he went on. "You are my eldest child, Miranda, but you are not a son. You cannot inherit Wyndsong, because the patent for the manor states that if there is no direct male heir, the present lord of the manor must designate from among his male relatives. I did so years ago, when the doctors said that your mother should not have any more children. The next lord of Wyndsong Island will be from the Plymouth branch of the family. You and your sister can inherit my personal wealth, but you cannot inherit Wyndsong."

"Not inherit Wyndsong?" Miranda was stunned. "You cannot simply give it to a stranger, Papa! Who is this cousin? Do we know him? Will he love Wyndsong as I do? No! No!"

"My heir is the younger son of my cousin, John Dunham. He has never been to Wyndsong. His name is Jared."

"I will *never* let him have Wyndsong! Never, Papa! Never!"

"Miranda, control your temper," said Dorothea Dunham in a firm voice. "You must marry. All young ladies of your class marry. Perhaps now, knowing that you cannot remain at Wyndsong, you will make a serious effort to find a proper husband."

"There is no one I love," came the icy reply.

"It is not necessary to love one's betrothed husband, Miranda. Love often comes afterward."

"Amanda loves Adrian," her daughter said flatly.

"Yes, she does, and how fortunate that the object of her affections has offered for her, and is suitable. Were he not, my dear, then no amount of love would matter."

"Did you not love Papa when you were first married?" Miranda persisted, and Dorothea felt irritation rising. How typical of her elder child to pursue a subject to the point of embarrassment. Why did she not simply understand how society operated? Amanda did. Dorothea began to suspect, as she so often did when locked in combat with Miranda, that her child understood quite well but was deliberately being difficult.

"I did not know your papa when we were first betrothed. Your grandparents, however, having made me a suitable match, gave us time to get to know one another. By the time Papa and I were wed I was beginning to love him, and not a day has passed in these last twenty years that I haven't loved him more each day."

"Did you not hate leaving Torwyck? It was your home."

"No. Wyndsong was your father's domain, and I wanted to be with him. Amanda will not regret leaving Wyndsong for Swynford Hall, will you, my love?"

"Oh no, Mama! I want to be where Adrian is!" was the instant reply.

"You see, Miranda? Once you have chosen a husband, where you live will matter little as long as you are with him."

"No," said Miranda obstinately. "It's different for both of you. Neither of you grew up loving your home as I love Wyndsong, nor did you grow up believing you would inherit, as I have believed. I do love Wyndsong, every bit of it! I know it better than any of you. Wyndsong is *mine*, whatever the original patent may say, and I will never let one of those prim and priggish Plymouth Dunhams have it! I won't!" Tears glistening diamond bright in her sea-green eyes, Miranda fled the room. Crying was not like her, and she was embarrassed to show such a feminine weakness.

"Oh, Mama! It is so unfair that Miranda is unhappy when I am so happy." Amanda stood up, and hurried after her sister.

"Well, Thomas?" Dorothea Dunham gazed accusingly at her husband.

He shifted uncomfortably. "I didn't realize she felt so strongly, m'dear."

"Oh, Thomas! You've spoiled Miranda to the point of overindulgence, although I can't blame you. She has always been a difficult girl. And frankly, I have not given her the attention I should have. It has always been easier to let her go her own way. Now I see that by doing so we have made a grievous error. Miranda's mind has been so filled with Wyndsong that there was room for nothing else.

"We must find a suitable husband for her, Thomas," Dorothea Dunham went on. "Lord Swynford is perfect for Amanda, but he will not wait forever. I cannot understand why you will not allow the engagement to be announced now." Her blue eyes were twinkling. "I went along with your decision about the eldest marrying first, and I certainly embroidered on it nicely, but I am at a loss as to when such a custom began in this family."

She paused and then said, "What is it you have done, Thomas, that you feel requires amending before you can allow Amanda's engagement to be announced?"

Thomas Dunham gave his wife an embarrassed grin. "You certainly know me well, m'dear. It's the only thing I've ever kept from you. It seemed like such a good idea at the time, but . . . I must change my will before we announce Amanda's betrothal to Lord Swynford." He ran a big hand through his iron-gray hair, and his blue eyes looked troubled. "You see, Doro, when I made young Jared Dunham the next lord of the manor, I gave into a bit of personal vanity.

"My will makes Jared my heir, but my personal wealth goes to you and the girls. Jared cannot maintain the island without money, however, so there is a clause stating that if I die before the girls are married, and he is unwed, my wealth and other than your widow's portion will go to him providing he weds with one of my daughters, the choice to be his.

"It isn't that I believe I'll die soon, but I wanted my blood to run in the veins of the future lords of Wyndsong. As my will provided a generous dowry for the remaining twin, who was I harming? Now I must change my will if Amanda is to wed Lord Swynford, for now only Miranda remains available."

"Oh, Thomas!" Dorothea put a plump, dimpled hand over her mouth, trying to hide her amusement. "And they say women are vain!" Then she said seriously, "Perhaps, my love, you have unwittingly solved our problem with Miranda. Why not make a match between her and Jared Dunham? Miranda would then be the first betrothed, your blood will run in the veins of the future lords of Wyndsong, and Amanda can wed Lord Swynford."

"By God, Doro, you're a shrewd one! Why didn't I think of that? It is the perfect solution!" He slapped his thigh enthusiastically.

"It is perfect, provided that Jared Dunham is not already betrothed, wed, or entangled."

"Well, I know he's not betrothed or wed. I recently had a letter from his father asking me to obtain a dinner service of yellow Jasper

Wedgwood for his wife's birthday. He mentioned that his eldest son, Jonathan, had become a father for the third time, and said he despaired of Jared's ever settling down. Jared is thirty now. This plan will please his father mightily. There is no time for me to send a letter ahead, for we sail in a few days, but I'll send a message once we are home."

"Then before we go home, you can announce Amanda's engagement, at least privately, to our families. It would be a mistake not to do so, Tom. Old Lady Swynford wants Adrian wed, and with an heir soon. I fear that she will seek elsewhere if some sort of announcement is not made."

"He's a poor-spirited lad if he lets her," remarked Tom Dunham.

"Thomas, he's only twenty. And his mama having had him so late in life—why, she was forty!—is doting. If his father were still alive he would be in his seventies. Poor Adrian is just now becoming his own man, but he is honorable, and he truly loves Amanda.

"If an announcement is made to the families now," she continued, "and then officially this winter, we may look to a wedding next June at St. George's in Hanover Square."

"What if Miranda refuses to cooperate, m'dear?"

"Miranda is a very intelligent girl, Tom, or so you are always telling me. Once she faces up to the fact that she cannot inherit Wyndsong, and that she must marry, she will see the wisdom of our plan. Only through Jared Dunham can she hope to become lady of the manor. I do not believe that she will allow some other woman to take what she feels is her rightful place."

Dorothea Dunham smiled at her husband. "You're an extremely sly old fox, Tom, and I love you."

Later, alone with his thoughts, Thomas closed his eyes and tried to picture what Jared looked like. He hadn't seen the young man for three years. Tall, yes, he was very tall, standing at least six feet three inches. Lean, with an oval, sculpted face that was more his mother's family than Dunham. Dark hair, and ... Good Lord! The boy had green eyes! Not the blue-green of Miranda's but a funny bottle-green color.

There was a feeling of elegance about him, Tom recalled. He remembered that Jared had, in the height of London society, been dressed in staid, old Boston clothes. He chuckled. Jared had a commendable streak of independence!

At twenty-seven, when Thomas had last seen him, Jared had been a man of breeding, education, and manners. Now, at thirty, would a chit of seventeen appeal to him? Would Jared Dunham welcome the match, or would he prefer to make an alliance elsewhere?

If Thomas Dunham felt any cause for concern he kept it to himself, and instead went about the business of preparing to return to America. He booked his family passage on *The Royal George*. It would sail south following the trades, stopping first at the islands of Barbados and Jamaica, and then at the Carolinas, New York, and Boston.

Thomas had arranged with the ship's owners for a special stopover off Orient Point, Long Island, so his yacht could pick the family up and ferry them around the Point to Wyndsong Island, two miles off the village of Oysterponds in Gardiner's Bay.

The farewell dinner was held, and the happy announcement of young Lord Swynford's engagement to Miss Amanda Dunham was made privately. The dowager Duchess of Worcester was the only outsider present. She was one of society's most powerful arbiters. With the duchess a witness to Lord Swynford's intentions, only death would be a completely acceptable excuse for either party's crying off.

Dorothea had chosen to garb her twin daughters in identical gowns of palest pink muslin. Amanda, of course, looked utterly adorable, her full young breasts swelling provocatively above the low, square neckline, her dimpled arms white and soft beneath the little lace-edged puffed sleeves. The neckline, the sleeves, and hemline of the gowns were embroidered in a charming band of dainty deeper pink rosebuds. The gowns were ankle length, and the twins wore white silk stockings with heel-less black leather slippers. Their jewelry, carefully chosen by their mama, was suitably modest, little hoop earrings of pink coral beads, and matching pink coral bead necklaces. Amanda wore a wreath of pink rosebuds atop her yellow-gold ringlets, but here Miranda had drawn the line.

She detested the baby pink of her gown with its sweet, girlish embroidery. She knew that pale pink was the wrong color for her

unusual coloring, but it was fashionable, and Dorothea insisted that
they be fashionable. When, however, the suggestion had been made
that she cut her long, heavy silver-gilt hair, Miranda had simply
refused in a tone even her mother quailed at. Mama might gown her
in ridiculous clothes, but she would not shear her like a sheep or
dress her head in silly ringlets.

Since Dorothea forbade Miranda a more adult hairstyle such as a
chignon, claiming it was not suitable for an unmarried girl, and since
Miranda would not wear childish braids, she was forced to wear her
long hair loose, confined only by a simple pink silk ribbon.

Miranda's only pleasure that evening was in her sister's joy. The
littler twin was radiant with happiness and Miranda knew she was
truly in love with Adrian Swynford, a fine-looking, blond young
man of medium height. She was happy and relieved to see that the
young English nobleman returned his betrothed's feelings, in equal
measure, his arm protectively around Amanda, mischievously stealing kisses from her when he thought no one was looking. Amanda
cast her swain adoring looks, hardly leaving his side all evening.
This forced poor Miranda into close proximity with her three female
cousins.

Caroline Dunham, who was also just finishing her first season,
was a haughty young woman of but average beauty. Her forthcoming
marriage to the Earl of Afton's eldest son and heir had only increased
her feelings of self-importance. She thought that her cousin Amanda
had made a very poor match compared with her dear Percival. But
then, cousin Amanda was only a colonial, and a baronet had
undoubtedly seemed very grand to her.

Caroline's two little sisters, Charlotte and Georgine, were gig-
glers. On the whole, Miranda preferred Caroline's coldness to the
younger ones' silliness. She was at least spared the company of her
boy cousins because the two eldest were deeply involved in talk of
gaming at White's horse auctions coming up at Tattersall's and
boxing matches scheduled at Gentleman Jackson's gym. Besides,
once they had discovered that their cousin Miranda was not about to
play kiss and cuddle in the darkened library, they quickly lost interest in her.

Thomas Dunham and his cousin, Sir Francis Dunham, stood talking earnestly by the fire. Dorothea, Lady Millicent, and the dowager Duchess of Worcester sat chatting amiably on a satin settee. Miranda glanced about, seeking Adrian's mama, and was surprised to find the lady at her elbow. Lady Swynford was a tiny old woman with bright, shrewd eyes under a purple turban. She smiled toothily at Miranda.

"So, my gel, your parents say they must marry you off before my son can have your sister. Have you some Yankee swain back in your America?"

"No, ma'am," Miranda answered politely, beginning to dread what was coming.

"Humph!" sniffed Lady Swynford. "I foresee a long and exhausting courtship for my son." She sighed affectedly. "Ah, how I long to dandle my grandchildren on my knee. I wonder if I shall live *that* long."

"I suspect you shall, ma'am, and even longer," answered Miranda. "The wedding is to be next June, after all."

"And will you be married by then, my gel?" Lady Swynford eyed her archly.

"Whether I am or not, ma'am, I promise you that Mandy and Adrian will be wed on schedule."

"You're no milk-and-water miss, are you, my gel?"

"No, ma'am, I am not!"

Lady Swynford chuckled richly. "I wonder," she said, "if they realize the woman they have in you."

"Ma'am?" Miranda was puzzled.

"Nothing, child," Lady Swynford replied in a more kindly tone, further confusing Miranda by patting her hand. "Why, I can see you don't even know it yourself yet."

The Dunhams sailed for America two days later, driving down from London to Portsmouth the day after the dinner party. The horses were changed four times. They stayed overnight in Portsmouth, putting up at the Fountain, and going aboard their ship the following morning to sail on the late-morning tide. The Dunhams

stood at the rail for a time watching the coast of England recede, but
then they went to their adjoining cabins. Amanda, gazing at the
perfect round sapphire surrounded by diamonds that Adrian had
given her, had become quite teary at the realization that she was
leaving her beloved. Miranda cared little, for she had not really
enjoyed her stay in London, and besides, she was returning home to
her own love, Wyndsong.

The Royal George sailed south under fair skies and brisk winds.
Captain Hardy declared he'd not seen such fine weather in all his
days on the Atlantic. They arrived at Barbados in record time, swept
across the Caribbean to Jamaica, and up the South Atlantic to
Charleston. At each port they lost passengers, gained passengers,
and discharged cargo.

Finally they arrived at New York. The ship stayed overnight
unloading cargo, taking on fresh water and foodstuffs, and being
loaded with cargo for England. The following morning, a bright blue
and gold October Day, *The Royal George* sailed up the East River
into the Long Island Sound. They would be home by the following
day.

Just before dawn on the day they would see Wyndsong, Miranda
woke Amanda.

"It isn't even light yet," protested the sleepy, smaller twin.

"Don't you want to see the sunrise over Orient Point?" Miranda
pulled the covers away. "Get up, Mandy! Get up, or I'll tickle you to
death!"

"I think I'm going to prefer Adrian as a bedfellow to you, sister
dear," muttered Amanda, climbing reluctantly out of her warm nest.
"Ohhh! This floor is like ice! You're absolutely heartless,
Miranda!"

Miranda raised a winged dark eyebrow in surprise as she handed
Amanda her lace-trimmed, white muslin undergarments. "Prefer
Adrian as a bedfellow? I am not sure if I am startled by your want of
delicacy, or simply shocked, Mandy."

"I may be younger, smaller, and slower than you, sister, but my
emotions are well developed. After all, I know what love is. You do
not. No one has ever touched your heart. Hand me my gown, will
you?"

Amanda stepped into the high-waisted, puff-sleeved gown of pink sarcenet, and turned her back so Miranda might button her up. She could not see the perplexed look on Miranda's face. Miranda felt very strange. She did not begrudge her sister happiness, but she had never not been first at anything. She quickly composed her face and, bending down, picked up her paisley shawl.

"Better take yours too, twin. It will be cold on deck."

They came out onto the deck just as faint color was beginning to show in the east. The water was black and mirror-smooth. There was a very faint breeze in the sails, and as they stood facing the bow of the ship, they saw the coast of Long Island to their right, through the gray mists of early morning. On their left, but farther away, the Connecticut coast lay shrouded in fog.

"Home," breathed Miranda, hugging her shawl around her slim shoulders.

"It really means that much to you, doesn't it?" said Mandy quietly. "Mother and Father are wrong, I fear. You will never love anyone as you love Wyndsong. It's as if you are part of the land itself."

"I knew you would understand!" Miranda smiled. "We have always understood each other. Oh, Mandy, I cannot bear to think that this cousin of Father's will inherit it someday. It should be mine!"

Amanda Dunham squeezed her twin's hand sympathetically. There was nothing she could do to change the situation, and nothing would soothe Miranda's troubled spirit.

"So this is where you two minxes have gotten to, and at such an early hour, too." Thomas Dunham flung his arms around his two daughters.

"Good morning, Papa!" they cried.

"And are my girls anxious to be home? Even you now, Amanda?"

They both nodded enthusiastically. Just then a brisk breeze suddenly sprang up and the remnants of fog disappeared. The sunrise spilled over the bluffs and dappled the green-blue waters with gold. The sky forecast a lovely, clear day.

"There's the Horton's Point lighthouse!" said Miranda excitedly.

"Then we're almost home, darlings!" laughed Dorothea Dunham, coming out onto the deck. "Good morning, my daughters!"

"Good morning, Mama," they called in cheerful unison.

"Good morning, m'dear." Thomas gave her a loving kiss, which she returned.

The ship's crew scurried around them, and Captain Hardy joined the Dunhams. "We'll come around Orient Point and anchor toward the bayside, so your yacht can come about more easily. Will your people be long? There's a good breeze with us, and if it keeps up I might make Boston by late tomorrow."

"My yacht should be standing off Orient now."

"Very good, sir. I appreciate your cooperation, and may I say it's been a great pleasure having you and your lady and daughters aboard my ship." He turned to Amanda. "I hope we'll have the pleasure of taking you back to England next summer, Miss Amanda."

"Thank you, Captain," said Amanda blushing prettily, "but it is not yet official." She fingered her ring.

"Then I shall not offer my felicitations until it is," he replied with a twinkle in his eye. "I have a wife and daughter myself, and I know how important it is to you ladies to have all the proper amenities observed."

"Sail ho!" came the cry from the crow's nest.

"Can you make her out?" called back the captain.

"Baltimore clipper, sir. American flag."

"Name and port?"

"She's the *Dream Witch* out of Boston."

"Hmmm." The captain thought for a moment and then ordered, "Keep your present course, Mr. Smythe."

"Aye, sir!"

They remained at the rail watching as the clipper made its way toward them. Suddenly a puff of whitish smoke came from the other vessel, followed by a dull boom that echoed across the water.

"By God! They've put a shot across our bow!" Captain Hardy was incredulous.

"Royal George! Stand to, and prepare to be boarded!"

"W-why, the insolence of them!" sputtered the captain.

"Are they pirates?" Miranda was fascinated, but Amanda shrank back next to her mother.

"No, miss, just the ragtag Yankee Navy being childish," said the captain. Remembering his passengers' nationality, he looked uncomfortable. "Begging your pardon." But the Englishman seethed. He more than outgunned the small, elegant ship now slipping alongside his, but he carried valuable cargo, and passengers. He knew full well that this was simply a retaliatory attack being carried out in revenge for some piece of idiocy committed by the Royal Navy. His owners had been quite specific in their orders. Unless life or cargo was threatened he was not to fire his guns.

The clipper's crew threw its grappling hooks into *The Royal George*.

"Make no resistance," called Captain Hardy to his crew. "No need for alarm, ladies and gentlemen," he reassured his passengers, who were now all milling around on deck.

When the two ships were safely locked together, a very tall, dark officer stepped aboard *The Royal George* from the American ship. The gentleman spoke to Captain Hardy, his voice low. At first they could not hear what he was saying, but then Captain Hardy's voice rose. "There are most certainly no impressed men aboard my vessel, sir! I do not traffic in captives, American or otherwise!"

"Then you will not mind assembling your crew for inspection, sir," the well-modulated voice replied.

"I bloody well do mind, but I'll do it to end this stupidity! Bosun! Pipe the crew topside!"

"Aye, sir!"

Thomas Dunham had been staring hard at the American naval captain, and now a broad smile lit his features. What a coincidence! He began to push through the assembled passengers, waving his silver-headed cane as he went, and calling out, "Jared! Jared Dunham!"

In the rigging of the clipper a sharpshooter placed there to oversee the decks saw movement in the crowd below. He saw a man push out onto the open deck and rush toward his captain, waving what appeared to be a glinting weapon. Being a hothead and a glory seeker, he waited for no order. Instead, he drew a bead on his target, and fired.

Thomas Dunham clutched at his chest as the echo of the shot rang out over the water. He had a look of stunned surprise on his smiling face as he glanced down and saw blood seeping between his fingers. Then he fell forward. For a moment no one moved, and there was complete silence. Then the English captain broke the spell, rushing forward, and bending down to seek for a pulse. There was none. He looked up, horrified. "He's dead."

"Thomas!" Dorothea Dunham fainted and Amanda collapsed with her.

The face of the American captain had turned dark with fury. "Hang that man!" he shouted, pointing up. "I gave specific orders that there would be no shooting!"

What happened next happened very quickly. From out of the crowd a tall girl with silver-blond hair launched herself at the American. *"Murderer!"* she shrieked, pummeling him. "You have killed my father! You have killed my father!" He tried to protect himself from her blows, catching at her arms.

"Please, miss, it was an accident. A terrible accident, but the culprit is already punished. See!" He pointed to his ship where the unfortunate sharpshooter was already hanging from the rigging, a frightening lesson to others who might be tempted to disobey orders. Harsh discipline was the law of the sea.

"How many other deaths are you responsible for, sir?" The hate emanating from her icy green-blue eyes shocked him. She was so painfully young to hate so fiercely. A strange thought flitted into his mind. Would she love as violently as she hated?

He had little time to wonder. She whirled away from him, turned, and whirled back as quickly. He felt a sharp pain in his left shoulder. For a moment his vision blurred, and with surprise he realized that he'd been stabbed. The blood was seeping through his jacket, and his shoulder hurt like the very devil.

"Who the hell is that wildcat?" he demanded as the English captain gently disarmed her.

"This is Mistress Miranda Dunham," said Captain Hardy. "It is her father, Thomas Dunham, the lord of the manor of Wyndsong Island, that your man shot."

"Tom Dunham of Wyndsong? Good God! He is my cousin!" The American knelt and gently turned the dead man over. "Dear Lord! Cousin Tom!" Horror passed across his face. Then Jared Dunham looked up. "There are two daughters," he said. "Where is the other?"

The surrounding crowd parted, and Captain Hardy pointed to two prostrate women being ministered to by other female passengers. "His wife, and Miss Amanda."

Jared Dunham stood up. He was pale, but his voice held authority. "Transfer them and their luggage to my ship, Captain. And the body of my cousin as well. I will return them to Wyndsong." He sighed deeply. "I last saw my cousin in Boston three years ago. I've never been to the island, and he asked me if I didn't think it was time I came to see it. I said no, that I expected him to live to a ripe old age. How macabre that I should first see my inheritance while bringing home my cousin's body."

"Your inheritance?" Captain Hardy was clearly puzzled.

Jared Dunham gave a bitter laugh. "My inheritance, sir. An inheritance I sought to avoid. Before you lies the body of the late Lord of Wyndsong Manor. Before you stands the new Lord of Wyndsong Manor. I was my cousin's heir. Is it not ironic?"

Miranda had been standing weeping silently since she had been disarmed. Now the full impact of his words penetrated her shocked, numbed mind. *This man!* This arrogant man who was responsible for her father's death was the Jared Dunham who was to take Wyndsong away from her!!

"*No!*" she shouted, and both men turned startled faces to her. "*No!*" she repeated. "*You cannot have Wyndsong!* I will not let you have Wyndsong!" and, hysterical, she began once again to flay wildly at him.

He was weak from his wound, which was already aching like Hades. He was somewhat in shock himself, and his patience was just about at an end, yet he heard the pain in her young voice. He had obviously taken more than her father from her, although he did not fully understand. "Wildcat," he said regretfully, "I am truly sorry," and then his fist made contact with her little chin, and reaching out swiftly with his good arm he caught her as she fell. For a moment he gazed down at her tear-stained little face, and in that moment Jared Dunham was lost.

His own first mate leapt forward, and he transferred his unconscious burden to the man with a sad reluctance. "Take her aboard the *Dream Witch*, Frank," and then he turned to Captain Hardy. "Do you think she'll ever forgive me, sir?" he asked.

"That, sir," said the Englishman with a half smile, "will depend on the size of her bruise, I fear."

❧ Chapter 3 ❧

Miranda opened her eyes. She was in her own bedroom. Above her was the dearly familiar green and white homespun linen canopy. She closed her eyes. Wyndsong! She was safely home with Mandy, Mama, and Papa. *Papa!* Oh, God, Papa! Memory returned.

Papa was dead. Jared Dunham had killed him, and was now going to take Wyndsong away from her. Miranda tried to sit up, but was assailed by a wave of dizziness. She lay back and breathed slowly, deeply, clearing her head. At last she was able to stand, and swinging her legs over the side of her bed, she slipped her slender feet into her shoes. Moving quickly across the room, she went through the connecting door into Amanda's room, but her twin was not there.

Miranda hurried through the broad, light upper hall of the house, and downstairs. She could hear the murmur of voices coming from the back parlor. Running, she burst into the room. Jared Dunham sat on the striped silk settee, her mother on one side of him, Amanda on the other. Fury filled her being. How dare that arrogant, beastly man be here in *her* house. As they all looked up at her, she snarled furiously, "What is *that* man doing here? He has no right here! I trust that someone has had the sense to send for the authorities. Papa's murderer must be punished."

"Come in, Miranda," said Dorothea Dunham quietly. Her blue eyes were red. "Come in," she repeated, "and make your curtsey to your cousin Jared."

"My curtsey? Mama, are you mad? This man killed my father! I'd sooner make my curtsey to the Devil himself!"

"Miranda!" Dorothea's voice was sharp. "Cousin Jared did not kill Thomas. It was a horrible misunderstanding that caused your father's death. It was not Jared's fault. It happened. It is over, and no amount of raging on your part will bring my Tom back to life! Now make your curtsey to our cousin Jared!"

"Never! Never to that usurper!"

Dorothea sighed. "Jared, I must apologize for my elder daughter. I should like to tell you that it is grief, but I regret to say that from babyhood Miranda has been a rude and headstrong girl. Only her father seemed to have any control over her."

"You need not apologize for me, Mama. I am aware that Mandy is your pet, and with Papa gone I am quite alone. I need neither of you."

Both Dorothea and Amanda burst into tears and Jared Dunham thundered at Miranda, "Apologize to your mother! Your papa may have cosseted you, but I won't!"

"Go to Hell, you devil!" she shot back, eyes blazing turquoise.

He was off the settee and across the room before she could move. He dragged her back across the room and sat down again, pulling her over his knee. Shocked, she felt her gown being raised and then his big hand descended on her little bottom with a loud smack. "Bastard!" Miranda shrieked, but the hand spanked her without mercy until she suddenly began to cry. Then she was sobbing wildly, all her grief out in the open. Then he gently pulled her clothing back down and, lifting her up, cradled her in his arms, wincing as she pushed her head against his injured shoulder. Miranda was weeping bitterly now.

"There, wildcat, there," he soothed softly, surprised at himself. This gilt-haired little bitch had touched him unbelievably. One moment she had him in a black rage and the next minute he felt fiercely protective of her. He shook his head slightly, and his eyes met Dorothea Dunham's. He was puzzled by the sympathetic amusement he saw brimming in them.

Miranda's sobs began to slacken. Suddenly aware of where she was, she scrambled from his lap, spitting like a wet kitten. "Y-you hit me!"

"I spanked you, wildcat. You were very much in need of a spanking."

"I have never been spanked in my entire life." His calm infuriated her.

"A vast oversight on the part of your parents."

Furious, Miranda turned on her mother. *"He hit me!* He hit me, and you let him!"

Dorothea ignored her daughter. "You have no idea," she said to Jared, "how many times I've wanted to do that, but Tom would never let me."

Outraged, Miranda slammed from the parlor and tore back up the stairs to her room. Amanda was close behind her twin, for she knew the signs of a terrible tantrum. "Help me with this damned gown, Mandy."

Amanda began to undo the buttons. "What are you going to do, Miranda? Oh, please don't be foolish! Cousin Jared is really very nice, and he is so upset that one of his men accidentally shot Papa. He has no wish to settle down yet, but now that Wyndsong is his responsibility it seems he must."

"I'll destroy the island," muttered Miranda.

"And where will we go? Cousin Jared has assured Mama that the island is still her home."

"We can go back to England. You'll marry Adrian, and Mama and I can live with you."

"My dear sister, when I marry Adrian no one is going to live with us except our children."

"What of old Lady Swynford?" Miranda was surprised by the firm tone in her quiet twin's voice.

"To the dower house at Swynford Hall! Adrian and I have already discussed it, and agreed."

Miranda yanked off her dress, undervest, and petticoat. "Then Mama and I will set up our own establishment! Hand me my breeches, Mandy. You know where they are." She opened her bureau drawer, drew out a soft, well-laundered cotton shirt, put it on and buttoned it up. Amanda handed her sister the faded dark green corduroy breeches, and Miranda pulled them on. "Stockings and boots, please." Amanda complied. "Thanks. Now run to the stables for me, darling, and tell Jed to saddle up Sea Breeze."

"Oh, Miranda, do you think you should?"

"Yes!"

Sighing, Amanda left the room. Miranda first drew on the light wool stockings, and then her worn but comfortable brown leather boots. Her backside still hurt, and she blushed with the sudden realization that Jared Dunham had seen her underdrawers! What a hateful beast he was, and Mama had allowed him to hurt her. In her whole life no one, certainly no man, had ever handled her so intimately.

She could not remain on Wyndsong for long. A self-pitying tear slipped down her pale cheek. When Papa's will was read they would be rich, and Jared Dunham could go to Hell. Now, she would enjoy *her* island. She slipped down the back stairs of the house, and out through the kitchen.

Jed had Sea Breeze already out of the stable. The big gray gelding danced at the end of his rein, eager to be off. Up on her own horse, the familiar salt air in her nostrils, Miranda could almost believe it was still all the same, and then Jared's voice cut into her dream.

"Where are you going, Miranda?"

She looked down, gazing at him full in the face for the very first time, and thought how incredibly handsome he was. His bronzed oval face was as angular as her own. It was a sensitive face. The dark hair was untidy, a lock that she longed to reach down and brush back tumbling over his high forehead. Beneath his bushy, black brows his bottle-green eyes glittered up from under heavy lids. The thin lips were slightly mocking.

A wave of something unfamiliar swept over her, and she felt her breath catch in her throat. But then anger and sorrow surfaced once more, and she answered rudely, "The horse is mine, sir. Surely you do not object if I ride it!" Then she yanked Sea Breeze's head about and cantered off.

He shook his head wearily. He had been in charge of a mission to stop any English vessels he encountered, search them, and rescue any impressed American seamen found on board. For the time being his missions to Europe were finished, and he was free of intrigue. Now, thanks to that constantly disobedient fool, Elias Bailey, a good man was dead and he was stuck with an inheritance he hadn't expected to have to cope with until late middle age.

Worse—far worse—he suspected that he was going to be charged with the care of his late cousin's family. Of course, that was the proper thing to do. The lovely widow, only twelve years his senior, would be no trouble. Neither would sweet, little Amanda, who would wed Lord Swynford in England next June. As to the other— Lord! What was he going to do with that headstrong, bad-tempered Miranda?

Thomas Dunham, eighth lord of Wyndsong Manor, lay in state for two days in the front parlor of the house. His friends and neighbors came from both forks of the Long Island mainland—from the villages of Oysterponds, Greenport, and Southold on the north shore, from East Hampton and Southampton on the south shore and from the neighboring islands of Gardiner's, Robins's, Plum, and Shelter. They came to pay their respects, to console Thomas Dunham's family, and to size up his heir.

The day of the funeral dawned gray, windy, and threatening. After the Anglican minister conducted the services in the parlor and Thomas Dunham was laid to rest in the family cemetery on a hill near the house, the mourners returned to drink a glass of wine in memory of Tom Dunham. Then everyone left. Only Lawyer Younge remained to read the will.

There were the usual bequests to loyal servants, and the official recognition of Jared Dunham as legal heir and next lord of Wyndsong Manor Island. Dorothea sat quietly, waiting for the revelation yet to come, but when it did it was worse even than she had known. For Tom, it seemed, had not told her everything. Thomas Dunham hadn't simply made the suggestion that his heir marry one of his daughters, he had made it impossible for Jared not to wed one of

them. Dorothea's widow's portion was safe but the remaining money
went to a local church unless Jared Dunham married one of Thomas
Dunham's twins. Only in that case would the wealth be divided
thusly: a generous dowry to the twin not chosen, and the bulk of
Thomas's wealth to the bride's husband.

The room's five inhabitants sat in stunned silence. Lawyer Younge
shifted uncomfortably, his brown eyes darting between the four
Dunhams. Finally Jared said, "And what the hell if I had already
been wed? Would the girls then have been penniless?"

"We changed the will regularly, sir," Younge replied.

"Tom knew you were not . . . involved with anyone."

"Then if I am to save the Dunham wealth from the church I must
marry one of these two girls."

"Yes, sir."

Jared turned to the twins, and appeared to study them very
carefully. Both quailed under his scrutiny. "Amanda is far sweeter
than her sister," Jared said, "but I fear that, without her fine dowry,
Lord Swynford will not be able to marry her. On the other hand, I
fear that even with a large dowry no one will have such a bad-
tempered wench as Miranda. It is quite a quandary."

His eyes flicked swiftly over Amanda to rest on her older twin,
and Miranda angrily felt herself blush. After a long silence, Jared
said, "Since Amanda is already promised, I will not make her
unhappy by forcing her into a marriage with me when she loves Lord
Swynford. I must therefore chose Miranda."

Thank heavens, thought Dorothea. Well, Tom, something good
has come from your terrible death.

Amanda sat, weak with relief, her legs shaking beneath her gown.
Thank God, she thought. June can't come soon enough for me!

Lawyer Younge cleared his throat. "Well, then, that is settled," he
said. "Mr. Dunham, I offer you my congratulations both on your fine
inheritance, and on your upcoming nuptials. There is one other
thing. Tom requested a one-month limit to mourning for him."

"In that case we will plan for a December wedding," said Jared
Dunham quietly.

"I have no intention of marrying you." Miranda finally found her
voice. "Father must have been mad to make such a will."

"If you refuse, you condemn your sister, Miranda."

"Mama can make up Amanda's dowry."

"No, Miranda, I cannot. If I am to take care of myself for the rest of my life I must hoard my widow's mite carefully."

"Oh," said Miranda brightly, "I understand now. Amanda is allowed to be happy. You, Mama, are also allowed to be happy. I, however, am to be the sacrificial lamb."

"You are seventeen, wildcat, and I am your legal guardian until you are twenty-one," said Jared. "I am afraid you must do as I dictate. We will be married in December."

Miranda looked to Lawyer Younge for confirmation. "He can do this to me?"

The lawyer nodded, his eyes not quite meeting hers. He damned well ought to feel ashamed, thought Miranda. This is no better than slavery!

"Would you all leave us, please," said Jared quietly. "I should like to speak with Miranda alone."

They all rose quickly, delighted to leave. Lawyer Younge took Dorothea's arm and escorted her from the room, Amanda following quickly.

The new lord of the manor waited until the door had closed behind the three. Then, reaching out, he pulled Miranda to her feet and drew her close to him. "Why are you fighting me, wildcat?" he asked gently.

A quick, cruel retort sprang to her lips only to fade as she looked up into his eyes. They were strangely tender. "Let us make the best of a difficult situation," he said. "Wyndsong cannot be without its lady, and I must have a wife. You love Wyndsong, Miranda. Marry me and it will always be yours. Many good marriages have come from less than we have, and I promise I will be good to you."

"B-but I don't know you," she protested, "and I don't love you."

"Couldn't you learn to love me, wildcat?" he asked softly, and then his mouth closed over hers. It was over in a moment. His lips, petal-soft, gave her her first kiss, a gentle, passionless kiss that nonetheless set her pulse racing.

"Why did you do that?" she asked, suddenly shy.

"I can't be hitting you forever," he answered, smiling down at her.

"Oh! You are hateful!" she cried, remembering clearly, and knowing that he remembered just as clearly her spanking of a few days earlier.

"You haven't given me your answer yet, Miranda," he persisted. "If you marry me Amanda will be able to wed Lord Swynford, and be happy. I know you love your sister."

"Yes," she snapped, "Amanda will have Adrian—and you will have Papa's fortune. Are you sure that is not your real interest?"

"Oh, wildcat," he laughed, "what a suspicious creature you are. I don't need your father's money. I inherited quite a nice fortune from my grandmother and I've tripled that money in the last ten years. If you marry me I'll put your father's money in trust for you. You will get half of it next spring on your eighteenth birthday and the rest when you turn twenty-one. It will all be yours."

"And if I refuse?"

"You, your mother, and your sister will always have a home here, but nothing more. I will not dower either of you."

"Then I have no choice but to marry you, sir."

"It will not, I assure you, be a fate worse than death."

"That remains to be seen," she answered tartly.

He laughed. "Life with you will not be dull, will it, wildcat?" he said, but she merely raised an elegant eyebrow in reply, and he laughed again. What an adorable witch she was, he thought, and what a woman she would be one day. "May I tell your mama that you have accepted my proposal, then?"

"Yes."

"Yes, *Jared*. I would like to hear you say my name, Miranda."

"Yes, Jared," she said softly, and he felt his heart quicken. It puzzled him. Why should she have that effect on him?

Dorothea and Amanda greeted their news with little cries of delight, which Miranda brutally stilled. "It is hardly a love match, Mama. He wants a wife, and has offered to put Papa's money in trust for me. I want Amanda happy with Lord Swynford. Jared will get his wife, I shall have the money, and Mandy gets Adrian. It is all quite businesslike."

Jared had to stop himself from laughing. Dorothea, his sweet but painfully proper mother-in-law-to-be, looked terribly embarrassed.

Miranda then turned her sharp tongue on her betrothed. "Will you remain on Wyndsong until we marry, sir, or rejoin your ship?"

"I am not a member of the Navy, Miranda, but I do hold the right to privateer for the government. In the last six months my ship has rescued thirty-three impressed American seamen from English ships. I want it to continue to sail even if I don't."

"You are quite free to follow the sea, sir," she said sweetly.

He lifted her hand to his lips, kissed it, and said smoothly, "I should not miss our honeymoon even for the honor of our beloved country, darling wildcat."

Blushing furiously, she shot him a venomous look, and he grinned back wickedly. He was going to enjoy watching her grow up, he thought, and he would particularly enjoy helping her become a woman. But first he would have to gain her trust, and that, he thought ruefully, would not be easy. "I will have to return to *Dream Witch* tomorrow, Miranda. I'll take her to Newport where I will turn her over to my friend, Ephraim Snow. He will captain her and continue her mission, but I will go overland to Plymouth to see my parents and inform them of our wedding plans. I think December sixth would be a good day for our wedding, if that suits you."

She nodded agreement. "Will your parents come to the wedding?"

"My whole family will come. My parents, brother Jonathan, his wife, Charity, and their three children, and my sister Bess and her husband, Henry Cabot, and their two children will all be there. I look forward to introducing them all to my adorable, sweet-tempered, well-mannered bride."

Miranda's green eyes glittered. "I promise not to disappoint you, Jared," she said innocently, and he laughed as Dorothea and Amanda looked at one another, confused, wondering what it was they did not understand.

The day had cleared. Jared looked at his defiant betrothed and asked, "Will you ride with me, Miranda? I would very much like to see the island, and I suspect that you know it best. Will you show me *our* domain?"

It was the right approach. With her father gone, Miranda was beginning to accept the fact that Jared Dunham was the new master of the island. But she was to be mistress of the manor, and wasn't that really what she wanted? She hadn't lost Wyndsong after all! A radiant smile lit her lovely face, the first real smile he'd ever seen on her, and again he foundered. "Give me a few minutes to change," she called, running from the room.

"If she knows you've fallen in love with her she will use you shamefully," said Amanda softly.

"Is it so obvious, pigeon?" He looked almost boyish in his chagrin.

Amanda's mouth turned up in a mischievous grin. "I am afraid so, brother Jared. Miranda can be the most awful bitch at times."

"Amanda Elizabeth Dunham!" Dorothea was shocked.

"Oh Mama, it's true, and you know it. Don't you think that Jared should be warned? I certainly do. You see," she said, turning an earnest face up to him, "Miranda has never been in love. I've been falling in love since I was twelve, but then I suppose it was necessary in my case if I was to know the real thing when it came along. I am much slower, you see, than Miranda. For her it will only be once. She's like that. So far, no one has touched her heart."

"Do you think I can, pigeon?"

"Yes, I do, but not if she knows you care. If she thinks she has the upper hand she'll trample your heart, and kick it aside, especially if she sees any weakness in you. The only prize worth having for Miranda is the one that is the hardest to get. You'll have to make her admit to loving you before you admit to loving her."

He bent and kissed her cheek. "I shall consider your advice carefully, pigeon, and I thank you for it."

Half an hour later, mounted on as fine a horse as he'd ever seen, he rode from the house, Miranda riding by his side on Sea Breeze. She was wearing the faded green breeches and white shirt he'd seen her in the other day. Her round young breasts gleamed like mother-of-pearl through the thin fabric. She was totally unaware of her own sexuality, or the sensuous effect her boyish costume was having on him.

"Would you, in future," he said evenly, "wear a vest beneath that shirt, Miranda?"

"Are you now an arbiter of fashion, sir?"

"It has nothing to do with fashion. I would prefer that no one but me enjoy the sight of your lovely breasts, which are quite visible through your shirt. You are not a child any longer, Miranda, although you often behave like one."

"Oh!" She glanced down, embarrassed, color flooding her face. "I never thought ... I've always worn this shirt riding."

He reached over and put a big hand over her small one. "You are really very beautiful, Miranda, and I am happy to see you are still innocent. A season in London did not coarsen you. I would have thought that the bucks would have turned your head." He had eased her embarrassment, and now he took his hand away. They rode knee to knee.

"I was too blunt to suit the London dandies," she said. "To be told my eyes are 'the green of a limpid pool in the August heat' annoys me rather than flatters me."

"I should hope so," he replied. "Limpid pools in August are usually green due to an overabundance of algae."

She burst into delighted laughter. "That's just what *I* thought, but you must realize that most of those elegant society gentlemen have never seen a real forest pool in August, as you and I have. Besides I am too tall and my coloring is all wrong. Amanda was the perfect incomparable. It was quite fashionable to be in love with her last season. She had over two dozen proposals, including the Duke of Whitley."

"I do not find you too tall, and your coloring is exquisite," he said quietly. "I will wager every beauty in London envied you your flawless complexion."

She looked at him carefully. "Are you flattering me, sir?" Was this what it meant to be courted?

He stopped also, and pretended to consider the matter. Then he said, "I believe I am flattering you, wildcat. I shall have to stop it." He was delighted to see her crestfallen look.

They rode in silence. Jared was impressed. The three-thousand-acre island was enormously fertile, with fields in one section that rolled down to the water's edge. The afternoon light on those fields was of such clarity and color that he wished he could paint. Nowhere else in the world had Jared seen such light, except the Low Countries of Europe and sections of the English coast.

Fat cattle grazed in the fields, and there were sleek horses. Wyndsong horses were well known in racing circles. The island was virtually self-sufficient, and some of the crops had already been harvested. There were four freshwater ponds on the island, several salt hay meadows, a hardwood forest filled with oak, maple, beech, birch, and chestnut trees, and a small pine forest.

The land rolled toward the north end of the island, and the manor house sat on the heights. Below it was a beautiful white sand beach, and a small, protected harbor known as Little North Bay.

The original manor house had been built of wood in 1663. Over the following fifty years it had been added to until there were several wings housing several generations of Dunhams—for the men of the family were particularly long-lived. In a violent summer storm in 1713 the house was struck by lightning, and burned to the ground. At that point the first lord of the manor was seventy-five years old, his son fifty-two, his grandson twenty-seven, and his great-grandson two years old. The very next week a kiln for making bricks was set up on the island.

The new house with its black, hand-cut slate roof was lighter and more spacious than its predecessor. It was a beautiful house, of three stories with chimneys at both ends. The front entry was centered, and flanked by long windows running the length of the house. The structure was divided by a center hall, on one side of which were two parlors, a formal one in front and a family one toward the rear. On the other side of the hall was a fine dining room. Behind it was a large kitchen. The second floor also contained a wide center hall with windows at both ends, and four large bedrooms, one at each corner of the house. The third floor was a large attic with several small rooms for children and servants, and much storage space.

Looking at the house from a nearby hill, Jared Dunham felt a strange pride well up inside him, and suddenly as his eye swept the island he understood Miranda's deep passion for this little kingdom, founded one hundred and forty-eight years ago by her ancestor. He also understood the sadness Thomas must have felt knowing that his line would end with him. And now at last, Jared fully realized why Thomas Dunham's will had forced a marriage between Miranda and himself.

He looked at the girl on her horse next to him. God, he thought, if she ever looks at me the way she looks at this island I will know I am well loved! The day had turned sharp and clear, and as they looked north and west from their vantage point on the hill, they could see the Connecticut and Rhode Island coasts, and just barely make out the hazy edges of Block Island.

"You must tell me everything about Wyndsong," he said. "By God, if there's a lovelier place on earth I do not know where it is!"

She was surprised by his vehemence.

"They say that when the first Thomas Dunham saw Wyndsong for the first time he knew he'd come home. He was English, and in exile. When the Restoration came he was given this island as a reward for his loyalty. The Dutch claimed this whole area, and how King Charles had the nerve to give Tom Dunham such a shaky land grant I don't understand."

She explained a great deal more and he said, "You certainly know your history. I thought girls only learned deportment, painting, singing, the pianoforte, and French."

She laughed. "Amanda is proficient in all those things. They gained her Lord Swynford. I, alas, have no manners—as you know. I have no talent for painting, I sing like a crow, and musical instruments cringe at my touch. But I do have an ear for languages, and I have been taught history and mathematics. Such things suit my nature better than watercolors and maudlin ballads." She looked at him through her lashes. "I hope you are an educated man, Jared."

"I graduated from Harvard. I trust that suits you, my love? I also spent a year at Cambridge, and another year touring Europe. I, too, speak several languages, and studied history and mathematics. Why are you concerned?"

"If we are to be wed we must know each other better. Knowing that you've been educated tells me we'll at least have something to talk about on cold winter nights."

"What?"

He looked to see if she was being deliberatively provocative, but she wasn't. In some ways she was still painfully young, and he said quietly as they rode down into the October forest, "I suspect you know very little about the relationship between a man and a woman, Miranda. Is that not so?"

"Yes," she said quite matter-of-factly. "Mama assured both Amanda and me that whatever we needed to know our husbands would explain to us. Amanda, with all her female friends in London, has learned a great deal this winter. I suspect she has practiced on Adrian."

"Not everything, I certainly hope," he said with mock severity. "I should be loath to have to call out our young Lord Swynford for debauching one of my wards."

"What on earth do you mean?"

"I think, Miranda, you had best tell me exactly what you do know." They had reached a lovely freshwater pond, and he stopped, dismounted, and helped her down. "Let the horses graze a bit, and we will walk around the pond while we talk," he suggested, taking her hand.

"You are making me feel like a gauche schoolgirl," she protested.

"I don't mean to make you uncomfortable, wildcat, but you are a schoolgirl, and we are just beginning to trust one another. If I mishandled you now I could lose that trust. In a few weeks we will be married, and oh, Miranda, there is more to marriage than you imagine. But trust is a very important part of it all."

"I guess I don't really know a great deal about what does go on between a man and a woman," she admitted shyly.

"Surely some of the London gentlemen you met at parties attempted to make love to you?"

"No."

"No? Incredible! Were they all blind?"

She turned her head away from him. Her voice was low as she said, "I was not a success in London. I am too tall as I have already told you, and my coloring is all wrong to be fashionable. It was Mandy with her peaches-and-cream skin, her pure-gold hair, and her lovely blue eyes they all sought. She is round, and petite, and quite appealing. The few men who sought me out did so hoping that I would plead their cases with Amanda."

He did not miss the hurt in her voice. "What fools they were," he said. "Your complexion is like ivory and wild pink roses, a perfect and fitting complement to your sea-green eyes and silver-gilt hair, which reminds me of a full April moon. I do not find you too tall." He stopped as if to illustrate his point, and pulled her against him. "You come just to my shoulder, Miranda. I think that you are absolute perfection, and even if Amanda had not been spoken for, I should have chosen you."

Startled, she gazed up at him, looking for any trace of mockery. There was none. His own bottle-green eyes looked steadily into hers, reflecting an expression she couldn't quite fathom. Suddenly blushing, she turned her head aside, but he caught her little dimpled chin and, tipping her face up, sought her lips.

"No!" she whispered breathlessly, her heart hammering wildly.

"Yes!" he answered huskily, capturing her face between his two hands. "Oh, yes, Miranda sweet!" and his warm mouth covered hers in a passionate kiss that set her trembling wildly. His lips consumed her as nothing had ever done before. His hands slid away from her face, but their lips remained together. Slowly one arm slid down to encircle her waist, and the other hand moved up to tangle in her hair.

Gasping, she tore her mouth from his, and flung back her head, but to her shock his mouth blazed a trail of fiery kisses down her throat, lingering in the soft hollow of her neck with its wildly leaping pulse. "Please ... " she pleaded, and through the mists of his desire, he heard the fright and confusion in her voice. He lifted his head slowly, reluctantly.

"It's all right, wildcat. You tempt me, God knows, but I promise to behave myself."

Her eyes were enormous and she touched her bruised lips wonderingly with trembling fingertips. "Is that what men do to women?"

"Sometimes. Usually they are driven to it. If I have frightened you, Miranda, I apologize. I could not resist you."

"Is that all men do?"

"No. There are other things."

"What other things?"

"Good Lord! Things I shall explain to you when we're married."

"Don't you think I should know before we're married?"

He chuckled richly. "I most certainly do not!"

"Why not?" The expression in her eyes now boded trouble, for it was extremely mutinous.

His own eyes narrowed. "You must trust my judgment in this, wildcat, for I have experience and you do not. Remember, my love, in a few weeks you will swear before God and man to obey me."

"And you, Jared Dunham, will swear to cleave only to me. I think if we are to be married we should learn whether we suit each other in all ways."

"You were half mad with fright just moments ago," he said softly.

She blushed, but pressed on. "Yet you tell me there is more. What more? Would you have me terrified on our wedding night when I can do nothing about it? Perhaps you are the sort of man who looks forward to a quailing, frightened bride."

"Do you wish me to seduce you, my love?"

"No, I do not wish to be seduced. One thing Mama is quite fond of telling us is that no one will buy the cow if they can obtain the milk for free."

He laughed. That sounded just like Dorothea Dunham. "Then what is it you want, wildcat?"

"I want to know what else is involved in making love! How can I learn if I don't know what to do? How do I know if I'll like *it* if I don't know what *it* is?"

He took her by the hand and drew her down to the mossy bank that edged the pond. "I must be out of my mind," he muttered. "Now I am a schoolmaster giving lessons in lovemaking. Very well, wildcat, come here to me, and we will resume where we left off." He put an arm around her shoulders and drew her back. The fingers of his other hand gently traced her jawline, sending little shivers along her spine. "You put a great deal of faith in my ability to control what are generally called my baser emotions."

"I trust you, Jared," she said softly.

"Do you, my dear? I wonder if that is wise." Then his mouth swooped down to cover hers in a burning kiss. To his surprised delight, she returned the kiss with a hesitant passion that blossomed until one kiss blended into another. Miranda began to feel dizzy with the honeyed sweetness suddenly pouring through her. She felt a delicious languor steal over her, and her arms slipped up around his neck.

Moments later, he gently raised her arms above her head and pressed her back against the bank. Her eyes were closed, the dark lashes fluttering against her pale cheeks. He gazed down at her for a moment, thinking how fair she was, how innocent. He was about to introduce her to her own sensuous nature, a nature that she probably didn't even know existed. He lay his dark head against her cotton-clad breasts, and heard her heart jump wildly.

For a few minutes he stayed quiet, letting her grow used to him, and then he raised his head and kissed her nipple. His face nuzzled her. The buttons of her shirt were suddenly open and his hot and hungry mouth was on her soft flesh. She cried out softly, and caught at his dark hair with her slender hands. "Jared!"

He sat up and looked mockingly into her eyes. "Do you know enough now, Miranda?"

She wanted him to stop, yet she didn't. "N-no," she heard herself say bravely.

He cradled her again in one arm while his long fingers moved lazily to caress her tender, round breasts. Her skin was silken, and warm beneath his touch, and she watched him through half-closed eyes, her breath coming in little gasps. Gently he cupped a breast, his thumb rubbing against the large, dusky rose nipple, and he felt the tremor from deep within her.

"A woman's breasts," he said, "are a part of her many charms. How beautiful yours are, my love."

"Is this all," she asked breathlessly.

"What a curious little wildcat you are," he chuckled. "I do believe that I should take you here and now on this mossy bank." And how easy it would be, he thought, aching terribly. "But I am too old to deflower virgins in secluded woodlands. I far prefer a beautiful candlelit chamber, a comfortable bed, and a bottle of good white wine with my seductions." He sat her up, buttoned her shirt, kissed her lightly, and stood up.

"You've shown me little!" she cried.

"Whether you like it or not, you will have to accept that I know best in this matter." He pulled her to her feet. "Now, show the lord of the manor the rest of his domain."

Furious, she ran to her horse, intending to canter off. Let him fend for himself. With luck he'd ride into a salt marsh! Laughing, he caught up with her. He spun her around and kissed her angry mouth. "I hate you!" she cried. "You're hateful, and too damned superior to suit me! We'll have a terrible marriage! I've changed my mind!"

"But I haven't! Having been tempted these last few days by the memory of your adorable bottom, I wouldn't cry off for a hundred island manors!"

She hit him. Hit him with all her strength, her slender hand meeting with his smooth cheek in a loud, smacking noise. Then she flung herself on Sea Breeze and galloped off through the woods.

"Damn!" he swore softly to himself. He hadn't meant to tease her. And now he'd offended her. She was a far more complicated creature than he had suspected, and as prickly as a little hedgehog. He smiled to himself as he rubbed his cheek. Despite her air of assurance, she had a vulnerability that he suspected stemmed from her London season.

He was surprised that those perfumed London fops had preferred the kitten-pretty Amanda to her ravishing sister. Miranda's beauty was unusual, and when she matured and learned how to dress she would be an elegant and formidable woman. Someday he would take her back to London and watch society acclaim her.

Right now, however, his task was to get them to the altar, and safely wed. Life! Who could predict it? A few short days ago he had been barely aware of the existence of Miranda Dunham, and now in a few weeks they would be man and wife. She was so young—perhaps too young—and she was much too willful. Yet he wanted her, and he found that intriguing in itself.

Even as a half-grown boy Jared had never lacked for women. He and his older brother, Jonathan, separated by but two years, had had many amorous adventures together until at age twenty Jonathan met Mistress Charity Cabot, fell head over heels in love, and—with their father's beaming approval—married the girl. Jared, however, continued to follow a pattern of brief amours, never caring deeply for the women involved.

But then love had happened to Jared, as it had to his brother. She had come at him, fists flying, silver-gold hair awhirl, scarcely a conventional meeting what with her father's dead body between them. He had fallen in love at first sight of the wildcat, but little Amanda was right when she warned him against wearing his heart on his sleeve. Until Miranda was ready to declare her feelings, he must not declare his.

Across the pond a big buck came loping down through the trees to drink. Jared sat quietly, barely moving, as the animal lowered his magnificent antlered head. He was at least an eighteen-point buck, deep brown and beautiful. Jared thought how very much this beautiful wild creature typified both Wyndsong and Miranda. The deer finished drinking and, raising his head, made a snorting noise. Immediately from behind the bushes a delicate doe and two fawns stepped forth and approached the water. When they had finished drinking, all four stole back into the forest, leaving Jared Dunham with a strange sense of loss.

He mounted his horse and rode back the way he had come, following Hill Brook, which fed into the pond, to Short Creek, which began two hills from the manor house. He had only seen about a third of the island, but there would be plenty of time to explore Wyndsong after they were married. It was growing late, the orange sun sinking lower with each passing minute, and a sudden chill was in the air. Nevertheless, he stopped for a moment on the crest of the hill above the house to look about him.

To the north the sky was already dark blue, the evening star rising sharp and jewel-like. The forest behind him was still bright, the setting sun reflecting back the red and gold of the autumnal trees. A soft purplish haze hung over the fields and marshes to the south and west. At the very tip of the island the pine woods seemed ablaze with golden sunlight. As he watched, a small flock of Canada geese whirled overhead out of the evening sky and settled down on Hill Pond near the house.

"Damn, I like this island!" he said softly.

"How fortunate since it is now yours," a tart voice replied.

"Where did you come from?" he asked, whirling around to face her. He was amused to have been caught.

"Oh, Sea Breeze and I rode off my bad temper. I came back to find you. It would hardly do if I lost you. God only knows who'd become lord of the manor then, and I'd stuck marrying *him*. At least with you I know what I've got. You're not *too* old, and I suppose one *could* call you reasonably attractive."

He hid a smile. She wasn't going to give an inch, but then he wasn't going to give one, either. "That was very kind of you, Miranda," he murmured. "Shall we continue on to the house?"

Their horses moved in tandem down the hill and up the next rise to the house where Jed, the stableman, was waiting for them.

"'Nother few minutes and I'd have come looking for you with the dogs," he said sharply.

"What on earth for?" demanded Miranda. "I've been riding this island all my life."

"He hasn't."

"He was with me."

"Yep," the taciturn man replied. "That's what I was worried about."

"You need have no fears for Miranda, Jed," said Jared quietly. "She has done me the honor of agreeing to become my wife. Our wedding is to be celebrated December sixth. Cousin Thomas asked that his mourning period be no more than a month."

"Ahhh," breathed the stableman with just a ghost of a smile on his weathered face. "That's different, Master Jared." He took the horses from them and turned away to the stables. "Good night to you both, then."

Jared chuckled. "He is more aware of the proprieties than you are, wildcat, even after your London season."

"I hated London!" she replied vehemently. "I could never really breathe. It was dirty, and noisy, and everyone was always in a hurry."

"That's the curse of all big cities, Miranda, but don't be too harsh on London. It can be a lovely place, and if this situation in Europe doesn't develop into a war I will take you back there one day."

"We must go back next spring for Amanda's wedding," she reminded him.

"Yes, there's that. But you will be too busy spending your time and my money shopping."

She grinned mischievously up at him. "Fashions change, sir. I shall be forced to purchase an entire new wardrobe. It would hardly do for the mistress of Wyndsong Manor to be seen in last year's clothes."

"Perish the thought," he mocked, casting his gaze heavenward.

They entered the house and were greeted by Dorothea, who asked, "When shall I tell Cook to serve dinner, Jared? It can be ready at any time."

"An hour, Miranda?"

She nodded, flattered that he had asked, and sped up the stairs calling to Jemima, the maid she shared with Mandy, to prepare a bath. But on entering her bedroom, she found the steaming tub already waiting. "How do you always do that?" she demanded.

"If I told you I'd have no secrets, now would I?" snapped the sharp-tongued Jemima, a tall, spare woman with iron-gray hair. "Phew, child, those clothes of yours stink to high heaven. You've been riding hard, Miss Miranda." She looked slyly at the girl as she pulled off her boots. "Did he catch up with you?"

Miranda kept her face carefully averted to hide her blushes. "No one, not even the new master of Wyndsong, can outride me, Mima. You should know that." She slipped behind the painted screen, pulled off her riding clothes, and tossed them to the maid. "Take those downstairs to be washed. I'll bathe myself, and ring when I need you."

Disappointed, Jemima left. She had been the twins' nursemaid, and had simply stayed on as they grew older, serving them as personal maid. It was hard for her to adjust to their being grown. She wanted their confidences as she had had them when they were children. Of course, Amanda was more inclined to confide in Mima than Miranda had ever been. Miranda had always been a very private person.

The bath stood waiting, and after testing it with her toe Miranda pinned her hair up, climbed in, and sank down into the perfumed water. The tub was cream-colored porcelain, decorated with tiny rosebuds. It had a high sloping back, and because it had been made especially for her in Paris, it was extra large and accommodated her long legs.

For a few minutes she sat quietly, letting the warmth of the water penetrate her body, her mind a blank. The air was warm, and redolent of her personal scent, sweet stock, a slightly exotic yet innocent perfume that strangely suited her. It was distilled and made for her in London.

As the tub began to cool she took up the stock-scented soap and quickly lathered and rinsed herself. Climbing out, she reached for the towel hanging on its rack before the fire, and slowly dried herself.

Her mind was beginning to clear. This afternoon had been quite a revelation, although she would never, ever admit it to Jared. Thank God the wedding was still six weeks away! How did women fight the feelings men caused in them? Would giving in to those feelings mean losing one's own self?

"I will not belong to anyone but myself," she said softly. "I won't!"

Naked, she walked across the room to the bed where fresh clothes lay, and dressed in white lawn drawers, white silk stockings with lacy garters, vest, and petticoat. All of the undergarments were edged in dainty, hand-made lace. She recalled the shocking new Paris fashion. French ladies had dispensed with undergarments, and were nude beneath their silk gowns! Some were even wetting their gowns so that they clung to their bodies!

Her dinner gown was of apple-green shot silk, which appeared silvery in certain light. Its neckline was square and low, its waistline caught beneath her breasts in the Empire style, its sleeves were short and puffy. She smiled, pleased with her image as she stood before the mirror and fastened a strand of pearls around her neck and matching pearl bobs in her ears. Pulling the pins from her hair, she brushed it vigorously, braided it, and affixed the braids neatly in a coronet atop her head. It was a severe style, but Amanda's confection of curls, the latest fashion, simply did not suit Miranda. Lastly she dabbed on essence of distilled stock flowers and, slipping on her heel-less apple-green silk shoes, left her room.

Knocking on her twin's bedroom door, she called out, "Are you ready, Mandy?"

"Meet you in the hall," Amanda called.

Amanda was dressed in her favorite pale pink, and together the sisters descended the main staircase of the house and entered the family parlor where Jared and their mother waited.

"Lord," murmured Amanda softly so only her twin could hear, "he is devilishly handsome . . . our guardian, your betrothed."

Then both girls chorused, "Good evening, Mama! Good evening, sir!"

Dinner was announced, and Jared took Dorothea's arm while the girls followed behind. The meal was a relatively simple one beginning with a thick cream of vegetable soup, followed by a ragout of breast of veal, a platter of partridges and quails stuffed with apricots, prunes, and rice, another platter of whole boiled lobsters, a soufflé of autumn squashes flavored with maple syrup and cinnamon, a bowl of late peas, and one of a whole cauliflower, the top of which was sprinkled with buttered crumbs. The second course consisted of apple fritters sprinkled with sugar, caramel custard, and almond cheesecake. Red and white wine were served with the first course, and coffee and tea with the second.

After dinner the four retired to the main parlor, and Amanda sang, accompanying herself on the pianoforte. Jared sipped an excellent brandy. Finally he put his snifter down after complimenting Amanda, and said to Dorothea, "I want you to plan Miranda's wedding as if Tom were still alive. Spare no expense, and invite whom you please."

"I don't want a large wedding," protested Miranda. "Can we please be wed quietly? Amanda's wedding will be the social event of the season, and that should be enough for us all."

"Amanda's being married in London, and none of our good friends and neighbors, as well as many of our relatives, will be able to come. You cannot deny so many people the chance to see one of you wed," said Dorothea.

"It's silly, Mama! This is a marriage of convenience, not a love match. I shall feel very foolish surrounded by a horde of people all burbling nonsense, and wishing me happiness."

"Because it is a marriage of convenience is no reason you cannot be happy," replied Dorothea sharply.

"Oh, do as you please!" snapped Miranda. "You will, anyway!" She stood up, and moved through the French doors out onto the terrace that jutted over the hill, giving a view of the sea. Her long, slender hands clenched and unclenched at the terrace's rough stone wall. She had always hated fuss, and this would become a monumental fuss. She shivered in the early October night, and was glad when a shawl was draped over her shoulders.

His arm slipped around her waist, drawing her back against him. She felt his breath warm against her ear as he spoke. "I thought all women loved planning their weddings."

"If they are looking forward to their weddings I imagine they do. But I don't love you. *I don't love you!*"

"You will, Miranda. You will," he said softly. "I will make you love me!" Turning her toward him, he bent and covered her mouth with his own.

It happened again! She shivered violently. Her heart began to race. The blood roared in her ears. *Fight!* said her brain. Fight, or be overcome! But her limbs were drained of strength. She melted against him, her lips returning his kisses. He raised his head from her mouth and kissed her closed, quivering eyelids. "You will love me, Miranda," he said huskily, "for I will it, and I am not a man to be denied!" Then he held her tenderly against him until her breathing quieted and she stopped trembling.

She felt so helpless against him, and wondered if it would always be like this between them. Why could he render her weak with just a kiss? It confused her, and she almost hated him for it.

"I will not see you in the morning, wildcat," he said gently. "We sail on the early tide, long before you'll open those sea-green eyes of yours. You have my permission to buy whatever you feel you'll need for the wedding."

She pulled away from him, and he immediately ached with loss. "Your permission? I do not need your permission to spend my money," she said angrily.

He couched his statement as diplomatically as possible. "I'm afraid you do, Miranda. You are legally underage, and I am your legal guardian."

"Oh."

He laughed. "Sweet Miranda, don't fight me so hard."

"I will never stop fighting you," she whispered suddenly, fiercely. *"Never!"*

"I think," he answered her seriously, "that there will come a day when you will have to, my dear." He bent, and sweeping her into his arms once more, took her lips in a swift, savage kiss that left her breathless. Then, setting her back on her feet, he said, "Good night, dearest wildcat. I wish you sweet dreams." And then he was gone.

She remained in the cool night air, clutching her shawl to her breasts nervously. It was all happening too fast. She was to marry a man she didn't even know, a man who could render her helpless with a kiss, and who promised—no, threatened in a voice that brooked no refusal that she would indeed love him one day.

Why was she so afraid that in loving him she would lose herself? Men, she had been taught, were superior to women. Did not the Bible teach that God created man first, and then woman as an afterthought? Miranda often wondered why, if women were so unimportant, God had bothered to create them at all. She wanted no master. She would marry Jared Dunham because it was the only way she might keep both Wyndsong and her father's fortune, but she would never love him. For to love him would be to give him an advantage over her.

This resolved, she returned to the parlor. It was empty, and lit only by dying embers, carefully banked for the night. In the hall outside, a lit chamberstick had been left for her, and taking it up she ascended the stairs. The house was quiet. She used the taper to light her own candles, and found her nightdress laid out, and a basin of lukewarm water.

Undressing quickly, for the air was chill, she bathed her face and hands and cleaned her teeth. Slipping beneath the covers, she was relieved to discover that Jemima had placed a flannel-wrapped hot brick at the foot of her bed.

"Miranda?" came the whisper.

"Mandy, I thought you asleep."

"Can I come in?"

"Yes," replied Miranda, throwing back the bedclothes. Amanda placed her chamberstick on the nightstand and hurried to climb into bed beside her sister.

"Are you all right, sister?" Amanda asked anxiously.

"Yes."

"Jared is most forceful. I am so relieved that I was previously contracted to my dearest Adrian. Did you swoon when he kissed you?"

"I did not say he kissed me."

"Well, I can't believe he didn't."

"Yes."

"And did you swoon?"

"Of course not!"

"Oh, come sister! I know for a fact that you've never been kissed until Jared. Are you going to tell me that you felt nothing? I won't believe you."

"I . . . I felt possessed! I didn't like it."

"Oh, Miranda, your feelings were shared by Jared, for if he possessed you, so you possessed him also. It is the way of a kiss between two people," said Amanda gently.

"You speak with such authority, little sister," was the mocking reply, but Amanda heard confusion in the mockery.

"Oh, Miranda, you are such a ninny! I should hope that I speak with authority since I have been kissing since I was twelve. In five and a half years I have learned something about kissing." She laughed softly.

"You must listen to me, sister, for Mama will tell you nothing on your wedding day but to obey your husband. And although men place a high price on their bride's virginity, total innocence can be dangerous. Our guardian is a magnificent creature, and I imagine that when the two of you finally make love it will be like a wild and wonderful storm!"

"Amanda!" Miranda was shocked, and suddenly shy of her twin who now seemed a stranger. "How can you have such knowledge? Surely you haven't dared to do anything improper!"

At first Amanda looked outraged, then she giggled mischievously. "Oh, sister, if you spent more time with females and less time by yourself and with books, you would know everything I do—and at no cost to your virtue. Women trade information."

"I'm sleepy, Mandy." Miranda was embarrassed.

"Oh, no, Miranda! You'll not escape my lessons. Come, dearest, did you not help me with our studies when we were younger? Let me return the favor now."

Miranda sighed. "If I must, I must. I can see you'll give me no peace until you've shared your knowledge." She sat up and, crossing her legs, began to braid her long hair, a task she'd neglected before climbing into bed.

Amanda hid a smile as she pulled the patchwork quilt over her shoulders to keep warm. Her little blond ringlets bobbed from beneath her white lawn and lace-edged nightcap. The cap was tied beneath her chin with pink silk ribbons. "Did Jared touch you?" she demanded.

"What?" Miranda's voice was absolute confirmation.

"Oh ho, he is a bold one!" murmured Amanda. "I almost envy you, but I do not believe I could withstand such passion as I see in those green eyes of his. Where did he touch you?"

"M-my b-breasts," came the whispered reply.

"Did you like it?"

"No! No! It made me feel hot and cold—and helpless! I don't want to feel like that!"

"He'll feel that way later on," came the surprising reply.

"He will?"

"Yes. First you must yield to him, and then he will yield to you, and finally together you will reach paradise."

"How can you know such things?"

"My friends in London, Miranda. The ones you think too silly to bother with."

"I think them even sillier having heard what you have to say so far, Mandy. How can you believe such drivel?"

"I know that when Adrian kisses me I die a thousand little deaths, and when he caresses my breasts I am in Heaven! I long for the day we may truly be one! I had hoped to have the opportunity to instruct you in these matters from personal experience, but suddenly you will be wed before I, so I can only tell you what I have experienced so far and what my married friends say."

"Let us go to bed, Amanda."

"No. Have you ever seen a naked man?"

"Good heavens, no!" Then, curiously, "Have you?"

"Yes!"

"Oh, Amanda, what have you done?!"

Amanda laughed delightedly. "Why, Miranda, I do believe I have shocked you!" She chuckled again. "Remember last summer when I went off with friends for a picnic outside London? There was a party of us, and Lord and Lady Bradley were the chaperones. It was a terribly hot day, and toward midafternoon we decided to go bathing in the stream that ran through the meadow in which we had been picnicking.

"The young men were to go around the bend in the stream while the ladies were to stay upstream. We'd taken off our gowns and petticoats, and were in our vests and drawers. Thanks to you I can swim, and so does my friend Suzanne. We decided to sneak downstream and peek at the men, which we did.

"We got a good deal more than we bargained for, I must say! The men were totally naked! Miranda . . . surely you have noticed the way horses are built?"

When her sister remained silent, Amanda went on. Miranda was keeping quiet either because she knew nothing or because she chose not to discuss what she had seen in the animal kingdom. Miranda being Miranda, she was not going to speak of it unless she wished to. Taking a deep breath, Amanda continued:

"Men have—well, appendages that hang from between their legs, the way animals do. Some are big and some small, some long and some short. But they all have them. And they have hair on their triangles, the way we do. Some even have hair on their chests and legs and arms."

"And you stayed there looking at them?" Miranda was shocked.

"Listen! Soon several girls came along. They were gypsies, I am quite sure—bold girls with big breasts and dark hair. They called to the men, joked with them, and the gentlemen invited them to swim. Well, Miranda, those girls threw off their blouses and skirts—they had no underdrawers, vests, or stockings on—and were quickly as naked as the men.

"They were not one bit shy about jumping into the water and splashing around with the men. For a while that's all they did, and then the men's appendages changed, becoming bigger, and sticking straight out from their bodies.

"Soon the girls lay on the grassy banks with their legs spread wide, and each man in his turn knelt between a girl's legs and pushed his stiffened appendage in and out of her body until he collapsed. The girls cried out, but they did not seem to be in pain. We saw that when the men stood up afterward their appendages were limp again."

"What was it the men were doing with the gypsies?"

"They were making love! Caroline says that to have a man inside of you is a delicious feeling, although I will admit that the gypsies looked kind of funny. So did the men. Anyway, Caroline says that there is pain the first time, when you are still a virgin, but that there is never any pain after that one time. And. . . ."

Here Amanda paused, nearly overwhelmed by her own knowledge. Then she added brightly, "Oh, yes! Babies are born through the opening we use for making love."

"But how can that be, Amanda?" Miranda was beginning to sound doubtful again. "A whole baby getting through there? That doesn't sound right."

"Caroline says the body stretches. She should know. She has a son!" Amanda stoutly defended her friend.

"Caroline is certainly full of facts," said Miranda. "I wonder she did not leave this to Mama to explain."

Amanda chuckled. "On the day you are married to Jared Mama will tell you nothing. She will tell you to trust in God, and obey your husband in all things. If she has had enough rum punch she may be bold enough to say that there are certain things in marriage that are necessary even if unpleasant. You will be left believing that babies are found under mushrooms, and in bluebells!"

Miranda was amazed. For all these years she had believed she was protecting Amanda, the gentle, slower twin, from the harshness of the world! Now it appeared that little Amanda knew far more than she did of things necessary to survival in a man's world. In her quiet way, Amanda had great strength.

"Do you have any questions?" asked Amanda matter-of-factly.

"No. You seem to have answered them all."

"Good! It really isn't fair to send a girl to her marriage bed with no real knowledge," said Amanda.

"One little thing, twin?"

"Yes?"

"If a girl is supposed to be a virgin on her wedding night, then how do men gain their experience?"

"Miranda, there are *good* girls, and there are *bad* girls in this world. Not all bad girls are necessarily gypsies."

The grandfather clock in the hall struck ten. "Go to bed, Amanda," said her sister.

"All right! I do feel ever so much better having spoken to you, Miranda." She slipped out of the bed, and picked up her half-burned candle. "Sweet dreams, dearest," she said, and then she was gone and Miranda heard the door close behind her.

Replumping the pillows, she yanked the crumpled quilt up over her shoulders. What a lot of bother this was going to be, she thought irritably.

I must be a woman now, she thought sadly, and I don't think I'll like it at all. But oh, Papa! I won't let Wyndsong down! I'll do what I must. And so resolving, she fell into a dreamless sleep.

❧ Chapter 4 ❧

"A tragic death, and so damned—your pardon, ladies—so damned unnecessary," said John Dunham. He stroked his thick gray sideburns. "So, Jared, you've come into your inheritance, and are now the lord of Wyndsong Manor. Have you had a chance to see where on the island we might place a boat yard? Don't worry about skilled workers, for we've more than enough to bring down; we'll build them their village right around the yard. I hear there's a vast forest on the island of both hard and soft woods. Good! We'll not have to import wood to build the ships."

Imagining Miranda's reaction to his father's speech, Jared almost laughed aloud. Instead he said quietly, "There will be no boat yard built on Wyndsong, Father. The manor is an extremely prosperous farm and the horses bred there are justly famous. A boat yard would in a few short years render a green and fertile land barren. My inheritance would have little value then. Perhaps that matters little to you, but it matters greatly to me. If I destroy Wyndsong, what will my sons have?"

"You must marry to have sons, Jared," said his mother, knowing an opportunity when she saw one.

"Another part of my news, Mother. I am to be married shortly. I came home particularly to invite you all to the wedding."

"Mercy!" Elizabeth Lightbody Dunham fell back in her chair, her slender bosom heaving. Instantly her daughter, Bess Cabot, and her daughter-in-law, Charity, were fanning her and patting her wrists.

"Congratulations!" grinned Jonathan. "I have no doubt that she's your match."

"Brother Jon, you have no idea how near the truth you are."

"You may be thirty, sir," boomed John Dunham, "but I must approve this match, or you'll not get my blessing. You've studiously avoided every respectable girl in Plymouth since you were breeked; now you come home to tell me you've inherited Wyndsong and you're getting married! Who the hell is this woman? Some fortune-hunting doxy, I've no doubt! You've never had any sense! Refusing to take your place in the yards here, running off to Europe all the time!"

Jared felt the anger well up in him, but he forced it down. It amused him to hear his father's threat about a blessing. The old man had been nagging him to marry for years.

"I think," he said, "you will approve my choice of a wife, Father. She is young, an heiress, and from a well-bred family whom you know personally. Like Jon, I fell in love at first sight."

"The name of this paragon?"

"Miranda Dunham, Cousin Tom's daughter."

"By God, I *do* approve, Jared!"

"I am delighted that my choice meets with your approval," said Jared wryly. The sarcasm eluded his father.

After a large family dinner the two brothers walked together in the back garden. Jared and his brother were almost identical in features. There was but a half-inch difference in their heights, Jared being a full six-feet three. Jared's dark hair was cut short à la Brutus, whereas Jonathan wore his long and clubbed back. There were subtler differences. Jonathan's step was not as long nor as confident; his hands were less elegant than Jared's, and his eyes were gray-green in contrast to the bottle-green of Jared's.

Jonathan Dunham came right to the point. "Love at first sight, Jared?"

"For me, yes."

"So fate has finally dealt you the blow you so richly deserve, my heartbreaking brother. Tell me about Mistress Miranda Dunham. Is she petite, and blond and round like her Van Steen mama?"

"Her twin sister, Amanda, is. Amanda is to be wed next summer to a wealthy English milord."

"If they are twins then they must look alike."

"They are twins, but as different as night and day. Miranda is tall and willowy with sea-green eyes and silken hair like a silvery-gold moon. She is a fairy child, as innocent as a fawn, as elusive as the wind. She is proud and defiant, and I will have my hands full, but I love her, Jon."

"Good Lord, Jared, you *are* in love. I certainly never thought to see you brought low by the tender passion."

Jared laughed good-naturedly. "She does not know how I feel, Jon."

"Then why did you ask her to marry you?" Jonathan was puzzled. His brother explained.

"So you've behaved like the perfect gentleman, eh, Jared?" Jonathan's mouth was twitching. "What if she'd been as ugly as sin?"

"But she isn't," said Jared.

"Only reluctant. That's a problem you've never faced before, brother."

"She's very young, Jon, and she's been very sheltered despite a season in London."

"And you love her! God help you, Jared!" Jonathan shook his head. "When is the wedding?"

"December sixth, on Wyndsong."

"Good lord, you're not wasting much time! What of the mourning period for Cousin Tom?"

"His will said he wanted no mourning past a month," replied Jared. "I can't leave the manor unattended over the winter, and I am too young to remain alone on the island with a lovely widow but twelve years my senior, and two young girls thirteen and a half years my junior. What a field day the gossips would have!

"So a wedding on St. Nicholas Day it will be for the fair Miranda and me, and you're all invited. I've planned for you to go overland to New London, where the yacht will be waiting to take you across the Long Island Sound to Wyndsong. I'd like you to be there a week before the wedding so you can visit with Miranda and her family."

"When are you going back?"

"In a few days. I'll need the time to gentle my wildcat before you come. It was hard enough on her that I inherited Wyndsong, but my being involved in her father's death was too much for her. We need to know each other better."

"You couldn't have found a sweet, quiet girl, could you, Jared?"

"Sweet quiet girls bore me."

"I know," grinned Jonathan Dunham. "Remember the time we followed Chastity Brewster. . . ." and he was off on a reminiscence that soon had both brothers laughing uproariously.

A few days later Jared Dunham left Plymouth, and returned to Wyndsong Island. He sailed on the Dunham family yacht that Dorothea had thoughtfully sent up the coast to Buzzards Bay. A crewman had ridden overland to inform him that his own ship awaited him. Jonathan's admiring glance surprised him, and Jared suddenly became fully aware of his new position.

The first time he'd approached Wyndsong he'd been too upset by his cousin's death to notice the beauty of the island. Now he stood in the bow of his yacht, a stiff north wind at his back, and watched the island appear on the horizon. He remembered what Miranda had told him—that the first time their ancestor Thomas Dunham saw Wyndsong, he felt he was coming home. And so do I, Jared thought, surprised. I feel like I'm coming home.

He came ashore after giving orders to berth the yacht. It was a late October day and the hillsides were ablaze with full autumn color. The maples had begun to shed some of their leaves, and they crunched beneath his feet as he walked to the house. The red oaks, however, still clung stubbornly to all their leaves. A jay screamed raucously at him from a gold birch tree. He laughed at the bird, then his eye caught movement at the top of the path. Miranda? Had she come to greet him?

In her hiding place behind the trees Miranda sat, holding Sea Breeze quiet, and watched him come up the path from the beach. She was unaware that he'd spotted her. She liked the easy, smooth way in which he moved. There was something reassuring about Jared.

Seeing him again after several weeks, her feelings became even more confused. She knew that Jared Dunham was a strong, good man with, she suspected, a spirit as proud and defiant as her own. He would be a good lord of the manor, and Papa had not been wrong in choosing him.

From a personal perspective, however, it was a different story. He threatened her, physically and emotionally, though she was loath to admit it even to herself. She had never battled feelings like this before. One moment she was lost in the memory of his kiss, and then she would recall her helplessness and become angry. If only he would give her time. But there was no time. Sighing, she rode into the woods, suddenly not wanting to see him.

She rode the island until late that day, and he, understanding her need, remained in the house. Dorothea and Amanda regaled him with plans for the wedding, and he felt a distinct sympathy for Miranda. She did not arrive home until they were at dinner, coming into the dining room in her riding clothes.

"Oh," she feigned surprise, "you're back." She slouched into her chair.

"Good evening, Miranda. I am delighted to be home, thank you," he replied.

"May I have some wine?" she said, ignoring his sarcasm.

"No, my dear, you may not. In fact you will leave the table, and have a tray in your room. I will permit riding clothes at breakfast and luncheon, but not at my dinner table. I also expect punctuality in the evening."

She gasped with outrage. "We are not married yet, sir!"

"No, we are not, Miranda, but I am head of this household. Now leave the table, miss!"

She stood abruptly and ran from the room and up the stairs to her bedchamber. Angrily she stripped off her clothes and bathed, swearing at the cold water. Later she put on her nightgown and climbed into bed. How dare he speak to her like that! She was being treated like a little girl! The door opened to admit Jemima with a tray. The maid placed her burden on the table by the fireplace.

"I've brought your supper."

"I don't want it!"

Jemima picked up the tray again. "It's all the same to me," she said, heading out the door with Miranda's supper.

Miranda scrunched back down in her bed, seething angrily. A few minutes later the door opened again, and she heard the sound of the tray being put back on the table. "I told you I didn't want any supper!" she said.

"Why?" came the sound of his voice. "Are you ill, wildcat?"

There was a long pause and then she said, "What are you doing in my bedroom?"

"I came to see if you were all right. You sent Jemima back with the tray."

"I'm all right." She was beginning to feel very foolish. She had attracted his attention when she hadn't meant to at all.

"Then get out of bed, and come eat your supper like a good girl."

"I can't."

"Why not?"

"I'm in my nightgown."

He chuckled at her modesty. "I have a sister, Bess, and many's the time when we were growing up that I saw her in her nightgown. Besides, we're being married in five weeks, Miranda. I think we might be forgiven a little informality." He walked over to the bed and, drawing the covers back, offered her his hand.

Trapped, she grudgingly took it, and slipped from the bed. Leading her over to the fireside table, he gallantly seated her, and then sat opposite her. She eyed the tray suspiciously, then lifted the napkin. There was a steaming bowl of clam chowder, a plate of fresh cornbread, a small dish of sweet butter and honey, a custard tart, and a pot of tea. "There was a joint of beef for dinner," she protested, "and ham, and I saw both apple and pumpkin pie."

"If you are late to my table, Miranda, you cannot expect to be fed from it. I had Cook send you something nourishing and filling. Now eat your soup before it gets cold."

She picked up her spoon obediently, but her sea-green eyes said to him what she dared not, and he repressed a chuckle. She ate quickly until the bowl was empty, then said, reaching for the cornbread, "Why do you persist in treating me like a child?"

"Why do you persist in behaving like one?" he countered. "You arrive late for dinner, pretending my presence is a complete surprise to you while we both know that you were in the woods above Little North Bay this morning, watching me land."

She flushed deeply. "Why did you say nothing?" Her eyes were lowered.

"Because, Miranda, I assumed you wanted to be alone. I was attempting to respect your wishes, my dear. I know this is not easy for you. But it is no easier for me. Did it ever occur to you that I did not wish to marry yet? Or that perhaps there was someone else in my life for whom I cared? You have, like the spoiled child you are, thought only of yourself. In the next few weeks before my family arrive you are going to practice behaving like the woman I know is beneath that bratty veneer," he finished firmly.

"I am afraid," she whispered low, her defenses suddenly crumbling.

"Of what?" his voice was gentle now.

She looked up at him, and to his surprise her eyes were filled with tears that suddenly spilled over onto her cheeks. She tried to blink them away. "I am afraid of growing up," she said. "I am afraid of the feelings you raise in me, for they are ambiguous and confusing. I am afraid I shall not be able to be a good lady of the manor. I love Wyndsong, but I was a terrible failure in society. Amanda knew just what to do in London, but despite the fact that I'd been taught the same things, despite the fact that I am thought to be smarter, I was gauche and awkward while my sister shone. How can I be your wife, Jared? We must entertain, and I am awful at small talk. I am too intelligent for a woman, and my speech is blunt."

A great wave of pity washed over him, but to offer her his sympathy would, he knew, only alienate her further. He wanted to take her onto his lap, and assure her that all would be well, but to encourage her childishness now would be a terrible mistake.

He leaned across the table and took her hands in his. "Look at me, wildcat, and listen. We both have some growing up to do. I've avoided the responsibilities of manhood rather successfully for more years than most. Suddenly I find myself responsible for this manor and its well-being when I'd rather be off chasing the British or outsmarting the French. But those times are over for me, as your childhood is over for you. Let's make a pact, you and I. I promise to grow up if you will."

"Is there someone?"

"What?"

"Someone else you'd rather marry?"

"No, wildcat, there is no one else." His eyes twinkled. "Are you relieved or disappointed?"

"Relieved," she answered simply.

"Dare I hope you are entertaining what is called in polite society a 'tender passion' for me?"

"No," she said, "I simply didn't want to lose my fortune."

He burst out laughing. "Good Lord, Miranda, your tongue *is* blunt! Hasn't anyone taught you tact? One may be honest without being quite so frank." He kissed her fingertips, and shyly she withdrew her hands from his.

"What should I have said?" she asked, daring to look him in the eyes.

He smiled at her. "You might have told me that it was much too soon to be sure of your feelings. A fashionable lady would have blushed prettily and said, 'La, sir! You are naughty even to ask such a question.' I realize that is not quite your style, Miranda, but you do understand what I am getting at, don't you?"

"Yes, although it seems rather silly to couch the truth in folderol."

"Silly, but sometimes necessary, wildcat. The plain truth frightens people. Trust me, Miranda, and we will grow together. Now," he stood up, and coming around the table drew her up so that they were facing each other, "about that other matter. You say you are afraid of the feelings I raise in you. Did you know that you raise the same feelings in me?"

"*I do?*" He was very close now. She could smell the male scent of him; feel the heat of his long, lean body; see the slow pulse beating at the base of his throat.

His big, elegant hand caressed her silver-gilt hair. "Yes, you do," his deep voice murmured as his arm tightened about her slender waist.

She almost stopped breathing. Her eyes widened and grew dark.

He bent and brushed those ripe lips gently, so very gently. "Oh yes, Miranda," he murmured against her mouth, "you very definitely set my senses awhirl." Tenderly he nibbled at her lips while one hand reveled in the silky texture of her lovely, long hair. He held her in a firm but easy embrace, and now with a soft little moan she fell back against his arm. He kissed the cleft in her chin, then traveled the satiny length of her throat downward to her breasts. The ribbons holding the two halves of the front of her nightgown together melted away. With a groan he picked her up, carried her across the room, and lay her on the bed.

He lay next to her fully clothed, and drew her into his arms. He kissed her with a passion that left her only semi-conscious, but still acutely aware of her newly awakened desires. She felt the thin hold she had on herself giving way as he buried his face in her breasts. A hungry, wet mouth closed over a swollen, aching nipple, and as he suckled eagerly, she felt with lightning-sharp awareness a corresponding ache in the hidden place between her legs. His fingers soon found that hidden place, and stroked her gently.

After what seemed a sweet eternity he rolled over on his back and, taking her slender hand, placed it on the covered badge of his gender. Wordlessly he taught her the rhythm, and shuddered beneath her delicate touch until finally he stopped her and said in a strangely hoarse voice, "You see, Miranda, if you are helpless beneath my touch, then so am I helpless beneath yours."

"I didn't know," she whispered.

"There are many things you don't know, wildcat, but I will teach you if you will let me." Then, leaning over her, he slowly retied the ribbons of her gown and, smoothing her tangled hair back, gently kissed her goodnight.

The door clicked shut behind him, and Miranda lay quivering for some minutes. So that was lovemaking! She realized that in being entirely truthful with him she had given him a powerful weapon against her. Still, he had not used that weapon. He had been equally truthful with her.

Being a married woman would entail responsibilities. Why, she might even be a mother by this time next year. *A mother!* The thought raised a host of new doubts. She certainly would have to grow up herself before she could nurture a child. Oh Lord! What was she letting herself in for?

For the next few days Miranda was strangely subdued, and her mother feared she was falling ill. She did not ride, but stayed indoors, poking around the manor and asking questions about the operation of the household. Amanda understood, and wondered what it was that Jared could have possibly said to turn her rebellious sister into such a docile creature. She also wondered how long it would last. The question was answered within the week, when Miranda, wilted and exhausted from a day of making grape conserves, burst into tears at the dinner table.

Jared leaped up, and was at her side immediately, his concern obvious, to Amanda's amusement.

"I cannot do it," Miranda sobbed. "I simply cannot do it! I detest homemaking! Oh Jared, how can I ever be a good lady of the manor? I burn the jam, I ruin an entire batch of cod by oversalting it, my pumpkin pies are overspiced, the soap I made smells more of pig than perfume, and my candles smoke!"

Relieved, Jared stifled his laughter. "Oh, wildcat, you misunderstood me. I don't want you to be what you're not. I only want you to understand how the manor is run. It is not necessary for you to make jam or soap, or salt cod. We have servants to do those things. You need only know how it is done so you can supervise." He took a slender hand in one of his, and placed a soft kiss on her upturned palm. "This sweet hand is far more skilled in *other* things," he murmured so that only she could hear, and a soft blush colored her cheeks.

Dorothea wondered about this intimacy between her daughter and Jared. True, they were to be wed shortly, but was it entirely proper that he put his arm around Miranda? She had learned from Jemima that he had taken the tray into Miranda's room the other night and not come out for a full half-hour. With surprise, Dorothea realized that she was envious. After all, she was still young enough to love. The sight of Miranda and Jared in close proximity pained her as she remembered how it had been between her and Thomas. She sighed softly. Had life stopped for her? She wondered.

The next few weeks sped by as final preparations for the wedding were made. These were mostly ignored by both bride and groom, who rode the island on good days and closeted themselves within the library on bad ones. Occasionally they were joined by Amanda, who was absolutely delighted to see how well suited the pair was.

The Plymouth Dunhams arrived *en masse*—six adults and five small children. After an initial uncomfortable moment both families settled down together. Elizabeth Lightbody Dunham and Dorothea Van Steen Dunham quickly became friends. Jared's mother was enchanted with Miranda, who was on her very best behavior. Dorothea was far better used to hearing Amanda accoladed, and she said so.

"Of course," agreed Elizabeth. "Your little Amanda is perfection, and she will certainly make Lord Swynford an ideal wife. But she would never do for Jared. Miranda has spirit. She will lead my son a merry dance, which is exactly what he needs. He will never be quite sure of her, and consequently he will always treat her well. Yes, my dear Dorothea, I am more than satisfied with Miranda."

St. Nicholas Day dawned clear and cold. The sun had barely peeped over the horizon, reaching with warm golden fingers across the cold blue waters of the bay, when boats set out from both forks of Long Island for Wyndsong Manor. Among the guests would be the Hortons, Younges, Tutills, and Albertsons; Jewels, Boisseaus, Lathams, and Goldsmiths; Terrys, Welles, and Edwardses. The Sylvesters from Shelter Island were coming, as were the Fiskes from Plum Island and the Gardiners from Wyndsong's neighboring island manor. The house was already filled with the Dunhams, and several days earlier Dorothea's relatives and close friends had begun arriving from the Hudson Valley and from New York City.

The twins' Van Steen grandmother, Judith, was still alive, her corn-colored hair now white, but her eyes as blue as ever. Like her daughter, Dorothea, and her granddaughter, Amanda, she was petite and plump. Her first glimpse of Jared elicited the comment, "He looks like a pirate—an elegant one, but a pirate nonetheless. He'll suit that vixen Miranda to a T, I've not a doubt."

"Good Lord, Mother! What a thing to say." Cornelius Van Steen the younger, current patroon of Torwyck Manor, looked embarrassed. "I must apologize for my parent, sirs and ladies," he nodded to the assembled gathering of Dunhams and Van Steens.

"No one, Cornelius, has to apologize for me," snapped old Mrs. Van Steen. "Bless me, but you're a prude! How I could have borne such a son is beyond me! I meant the observation as a compliment, and Jared knew it, eh, my boy?"

"Indeed, ma'am, I understood exactly what you meant," replied Jared, his green eyes twinkling, and he raised her plump white beringed hand to his lips and kissed it.

"Bless my soul! A rogue as well!" exclaimed the old lady.

"I am that too, ma'am," came the reply.

"Heh! Heh! Heh!" chortled the elderly woman. "If I were thirty years younger, my boy!"

"I've no doubt of it, ma'am," was the smooth answer. He punctuated his remark with the lift of a bushy black eyebrow.

Miranda chuckled, remembering the incident. She was standing looking out her bedroom windows at the dawn sky. It was going to be a beautiful day. Behind her, the fireplace crackled with a sharp snap as the applewood burned. Amanda inquired sleepily from the bed, "Are you up already?" The press of guests had made it necessary for them to share a bed these last few days.

"Yes, I'm awake. I couldn't sleep." Miranda glanced around her bedroom. Tonight she would sleep in the newly decorated master suite of the manor, and for days she had lived with that thought. All her life this had been *her* room. Her double-sized tester bed with its lovely green and white linen homespun hangings. The posts on the cherry-wood bed were turned, and as a child she had lain in bed imagining what it would be like to slide down the turning, going round and round and round until she slid dizzily into sleep. There was a beautiful cherry-wood chest-on-chest with flame finials on one wall of her room, the brass pulls always kept shining. Her dressing table had been made especially for her fourteenth birthday, its built-in mirror of precious glass, perfect and unflawed. There was a round piecrust table to one side of the fireplace, and on the other side, an armed ladder-back chair with a green velvet cushion.

The master bedroom had been entirely redone for her and Jared. The work had been going on for weeks. She had no idea what it would look like, for he wanted it to be a surprise. At least it hadn't been her parents' room, she thought with relief. When Thomas and Dorothea were married both of her grandparents and her great-grandfather had been living in the house. Her great-grandfather had died in 1790, and her grandparents had moved into the master suite. But when her Dunham grandmother passed on, her grandfather had not relinquished the room. When he died, four years earlier, her parents had decided to stay in their bedroom of over twenty years. So it was actually her grandfather's room that was being redone for her and Jared.

The little clock on the mantel with the painted face chimed half-past seven, and Amanda muttered, "Why on earth did you chose ten o'clock in the morning for your wedding? I do not intend being married until late afternoon."

"It was Jared's idea."

"What kind of a day is it?"

"Clear. Bright blue sky, no clouds, sunny. The bay is full of boats coming from all directions. It reminds me of the hunt breakfasts Papa used to have."

Amanda got reluctantly out of bed, squealing at the icy floor. "We had better consider getting ready," she said.

Just then Jemima arrived with a heavily ladened tray. "Don't tell me you can't eat, for Lord knows when you'll get to eat again, especially with those locusts arriving downstairs. 'Serve a light breakfast,' says your mama, so Cook does six hams, plenty of eggs, hot breads, coffee, tea, and chocolate. Three of the hams are gone already and not half the guests here yet!" She plunked the tray down on the table. "I'll have the hot water for your baths brought up in an hour," and she bustled out.

"I'm starved!" announced Miranda.

"You are?" Amanda was aghast. "You're really hungry on your wedding morning? You always did have nerves of iron, twin."

"You can be nervous for me, Mandy, and I'll eat your portion too!"

"No, you won't! It's not my wedding day!" laughed Amanda, and she snatched the napkin from the tray. There were two plates, each filled with fluffy scrambled eggs and thin slices of pink ham. "Ummm, delicious! I've never tasted eggs like Cook makes anywhere else," she said.

"It's the heavy cream, the farmer's cheese, and the chives," answered Miranda calmly, buttering a flaky croissant, and spreading it lavishly with raspberry jam.

Amanda's mouth fell open. "How on earth did you know that?"

"I asked. Pour me some chocolate, will you, dearest? The secret to the chocolate is the touch of cinnamon."

"Good Lord!" said Amanda.

Breakfast eaten, the sisters' porcelain baths were set up and filled with hot water. They had washed their hair the day before, knowing there wouldn't be time in the morning. Dry again, and in their chamber robes, they waited for their gowns to be brought to them. The clock struck nine-thirty and the door opened to admit Jemima and two maidservants carrying their gowns. Dorothea had wanted Miranda to wear her own wedding gown, but the bride was too tall and too slender. If the gown had been altered to fit Miranda, then Amanda would not be able to wear it the following June, and as it was the gown fit Amanda perfectly. So Madame duPré, a well-known New York City dressmaker, had been brought all the long way from town to do Miranda's wedding gown, Amanda's gown as maid of honor, and the trousseau.

Pure white was not Miranda's color, and so her gown was of a creamy ivory velvet. The dress was in the height of fashion, with short, puffed sleeves edged in lace and a waistline set just below her breasts. The neckline, deep and square, was edged in lace and at the bottom of the gown was a two-inch hem of swansdown. Miranda wore a single strand of perfectly matched pearls around her slender neck.

Miranda's pale-gold hair was parted in the center and drawn into a chignon at the nape of her neck except for a small tendril of curl on either side of her heart-shaped face. Crowning her was a wreath of small white roses to which was attached a floor-length veil so fine that it looked spun from thistledown. The rose wreath had come from the manor's small hothouse, and matched her bouquet, which contained green fern as well as the small white roses. The bouquet was tied with silver-gilt ribbons.

The petite Amanda looked like a delicious bonbon in a pale-pink velvet gown that was identical in design to her sister's. The roses atop her fair head were Chinese red, as were the roses mixed with pine that she carried.

At ten minutes to ten o'clock the twins were ready, and Amanda commanded, "Call Uncle Cornelius, and let us begin the ceremony now."

"Early?" Miranda looked amused despite the butterflies that had suddenly taken up residence in her stomach. "Are you afraid I'll cry off, Mandy?"

"No! No! But it's good luck to begin a marriage while the clock hand sweeps upward, not downward."

"Then by all means let us begin! Besides, all the local gossips will say how eager I am to wed Jared. I would disappoint them if I did the expected."

Amanda laughed delightedly. This was the sister she knew and loved. She ran to fetch their uncle, who protested the early start until Amanda mischievously suggested that the bride was debating backing out. Horrified by the possibility of scandal, the prim and proper Cornelius Van Steen hurried to escort his niece to the altar, grateful as he did so that the Lord had given him only docile daughters.

The wedding ceremony was held in the main parlor of the house. The room, a retangular corner one, was painted palest yellow and was quite bright and cheerful. It had plaster ceiling moldings in a simple leaf design, and an ornate plaster ceiling centerpiece with an oval decoration with rosettes in high relief.

The long windows, two facing south and three facing east, were draped in yellow and white satin. The polished, wide-board oak floors were covered by a rare sixteenth-century Tabriz carpet embroidered in all sorts of animals. For the wedding the mahogany Queen Anne and Chippendale furniture and the upholstered pieces had been removed from the room. A small altar had been set up before the blazing fireplace, either side of which was decorated in large white willow baskets filled with roses, pine, and holly. From the mantel of the fireplace hung a garland of pine, gilded nuts, and pine cones, and above the fireplace hung an enormous wreath done in the same motif.

The room was crowded now as Amanda, demure and sweet, preceded her sister through the room toward the altar, where Jared and Jonathan and the minister waited. The little twin elicited gasps of envy from the young ladies attending the ceremony, and sighs of regret from the local swains who had already learned that Amanda Dunham's heart and hand belonged to an English milord. The bright morning sunlight filled the lovely room, making candles unnecessary. The heat from both the fire and the sun coming through the windows combined to make the room quite warm, and the floral decorations opened eagerly to scent the room.

All eyes turned eagerly to the doorway of the drawing room where the enchantingly lovely bride appeared on the arm of her nervous uncle, and floated forward to meet her destiny. Dorothea, Elizabeth, and the elderly Judith sniffed audibly as the bride moved past them and Jared's sister, Bess, and his sister-in-law, Charity, dabbed daintily at their eyes with showy bits of lawn and lace. Miranda glanced around at the room full of people, marveling that a wedding had brought them across several miles of open water on a December day.

Jared stood quietly watching her come toward him, wondering what was going on in her mind. His throat had tightened at the sight of her, for she was lovelier today than he had ever seen her. There was an elegance about her, a serenity he had not seen before, and it pleased his vanity to believe that he might be partly responsible for this new beauty.

Miranda came out of her reverie as they approached the little altar. How handsome he looked! She saw several girls eying him with envy, and she smiled to herself. He truly was a fine figure of a man. She had never paid a great deal of attention to his clothes, but of course today was different. He was wearing fitted, tight, white knee breeches, and his high black leather boots had been polished till they glistened. She wondered if he used a mixture of champagne and bootblack, as they did in London. His white shirt was the latest fashion in England, with its high collar. His fitted coat was of dark green velvet, bobtailed in back, cut short in front, and decorated with gold buttons. His stock was tied in the style called the Waterfall.

Next to Jared stood Jonathan, whose dress echoed his brother's. Miranda had discovered that some could hardly tell the two apart, but for her they were as different as day and night.

With a start, Miranda felt her hand transferred to Jared by Uncle Cornelius.

"Dearly beloved," began the Anglican minister. He had come from Huntingtontown to perform the ceremony, for the Wyndsong Dunhams were Church of England. Miranda was so intent on the words that she had no chance even to glance at Jared.

"I require and charge ye both, as ye will answer at the dreadful Day of Judgment when the secrets of all hearts shall be disclosed," pronounced the clergyman ominously, and Miranda's pulse quickened. She had never thought of marriage quite so seriously. All she wanted was Wyndsong, and Papa's fortune, which would mean Amanda's happiness with Lord Swynford. Was she doing the right thing in marrying Jared when she didn't love him? Well, at least she didn't hate him any longer.

As if he understood her thoughts, the man by her side squeezed her hand reassuringly.

"Jared, wilt thou have this woman to be thy wedded wife, to live together after God's ordinance in the holy estate of matrimony? Wilt thou love her, comfort her, honor, and keep her in sickness and in health and, forsaking all others, keep thee only unto her, so long as ye both shall live?"

"I will!" his deep voice echoed loudly and firmly.

"Miranda Charlotte..."

She started, hearing her full name, and for a moment she lost her concentration.

"Wilt thou love him, comfort him, honor and obey him..."

I don't *know!* Yes, yes...but not always, not if he's wrong and I'm right, she thought frantically. Oh God, why do you make it so harsh?

"...so long as ye both shall live?" finished the cleric.

The answer stuck for a moment in her throat as the terrifying thought, *This is forever,* crossed her mind. Frantically she gazed through fogging eyes at her uncle and her sister, both of whom looked as if they were expecting a volcano to erupt. Her eyes swung up to Jared, and although his lips never moved she later swore that she heard the soft words "Easy, wildcat." Reason returned.

"I will," she said softly.

The ceremony continued. A beautiful gold wedding band with tiny diamond-chip stars was placed gently on her finger and, for some reason, she felt tears pricking her eyelids. Finally they were pronounced man and wife, and the beaming clergyman said to Jared, "You may kiss the bride, sir," and Jared bent and gently kissed her while around them the onlookers cheered.

In a few minutes they were standing at the entry to the parlor, receiving congratulations. Miranda was soon rosy with kisses from the male guests, all of whom insisted on the traditional bride's kiss for luck. She stood through it all, graciously acknowledging each guest, each tribute, with a personal word for everyone. Jared was very proud of her. Given a challenge, she had responded well. Some of her female acquaintances jealously attempted to bait her into a show of her famous temper, but Miranda handled them like a veteran.

"My goodness, Miranda," murmured Susannah Terry sweetly, "such a quick courtship! But trust you not to do the conventional thing."

"Papa wanted it this way," returned Miranda just as sweetly. Then, "Are you still waiting for Nathaniel Horton to propose, dear? How long has it been since he started courting you? Two years?"

Susannah Terry moved quickly on, and Miranda heard her husband chuckle. "What a venomous tongue you have, Mistress Dunham."

"La, sir, I attempt only to protect our reputation. Susannah is a notorious gossip."

"Then let us give her something to gossip about," he murmured, nuzzling her neck so that she blushed. "It will be said that I lusted after my wife, with the ceremony barely over."

"Jared," she pleaded.

"Is this person bothering you, ma'am? He always was a cheeky fellow. Good grief, brother, restrain yourself."

"The wench drives me wild, Jonathan."

"Will the two of you stop it? You are both embarrassing me," Miranda protested. "I shall leave you to mingle with our guests before the buffet is served." She moved away into the crowd of guests.

"I've been watching you with her all week, Jared, and this morning when she had that moment of panic, I've never seen you look so stricken. You love her, man, but she doesn't yet love you. Does she know how you feel?"

"No. On advice of the fair Amanda, I am not to tell her until she admits similar feelings for me. She's so damned innocent, Jon, I don't want to frighten her off."

"You were always too much of a romantic, Jared, but if it were me I'd get her with child as quickly as possible. Nothing settles a woman faster than a baby."

Jared laughed. "That's all I need, Jon, a child-wife with a child. No, thank you, I intend spending the next few months courting my bride."

"The courtship usually comes before the wedding, Jared, not after."

"Only when you're dealing with an ordinary girl, and I think we both agree that Miranda is not ordinary. Nor was the situation. Now, brother, as dear as you are to me, I know you'll excuse me if I join my bride."

Jon watched his brother affectionately. He had no doubt that given enough time, Jared would win over the prickly Miranda. He himself didn't know if he'd have that much patience. He far preferred his sweet, even-tempered Charity. Complicated, intelligent women were such a trial. Seeking his wife, he found her with Cornelius Van Steen's wife, Annettje, comparing recipes for potpourri. Sliding his arm around her comfortable middle, he kissed her cheek, and she flushed with pleasure.

"What on earth is that for, Jon?"

"For being you," he answered.

"Have you been in the rum punch?"

"Not yet, but an excellent idea! Ladies," he gallantly offered his arm to them, "allow me to escort you to the buffet."

The formal dining room at Wyndsong was opposite the main parlor across the center hall of the house. The wide doors were now opened back. The room was powder blue, with white plaster detail. The long windows were draped in a slightly darker blue satin sprigged with a buff color, and the crystal chandelier with its mouth-blown hurricane lamps was relatively new, having been a tenth-anniversary gift from Thomas to Dorothea. The mahogany Hepplewhite table and chairs came from the New York shop of Duncan Phyfe. The chair seats were upholstered in blue and buff satin. The New York Hepplewhite sideboard of inlaid mahogany had come from the Maiden Lane Shop of cabinetmaker Elbert Anderson. On either end of the sideboard were fine mahogany knifeboxes with silver escutcheons.

A large buffet had been set up on the table in the center of the room. Covered in a white linen cloth, the table held a centerpiece of pine, holly, and red and white roses arranged in an enormous pewter bowl. It was flanked on either side by elegant silver candelabra burning bayberry-scented white beeswax tapers.

On the table were bowls of oysters, mussels, and clams, small lobsters and crab claws done with mustard sauce, as well as broiled in herb butter. There was even a platter of cold crabmeat, accompanied by a pewter dish of mayonnaise. There were several varieties of cod, flounder, and bluefish, Wyndsong waters abounding with fish.

Four large hams had been baked in brown sugar and all were studded with precious, difficult-to-obtain cloves. There was an entire side of beef and a side of venison, as well as Miranda's favorite, stuffed turkey. There were two geese, both roasted to a crisp brown and stuffed with wild rice.

The vegetables alone looked like a painting of the horn of plenty. Besides large white china bowls of yellow squash topped with melting butter, there were green beans with almonds, whole cauliflowers, onions boiled in milk and butter and black pepper, and succotash. Dorothea's recipe for pumpkin squash was the one the cook had followed, as it was a family favorite.

There were five red-and-white-striped china bowls of macaroni and grated sharp Cheddar cheese, another of Miranda's best-loved dishes, as well as potatoes in Hollandaise, mashed potatoes with butter, and potato puffs, Cook's jealously guarded secret.

Even though it was winter, there were large china serving platters of lettuce and cucumbers in a delicately flavored piquant white sauce, made with just enough vinegar to wake the palate.

The wedding cake—a light fruit cake covered in sparkling white frosting—commanded the most attention. On the sideboard surrounding the cake were pineapple creams, apricot fritters, three kinds of cheesecake, and caramel custard. Guests exclaimed over the spongy Genovese cakes filled with coffee cream, and despite the recent appearance of mince and pumpkin pies on everyone's Thanksgiving tables, these disappeared as quickly as did the assortment of lemon and raspberry tarts, the soufflés, and the tiny *pots au chocolat,* which Miranda had always loved and which, though not officially part of the menu, Cook had decided were just what Miranda needed on this day of great changes.

Even these guests, all of whom dined well at home, were delighted by the variety of food and the elegant display of every dish. Dorothea, a little more relaxed now, watched them with amusement and affection, finally taking a plate for herself and heaping it with turkey, pumpkin soufflé, ham, and rather more salad than she usually ate. It had been a long week, and she wanted a taste of spring. Somehow, cucumbers always reminded Dorothea of spring.

Liquid refreshments were equally lavish, which pleased the gentlemen especially. There were several wines, both red and white, beer, cider, applejack, rum punch, tea, and coffee.

Small tables had been set up in the hall, the drawing room, the library, and the family parlor. The guests, clutching well-filled plates, were fast finding seats. The bride and groom were seated at a trestle table made of oak with a pine top that had been set before the fireplace in the library. The table, made in the mid-1600s, was one of the few pieces that remained from the original manor house. Also

seated at the table were Jonathan Dunham and his wife, John and
Elizabeth Dunham, Bess Dunham Cabot and her husband, Henry,
Amanda, Dorothea, Judith, Annettje and Cornelius Van Steen.

Miranda sat back in her chair and viewed the guests with
amusement. The enormous amount of food that the Wyndsong cook
and her helpers had so painstakingly prepared was being quickly
demolished.

"When do you think they last ate?" queried Jared solemnly, and
Miranda giggled.

"That's a nice sound, wildcat. Dare I hope it's a happy day for
you?"

"I am not unhappy, sir."

"May I get you something to eat, madam?" he inquired solicitously. "I have promised to cherish you, and I believe that covers
feeding."

She flashed him a genuine smile, and his heart contracted
painfully. "Thank you, sir. Something light, if you please, and some
white wine."

He brought her back a plate with a slice of turkey breast, a
miniature potato soufflé, some crisp green beans and yellow squash.
On his plate were oysters, two slices of ham, green beans, macaroni
and cheese. Putting the plates down, he disappeared into the dining
room, then returned with two glasses of wine, one red, the other
white.

She was silent as she ate, and then suddenly she said softly to him,
"I wish they'd all go home. If I must smile sweetly at one more old
lady, kiss one more slightly tipsy gentleman . . ."

"If we cut the cake," he said, "and then you throw your bouquet a
little while after that, they will have no excuse to stay. Besides, it
will be dark early, and our guests will want to be off the water, and
safely on dry land by then."

"Your sound logic amazes me, *husband,*" she said low, blushing
at her daring use of the word.

"I long to be alone with you, *wife,*" he returned, and her blush
deepened.

They cut the wedding cake with the usual ceremony, and as the
desserts were offered to the guests, a maid passed among them with

a tray of specially boxed tiny pieces of cake for the ladies to take home so they might dream of their true love. Miranda allowed a decent interval to pass, and then she ascended partway up the stairs with much hoopla and threw her bouquet. It flew straight into Amanda's outstretched hands.

Shortly afterward she and Jared stood at the front door of Wyndsong House bidding their guests farewell. It was only three-thirty in the afternoon, but already the sun had begun to sink into the west over Connecticut.

Then the house was quiet, and she looked up at Jared with an expression of great relief. "I warned you that I hate big parties," she said ruefully.

"Then we shall not give them," he answered.

"I imagine I should see to the servants."

"It is not necessary today. They have their instructions."

"I should give Cook the menu for dinner."

"She has it."

"Then I shall join the ladies, sir. I assume they are in the family parlor."

"Everyone is gone, Miranda. Your mother and sister left with your grandmother, your aunt and uncle, and your cousins. They will be spending the rest of the month at Torwyck, with the Van Steens. Your mother is especially eager for a long visit with her brother."

"We are *alone?*" She edged nervously away from him.

"We are alone," he said quietly. "It is, I believe, the usual state for a bride and groom on their honeymoon."

"Oh." Her voice was suddenly very small.

"Come!" He held out his hand to her.

"Where?"

His bottle-green eyes swept toward the staircase.

"But it's still light," she protested, shocked.

"Late afternoon is as good a time as any. I don't intend to be bound by the clock when it comes to making love to you, my dear." He took a step toward her, and she retreated farther.

"But we don't love each other! When this marriage was first agreed upon I attempted to gauge our suitability in intimate matters. You were not interested! You laughed at me, and treated me like a child! I assumed, therefore, that this marriage would be in name only."

"The hell you did!" he growled, striding forward, and swept her up in his arms. Christ, she was a warm armful. For a moment he buried his face in her cleavage, and breathed the sweet scent of her. She trembled against him and, raising his dark head, he muttered fiercely, "Not for one minute have you ever believed in your heart that this would be a marriage in name only, Miranda!" Then he mounted the stairs, carrying her, and strode down the hall to their bedroom. Kicking the door open with his booted foot, he set her firmly on her feet; spinning her around, he began to undo her gown.

"Please!" she whispered. "Please, not like this!"

He stopped, and she heard him sigh deeply. Then his arms went around her, and he said softly against her ear, "You drive me to violence, wildcat. I will call your maid to help you, but I will not wait long."

She stood rooted to the floor as she heard the door close. She could still feel his arms around her, strong arms, arms that would not be denied. She thought about what Amanda had told her of lovemaking, and she thought of the terrible feelings Jared caused in her.

"Madam? Madam, may I help you."

She whirled about, startled. "Who are you?"

"I am Sally Ann Browne, ma'am. Master Jared chose me to be your maid."

"I have not seen you on Wyndsong before."

"Lord no, ma'am. I'm Cook's granddaughter from Connecticut." Sally Ann went behind Miranda and began unfastening her gown. "I'm sixteen, and I've been working for two years now. My old mistress, she died, poor soul, but then she was near eighty. I came over the water to visit my granny before I looked for a new position, and lo and behold there was a place available right here." She drew the gown down, and helped Miranda step out of it. "I'm a good seamstress, and I do hair better than anyone. Despite her age, my old mistress was one for keeping up with the latest fashions. God rest her."

"My h-husband engaged you?"

"Yes, ma'am. He said he thought you'd be happier having a maid of your own, and one nearer your age. My word, that old Jemima was put out at first, but your sister says to her, 'And who'll take care of me, Mima, if you don't?' Well, that pleased Jemima so much she never gave me another thought!" Sally Ann worked as quickly as she talked and soon, embarrassed, Miranda found herself nude. The maid handed her a lovely simple white silk nightgown with a deep-scooped neckline and long, flowing sleeves edged in lace. "There now, sit down at your dressing table, and I'll brush your hair. Lord, what a lovely color it is, like silver gilt."

Miranda sat silently as Sally Ann chattered on, and her sea-green eyes began to focus on the room. The deep-set windows with their cushioned, creweled window seats faced west. The walls were painted a pale gold with off-white ceiling and woodwork. The furniture was all mahogany, the largest piece within the bedroom being a bed in the Sheraton style with tall reeded and carved posts. The festooned canopy and skirt were a cream-colored printed French cotton with a tiny lime-green sprig called toile de Jouy. For a moment Miranda could not take her eyes off the bed. She had never seen anything so big! With an enormous effort of will she tore her eyes from the bed to concentrate on the room's other furnishings. There were candlestands on either side of the bed, each with its own silver candlestick and snuffer. Across from the bed was the fireplace with its lovely white Georgian mantel, and a facing done in tiles painted with examples of local flora. To the left of the fireplace was a large wing chair upholstered in dark gold damask satin. To the right of the fireplace was a Philadelphia piecrust tripod tea table of Santo Domingo mahogany with three carved ball feet, and two New York mahogany side chairs with seats upholstered in a green-sprigged cream-colored satin. The window hangings matched the bed hangings, and there was a beautiful, rare Chinese rug done in gold and white on the floor.

"There you go, ma'am. Lord, if I had such hair, I'd be a princess!"

Miranda looked up at her maid, really seeing her for the first time. She smiled. Sally Ann was a big-boned, gawky girl with a homely face and an engaging grin. Her hair was carrot red, her eyes brown.

She was freckled, and altogether as plain as white cotton. "Thank you, Sally Ann, but I think my hair an odd color."

"Is moonlight odd, ma'am?"

Miranda was touched. "There's a bit of the poet in you," she said.

"Will there be anything else, ma'am?"

"No. You may go, Sally Ann."

The door closed behind the maid, and Miranda rose from her dressing table to explore further. To the left of the fireplace was an open door; peeping in, she saw what would now be her dressing room. It was newly furnished in a Newport highboy and a bombe chest. She ventured further, and discovered that his dressing room, with a Charleston chest-on-chest, was behind hers. The room smelled of tobacco and man, and she nervously fled back to the bedroom and sat on the window seat. The sky was flame and lavender, peach and gold with the sunset, and the bay was dark and calm. The trees, leafless now, stood in black relief against the sunset.

Hearing him quietly enter the room, she remained motionless. He crossed the floor noiselessly and sat next to her, his arm slipping around her waist, drawing her back against him. Silently they watched the day flee west and the night fill the sky, turning it deep blue, the horizon edged in red gold, the evening star silvery bright. His fingers drew her gown down from a shoulder, his lips pressed a kiss on the soft skin. She shivered, and he murmured, "Oh Miranda, don't be afraid of me. I only want to love you."

She said nothing, and the other side of her gown was lowered to meet the first, then pulled quickly away to her waist. His big hands were cupping her breasts, gently crushing the soft flesh, and she gasped as he turned her toward him, and began kissing the twin delights. "Ohh, please, Jared! Please!"

"Please what?" he muttered thickly.

She smelled the brandy on his breath, and was surprised. "You've been drinking!" she accused, feeling braver, and pushing him away.

He gazed up at her, and she started at the look in his eyes. "Yes, I've been drinking, wildcat! Dutch courage, they call it."

"Why?"

"So I won't lose my nerve with you, my bride. So your pretty protestations followed by your quick temper will not deter me from my purpose. Oh, I'm not drunk, Miranda, far from it. I've had only one snifter, just enough to harden my heart against your pleas."

"How can you want me, knowing that I don't want you?" she demanded.

"My dear, you don't know what you want. Virgins, it has been my experience, are at best a capricious lot. Let us rid you of that disadvantage, and then we'll see!"

He stood up, pulling her after him, and the loosened gown fell to her feet. Then he swept her up and carried her to the bed, where he dumped her unceremoniously. She scrambled to get up, and he, half out of his dressing gown, was caught at a disadvantage. She looked around frantically, but there was no refuge. Warily, they faced each other across the bed, she on one side clutching at the coverlet to cover her nakedness, he on the other, massive and nude.

She eyed him defiantly and he was entranced by her beautiful little breasts with their big nipples. They heaved with outraged passion, and to possess them once more he was tempted to mayhem. Miranda, seeing his preoccupation, sneaked her first hard, close look at a masculine body. His shoulders and chest were quite wide, tapering to a flat belly and slim hips. His legs were very long, as were his narrow feet. His chest was lightly furred in dark hair which turned into a narrow strip running down from his navel to the darkened triangle between his legs. She pulled her eyes quickly away, avoiding his sex, and looked up into his cool, level gaze.

She stood rigidly as he walked around the bed and pulled her into his strong arms. His mouth found hers, and when he felt the first measure of response he gently forced her lips apart and tenderly took her mouth. His silken tongue caressed hers with an ardor that left her faint.

She was weakened by her own passion. Feeling it, he fell with her back onto the bed, never taking his lips from hers. She lay atop him and, shocked, felt his hard, masculine body beneath hers. His muscled thighs were covered sparingly in soft, dark hair, and she swore she could feel the blood pumping in his legs. The softness of her belly lay atop the hardness of his. His hand caressed her long back, her rounded buttocks, and she struggled to escape his touch, tearing her head away from him with a sobbing, *"No!"*

In answer he rolled over onto his side, pinioning her beneath him. He kissed her eyes, her nose, her mouth, her breasts, his lips traveling to her belly. She caught at his dark head with frantic fingers, and he groaned with frustration, but moved upward again to nurse on her lovely breasts as his fingers searched for her. When those elegant fingers found what they sought, she bit her lip to keep from crying out.

"Easy, wildcat," he soothed. "Easy, my little love."

"Oh don't! Please don't!" she begged, half sobbing.

"Shh, shh, wildcat, I won't hurt you, but I must know." His fingers gently probed her.

"K-k-know w-what?" Oh God! She was beginning to ache so terribly. "No!" A finger thrust into her, and gently moved back and forth with a tantalizing motion that she imitated with her hips, involuntarily pushing up to meet him.

He kissed her mouth, tasting the salty blood where she'd bitten her lips. "I must know," he answered her, "how tightly lodged your virginity is, Miranda. I don't want to hurt you any more than I have to, my love."

"H-hurt me?" Her voice was edged in hysteria, and Jared heard it.

Gently he withdrew his finger from her trembling body. "Did your mother speak to you of a wife's duties, Miranda?"

"No. She said only that when Amanda and I wed, our husbands would tell us all we need to know."

He swore softly. His bubbled-headed mother-in-law might have eased the way. And then his bride said:

"Amanda has told me some of the facts of life."

"What has she told you?" he asked, prepared to hear a babble of nonsense, and when she repeated her sister's tale, he nodded, surprised. "Amanda's story is basically correct, wildcat. One thing I do want to tell you now is that the first time is hard, for the shield of your virginity must be broken and it will hurt you." She trembled, and he reassured her, "Only for a moment, my love, just a moment. Here, my darling, touch me as sweetly as you did a few weeks ago." He guided her hand to his manroot, and she caressed him, brave again.

He was already hard, and her soft touch brought a groan from him. "I want you to look at it," he said. "Only the unknown is fearful, my darling. I want to love you, not frighten you."

She raised her head, and her eyes traveled fearfully downward, widening as they reached their goal. The banner of his manhood stood tall, a pale tower of ivory, veined in blue. "It's so big," she whispered, and he smiled in the dimness of the firelit room. In her innocence she was unaware of the truth of her words, for he was bigger than most men.

He reached up and caressed her face. "I want to love you," he said in a deep passionate voice that sent a thrill through her. "Let me love you, my darling." The hand slipped down to her shoulder, her arm, to the curve of her hip. Gently he pressed her back among the pillows, and placed tender little kisses on her lips and quivering breasts. "Don't be afraid of me, Miranda."

She found her resistance weakening. At that very moment she couldn't understand why she was fighting him. She wanted to be done with her damned virginity, and have the mystery solved. Once it was, she would surely be free forever of this hunger that raged in her. Placing her palms flat on his chest, her sea-green eyes gazed into his bottle-green ones, and she was amazed by the intensity of passion she saw there. She realized with surprise how great his restraint actually was just then, and the realization touched her.

"Love me," she whispered to him, "I want you to love me."

As he swung over her his eyes glittered in the reflecting firelight. He sat back on his heels, letting his hands wander over her, and Miranda grew warm and languorous at his touch. She watched as if her mind were separated from her body, and he smiled at her curiosity. His fingers teased her nipples, and they grew small and tight, and hard. His hands continued to caress her, moving constantly over her excited body. Her breathing began to quicken as did his hunger to possess her. Still, he restrained himself.

Her long, pale-gold hair was tangled now, and a fine moist sheen covered her body. Very gently, his hand slipped between her thighs, and she cried out softly. "Easy, my love," he gentled her, and his fingers sought to again part her nether lips. She was trembling, and he knew that to delay any longer would be cruel. Guiding himself to the portal of her innocence, he gently thrust forward. She cried out in pain and he stopped, giving her body a chance to grow used to his invasion.

"Oh, my love," he whispered hungrily, "just a little more pain, only a little more and afterward I swear it will be only sweet." And then his mouth covered hers, absorbing her sob of pain as he drove through her maidenhead, sinking his manhood to its hilt into her tender body. He kissed the tears from her cheeks, gently moving back and forth until, to his intense delight, she began to imitate his movements, pushing her slender hips up to meet his downward motion.

The pain had been terrible, and when his great shaft first invaded her, she did not think she could bear it. But the pain began to fade, and in its place grew a delicious, stormy passion. It overtook her. Suddenly she wanted him. *She wanted him!* She wanted this proud and tender man who rode her so gently. She wanted to pleasure him, she wanted to be pleasured.

She sank her little teeth into the fleshy part of his shoulder, and he laughed softly and increased the pace of his thrusts. Her nails raked his back, and he teased, "So you bite and scratch, eh, wildcat? I can see I must tame you into a house kitten."

"Never!" she whispered fiercely.

"Yes!" he said, and his body took control of hers, thrusting deeply, quickly, until she surrendered with a little cry and slid rapidly away into a shining, whirling world.

He had meant to hold back at her first climax, meant to double the delight for her, but it was too much for even such a skilled lover as Jared Dunham. The look on her face, a look of disbelief and wonderment followed by total joy, destroyed his control, and his warm seed flooded her. "Oh, wildcat!" he groaned.

His recovery was far quicker than hers, and as he rolled away from her she lay half-conscious, barely breathing, her lovely body still vibrating. Plumping the big goose-down pillows, he moved himself into a sitting position, drew her into the protective circle of his arms, and pulled the bedclothes over them, noticing as he did the blood on her ivory thighs. Oh wildcat, he thought, I've taken your innocence, and your girlhood is really gone. You must be a woman, now, and I wonder if you'll ever forgive me. I tried to be gentle, for, God help me, I love you.

She stirred against him, and her sea-green eyes slowly opened. Neither of them spoke for a moment. Then she reached up and caressed his cheek. He shuddered slightly, and she said softly, "Do I really do that to you?" He nodded, and although her face remained unchanged, a tiny look of triumph flickered in her eyes. "Did I please you, Jared?"

"I wasn't aware you wanted to, Miranda."

"Not until the end," she admitted candidly. "Not until I began to see how wonderful it could be, and then I wanted it to be wonderful for you, too! Oh, Jared!"

"You pleased me, Miranda. You pleased me very much, but it's only the beginning. There is more ... much more, my love."

"Show me!"

He laughed. "I'm afraid, madam, that you'll have to give me a few moments to recover. Besides," and he became serious, "you're but newly opened, my darling, and may yet be tender."

She had already forgotten the pain of her deflowering. Hot passion racing through her veins, she was eager for more love. Pulling back the bedclothes, she playfully reached for his manhood, but suddenly a look of horror crossed her face. "Jared! You're bleeding!"

He swallowed his laughter, silently cursing her mother again, and said, "No, sweetheart, I am not bleeding. It was you, but it won't happen again. It was only the proof of your virginity."

She looked down at her thighs, blushed furiously, and said, "Oh, I forgot!" and then: "Dammit, Jared, I am weary of all this innocence! What else don't I know? Are all girls my age such ninnies on their wedding nights?"

"You are more innocent than some women your age, Miranda, but as your husband my vanity is better served by it than by too great a knowledge. From now on you may ask me anything that puzzles you and I will do my best to teach you all I know, my darling." He kissed the tip of her nose, and was flattered when she returned his kiss, her ripe mouth pressing against his mouth, tasting him, nibbling at the corners of his lips. He let her have her way, thinking as he lay back what a daughter of Eve she really was.

Her newly awakened ardor increased until he could no longer ignore it, and he quickly shifted so that she found herself beneath him. He teasingly nuzzled at her breasts, and was surprised when she drew his head down, murmuring, "Please." He willingly obliged her, suckling on the sweet fruits until she moaned and writhed against him, pulling him atop her, spreading her slim legs in invitation.

"Oh, wildcat," he murmured, touched by her eagerness, caressing her tenderly in an effort to take the edge off her highly excited state.

"Take me, Jared," she said urgently. "Oh God, I burn!"

She was not to be denied. Amazed by her passion, he drove deep into her eager body, reveling in the softness of her. He gloried in her tight sheath, which enclosed his pulsing shaft in a passionate embrace. Then through the fires of his lust he heard her cry out. Her body arced and, for a moment, their eyes met and he saw the dawning of knowledge in those sea-green depths before she fainted with the force of her orgasm.

Passionlessly he released his seed, and withdrew from her. He was stunned, amazed by the woman who lay so motionless, barely breathing, caught in the throes of *la petite morte*. An hour ago she had been a trembling virgin, and now she lay unconscious as a result of intense desire. A desire that she might not truly understand yet.

Again he took her in his arms, holding her close, warming her fragile body with his own. She was so young, so new to passion, but when she woke it would be in the tender safety of his love.

She moaned softly, and he brushed a tangle of hair back from her forehead. The sea-green eyes opened, and as the memory of her recent passion returned she flushed pink. Jared laughed softly, reassuring her, "Miranda, my sweet and passionate little wife, I fall at your feet in rapt admiration."

"Don't mock me," she said shyly, hiding her burning face in his chest.

"I'm not, love."

"What happened to me?"

"La petite morte."

"The little death? Yes, it was like dying. It did not happen the first time."

"It doesn't always happen, my love. You were overwrought with desire. I am quite impressed with you."

"You are laughing at me!"

"No, no," he hastened to reassure her. "I am simply astounded by your reaction tonight."

"Then it was wrong?"

"No, Miranda, my love, it was very right." He dropped a kiss on her forehead. "I want you to go to sleep now. When you awake we will have a late supper, and afterward, perhaps we shall work on refining your marvelous natural talent."

"I think you are very wicked," she said softly.

"I think you are very delicious," he returned, laying her back against the pillows and tucking the bedclothes around her.

She fell asleep almost immediately, as he had known she would. He lay next to her, and shortly joined her.

There was no late supper for them, for Miranda slept through the night, and, to Jared's surprise, so did he. He awoke when the first gray light of dawn lit the room. He lay quietly for a moment, then realized that she was gone. His ear caught the sound of activity in her dressing room. He stretched lazily, rose from the bed, and padded on bare feet into his own dressing room.

"Good morning, wife," he called cheerily as he poured water from the porcelain pitcher into the matching basin.

"G-good morning."

"Damn! This water's cold! Miranda..." He stepped into the connecting door.

"Don't come in here!" she cried out. "I am not dressed!"

He yanked the door open, and strode through. She clutched a small linen towel to her body, and he yanked it away. "There will be no false modesty between us, madam! Your body is exquisite, and I take great pleasure in it. You are my wife!"

She said nothing, but her eyes widened and she stared at his midsection. He looked down at his swollen manhood and swore softly. "Damnation, wildcat, you certainly have a powerful effect on me."

"Don't touch me!"

"Why ever not, *wife?*"

"It's daylight!"

"Indeed it is!" He took a step toward her, and with a shriek she ran from the dressing room. With a shrug he picked up her half-filled pitcher of warm water and, whistling, carried it back into his dressing room, splashing the contents into his basin. He washed himself, then strolled with feigned casualness back into the bedroom where she was frantically trying to dress.

He slipped up behind her, put an iron arm about her, and with mischievous fingers pulled open her blouse and fondled her left breast.

"Ohh!"

The blouse came off, as did her breeches and lacy little drawers. He turned her around to face him, and she beat on his chest.

"You are a monster, sir! A beast! An animal!"

"I am a man, madam! Your husband! I wish to make love to you, and by God I shall!"

His mouth came savagely down on hers, forcing her lips apart, his tongue seductively caressing, forcing the honeyed fire into her veins. She pounded against him, but he ignored her as if she were an insect and forced her back onto the bed. His body lay the full length of hers, and she was pinioned between his strong arms.

This time his mouth grew soft and passionate, coaxing the sweetness from her until she moaned. His hands roamed freely, sliding beneath her, down her long back, cupping her buttocks, drawing her against him in an embrace so torrid she actually felt her body was being scorched by his.

She tore her head from his, gasping for breath, and while she was distracted he moved low, his lips teasing her shrinking belly, his tongue flicking out suddenly to taunt the inside of her thighs.

"Jared! Jared!" she whispered, pulling at his thick, dark hair.

He shuddered. "All right, my love," he said reluctantly, "but damn, you're so lovely there. One day I won't heed your pleas, and then you'll want it as badly as I do!" He pulled himself up and, straddling her quickly, took her with a restraint and tenderness that amazed even him. "Come with me, my love," he crooned, moving smoothly, feeling the storm building within her. At the moment she crowned the tip of his pulsing shaft with her love juices, he released his own boiling tribute.

Miranda felt drained, yet full; battered, yet cherished; weak, yet strong. A great calm filled her, and she slid her arms around him. "You're still a beast," she murmured weakly in his ear.

He chuckled in reply, "I've loved you well, madam, in full daylight, and the house still stands."

"Villain!" she hissed, squirming away from him. "Have you no shame?"

"None, wildcat! None at all!" He rolled over and looked down at her. "I'm hungry," he said.

"What, sir! You are insatiable!"

"For breakfast, my love, though I regret to disappoint you."

"Ohh!" she turned pink.

"I'll be happy to oblige you again afterward," he promised, climbing out of bed, chuckling at her look of outrage. "I'll have Cook send you a tray, for you'll need all the rest you can get, Miranda. I intend making the most of our time alone before your Mama and sister return."

She watched him disappear back into his dressing room. Laying amid the tumbled bedding, she felt strangely relaxed. He was a rogue, she thought, but then—and a small smile lifted the corners of her kiss-bruised mouth—she was finding she had a weakness for rogues. Not that she'd admit that to him—at least not yet!

❧ Chapter 5 ❧

Each day of their honeymoon was better than the previous one had been. Miranda, at first as skittish as a young filly, began to gentle somewhat as she became used to Jared's presence at Wyndsong, in their bedroom, and in her life. He awoke Christmas Day to find her propped on one elbow studying him in the half-light of early winter morning. He watched her through slitted eyes, feigning sleep. She was very lovely in her pale-blue silk nightgown with its long sleeves and modestly buttoned high neckline.

Her pale-gold hair hung loose after last night's sweet combat between them, although she had come to bed with it plaited into two long neat braids. He didn't know what it was about the sight of those braids that roused him so thoroughly, but they did. He had undone them, letting her beautiful thick silvery hair pour through his fingers, becoming excited by the soft, scented tresses, and she had laughed at him. He had taken her then and there, and she had continued to laugh into his face, a soft and seductive woman's laughter, until she had finally yielded her body. He felt that she had yielded him nothing else this time. Miranda was growing up.

He continued lying quietly, and she reached out a slim hand to touch his face gently. In her sea-green eyes he saw puzzlement yet tenderness, and he thought, with amazement, She's falling in love with me! Women who clung had always bored him, but he wanted this one to cling a little. He didn't want her helpless, but he did want all of her. Reaching up, he caressed her face in return.

"Ohh!" She colored guiltily. "How long have you been awake?"

"Just now," he lied. "Happy Christmas, Miranda."

"Happy Christmas to you, sir." She scrambled from bed, and ran into her dressing room to reappear a moment later with a gaily wrapped package. "For you, Jared!"

He sat up and accepted the gift. Unwrapping it, he found a beautiful buff-colored satin vest, embroidered with dainty sprigs of gold flowers with green leaves. The buttons were polished green malachite. There were also several pairs of well-knitted heavy wool stockings. He knew from the anxious look on her face that she had made both the vest and the stockings. Carefully he lifted the vest from its nest of wrapping and examined it. It was amazingly well done, and he was deeply touched.

"Why, madam, how marvelous," he said. "I commend your needlework. I shall certainly take this excellent garment to London next spring, and be the envy of every gentleman at White's."

"You really like it?" Dear Lord! She sounded like a ninny! "I trust the socks also meet with your approval, sir," she finished severely.

"Most assuredly, madam. I am flattered that you took the trouble to make me these gifts." He reached up and drew her down to him. "Give me a Christmas kiss, my love."

She brushed his mouth sweetly with her own, then said, "Have you nothing for me, sir?"

He chuckled. "Miranda, Miranda! Just when I believe you're growing up, you become a child again." She looked piqued, and he continued, "Yes, you greedy little puss, I have something for you. Go into my dressing room, and you'll find two boxes in the bottom drawer of my chest-on-chest. Bring them here so I may present them to you properly."

She was back in a moment with the boxes, which she handed to him. One was large, and the other small. He put them before him on the bed, and she studied them. The larger box bore the name of a Paris shop on it, the smaller the label of a London jeweler.

"Well, Miranda, which one first?" he teased.

"The smaller is bound to be more valuable," she teased back, and he laughed as he handed it to her.

"Oh!" she breathed delightedly as she opened the box. Within the white satin nested a large cameo brooch, showing creamy-colored head and shoulders of a Grecian maiden with upswept and beribboned curls on a coral background. The maiden wore about her own neck an exquisite tiny gold chain with a single perfect diamond. It was a very unusual piece, and Miranda knew it must have cost him a pretty penny. She lifted it from its box and sighed with pleasure. "It's the loveliest thing I've ever owned," she said, pinning it to her nightgown.

"I saw it last year in London, and sent for it right after we met. The jeweler was told to make me another, if he'd sold the original. I wasn't at all sure it would be here in time for Christmas, but the fates must have heard my pleas. Open the other, my dear."

"I have not thanked you yet, sir."

"Words are not necessary, Miranda. I see the thanks in your beautiful eyes. Open the box from Madame Denise's."

Again her pretty mouth made an O of delight, as she excitedly lifted the garment from its box. "Pray, sir, tell me if you saw this in Paris last time you were there?" She stood up and held the exquisite lime-green silk and lace Circassian wrapper against her slender form.

His green eyes were smoky with amusement. "I have bought similar garments before from Madame Denise's. For Bess and Charity, of course," he added mischievously, and knew by the elegant lift of her eyebrow that she did not believe him.

"I do believe Grandmother Van Steen is right about you, Jared. You are a rogue!"

The new year of 1812 came, and with it strong winter storms. A coastal packet from New York brought a letter from Torwyck saying that Dorothea and Amanda were snowbound, and would not even attempt returning before spring when both the river and the Long Island Sound would be free of ice.

The world about them was white and quiet, some days brightened by sunshine and skies so blue that one could imagine it was summer. Other days were windswept and gray. But there was a hint of spring in the air. The forest stood black and still, except for the evergreen pines, moaning and whispering their loneliness around Long Pond at the west end of the island. The salt marshes were frozen over on dark February mornings with a skim of ice, and the purity of the meadows broken only by occasional paw prints. On the four freshwater ponds the Canadian geese, the swans, and wild ducks—mallards, canvasbacks, buffleheads, and redheads—wintered in relative peace. In the manor barns the horses and cattle lived dull lives, dreaming of warm summer meadows, the chill monotony broken only by daily feedings and the friendly company of several barn cats. Even the barnyard fowl kept pretty much indoors.

At first Miranda had felt strange being cut off from her family. She had never been away from them in her entire life, and now even Wyndsong was beginning to seem different, too. She had found it difficult at first to believe that it was she, and not Mama, who was mistress here. She had reconciled herself to Jared's place as lord of the manor, but her own place was harder to accept. With his gentle guidance, however, she began to take up the reins of authority that were hers as chatelaine.

March came, and with it the thaw. They were, it seemed, an island of mud in a bright blue sea. Suddenly, toward the end of the month, a small flock of robins appeared, the hills were polka-dotted with yellow daffodils, and the land began to green once more. Spring had come to Wyndsong. From the shelter of their barns the livestock joyfully emerged. The colts and calves were bewildered at first, but soon gamboled across the meadows beneath the benign gaze of their proud parents.

Miranda celebrated her eighteenth birthday on April 7, 1812. Her mother and sister had arrived home late the day before on the Wyndsong yacht, *Sprite*. The twins had celebrated all their birthdays together, even the year Amanda had had the measles, and the one when Miranda was covered in chicken pox. Then it had been their father who sat at the head of the table, their mother at the foot, the twins on either side. Tonight Jared sat at the table's head, and Miranda at its foot, wearing her birthday present from her husband, an emerald necklace.

The master of Wyndsong sat quietly amused by the endless chatter of the three ladies who had already spent the day catching up on the news of the last four months. Miranda, according to her mama, had missed a wonderul winter at Torwyck.

"I have had a wonderful winter here," said Miranda. "It is really preferable, Mama, to spend one's honeymoon with one's husband."

Amanda giggled, but Dorothea looked shocked. "Really, Miranda, I cannot imagine Jared approves of your immodesty."

"On the contrary, my dear Doro, I encourage my wife in such immodesty."

Miranda blushed, but her lips twitched with suppressed mirth. Since she had returned home Dorothea had attempted to force Miranda back into being just a daughter, thus unwittingly undermining Miranda's position as mistress of Wyndsong. Jared's remark annoyed her. Amanda, her cornflower-blue eyes round with delight, was obviously in cahoots with *them*, and it made Dorothea feel old, which she most certainly was not. At that moment, Dorothea decided it was time for *her* news.

"Well," she said, her pretty, plump, dimpled hands fussing with the snow-white linen napkin, "I shall not remain here at Wyndsong much longer, my dears. A mother-in-law is a welcome guest only if her visit is a short one."

"You are welcome here always, Doro. You know that."

"Thank you, Jared. But I married Tom young, and I am still young, though I am a widow. This winter at my brother's home I had the opportunity to spend a great deal of time with an old friend of the family's, Pieter Van Notelman. He is a widower with five fine children, of whom only the eldest is married. Just before we returned to Wyndsong, he did me the honor of asking me to be his wife. I have accepted."

"Mama!" the twins exclaimed at once.

Dorothea looked extremely pleased at the reaction she had elicited from her daughters.

"My felicitations, madam," said Jared gravely. He had been willing to offer his mother-in-law a permanent home until he saw her effect on Miranda. Dorothea could not live comfortably at Wyndsong, now that her daughter was its new mistress. It would be far better this way.

"I do not recall Mynheer Van Notelman, Mama," said Miranda.

"He owns Highlands. You and Amanda were there for a party four years ago."

"Ah, yes! The great house on the lake up in the Shawgunk Mountains behind Torwyck. As I remember, there was a son who looked like a large frog, and was always trying to get Mandy and me into dark corners where he might kiss us."

Amanda took up the story. "He managed one wet kiss, I shrieked, and Miranda came flying to my rescue. She blackened his eye. He spent the rest of the party telling people he'd walked into a door."

Jared laughed heartily. "I think, pigeon, that a kiss from you would be worth it. Lord Swynford is a fortunate man."

Dorothea spoke again. "I am distressed to hear, even at this late date, of such an unsavory incident," she chided her daughters. "The young man of whom you speak died in a boating accident on the lake three years back. It was his demise that brought on the death of Pieter's first wife, from melancholia. The boy was, you see, the only son."

"And of the five remaining daughters one is plainer than the other," said Amanda mischievously.

"Amanda, that is unkind!" scolded Dorothea.

"Have you not taught me to be truthful, Mama?" answered Amanda demurely while Jared and Miranda chuckled.

"When is your wedding to take place, Mama?" asked Miranda, not wishing to distress her mother.

"In late summer, when we return from London, dear. I would not think of marrying Pieter until I have Amanda safely settled with Adrian."

Jared took a deep breath. He hadn't intended to speak of this tonight, but now he had no choice. "Amanda cannot go to London. In fact none of you can. Not right now. With President Madison's decree against trade with England there are no ships sailing for London. The French are still seizing American vessels. It's much too dangerous, ladies. I received the New York papers today, and our minister to England has returned home. It's not possible for us to go to London now."

"Not possible?!" Miranda's eyes were blazing. "Sir, we are not speaking of a casual pleasure trip! Amanda must be in London on June twenty-eighth for her wedding!"

"It is impossible, wildcat," he answered with such finality that Amanda began to weep. Jared looked at her pityingly. "Pigeon, *I am sorry.*"

"Sorry!" shouted Miranda. "You're deliberately destroying my sister's life, and you say you're sorry?! The church was booked a year ago! Her trousseau awaits its final fitting at Madame Charpentier!"

"If he loves her, Adrian will wait. If not, it's better the wedding be cancelled entirely."

"Ohh!" wailed Amanda.

"Adrian would wait," snapped Miranda, "but his mama will not. She was furious at his engagement to an American colonial as she insists on calling us. Adrian adores Amanda, and he is perfect for her, but Lady Swynford is strong-minded. If Amanda postpones the wedding Lady Swynford will use it as an excuse to separate them forever. Adrian will find himself married to some meek miss more acceptable to his mama."

Amanda sobbed loudly.

"War may break out any minute between England and America," said Jared.

"All the more reason for Amanda to get to London on time. War has nothing to do with us. If the stupid governments of England and America wish to fight, then let them. But Amanda and Adrian will be happily wed."

"There are no ships," replied Jared irritably.

"You have ships! Why can't we sail on one of them?" she persisted.

"Because I will not lose a valuable vessel and endanger a crew even for you, my dear wife!"

"We will go!" she yelled.

"You will not!" he thundered back.

"Miranda! Jared! This is most unseemly," chided Dorothea.

"Mother! Be silent!" snarled Miranda.

"Oh, Adrian! Oh! Oh!" hiccoughed Amanda.

"Dammit, be quiet, all of you! I will have peace in my own house!" roared Jared.

"There'll be no peace in any part of this house, Jared Dunham, unless you get us to England by June," Miranda warned ominously.

"Madam, are you threatening me?"

"Was I not clear enough, sir?" she replied with false sweetness.

With a final wail Amanda fled the table. Miranda, with a furious look at her husband, followed her sister.

"I suppose we must postpone the birthday cake," said Dorothea seriously, and when Jared burst out laughing she looked at him strangely. This was not the Wyndsong she was used to.

In Amanda's room Miranda comforted her twin. "Don't worry, Mandy, you'll be safely wed to Adrian. I promise you."

"H-how? Y-y-you heard what Jared said. There are no ships!"

"There are ships, twin. One simply has to find them."

"Jared will stop us."

"Jared must go to Plymouth. He held off on the trip because of our birthday, but he'll be gone within a few days. When he returns, we will be gone. You'll be married at St. George's, Hanover Square, on June twenty-eighth, as planned. I promise you."

"You've never made me a promise you didn't keep, Miranda. This time, however, I fear you'll not be able to keep it."

"Have faith, little twin. Jared believes I've become a tamed house cat, but I'll soon show him how wrong he is." Miranda smiled a strangely mischievous and seductive smile.

"We have no money but what he gives us," said Amanda.

"You forget that today half of Papa's wealth became mine to do with as I please. I will inherit the rest when I am twenty-one. I am a rich woman, and rich women always get what they want."

"What if Jared is right, and there is war between England and America?"

"War, fiddlesticks! Besides, if we do not get to England you will surely lose Adrian. Jared is being a fussy old man."

There was a knock, and Jemima's head popped around the door. "Master Jared says you're both to come downstairs for dessert and coffee in the front parlor."

"We'll come directly, Mima." The door shut firmly. "Pretend to be devastated, but resigned to Jared's wishes, Mandy. Just follow my lead."

The sisters descended to the main parlor of the house, where their mother and Jared awaited them. Miranda seated herself regally at the dessert table and sliced the cake. "Mama, will you pour for me?"

"Of course, dear."

Jared looked at his wife suspiciously. "Surely you cannot be resigned to my wishes so quickly, Miranda?"

"I am not resigned at all," she answered pertly. "I believe you are wrong, and I think you are ruining Amanda's happiness. But what can I do if you won't take us to England?"

"I am relieved to find that you are maturing enough to accept my decisions."

"Please reconsider," she said quietly.

"My darling, the seriousness of the times—not I—have made the decision. I am going up to Plymouth tomorrow, but when I return in around ten days, if the situation has eased we'll sail for England immediately. If war still seems imminent I'll write to Lord Swynford myself on Amanda's behalf."

The Dunham family yacht had barely cleared Little North Bay the following morning when Miranda was riding across the island to Pineneck Cove, where she kept her own catboat anchored. Leaving her horse to graze by Long Pond, she sailed across the bay to Oysterponds and, tying her catboat at the village dock, made her way to the local tavern. Despite her boy's garb, it was obvious that she was a woman and she received much clucking disapproval from the village wives as she passed. She strode into the Anchor and the Plow, much to the consternation of the landlord, who hurried toward her from behind the bar.

"Here now, miss, you can't come in here!"

"Indeed, Eli Latham, and why not?"

"By cricky, 'tis Miss Miranda, or rather Mistress Dunham. Come round to the dining room, ma'am. It's not seemly you bein' in the taproom," said the older man nervously.

She followed him into the sunshine-filled room with its mellow golden oak tables and benches. The shelves were filled with polished pewter tankards and chargers, and there were blue glass vases of yellow daffodils on either end of the carved oak fireplace mantel. Eli Latham and his wife, Rachel, were proud of their dining room. The Lathams fed travelers going across the water to and from New England.

Miranda and the Lathams sat down at a table in the empty room and, after declining cider, Miranda asked, "What English ships lie just out of sight of the coast, Eli?"

"Ma'am?" His bland face looked innocently at her.

"Dammit, man, I'm no customs agent! Don't tell me your tea, coffee, and cocoa tins are bottomless, for I know better. English and American trading vessels lie off this coast despite the blockade. I need a reputable English ship."

"Why?" asked Eli Latham.

"Amanda's wedding is scheduled for June twenty-eighth in London. Because of this damned blockade my husband says we cannot go, but we must!"

"I don't know, Miss Miranda, if yer husband says no..."

"Eli, please! For Amanda. She is devastated, and I fear she will pine away entirely if I cannot get her to England. Lord, man, what do we care for politics?"

"Well, there is one ship I'd trust to carry you safely. He's some highborn milord so's I expect he's all right."

"His name?" she asked eagerly.

"Now hold on, Miss Miranda. I can't be givin' his name to you unless I'm sure he'll be willin' to take on passengers," said Eli, glancing at his wife.

"Then have him contact me at Wyndsong."

"The house?"

"Of course at the house, Eli." Then she laughed, realizing his predicament. "My husband left today for Plymouth and won't be back for ten days."

He demurred. "I just don't know if it's the right thing to do, Miss Miranda."

"Please, Eli! It's not for a silly whim. It's for Amanda. I'd as soon never see London again. It's a fearfully dirty and noisy place. But my sister will die of a broken heart if she cannot marry Adrian Swynford."

"Contact the Englishman, Eli! I'll not have that sweet child's sorrow on my conscience," said Rachel. "Morning, Miss Miranda."

"Morning, Rachel, and thank you for sticking up for us."

"Yer mama know ye're doin' this?"

"She will. I'm taking her with us. We can't go without her chaperoning us."

"She'll not be happy 'bout it. I hear she's planning to marry again."

"How on earth did you—Oh! Jemima, of course."

"Well, she is my sister, and lives with us when she's off-island. You go on back home now, Miss Miranda. Eli here will get in touch with the ship we got in mind, and her captain'll come to see you."

"I don't have much time, Rachel. I'd as soon be gone a good week by the time my husband returns."

"He'll come after you. Never saw a man so plum crazy 'bout a woman as he is 'bout you."

"Jared?" Miranda looked genuinely surprised.

"Lord, girl, ain't he never told you he loves you?"

"No."

"You ever tell him you love him?"

"I don't."

Rachel Latham laughed heartily. "It's as plain as the nose on yer face that ye're in love with the man, and he with you, and both of you prob'ly too stubborn to admit it to the other. Didn't that featherhead mama of yers ever tell you that honesty is the firmest cornerstone on which to build a good marriage? When he catches up with you, girl, tell him you love him, and I guarantee you'll escape the trashing he'll have been planning to give you." The older woman gave Miranda a hug. "Run along home now, girl. Eli will help make everything right."

Miranda sailed her little boat back to Wyndsong, and moored it at its dock in Pineneck Cove. She found her horse browsing by Long Pond where she'd left him. Mounting, she rode slowly home musing on what Rachel Latham had said. Jared in love with her? How could that possibly be? He never said so, and he was always teasing or criticizing her. She hardly considered that love, and as for Rachel's silly accusation that she, Miranda, loved Jared, it was poppycock! He was an arrogant, stubborn man, and while she didn't hate him, she—she—Miranda stopped her horse, confused. If she didn't hate him, what *did* she feel? She guessed she didn't know any longer. Annoyed with herself, she kicked Sea Breeze into a canter, and hurried home to tell Amanda the news.

"Who is this captain?" was her twin's first question.

"The Lathams wouldn't tell me, but they feel he's reliable."

"What if he isn't? We could be ravished, and sold into slavery. I hear there are plantations in the West Indies that breed white slaves, and they're always looking for beautiful women to . . . to use."

"Good Lord, Amanda! Whoever told you a thing like that?"

"Suzanne, of course. A young girl in the village where their country house is located was accused of stealing a squire's horse. She hadn't really, she'd only borrowed it on a dare, but the squire pressed charges and she was sentenced to be sold as a bondslave in the West Indies. When she finally was able to smuggle a letter to her family two years later, she told of being forced to mate with certain white slaves in order to produce other slaves for their master. She already had one child, and was expecting another."

Miranda shuddered. "That is disgusting," she said. "I am appalled at Suzanne's repeating such a tale. I am sure it is not true at all. And besides the captain Eli has in mind is an English nobleman. Perhaps he even knows Adrian."

"Have you told Mama yet?"

"No, and I shall not until it is all settled."

They were at dinner that night when Jemima appeared, pursing her lips with disapproval, and announced in a tart voice, "There's a man here to see you. I put him in the front parlor."

"Do not disturb us," said Miranda, rising from the table and hurrying out of the room. She smoothed her fair hair as she went, and brushed crumbs from her sapphire gown. Placing her hand firmly on the parlor doorknob, she turned the handle and walked confidently into the room.

A man of medium height with wavy ash-brown hair styled, amazingly, in the London fashion stood by the fireplace. He turned and came toward her smiling a sweet smile, and she noticed how perfect and white his teeth were. He appeared to be a little under thirty years old, and his dark blue eyes sparkled with good humor.

"Mistress Dunham, I am Captain Christopher Edmund of the *Seahorse,* out of London. I've been given to understand that I may be of aid to you." His dark eyes quickly took in her youth, her unusual beauty, the expensive gown with exquisite handmade cream-colored lace at its high neck and at the ends of the long, tight sleeves. The cameo brooch at her throat was magnificent, of the best workmanship.

"Captain Edmund, how do you do." She offered her hand, he kissed it politely, and then she waved him to a chair. "Pray be seated, sir. May I offer you a brandy?"

"Thank you, yes, madam."

She walked slowly to the table that held the decanters and glasses, poured the amber liquid into a Waterford snifter, and served him. He sniffed and his eyes widened in appreciation. She smiled. Putting the liquid to his lips, he sipped, and then said, "Now, ma'am, how can I be of service to you?" He had the speech of a highborn English gentleman. Relaxing a little, Miranda sat down across from him in a matching cream brocade chair.

"I need immediate passage to England, sir, for myself, my sister, and my mother."

"I am not a passenger vessel, ma'am."

"We *must* get to England!"

"Why?"

"I am not in the habit of discussing personal business with a stranger, Captain. Suffice it to say that I will pay you double the usual passage, and supply our own provisions and water."

"And I am not in the habit of taking a beautiful woman aboard my ship without knowing a bit more than 'I must get to England.' I repeat, ma'am, why?"

She threw him a furious look, and he almost laughed, for he could see she was trying very hard not to lose her temper. He liked her spirit. Sighing, she said, "My sister is scheduled to be married the twenty-eighth of June to Adrian, Lord Swynford. Because of this stupid blockade we cannot get to England, and if we don't—"

"The dowager dragon will use it as an excuse to marry young Adrian to another heiress."

"How do you know that?!" Slowly, comprehension dawned. "Christopher Edmund! Pray, sir, are you by chance related to Darius Edmund, the Duke of Whitley?"

"I am his brother, ma'am. The second brother. There are two after me. Surely you know the silly rhyme they have about us. 'One for the title, one for the sea, one for the army, the last's the clergy.'"

She laughed. "I have heard it, but I have met your eldest brother, sir. He was one of Amanda's suitors last season. But, of course, there was no one but Adrian from the moment they met."

"My brother was quite disappointed, I know, but your sister is better off with young Swynford."

"How disloyal of you, sir!" she teased.

"Not at all, ma'am. Darius is ten years my senior, a widower of rather eccentric habits. Were he of a more winning nature I'm sure your sister would have chosen to be a duchess rather than a simple lady."

"My sister is marrying for love, sir."

"How refreshingly novel, ma'am. And did you also marry for love?"

"Is that information necessary to obtain our passage, Captain?"

He laughed. *"Touché,* ma'am! Well, despite your sister's cruel treatment of my older brother, I shall be happy to give your family passage. But I sail on tomorrow night's tide. It's becoming far too risky hanging about your coast." He grinned mischievously. "Besides, I've traded off all my goods, and my hold is just about chock full of American merchandise. I am now ready to sail home, make a fat profit, and spend the next few months enjoying the gaming halls, and the charming Cyprians of London. On my way home, I shall more than enjoy the company of three elegant ladies of the bon ton."

Miranda was elated. It had been so simple, and she was sure now that Jared was merely being difficult in refusing to take them to London. Captain Edmund was obviously not concerned about danger. "If you think it safe, Captain," she said, "you may anchor your ship in Little North Bay below the house. It's a deep but well-sheltered harbor, and you can fill your water casks here on Wyndsong. I regret it is too early in the year for me to offer you any fresh produce, but only daffodils grow here in early April."

"Most kind of you, ma'am. I shall certainly take the opportunity to bring *Seahorse* into the safety of your bay tonight under cover of darkness."

Miranda rose. "I should like to introduce you to Mama and Amanda now. Will you take coffee with us?"

He stood. "Yes, ma'am. Most kind."

She jerked at the bellpull, and Jemima nearly fell through the door. Miranda took a quick breath so she wouldn't laugh, and said in a cool, level voice, "Please tell my mother and sister that I would like them to join us here for coffee."

Taken aback by Miranda's tone, Jemima bobbed a curtsey and answered in a subdued voice, "Yes, ma'am." She backed out and closed the door.

Miranda wished to know more about her rescuer.

"So you are one of four brothers, sir?"

"Four brothers and three sisters. Darius, of course, is the eldest, and then came the three girls, Claudia, Octavia, and Augusta. Mama finished her classical period with the girls, and the three boys that followed have reasonably English names—Christopher, George, and John. John, by the way, was at Cambridge with Adrian. He's to be the clergyman, and George is the soldier. Prinny's regiment."

"You seem to be well taken care of. I was not aware that Whitley was such a wealthy dukedom." Miranda stammered, realizing too late that she was being rude.

"It isn't really. Darius is just your usual well-to-do peer, and much of that is due to his first wife. Our mother, however, had three brothers, all titled, and all bachelors. Each uncle was given a younger Edmund as a godson, and we were each named heir to our godfathers. I'm the Marquis of Wye, George is Lord Studley, and young John will one day be a baron, though I imagine he'd prefer a bishopric," laughed Christopher Edmund. He liked this friendly young woman, and hadn't at all minded her remark about his family's wealth.

The parlor door opened and the captain rose to his feet as Dorothea and Amanda entered.

"Miranda, who is this gentleman?" demanded Dorothea, attempting, as she sometimes did, to regain her old authority.

Miranda ignored her mother's tone, saying smoothly, "Mama, may I present Captain Christopher Edmund, the Marquis of Wye. Captain Edmund has agreed to give us passage to London aboard his ship, the *Seahorse*. We sail tomorrow evening and, with good winds and no storms, I imagine we should make England by the middle or the end of May—in plenty of time for Mandy's wedding. Captain Edmund, my mother, also Mistress Dunham. I think that to avoid confusion it would be permissible for you to address me by my given name in private."

"Only if you will return the compliment and call me Kit, as all my friends do." He turned to Dorothea and, bowing elegantly, took her hand and kissed it. "Mistress Dunham, I am delighted, ma'am. I believe my mama had the pleasure of taking tea with you last season when my brother Darius was so smitten with Miss Amanda."

Totally taken aback, Dorothea gasped. "Indeed, sir. Very cordial, your mama."

"And Captain, my twin sister, Amanda, who is soon to be Lady Swynford."

Again Kit Edmund bowed. "Miss Amanda, having met you at last, I must pity my poor brother Darius his great loss. But I congratulate you on your good sense in turning him down."

Amanda's two dimples appeared as she smiled. "La, sir, how naughty you are." Then she became serious. "Are you really going to take us to England?"

"Yes, I am. How could I refuse your sister's plea, and how could I ever face Adrian Swynford again if I didn't take you?"

"Thank you, sir! I know it's dangerous for you, but—"

"Dangerous? Nonsense! Nothing to it. Britannia rules the waves, y'know."

"We are most grateful, sir."

Jemima flounced in bearing the coffee tray. "Where do you want it?" she demanded.

"Captain . . . Kit, would you set up the tea table by the fire? Thank you so much. Put it there, Mima, then you may go. Mama, will you pour? Oh, dear, no, you can't, can you? I can see you're much too overcome by our good fortune." Miranda seated herself calmly at the tea table and, lifting the silver coffeepot, poured some of the velvety dark liquid into a dainty porcelain cup. "Give this to Mama, please, Amanda," said Miranda sweetly, gazing innocently over at Dorothea, who had collapsed in a sidechair.

"Will your father and husband be accompanying you, Miranda?" asked Kit Edmund conversationally as she handed him his coffee.

"Papa passed on some months now, Kit. And unfortunately, my husband cannot come due to the press of business."

"Miranda!"

"Mama?"

Dorothea was rapidly recovering. "Jared has forbidden this trip!"

"No, Mama, he has not. He has said only that there are no ships because of the blockade, and that he does not choose to risk one of his own vessels. At no time did he say that we could not go."

"Then why this unseemly haste? Wait until Jared returns."

"Captain Edmund cannot wait a week or more, Mama. We are fortunate to have found a ship at all, and I am extremely grateful that Kit is willing to take us."

"I shall not accompany you! I will not be party to your unseemly behavior," snapped Dorothea.

"Very well, Mama, we are then faced with a choice. Amanda and I can cross the ocean *unchaperoned,* which will, of course, seem very strange to our family and friends in England. Or," here she paused for effect, "or Amanda can go to live with you and your new husband at Highlands. I doubt, however, that either Mynheer Van Notelman or his ugly daughters will be overly thrilled to have such a beauty in their midst, stealing all the beaux. The choice, Mama, is yours."

Dorothea narrowed her gaze, looking from Miranda to Amanda. Both wore angelic expressions. She turned to Captain Edmund, who quickly lowered his blue eyes, but not before she'd caught the gleam of amusement dancing in them. There was really no choice, and both she and her daughters knew it. "You really are a bitch, Miranda," she said levelly. Then, "What sort of accommodations can you offer us, Captain Edmund?"

"Two connecting cabins, ma'am, one relatively large, the other small. I can't allow you much space, for I'm not really set up to carry passengers."

"Do not worry, Mama. And we shall all have brand-new wardrobes in London."

"You seem to have an answer for everything, Miranda," said Dorothea tartly, standing up. "I will bid you good evening, Captain, as I find suddenly that I have a great deal to do in a short time."

Christopher Edmund rose to his feet and bowed. "Mistress Dunham, I shall look forward to having you aboard the *Seahorse*."

"Thank you, sir," said Dorothea. Without so much as a glance at her daughters, she left the room.

"You are a hard opponent, Miranda," remarked the Englishman.

"I want my sister happy, Kit."

"Has your husband forbidden you this trip?"

"No. It is as I said."

He laughed softly. "I somehow think that what your husband forgot to say is, nevertheless, what he intended."

"Oh, please, Captain!" begged Amanda. "You must take us!" Her blue eyes glittered with crystalline tears.

"I have given my word, Miss Amanda," he replied, envying young Adrian Swynford more as each minute passed. Perhaps he'd do well to stay in London next season and find a sweet young thing. Perhaps he needed a wife.

"Amanda, please don't cry. You have quite stricken poor Kit helpless already. He could not possibly refuse you now." Miranda laughed. "Run along, and see to your packing while I complete the financial arrangements."

"Oh, thank you, sir," replied Amanda, a small smile beginning to turn up the corners of her rosebud mouth. She curtseyed prettily, and flew from the room.

"What a perfect nobleman's wife she'll make," sighed the young captain.

"Indeed," murmured Miranda, her sea-green eyes dancing with amusement. It was happening all over again. Strangely, the hurt she might have felt a year ago at being so blatantly overlooked was gone. Jared had been right. Jared! She felt a twinge of guilt, which she pushed quickly away. She *was* going to London! Moving to the desk, she opened the secret drawer at the center and took out a small pouch. "This should more than cover our passage, I believe," she said, handing it to him.

He accepted the little velvet bag and knew from its weight that she was being quite generous. "We'll be anchored in your bay by dawn, Miranda. You may begin bringing your supplies aboard then.

"Miranda, I must ask one thing of you. My crew are not gentlemen. In fact, they are quite rough. You will have to confine yourselves pretty much to your cabins during the crossing, and when you do walk out for exercise I ask that your dress be quite modest and that your hair be covered as well. A woman's long hair blowing carelessly in the sea breeze can be quite tantalizing."

Miranda felt a chill of fear. "Are you saying, Kit, that your crew are dangerous?"

"My dear, I thought you understood that. His Majesty's Navy has taken every decent sailor available. What's left for the privately owned ships, the blockade runners like myself, are the dregs of the waterfront. I have a first and second officer, and a bosun I rely on, and Charlie, my cabin boy. We keep the rest of the crew in check by fear, by intimidation, and the promise of riches at the end of the voyage. Even so, we officers are outnumbered. The least incident could set off a mutiny. That is why I must ask that you be discreet at all times."

Suddenly Miranda realized the possible consequences of her reckless actions. Jared had not been unreasonable. It was dangerous. Yet, if they did not go with Kit, Amanda could lose Adrian. I want her to be happy, as I am, thought Miranda, and then she realized what she'd said. *I am happy!* Yes, I am! Perhaps Mistress Latham is right. Perhaps I do love Jared. It was the first time she'd ever considered such a thing, but she did not shy away from the idea.

Still, she must do this for Mandy. Amanda must have her chance at happiness, too.

"We will be most discreet, Kit, but because of what you've told me I want you to anchor in Big North Bay instead of the little bay below the manor house. My people will guide you to Hidden Pond and Hill Brook to fill your water casks. Bring your ship around Tom's Point at sunset, and our luggage and supplies will be loaded just before we come aboard, under cover of darkness. We will not be visible to your crew if we do it that way."

"Excellent! You've a good head on your shoulders for a woman. Wouldn't have expected it!" He rose. "My thanks for your hospitality, Miranda. I'll look forward to seeing you aboard *Seahorse*."

As Kit Edmund returned to his ship he mused over the last hour. Miss Amanda Dunham was an adorable young woman without a doubt, but a man would be foolish to overlook Mistress Miranda. There was a young woman with beauty and character, and he promised himself that he would get to know her better during their voyage. He suspected that she could talk to a man about things that would interest him, and that she did not engage in the silly prattle that, with most females, passed for conversation.

Miranda had seen Kit to the door, and then returned to the parlor to snuff the candles. Seating herself in a wing chair before the crackling fire, she listened to the rising wind in the bare oak trees outside. They were always late to leaf, and always late to lose their leaves. The willows and the maples were already greening. She would miss spring on Wyndsong, but as soon as Amanda was safely wed she'd be on the first ship back she could get. By late summer she'd be safely home on Wyndsong, safe with Jared. Never again would she leave him or Wyndsong.

She wished she had realized sooner that all those strange and conflicting feelings she had felt were the beginnings of her love for him. Did he really love her, as Rachel Latham believed. She closed her sea-green eyes, and pictured him, remembering his green eyes growing dark with lust, his tanned, hawklike visage, the thin, sensuous lips bending over her. Her face grew warm; and she could almost hear his deep voice saying, *"You will love me, Miranda, because I will it, and I am not a man to be denied."* She shivered. Why had he said that? Was it because he loved her? Or was it only his pride demanding she love him? Could it have been only that?

"Damn!" she swore softly. She wished she knew the answer. Standing up, she paced back and forth in the dark for a few minutes before lighting a chimney lamp, setting it on the desk, and sitting down to write to him. Drawing a sheet of cream-colored vellum from a drawer, she picked up the quill.

The wind howled mournfully in the tall oaks, and long dark clouds skipped across the sky playing hide and seek with the quarter moon. A log snapped loudly, and crashed into the grate in a shower of sparks. She jumped, the pen slipping from her hand. Then as the tension began to drain from her, she laughed. Picking up the quill again, she began writing swiftly with sure, clear strokes.

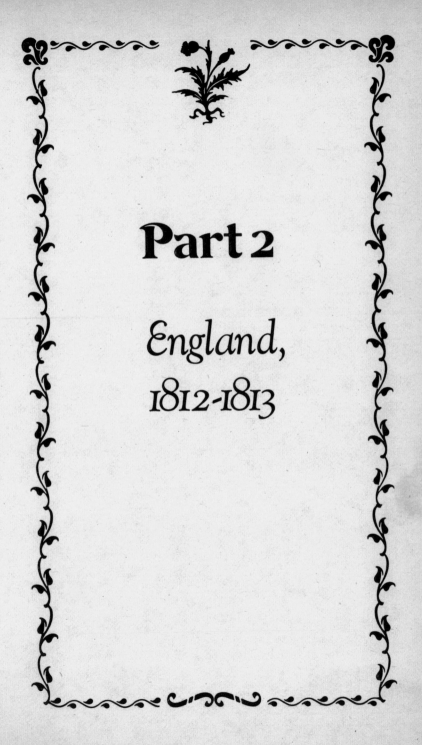

Part 2

England,
1812-1813

❧ Chapter 6 ❧

My dear husband, I love you, and because I do, it makes it hard to write what I must write. As you read this, Amanda, Mama, and I are a quarter of the way across the ocean to England. We have sailed from Wyndsong this tenth day of April aboard *Seahorse*, an English vessel owned and captained by Christopher Edmund, the Marquis of Wye, who is the brother of one of Mandy's discarded suitors. I could not let my sister lose Adrian Swynford, for she loves him deeply. As I now understand what love is and how she feels, I could not bear to see her unhappy. I am unhappy for her. I ache for her. And I am afraid, too—afraid that having finally found you, I shall lose you. Please don't be angry with me. I shall hurry home immediately after the wedding, I promise you. Wait for me.

Your loving wife, Miranda

With a smothered curse Jared Dunham crumpled the letter and glared at Jed. "Couldn't you have gotten here sooner?" he demanded.

"Two and a half days from Wyndsong to Plymouth ain't poor time, Master Jared."

"Two and a half days!" Jonathan Dunham whistled admiringly. "Damn, man! Did you fly?"

The weathered stableman grinned. "Thought I was flyin' at times, 'stead of sailin'. Came closer to being seasick than I've ever been in m'life. Had a helluva south wind pushing us right along. I rode overland from Buzzards Bay. You owe Barnabas Horton five dollars for bringing me up, Master Jared. Figured you'd want me to take *Sprite* back to Wyndsong, 'cause you'll be goin' after Miss Miranda in a bigger ship."

"You're damned right I will!" roared Jared, and Jonathan chuckled despite his brother's outraged glower. "Did my wife give you this note?"

"Nope. Miss Dorothea sent me to tell you they'd gone. Jemima give me the note. Said you ought to hear yer lady's explanation, and then maybe you wouldn't beat her too bad when you caught up with her."

Jonathan whooped with laughter, only to be silenced by a look from Jared.

"I'll need a ship, Jon, and a crew willing to run that damned blockade. She may get to England safely, but getting back to Wyndsong's another matter."

"*Dream Witch* is finished in dry dock, Jared. A few touches, and we could rig her out to look like a private, seagoing yacht. There are a number of seamen here in Plymouth who would be more than willing to sail with you as crew."

"Anyone sailing with me will be well paid, Jon. I want *Dream Witch* ready in twenty-four hours. With luck I can make England just before that headstrong vixen I married." He turned to Jed. "Go to the kitchen and get Martha to feed you, then get a night's rest. There are extra rooms above the stable. I'll have a letter of instruction for Captain Browne in the morning. Go along now."

"Yes, sir." Jed left the room.

"Is your business finished here, brother Jared?" asked Jonathan softly.

"I thought it was, Jon. I had told them that, now that I was a married man, I could no longer work for them as I had in the past. They wanted me to make one more trip to Europe, and I said no. But I've changed my mind. I shall go back to them tonight and say that I will. If a war between England and America can be prevented, I will feel it work well done. Despite what President Madison feels, Napoleon means us no good. He has been badly advised in this matter. All those young, ill-educated congressmen from the Western territories are so eager for a war. To them, another war with England is no more than a good barroom brawl, and they're spoiling for a fight. How glamorous it seems in retrospect! Little David challenging and defeating Goliath. God, how sick I am of wars, big and small! If this country is to grow and thrive we must build a strong economy, and war only wastes lives." Then he laughed at himself. "Jon, you got me going again."

"You should run for Congress yourself, Jared. I've said it before."

"Perhaps I will someday, but at the moment I seem to have little control over my own home," he answered ruefully.

"It was not a mistake, then? You really do love her?"

"God, yes! So much that she can drive me to anger as quickly as she can to passion. You know, brother, in the four months we've been married she has never admitted to the slightest affection for me, but the first three words of her letter are 'I love you.' Does she mean it, or does she mock me? I intend to find out, and as quickly as possible." Again, his fist tightened around her letter.

His temper had not improved when, several weeks later, he stood on the West India Company docks in London and watched *Seahorse* being made fast. He had left Plymouth on the fourteenth of April and, by a combination of favorable winds, expert sailing, and the fact that his *Dream Witch* was sleeker and built for speed, managed to arrive in London three days ahead of his quarry. Roger Bramwell had been quite surprised to see him, but with his usual efficiency had gotten Jared's London house running smoothly.

"M'lord, it is good to see you," the secretary had greeted him. "I didn't expect you back for some time."

"My ward's wedding to Lord Swynford draws me, Bramwell. And why the 'm'lord'?"

"Your title, sir, 'lord of the manor,' was a royal grant. You are entitled to use it here in England. I suggest that in the interest of your business and your social position you do use it. As to Miss Amanda Dunham's wedding, the gossip, thanks to the dowager Lady Swynford, has it that the match is off. Lord Adrian is going about with a very long face, and the mamas of several eligible heiresses have been seen at Almack's in deep conversation with Lady S. Everyone assumed the political troubles between England and America would prevent your coming."

"It might have, Bramwell, were my wife not so stubborn. Send a note around to Lord Swynford asking him to dine with me tonight. Say that my ward is en route to England now. Best to put him out of his misery quickly. Be sure the note is delivered to Lord Swynford personally and not to anyone else."

Miranda had been correct, Jared mused, and had she not taken the initiative her sister might indeed have lost young Swynford.

The wind blew the stench of the river at him, and Jared lifted a scented handkerchief to his nose. Adrian Swynford had arrived promptly at seven o'clock that evening, and never had Jared seen such an eager young man. He smiled at the recollection. Lord Swynford was of medium height and build. His eyes were cornflower blue, his hair a dark blond, clipped short in the back, a deep wavy curl falling across his high forehead. He had a fair English complexion with ruddy cheeks that bespoke his good health. His eyes were intelligent. He had a straight nose, well-shaped mouth, and firm chin. It was a pleasing face.

His dress was the height of current London fashion, ankle-length dove-gray pantaloons, sky-blue long-tailed coat, a simple white silk shirt, a pale-rose satin brocade waistcoat, a white cravat tied in the fashion known as "Love Lost," and high black boots. His dress declared that he had taste, but was no dandy.

"Lord Dunham?" He had come toward Jared, his hand held out. "I am Adrian Swynford. Your note said Amanda is on her way to England. Why has she not come with you?"

"Because," said Jared, taking the outstretched hand and shaking it, "I forbade the journey. But my wife—you do remember Miranda?—disobeyed me, and ran off with her sister and mother as soon as I was safely out of the way. Sherry?"

"Good Lord!" Adrian Swynford slumped into a chair.

"Sherry?" repeated Jared, holding out a Waterford glass of the amber liquid.

"Yes! Yes, thank you, sir!" Adrian took the glass, sipped, and, leaning forward, said anxiously, "Do you object to me as Amanda's husband?"

Jared sat down in the brocade wing chair opposite his guest. "Not at all. For months my wife and her mother have been singing your praises and Amanda has been quite frank about her feelings. I did not forbid your marriage, I forbade the women from making an Atlantic crossing because of the unfavorable political climate between our countries. Miranda, however, was determined that your wedding not be postponed, and in my absence she arranged passage on a British blockade runner."

"My God!" ejaculated Lord Swynford. "How irresponsible! What utter madness! Has Miranda no idea of the kind of men who run blockades?"

Jared smiled ruefully. "I must admit to blockade running also, m'lord. Nevertheless, I agree with you. My wife's naiveté is amazing. However, the captain of her ship is Christopher Edmund, the Marquis of Wye. I believe his older brother was also a suitor of Amanda's. I assume they are relatively safe."

"If you left after Amanda then why are you here before them?"

"My yacht is sleeker and swifter."

"And you are most determined, eh, m'lord," chuckled Adrian Swynford.

"Much more determined," said Jared softly. "Since we are to be brothers-in-law, I hope you will call me Jared, and I may call you Adrian. Now, before my cook has apoplexy, let us go in to dinner."

The twenty-year-old English lord and the thirty-year-old American became friends. Adrian Swynford saw that he had a strong ally against his tiny but formidable mother when, the very next day, she looked down her lorgnette at the upstart American and found herself charmed by him despite herself.

"His manners are impeccable and he is amazingly genteel," she told an acquaintance.

"For an American, you mean," came the reply.

"For *any* real gentleman," said the dowager Lady Swynford.

Three days after their meeting, two gentlemen stood on the rainswept docks of the West India Company watching as the gangway of the *Seahorse* was lowered. The captain appeared at the top of the gangplank, Miranda on his arm. Behind her were Dorothea and Amanda. As they came down the gangplank Miranda said gaily,

"La, Kit, how can we thank you for getting us here so quickly and safely? I shall be eternally grateful."

"Having you aboard has been a pleasure, ma'am, but if you truly wish to thank me then a kiss will do quite nicely."

They had reached the bottom of the gangway.

"Fie, sir! You are most wicked!" scolded Miranda, but she was smiling. Then she kissed him quickly on the cheek. "There, Kit!"

"You are well rewarded, sir," said Jared smoothly, stepping out from the warehouse porch. "Welcome to London, madam."

"Jared!" The look of utter astonishment on her face was his reward. Never again did he expect to have such an advantage.

"Amanda!" cried Jared's companion.

"Adrian! Oh, Adrian!" Amanda flew into her betrothed's arms, and was soundly kissed.

"Thank heavens you are here, Jared," said Dorothea. "Perhaps now you can talk some sense into Miranda."

"What would you have me say, Doro? She has already accomplished her objective." He turned to his wife. Miranda's heart was pounding wildly as his fierce green gaze held her captive. "Did you mean what you wrote me?" he asked her in a deep, intense voice.

"Yes," she said in a low voice.

Slowly he lifted her gloved hand to his lips and kissed it. "We will talk later, my love."

"Yes, m'lord," she murmured, wondering if he was very angry with her. Knowing she loved him, she wanted to please him, and she had matured enough to realize she could do so without losing her own being. She was so very happy to see him.

"Miranda, m'dear, I believe you should introduce me to Captain Edmund," said Jared, and she came out of her reverie.

"Kit, may I present my husband, Jared Dunham, the lord of Wyndsong Manor. Jared, Captain Christopher Edmund, the Marquis of Wye."

As the two men shook hands, Kit said, "I was given to understand that the press of your other affairs would keep you from England, m'lord."

A smile played at the corners of Jared's mouth. It was plain to see the young puppy fancied himself in love with Miranda. Undoubtedly he had intended to squire her all over London in her husband's absence. "I was able to conclude my business far in advance of my expectations," he replied smoothly. "I owe you a great debt, m'lord, for transporting my ladies in safety. I hope you will favor us at dinner one night soon. And, of course, we shall expect you at the nuptials."

"Thank you, sir. It was an honor to have Mir—Lady Dunham and her family aboard." He turned to the others. "Ladies, m'lord, your servant. I must now see to my ship."

"I would add my thanks too, Edmund," said Adrian. "I owe you a greater debt than I can ever pay," and he smiled happily into Amanda's radiant, upturned face.

Kit smiled back at the lovers. "I am more than well rewarded, seeing you together," he replied graciously. Then, bowing smartly at the assembled group, he walked back to his ship.

"I've brought the coach," said Jared, offering his arm to his wife and mother-in-law. "What of your luggage?"

"We've very little," Miranda replied. "There was no room aboard for luggage. Besides, Amanda's trousseau was ordered from Madame Charpentier before we left London. All that is necessary for her is to send to Madame for delivery."

He smiled. "Amanda cannot wear her trousseau before the wedding. Neither can you and Dorothea be seen in society in last year's fashions. I suggest that when Madame Charpentier delivers Mandy's trousseau, she fits you all for a London wardrobe."

"But we are returning to Wyndsong immediately after Mandy's wedding, aren't we?"

"I have business here, my dear, which may not be concluded by then. Since you have gone to such trouble to get to England, you may as well enjoy it. Besides," and here he lowered his voice, "I am not sure how easy it will be for us to get home."

"Do we not have *Dream Witch?*" she asked in the same tone.

"The British could impound it and all other American property if the situation between our countries grows more serious. That was another reason for my hesitating to make this trip."

"I am glad we came!" she said. "Do you see how happy Amanda is?"

"Yes, I do, but you are still not excused for disobeying me, wildcat. We will speak of this later."

The coach was black and ivory with a gold-velvet-draped coach-

man's seat, pulled by two perfectly matched gray horses. Two
lackeys in green and white livery were helping a sailor load their
baggage into the boot beneath the driver's seat. As Jared approached,
one of the lackeys turned and opened the coach door, pulling down
the folding steps.

"We will sit with our backs to the coachman," said Adrian,
helping Amanda into the vehicle.

Jared helped Dorothea up, and then Miranda, following and
closing the door behind him. The coach moved at a sedate pace off
the West India Company docks and into the London traffic.

"I've never been so relieved to see dry land in my life," announced Dorothea.

"Was the crossing so unpleasant then? I ran into no foul weather
with *Dream Witch*," replied Jared.

"The weather was unusually fine. In fact, I've never had such a
smooth trip. But I lived in terror of the French catching us, or an
American patrol boat." She sighed mightily and her ample bosom
heaved. "How, my dear Jared, could we have explained our presence
on a British ship to our fellow Americans? I shudder even to imagine
it. Then, when I decided we were safe from our own people, I had
the Barbary pirates to worry about."

"The Barbary pirates don't often attack English ships, Doro."

"Nonsense! They are savages! The sailors on board the *Seahorse*
told me the Turks *love* blondes. Why, we could all have ended up in a
harem! Thank God that we are safely here in spite of Miranda's
wilfullness." She sighed again and leaned back against the tufted
gold velvet seat. "I am utterly exhausted. I shall sleep for three
days!" Her eyes closed, and within minutes she was snoring softly.

On the opposite seat Amanda giggled and snuggled next to
Adrian. "I almost believe Mama is sorry we arrived safely."

"Nevertheless, you took a serious risk," said Adrian gravely.

"Had my sister not been bold enough to take the risk I should not
be here with you now," replied Amanda pertly, and Jared raised an
amused eyebrow. The kitten had claws.

"If I had lost you..." began Lord Swynford.

"But you didn't! Now please kiss me again, Adrian. I have missed being kissed for these last nine months."

Lord Swynford willingly complied with his betrothed's request, and Jared turned to his wife and tipped her face up to his. Her sea-green eyes regarded him warily. "I have spent the last several weeks debating whether I should kill you or kiss you when we met again. Adrian is right. You took a serious risk."

"I would not have gone aboard the *Seahorse* if I had not felt Kit a trustworthy captain," she said in a low voice.

"You would have sailed with the Devil himself to get Amanda here, my dear, and we both know it." She had the good grace to blush, because it was true. He continued, "Will you be as loyal to me as you have been to your sister, Miranda?" She had barely time to murmur yes before he kissed her passionately, his lips branding her. She boldly sucked on the velvet of his tongue, and he pulled her roughly into his lap, his hands seeking her perfect little breasts.

"Jared!" she whispered frantically, "not here, m'lord!"

He bit her neck gently, and said roughly, "Mama is sleeping, and Amanda and Adrian are far more involved than we are, m'lady." Undoing the strings of her bonnet, he pulled it off, and pushed it aside. His hands tangled in her pale-gold hair, drawing the pins out, letting it fall around them like a curtain. "Oh, wildcat, if anything had happened to you!" and his mouth found hers again, bruising her soft willing lips.

The carriage came to an abrupt halt, and the embracing couples parted, flushed, their breathing rapid. Adrian pulled down the window and leaned out. "Oh, blast! It's Prinny's coach, and he's driving slowly so the crowds can see him."

"Have Smythe take one of the side streets," replied Jared. "It isn't necessary for us to have a tour of London. Besides," and here his dark eyebrows waggled ferociously, causing both sisters to giggle, "I suddenly find myself eager to be home."

"And I find myself eager to be married," laughed Adrian.

"You should be ashamed of yourselves," said Miranda with mock severity, rearranging her long hair back into its chignon.

"They are both as randy as billy goats," remarked Amanda innocently. There was a shocked silence quickly followed by a burst of laughter.

"My dear young sister-in-law, as your guardian I am strongly tempted to spank you. Your manner of expression is shocking. However, since you are quite right in my case, and, I suspect, in Adrian's case, I can hardly punish you for telling the truth."

"I shall endeavor to be more tactful in future, sir," promised Amanda. Her cornflower-blue eyes were dancing merrily.

"Very good," he answered, his eyes bright with amusement.

"Where are we going?" asked Miranda.

"To my house," said Jared. "It is on a small square near Greene Park. Where had you expected to stay? Surely not at a hotel?"

"We were going to Sir Francis Dunham's home. I knew you had a house in London, but you never told me where, and I didn't know whether you kept it staffed or let it out."

"You are definitely not an organized traveler, wildcat," he teased her.

"We did come away in a bit of a hurry."

"Indeed you did, and what provisions, pray, did you make for the running of Wyndsong?"

"I expected you to go home, Jared," she answered, "but even so, Peter Moore, the manor foreman, is quite capable of running the farm and seeing to the horses. I told him to continue as my father had unless you gave him other instructions. Were you in such a hurry to come after me, m'lord, that you sailed off and forgot Wyndsong?"

"Do not provoke me, madam. My revenge will be fierce."

"Do your worst, m'lord. I am ready to battle with you," she challenged. Her look was smoldering.

Gracious, thought Amanda, snuggling close to Adrian, I far prefer my quiet love. They are both so strong, and so wild.

The coach turned into a small square a block off the park. There were only eight houses around Devon Square, and the center had a planted miniature park of its own with chestnut trees at each corner. A carefully raked gravel walk in the shape of a cross bisected the area into four sections of green lawn edged with bright flower beds. The center of the cross held a greenish-bronze lily-shaped fountain from which spouted a column of water. There were four curved white marble benches in the classical style around the fountain.

The houses were all a mellowed red brick, with dark gray slate roofs and high, white marble stoops. The Dunham carriage pulled up before a house on the east side of the square, and the two footmen leaped down from their perch behind the coach and hurried to open its street-side door. Two other footmen came from the house to carry the luggage.

Dorothea awakened with a start. "Wh-where are we?"

"We are at our London house, Mama," soothed Miranda. "In a few moments you'll be in a nice hot tub, and you'll have a pot of China Black all to yourself. It will ease your headache." She reached for her bonnet, put it on, and tied the strings.

The gentlemen escorted the ladies up the steps and into the house. To Miranda's surprise, the entire staff was assembled. She was not used to such formality, but then this was England, not America. She lifted her chin. Feeling the warm pressure of Jared's hand on hers, Miranda was strengthened. Roger Bramwell stepped forward.

"Miranda, this is my secretary, Roger Bramwell. He keeps everything going for me here in England. Roger, my wife."

She held out her gloved hand to shake his, but instead he turned it deftly, and kissed it in the European manner. "M'lady, it's a pleasure to welcome you to London."

"Thank you, Mr. Bramwell," she replied, withdrawing her hand.

"Allow me to present the staff," he said. "Simpson, the butler."

"Simpson."

"Welcome, m'lady," said Simpson, a very tall, large, dignified man.

"Mrs. Dart, the housekeeper."

"We're delighted to have you with us, m'lady," said Mrs. Dart, as tiny as the butler was large, and sweet-faced.

"Thank you, Mrs. Dart."

"The treasure of our household, m'lady—Mrs. Poultney, the cook."

"Heh! Heh!" chortled the red-cheeked plump woman, her four chins jiggling. Then she bobbed a curtsey. "Happy to serve you, m'lady."

"I shall depend on you, Mrs. Poultney."

"M'lord's valet, Mitchum."

Miranda nodded at the tall, rapier-thin man.

"And this is Perkins, m'lady. I've chosen her to be your personal maid. Her references are excellent."

"I'm sure they are," replied Miranda. "I know we shall get along famously," she said to the maid, who curtseyed pertly. Good, thought Miranda, this one is no simpering girl. "Mr. Bramwell, I shall need someone to look after Mama and Amanda while we are here."

"I shall see to it, m'lady."

The rest of the staff were quickly introduced: Smythe, the coachman, the four footmen, the two parlor maids, the two upstairs maids, the laundress, young Walker, Jared's tiger, the two stable grooms, the tweeny, and the potboy.

"We've prepared the rose bedroom for Miss Amanda, m'lady, and the tapestry bedroom for Mistress Dunham," said the housekeeper to Miranda.

"Very good, Mrs. Dart. Will you see that the baths are brought up to the bedrooms? I shall also require a pot of tea, China Black, if we have it, for Mama. As soon as I've bathed I should like to see today's menus, and perhaps one of the upstairs maids can help my mother and sister until we have someone for them."

"Yes, m'lady!" Mrs. Dart was impressed by Miranda's quick authority. "Violet!" she gestured to one of the upstairs maids. "Show the ladies to their bedrooms."

"You will, of course, join us for dinner, Adrian," said Miranda.

He nodded, and she turned to follow her mother and sister up the oak staircase.

"M'lady," said Jared.

"M'lord?"

"I will attend you shortly," he said.

"I shall await you, sir."

The staff went back to their duties, and to gossip about their new mistress. The gentlemen repaired to the morning room, and were served coffee.

"I've obtained the necessary vouchers to Almack's for the

ladies," said Roger to Adrian and Jared. "Princess de Lieven and Lady Cowper send their kind regards. They say you've broken half the hearts in London by marrying. They also say that they do not remember your wife from last season. They recall Miss Amanda, but not her sister. They say they look forward to meeting Lady Dunham."

"I'm sure they do," grinned Jared. "I hope they managed to mask their eagerness."

Roger chuckled. "Not too well. Mostly they speculated on how Lady Gillian Abbott would take the arrival of you *and* your wife."

"I say! were you involved with Gillian Abbott?" said Adrian. "She's a bit of a high flyer, but then old Lord Abbott don't care what she does as long as she's discreet, and brings home no bastards."

"Lady Abbott and I were friends," replied Jared. "She was not in a position to offer anything other than friendship; and I certainly had no intention of offering anything else, even under other circumstances."

"Certainly not, Jared. Even before she married old Abbott she wasn't a particularly good match. Only thing she's got is her beauty. The old man was eighty when they were married three years ago. Didn't think he'd last this long."

To change the subject gracefully, Roger Bramwell said, "You have several invitations, Jared. Sir Francis Dunham and his wife, the dowager Lady Swynford, the dowager Duchess of Worcester. I tendered your acceptances for those three. The others you will have to look over and decide on yourself."

"Nothing too soon, Bramwell. The ladies haven't an extensive wardrobe. In fact I want you to send one of the footmen around to Madame Charpentier's and say that Miss Amanda Dunham is here. We'll want Amanda's trousseau delivered, and fittings for my wife and her mother for entire new wardrobes. And Miss Amanda will need a few things to tide her over until the wedding. Send the payment for what's already done, and give Madame a deposit for what she's about to do. That should bring her posthaste," he grinned. "Now, gentlemen, I have something to discuss with my wife. I'll see you tonight. Adrian..." He bowed and left the morning room.

Miranda was delightedly exploring her bedroom. Done in turquoise velvet and heavy cream satin, it had beautiful mahogany furniture in the Chippendale style. The carpet was Chinese, a thick turquoise blue wool

with a cream geometric design. The two long bedroom windows
overlooked the garden, which was abloom now with multi-colored
flowers. The fireplace had a marvelous Georgian mantel that sported
exquisite tall pink and white Sevres vases on either end, and a matching
pink Sevres porcelain mantel clock in its center. On a piecrust table by
the window was a large Waterford crystal bowl of pink and white roses.

"Shall I see to your bath, m'lady?" asked Perkins.

"Oh, please, yes! I haven't had a freshwater bath in almost six weeks.
Is there any bath oil in the house? No, wait, I've some in the little trunk.
It's my own blend." She sat down in a wing chair by the window and
waited.

Perkins bustled around the room unpacking Miranda's things,
placing her silver brushes on the dressing table, clucking over the
condition of her crumpled, trunk-bound clothing, directing with firm
authority the grunting footmen who brought in the porcelain tub and
buckets of hot water. She was as tall as her new mistress, as big-
boned a girl as Miranda was slender. She had neatly braided nut-
brown hair framing her round face. It was a sweet face with large
gray eyes, a wide mouth, and an upturned nose. She was dressed
plainly in an ankle-length gown of good-quality gray kerseymere
with a spanking white collar and matching cuffs. She shooed the
footmen out, closed the bedroom door firmly, and, taking the
carefully hoarded supply of Miranda's bath oil, poured a generous
dollop into the tub, noting the London label on the small flacon.

"I'll send one of the men around to Mr. Carruthers' chemist shop
tomorrow, m'lady, and get you more of this. Sweet stock, isn't it?"

"Yes. You've a good nose, Perkins."

Perkins grinned her infectious grin. "I should hope so, m'lady.
My family grows flowers for sale, right outside of London. Stand up
now, and let's get those poor, travel-stained clothes off you." She had
Miranda stripped and into her tub in a minute. "Now you just lay
there and relax, m'lady, while I get these things to the laundress. I
won't be but two minutes," and she was gone.

Miranda sighed at the welcome luxury of the privacy and the even
more welcome hot tub. During the voyage they could bathe only with

salt water, and never in a tub, naked. They had taken what Mama referred to as "birdbaths," and the cold salt water left them feeling more sticky than clean.

Miranda felt her entire body relaxing, and without even opening her eyes she laved the sweet, oiled water over her shoulders.

"I can almost hear you purring, wildcat." His deep voice held an amused note.

"I am purring," she said, still not opening her eyes.

"You make a fetching sight, m'lady. I can only regret that your tub is too small for both of us. I far prefer the tall old-fashioned oak tubs where two can bathe together."

"Somehow I don't believe bathing is on your mind, m'lord."

"Indeed, madam?"

"Indeed, sir."

"*Say it!*" He dropped the bantering tone, and his voice suddenly had a ragged sound.

"Say what?"

"Say it, dammit!"

She opened her sea-green eyes, and looked up into his face. His bottle-green eyes were blazing with gold lights. She could sense the barely restrained violence. "I love you, Jared," she said clearly. "I love you!"

He reached down and lifted her, sleek and dripping, from the tub. She was clasped against his hard body; his mouth came down fiercely on hers, and she kissed him back just as passionately, finally tearing her head away to gasp for air. "Say it," she commanded.

"Say what?"

"Say it, dammit!"

"I love you, Miranda! Dear God, how I love you!"

The door flew open. "There, m'lady! I'm back! Ohh! Oh, m'lady! I beg your pardon. I—I—"

Jared calmly lifted Miranda back into the tub. She was shaking with laughter. "Finish attending your mistress, Perky," he said calmly. "I just came to tell her that the dressmaker will be here shortly." He turned, and Perkins's eyes widened, for Jared's clothes

were soaked through from chest to knee. "I shall rejoin you when
Madame Charpentier arrives, my dear," he said, going through the
connecting door between their rooms.

"Will you please wash my hair, Perkins? It's really quite disgrace-
ful," Miranda murmured. "What was that my husband called you?
Perky? How charming, and it does suit you better. You're far too
young to be a Perkins. Perkins is an elderly, gray-haired lady with a
flat chest." The maid giggled, beginning to recover somewhat. "I
am going to call you Perky," said Miranda firmly.

An hour later, Miranda's hair had nearly dried and she felt
deliciously clean. A knock on the door sent the maid to answer it and
admit the volatile Madame Charpentier with her two assistants. A
tall, gaunt woman of indeterminate years, always dressed in black,
she was the most sought-after dressmaker in London. Looking down
her long nose at Miranda, she said, "Mees Dunham, it is nice to see
you once more."

"It is *Lady* Dunham," Jared interjected quietly, coming in behind
Madame Charpentier.

The dressmaker ignored him. Husbands, she had long ago decided, were of little account, good only for paying the bills.
"Clarice! Ze Tape!" she ordered an assistant, and went quickly
about the job of measuring Miranda. "You 'ave not changed, Mees
Dunham. Your measurements are ze same. We will use ze same
colors as last year, pale pinks and blues and greens."

"No!" said Jared firmly.

"M'sieur?"

"You are not dressing Miss Amanda, Madame de Charpentier. My
wife is totally different from her sister. Pale colors are not suitable
for her."

"M'sieur, it ees the fashion!"

"The Dunhams of Wyndsong make their own fashions, Madame
Charpentier. Are you equal to such a challenge? Perhaps I should
have Simone Arnaude dress my wife."

"*M'sieur!*" The gaunt dressmaker had the look of an outraged
chicken, and both her mousy assistants were pale and gasping.

"Look at Lady Miranda Dunham, madame!" One elegant hand

reached out, and lifted her hair to let it sift through his fingers. "Her hair is gilt, her eyes sea-green, her coloring wild roses and cream. Every bit of her is exquisite, but dress her in the pale fashionable colors of today and she fades into the background. I want to see color! Turquoise! Burgundy! Garnet! Emerald! Sapphire! Black!"

"*Black*, m'sieur?!"

"Black, madame! We will be going to Almack's this Wednesday night. I want my wife's gown to be made of black silk to set off not only her fair skin, but the diamonds she'll be wearing."

"Black," mused the dressmaker. "Black." She looked long and hard at Miranda, causing her to flush, then a note of respect crept into her voice. "M'lord Dunham ees correct, and I am certainly not too old to learn. M'lady will be *ravissante*, I promise! Simone Arnaude, indeed! Come, Clarice, Marie!" And gathering up her tapes, and pads, she stalked regally from the room, her two assistants fluttering in her wake.

"What diamonds?" demanded Miranda.

"Perky, out! Don't come back till you're called."

"Yes, m'lord!" cried Perkins, giggling as she left the room.

"What diamonds?" repeated Miranda.

"The ones I'm going to buy you tomorrow. Get into bed!"

"In my undergarments?" she teased him, feigning shock.

He calmly tore her chemise from her, and dropped the two pieces on the floor. With equal calm she reached out and ripped his shirt off, dropping the two pieces next to the remains of her chemise. But when her hands reached for the waist of his breeches he caught them.

"Oh, no, m'lady! I have plenty of shirts, but with every tailor in London booked for the season and decent fabric for breeches at a premium..." He undid the offending garment and stepped out of it. Then, with a swift movement, he swept her up and carried her to the turquoise-satin-hung bed. Cradling her in one arm, he drew back the covers and gently deposited her. He stood by the bed for a moment looking down at her, drinking in the perfection of her beautiful body. The small, yet perfectly formed breasts, the slim, exquisitely molded waist, the long, slender legs. Jared ached, not simply with his desire but with another sort of longing, a longing so elusive he could not even put a name to it. She held up her arms to him, and with a groan he entwined his body with hers. Their mouths touched, gently, tenderly, and he held her so tightly she could barely breathe.

"Oh, wildcat, I love you!" he murmured helplessly. "You must be a sorceress to have woven such a tight web of enchantment around me. I am a fool to admit my weakness to you, but then I suspect you knew all along that I loved you." His big, bronzed hand caressed her silky hair.

"I did not guess, Jared," she answered softly. "How could I have? I was far too wrapped up in myself to really see you. The night before we left Wyndsong I sat awake, in the dark, listening to the wind in the oaks, and for the first time I faced myself and the seriousness of the decision I was making in sailing to England. It was only then that I realized I loved you and needed you; that I was but a half-thing without you and your love to make me whole. I love you, my darling! I hope the web I have woven around you is indeed magic. If it is, it will never break!" She took his dark head in her hands and, drawing it down to hers, kissed his eyelids, his mouth, his sharply molded high cheekbones. "Love me, my darling! Oh, please love me!" she whispered softly in his ear, sending hot desire through him.

She lay pinned between his muscular thighs, and his hands skillfully caressed her warm flesh. She drew his head down to her breasts murmuring "Please!" and he was delighted that she felt easy enough with him to tell him what pleased her. His mouth closed over a pertly thrusting pink nipple, and she cried out sharply. He nursed hungrily on one sweetly rounded breast and then the other. He let his lips travel downward to the soft, mossy grotto between her legs, strangely dark in contrast with her silver-gilt hair.

Miranda was more than a little frightened as the wildly beating pulse in her throat gave evidence. But she let him love her as he so desperately wanted to do. A gentle tongue tasted of a hitherto forbidden sweetness, sending her into a near swoon. His deep voice crooned. "Ah, wildcat, you're as beautiful there as I suspected," and she felt the heat of her own blush.

Passion cradled her, and lifted her high above the world of mere mortals. She floated. He slid his hands beneath her to lift her up and thrust deep into her, and Miranda felt the tears sliding down her cheeks as he filled her with his bigness, his warmth. He kissed and licked the wetness away, all the while his body moved rhythmically within her, gently yet insistently, until they reached a simultaneous crest.

His panting, big body covered her shuddering, slender one until the spasms passed. Then he reluctantly withdrew from her. Wordlessly he pulled the bedcovers over them and cradled her in his arms. She sighed contentedly, and shortly her even breathing told him she was asleep. Jared smiled to himself in the firelit room. How very like her was this sudden passionate declaration of her love for him.

The Sevres clock on the mantel woke him as it chimed seven o'clock. "You're awake," her quiet voice startled him.

"Um, best sleep I've had in months," he rumbled.

She chuckled. "Best sleep I've had in months, too!"

"I think we're going to have to get up, Miranda. I don't care about the servants, for they will gossip anyway. But I do feel poor Doro will be quite shocked if we do not appear for dinner."

"I suppose so," she murmured, flipping onto her stomach and trailing her fingers across his furry chest, moving dangerously downward.

"Madam!" he growled at her.

"Sir?" Her sea-green eyes were narrowly slitted, catlike, and her nails sent shivers down his spine. He grasped her wrist tightly.

"Dinner, madam. Our houseguests. Remember?"

She made a little moue with her mouth. "Thank God both Mama and Amanda are being married! The sooner the better!"

He laughed loudly. Releasing her wrist, he rolled out of bed and yanked at the bellpull. "Practice nonchalance with Perky while I call Mitchum to help me bathe and dress."

That was Saturday evening, and the only public appearance the Dunhams made over the weekend was at early church on Sunday.

On Monday, Jared Dunham disappeared for several hours. The ladies occupied themselves with the constant fittings insisted upon by Madame Charpentier who began arriving with her two nervous assistants and six sewing girls early each morning, never leaving until late evening. Miranda, pitying the half-starved, overworked young seamstresses, all of whom were just barely out of childhood, instructed the cook to feed them well and insisted they stay in the empty attic servant's room.

"If they can sew as good as they can eat, you'll be the best-dressed lady in London," observed Mrs. Poultney to her mistress.

"I begrudge them nothing," replied Miranda. "Two of those poor girls had tears in their eyes when the footman carried away the tray with the remains of our tea."

"Hungry or no, they're the lucky ones," said Mrs. Poultney.

"Lucky?"

"Aye, m'lady, lucky. They've a trade, and a job. It's more than most. Times ain't good with us and the froggies fightin' all the time. There's many going hungry."

"Well," sighed Miranda, "I cannot feed them all, but I can feed Madame Charpentier's sewing girls while they're here."

"Voilà!" cried Madame late Wednesday afternoon. "Eet ees finished, m'lady, and eef I do say so, eet is parfait! You weel be the envy of every woman at Almack's tonight."

Miranda stared silently at herself in the long looking glass, and was amazed at the image she saw staring back. My God, she thought, *I am beautiful!* Its waist high with thin silver ribbons that tied beneath her breasts, the gown was exquisite.

The gown was made of several layers of pure, sheer black silk. It had short, puffed sleeves and a long straight skirt embroidered in dainty diamanté flowers. The back was cut low, the neckline lower yet. Seeing the clear dark color against her flesh, Miranda realized why Jared had chosen it. It made her skin as translucent as the finest Indian ocean pearls.

The dressmaker's discreet cough caught Miranda's attention. "I am stunned, Madame Charpentier," she said softly. "The dress is quite magnificent."

The Frenchwoman bridled with pleasure. "The accessories for thees gown include elbow-length, black silk gloves, black silk roses with silver leaves for your hair, and a small black swansdown muff."

Miranda nodded absently, still somewhat bemused by the woman in the mirror. Was it really she? Miranda Dunham of Wyndsong Island? She turned slightly, lifting her chin, and gazed again at her mirror image. A small smile lifted the corners of her mouth as she began to grow a bit more accustomed to the beautiful woman in black with the porcelain skin, the pink-flushed cheeks, and the clear sea-green eyes. By God, she thought, I'll give those dainty beauties a run for their money tonight!

At nine o'clock that evening the Dunhams, Lord Swynford, and the dowager Lady Swynford gathered in the foyer of the mansion preparatory to leaving for Almack's. The gentlemen were elegant in the required knee breeches. Amanda was adorable in a baby-blue gown, a strand of perfectly matched pearls about her throat. The two older women were in gray and dark green gowns, respectively, matching turbans on their heads. They turned and gasped as Amanda squealed, "Oh, Miranda! You are absolutely stunning!"

"Miranda! What has possessed you to wear such a gown? It is highly unsuitable for a young girl," said Dorothea sharply.

"I am no longer a young girl, Mama. I am a married woman."

"But pastels are fashionable now," protested Dorothea. "Black is not at all fashionable."

"Then I shall make it fashionable, Mama. Milord! Where are the diamonds you promised me?"

His bottle-green eyes slowly raked her from the top of her silvery-gilt head to the toes of her kid shoes, lingering appreciatively on her creamy breasts, which swelled perhaps a trifle too provocatively above the low, black silk neckline. Then their eyes met in a look of private understanding, and he reached into his jacket and drew out a flat, Morocco leather case. Proffering it, he said, "Madam, I always keep my promises."

Miranda opened the case. Her eyes widened but she said nothing, staring at the chain of tiny diamonds with its heart-shaped diamond pendant. He took it from its satin nest and fastened it around her throat. The diamond heart hung just above the cleft between her breasts.

"You'll have to do the earbobs yourself, m'lady. I'd be all thumbs."

"It's so beautiful," she said to him quietly. It was as if no one else were in the room with them. They gazed intently into each other's eyes for a moment, and then Miranda said, "Thank you, m'lord."

He bent and placed a burning kiss on her half-bare shoulder. "We will discuss your gratitude in private, Miranda, at a later date," he murmured.

"Oh, I do hope you're going to buy me diamonds too when we're married," said Amanda mischievously.

"Amanda, you are becoming as undisciplined as your sister!" snapped Dorothea. "Diamonds are not suitable for the young."

"Diamonds," replied Amanda, "are suitable for whomever is fortunate enough to have them."

The men laughed and even the dowager Lady Swynford allowed herself a small smile before saying, "Are we to stand here all night discussing the merits of fine jewelry, or are we to go to Almack's? Must I remind you all we will not be admitted after eleven?"

They arrived at Almack's shortly after ten to find the dancing in full swing. Almack's was actually three rooms consisting of a supper room, a reception area, and a large ballroom where most of the activities took place. The ballroom was a hundred feet long and forty feet wide, and was a chaste cream color. It was decorated with gilt columns and pilasters, classic medallions, and mirrors. Almack's boasted the newest gas lighting, in cut-glass lustres. All around the dance floor were pale-blue velvet and gilt chairs, and tubbed palms. The orchestra was set in an open balcony above the dance floor. It was London's most elegant scene.

Tonight the only patronesses present were Lady Cowper and Princess de Lieven. Miranda and Jared moved across the ballroom to pay their first respects to these two powerful social arbiters, both men bowing elegantly, a fact noted with approval.

"So, Jared Dunham," said Emily Mary Cowper, "you return to us in full possession of your inheritance, *and* with a bride."

"I do, m'lady. May I present my wife, Miranda."

"Lady Dunham." Lady Cowper looked closely at Miranda and her blue eyes widened. "Ah, of course! I *do* remember you! You were the plain, sharp-tongued little girl who pushed that idiot Lord Banesford into a fish pond last season."

"He attempted to take liberties, madam," said Miranda smoothly.

"You were quite right," agreed Lady Cowper. "Bless me, you're not at all plain either, are you? That dress is simply stunning. Much more stylish than all these flowery colors. I do believe you'll start a fashion."

"Thank you," replied Miranda.

The other introductions were made, and the young people moved on to the dance floor, while the two mamas sat gossiping. Emily Mary Cowper watched for a while then said to her friend, Princess de Lieven, the wife of the Russian ambassador, "the little Dunham girl will make young Swynford a perfect wife. She has a nice fortune too, I hear."

"What do you think of our Jared's wife?" asked the princess.

"I think if she'd dressed like that last season, she'd have had a duke instead of a Yankee lordling. I've never seen a light hidden so successfully beneath a bushel. She is a beautiful young woman. That gorgeous hair! Those eyes! Her rose and cream coloring! And worse, it's natural!"

The princess laughed. "I'd like to get to know her better. I suspect a mind there. She's no vapid miss. Let's have her to tea."

"Yes, I shall ask her tomorrow," replied Lady Cowper. "Is Gillian Abbott here tonight?"

"Not yet." The princess laughed again. "She's going to be furious, isn't she? Old Lord Abbott is on his last legs, I hear. I do believe that she had Jared Dunham singled out to be her next husband. After all, her reputation among the ton is only slightly better than a demirep; and what gentleman with enough money to support her would marry her when so many young ladies of better families *and* unblemished reputation are available?"

"Well, I do hope she comes tonight, for I should adore to see *that* confrontation."

"Dear heavens!" exclaimed the princess. "You must be a favorite of the gods, Emily Mary! Look! She is here!"

The two patronesses turned to the ballroom door, where Gillian, Lady Abbott, stood with three escorts. She was of medium height and perfectly proportioned with a long, swanlike neck and high, cone-shaped breasts. She had ivory skin, short dark red curls, and oval-shaped amber-gold eyes edged in long, thick black lashes. Her gown was pale pink, and quite diaphanous, and she wore the famous Abbott rubies, large glittering stones in an ugly old-fashioned red-gold setting.

Certain that she had been noted by everyone present, Lady Abbott advanced into the ballroom, trailed by her escorts. She made an elegant but sketchy curtsey to Countess Cowper and Princess de Lieven. "M'ladies."

"Lady Abbott," murmured Lady Cowper. "How is dear Lord Abbott? I had heard he is quite low, these days."

"Indeed," came the reply, "he is. But nothing would do but I come and enjoy myself. 'I'm an old man,' he said to me, 'but you are young, and mustn't concern yourself with me, Gillian.' How the dear man dotes on me. I could not disappoint him, for he so adores the gossip I bring back."

"How nice for you," said the princess sweetly. "Let me give you some gossip then. Jared Dunham has returned to London, and is now Lord Dunham, having inherited the island he expected to inherit one day."

"I did not know that," exclaimed Lady Abbott.

"He is here tonight," said Lady Cowper, "with the old Lord's two daughters. The younger is to marry Lord Swynford in a few weeks."

Gillian Abbott turned abruptly and surveyed the room. Spying her quarry, she glided off toward it.

"Emily! You didn't tell her that Jared is married!"

"No, I didn't, did I?" said Lady Cowper innocently, her eyes bright with anticipation.

Gillian Abbott patted her curls self-consciously, ignoring her swains, who stumbled after her. *He* was back, and Horace was surely on his deathbed this time. Gillian, Lady Dunham, she thought smugly as she skirted the dancers and scanned the room for Jared. What was the name of his American holding? Windward? Something like that. Not that it mattered. She had no intentions of living in that savage land. He had a decent town house on Devon Square and she'd get him to buy a country place. There he was! God, she'd know that broad, muscular back anywhere!

"Jared!" she cried in her low, husky voice. He turned. "Jared, darling! You're back!" She flung herself into his arms, pulling his head down for a passionate kiss. There! He would be publicly committed! she thought triumphantly.

With a suddenness she hadn't anticipated, Gillian Abbott found herself removed from the embrace she had so carefully engineered, and pushed firmly away. Jared Dunham was looking at her with that damned sardonic look she'd always hated.

"Gillian, my dear," he said. "Do try and behave yourself."

"Aren't you happy to see me?" she pouted. Gillian's pouts had been known to drive men wild.

"I am delighted to see you, *Lady* Abbott," he said. "May I present my wife, Miranda? Miranda, my dear, Lady Abbott."

Gillian felt a chill begin. He couldn't have married, she shrieked silently to herself, she had plans! She glowered at the tall beautiful woman in black by Jared's side. Unimpressed, the beauty dared to glower back! Lady Abbott struggled to get hold of herself for it seemed that the entire room was watching the exchange. Damn Emily Cowper and Dariya de Lieven for the two bitches they were.

"I wish you happy, Lady Dunham," she managed to choke.

"I am quite sure you do," was the clear reply. A subdued titter ran through the room.

Gillian felt a red-black rage well up inside her. What right had this smug-faced Yankee chit to speak to her in such a fashion! "What on earth ever possessed you to marry an *American*, Jared?" Her voice dripped acid.

The room grew hushed. Though the English and the Americans were feuding again, neither side felt a true animosity toward the other. It was simply another round in the seemingly never-ending battle between parent and child. The insult was, therefore, only the frustration of an embittered woman, yet the ton gathered at Almack's that evening knew that unless young Lady Dunham met the challenge flung down by Gillian Abbott, she would be socially damaged.

Miranda drew herself up to her full five feet eight, and looked down her aristocratic nose at Lady Abbott. "Perhaps my husband married me," she said with devastating sweetness, "because he felt the need of a *real* woman."

Gillian Abbott gasped as the barb hit its mark. "You . . . you . . . you . . . " she sputtered furiously.

"American?" supplied Miranda cheerfully. Then she turned to her husband. "Did you not promise me this dance, sir?" As if on cue, the orchestra struck up a sprightly country tune.

"Well, well, well," chuckled Lady Cowper, grinning at her dearest friend, Princess de Lieven. "It appears the last of the season shall not be dull after all."

"It was really quite awful of you not to tell Gillian Abbott of Lord Dunham's marriage, Emily," the princess scolded. Then she laughed and added, "The young American is quite an elegant fighter, isn't she? A really perfect match for Jared."

"You knew him in Berlin, didn't you, Dariya?"

"And St. Petersburg, too." She lowered her voice. "On several occasions he's acted for certain interests in his government as an unofficial ambassador-courier-spy."

"I knew."

"I wonder why he's in London."

"His sister-in-law's wedding, of course. She is to be married at the end of June."

"Perhaps," said Princess de Lieven. "But I'd wager there is more to this visit. England and America are again close to war thanks to Napoleon's meddling, and President Monroe's innocence of European politics. Jared has always sided with those in his government who want peace with honor, and economic prosperity. That is how America will thrive. It's a vast, rich country, and one day it will be a power to be reckoned with, Emily."

"I will ask Palmerston," said Lady Cowper. "He will know."

The dance was ending and the dancers moved off the floor, finding refreshment before sitting down. Amanda, though soon to be Lady Swynford, was surrounded by admirers to whom she parceled out dances with a twinkling charm, while Adrian stood adoringly by. On gilt and velvet chairs the dowager Lady Swynford and Dorothea conversed busily as they planned the wedding and exchanged gossip.

In the dimness of a secluded box Miranda sipped at the warm lemonade and nibbled at the stale cake that constituted Almack's effort at refreshments. She was furious, and his cool, amused attitude outraged her. Finally she could no longer bear the thick silence between them, and burst out, "Was she your mistress?"

"For a time."

"Why did you not tell me?"

"My dear wildcat, no gentleman discusses his mistress with his wife."

"Did she expect you to marry her?"

"That would be quite impossible for several reasons. The lady is already married, and I never offered her the hope of anything other than a brief friendship. That friendship ended when I left London last year."

"She certainly didn't seem to think so," muttered Miranda.

"Are you jealous, wildcat?" he teased.

"Yes, dammit. I am! If that yellow-eyed cat comes near you again, I'll claw her eyes out!"

"Be careful, m'lady. You're behaving most unfashionably. Showing affection for one's husband is considered very bad form."

"Let's go home," she said softly.

"We've only danced one dance. I fear we'll cause a minor scandal," he replied.

"Good!"

"I am putty in your hands, m'lady," he replied. His green eyes narrowed. The dimness of the box hid them as he pulled her against him. *"Say it!"* he commanded, brushing his lips against hers.

"I love you!" she murmured.

His arms tightened about her. "I will never tire of hearing you say that, wildcat," he muttered roughly.

"Say it!" she now demanded.

"I love you," he replied unhesitatingly. "I love you the way I have never loved anyone. I loved you from the moment I first saw you and I shall always love you, even if you are the most unpredictable, impossible creature I've ever known."

"O Fiend! You spoiled it!" She hammered against his chest, and his body rocked with laughter.

"Now, wildcat, it wouldn't do for you to become overconfident," he chided mockingly. "Oh, no, that wouldn't do at all."

❧ Chapter 7 ❧

The highlight of the season's end in 1812 was the celebration of the marriage between Adrian, Baron Swynford, and the American heiress Miss Amanda Dunham. Not only did the bride rank among the year's "incomparables," but she was rumored to have an income of three thousand pounds a year. Small wonder, said the wags and wits, that her unfortunate nationality had been overlooked by the Swynfords.

The young couple had been fêted for several weeks prior to their wedding day, the largest party—a ball—given by Jared and Miranda two nights before the nuptials. Invitations had been at a premium, but the greatest honor done the young people was the attendance of George, the Prince Regent, himself.

The virtual ruler of England now that his father, George III, had been declared mad, the Prince Regent—or Prinny, as he was known by all—was not as popular as he had once been. Confirmed by Parliament to rule in his father's place, he had asked the Tories to form the government, thus alienating the Whigs, who had supported him for years and had expected to ride to power on his coattails. The Tories had no love for Prinny either, and the common people saw only his excesses. To their minds he ate too much when many starved. He squandered money on women, paintings, furnishings, houses, and horses. His marriage was an open scandal although he partly redeemed himself by his adoration of his only child, the Princess Charlotte. Only among his peers was the Prince Regent at ease, for whether they liked him or not, being in favor with the prince was the pinnacle of social success.

He arrived at Dunham House at precisely eleven o'clock the evening of the ball, accompanied by Lady Jersey. He was a tall, full-figured man with carefully coiffed dark brown hair and watery blue eyes. The eyes swept approvingly over Amanda, for the Prince Regent liked his women dimpled and buxom. Still, he was strangely taken by his willow-slim hostess, whose sea-green eyes matched her gown. The Prince Regent, who had expected to stay only half an hour, had such a good time that he stayed for almost the entire ball, thereby guaranteeing its success.

The family had expected to spend the next day recovering from their evening and resting for the wedding, which would take place the following day; but a visitor at ten o'clock in the morning brought the four Dunhams to the main drawing room in various states of dishabille.

"Pieter!" shrieked Dorothea, joyously flinging herself into the arms of a big, tall, red-cheeked gentleman.

"Then you still love me?" whispered the gentleman anxiously.

"Of course I do, you foolish man," replied Dorothea, blushing prettily.

"Good! I have obtained a special license for us to marry, and I intend we use it today!" he cried.

"Oh, Pieter!"

Jared stepped forward. "Mr. Van Notelman, I presume? I am Jared Dunham, lord of Wyndsong. This is my wife, Miranda, and my ward, Amanda."

Pieter Van Notelman took the outstretched hand and shook it. "Mr. Dunham, you'll forgive my unorthodox behavior but I received a note from Dorothea saying that she must, despite the hostilities between England and America, go to London and see to her daughter's wedding. Frankly, I became worried, so I arranged to have a cousin look after my children, and I found a ship sailing from New York to Holland. From Holland I managed to get a fishing boat to bring me to England."

"And once here, you immediately managed to obtain a special wedding license," said Jared drily, his eyes twinkling as he rang for the butler.

"I have friends here too, m'lord."

"But, Pieter, tomorrow is Amanda's wedding! We can't be married today."

"Why not?" chorused the twins.

"We must marry today, Dorothea. I have booked us passage on a West Indiaman sailing tomorrow night for Barbados. From there we will connect with an American ship, and be home before summer's end. I cannot leave the children long, and I should not have left Highlands to be managed by others."

The drawing-room door opened, and the butler entered. "Sir?" he inquired of Jared.

"Send a footman around to Reverend Mr. Blake at St. Mark's. Tell him we'll need him to perform a wedding ceremony at half after eleven. Then beg Mrs. Poultney's indulgence, and say we should like a festive luncheon at one to celebrate the wedding of my mother-in-law and her new husband."

"Very good, m'lord," murmured Simpson impassively, his face betraying neither surprise nor disapproval. He turned and left the room.

"Jared!" squeaked Dorothea.

"Now, Doro, my dear, you have told us of your intention to marry Mr. Van Notelman. Have you changed your mind? I certainly won't force you into a distasteful marriage."

"No! I love Pieter!"

"Then go upstairs and get ready for your wedding. You have heard Mr. Van Notelman's explanation for the haste. It is quite reasonable. And just think, Doro! You will have both your girls with you on this happy day. If you had waited, neither of them would have been with you."

Lord Swynford was hastily summoned, and at eleven-thirty that morning Dorothea Dunham became the wife of Pieter Van Notelman in the presence of her two daughters, her son-in-law, her about-to-be son-in-law, and the personal secretary of the Dutch ambassador, who happened to be a Van Notelman cousin, and had been the one responsible for obtaining the special license.

They returned to the house to find that Mrs. Poultney, though she was deep in preparations for Amanda's wedding feast, had prepared an admirable luncheon. Laid out upon the sideboard in the dining room were a turkey stuffed with chestnut and oyster dressing, a juicy loin of beef, a pink ham, and a large whole Scots salmon *en gelée*. There were bowls of vegetables, whole green beans with almonds, carrots and celery in a dilled cream sauce, a cauliflower with a cheese sauce, Brussels sprouts; little whole new potatoes, potato soufflés, and a marrow pudding. There were tiny roast larks, pigeon pâté, and rabbit pie, as well as a large salad of young lettuce, small radishes, and little green scallions. At the end of the sideboard were an apricot tart, a small wheel of Stilton, and a bowl containing peaches, cherries, oranges, and green grapes. To everyone's amazement and delight, there was even a small two-layer wedding cake.

Brought forth to be complimented on her marvelous achievement, a flushed and beaming Mrs. Poultney explained that she had accomplished the miracle of the wedding cake by the simple process of removing the top two layers from Amanda's cake.

"There's time to redo them for ye, miss. In fact the new layers is already baked and cooling."

She was roundly applauded for her cleverness, and returned to the kitchen richer by a gold sovereign discreetly pressed into her hand by her pleased employer.

The Dutch ambassador's secretary departed in late afternoon, and so did Lord Swynford, who hoped to catch a catnap before his bachelor fête that evening. Jared also napped.

Amanda had attempted to, but she shortly returned downstairs to join her sister in the library overlooking the garden. Secluded up in the little loft balcony, Miranda was reading when she heard her sister calling.

"I'm here," she called back.

Amanda clambered up the teetery library steps to join her twin. "Here again? Lord, Miranda, you will get lines before your time reading so much!"

"I like to read, Mandy, and this is the most marvelous library! I am really going to insist we move it to Wyndsong."

Amanda sat down on a tufted stool facing her sister. She had a strange expression on her face, and Miranda asked, "Why can't you sleep? Bridal nerves?"

"Mama and her new husband."

"Mama and Mr. Van Notelman!?"

"They did not even wait for tonight, Miranda!"

"What?"

"They are...they are..." Her pretty little face grew pink with embarrassment. "The bedsprings squeak, and I heard Mama cry out! It is still daylight, Miranda!"

Miranda choked back her laughter. She remembered her shock the first time Jared made love to her in daylight. Still, her sister needed reassurance. "Don't be shocked, darling," she said. "Husbands have the disconcerting habit of making love to their wives when the spirit moves them. Lovemaking is not necessarily confined to the evening hours."

"Oh." Amanda's rosebud mouth turned down, and once again the perplexed look filled her eyes. "But Mama? I thought she was too old! Surely Mr. Van Notelman is! He must be close to fifty!"

"Age, so Jared assures me, has little to do with it, Amanda."

Amanda was silent for a few moments, and then she said, "What is it like?"

"After the first time, delicious! There is no other word to describe lovemaking. The violation of your maidenhead will hurt, but afterwards..." She smiled dreamily.

"Delicious? Is that all you can tell me, sister?" Amanda was beginning to sound piqued.

"It isn't that I don't want to tell you, Mandy, but there are no suitable words to describe it. It is something you must experience for yourself. All I can do is tell you not to be frightened, and to trust

Adrian. I suspect he has had considerable experience in these matters. Simply allow yourself to enjoy the myriad delicious sensations that will overtake you."

"It *is* nice?" came the hesitant query.

Miranda leaned down and hugged her younger twin hard. "Yes, sister, it is *very* nice."

Very nice indeed, she thought to herself later that night when Jared returned from Lord Swynford's bachelor party and stumbled, shirtless, shoeless, and smelling of a great deal of wine, into her bed to nuzzle at her breasts. "You're drunk!" she accused him, amused.

"Not so d-runk that I can't make love to my wife," he muttered, squirming out of his tight breeches.

Very, *very* nice, she thought afterward, drowsy and satisfied, as he snored lightly next to her.

The following morning dawned bright and clear, a perfect June day. The wedding went perfectly. Amanda's gown, yards of pure white silk draped over a hoop in the style of her grandmama, had a tiny waist and a round low neckline that extended off her shoulders. Little white silk bows embroidered with individual pink silk rosebuds festooned the full skirt with its panniers. The sleeves of the dress were long and loose, with layers of lace at the ends. The hem was edged in lace ruffles and a long train in the back was held up by two of Lord Francis and Lady Millicent Dunham's grandchildren, a boy and girl, ages three and four. The bride wore a lovely strand of perfectly matched pearls about her slender neck, a gift from her mother; and her short, golden blond curls were topped with a dainty diamond tiara, a gift from her mother-in-law, to which was attached a long, sheer lace veil. She carried white roses tied with pink silk ribbons.

Amanda was attended by three bridesmaids, her cousins, the Honorable Misses Caroline, Charlotte, and Georgina Dunham, suitably gowned in sky-blue silk dresses with wreaths of pink rosebuds on their heads, and carrying baskets of multicolored early-summer flowers. The matron of honor, the bride's unusual-looking sister, was very striking in a deep-blue silk gown.

Afterward everyone invited to the church returned to the Devon Square house to toast the couple and eat wedding cake. The guests filled the ballroom, the drawing room, and the garden. The cream of

London society, they resembled a flock of brightly plumed birds chattering madly, making and destroying reputations in one sentence. They lingered into the late afternoon, the last of them finally leaving with the lavender dusk even though the bride and groom had departed long before in a high perch phaeton, bound for a secret destination.

There was a second good-bye, for Dorothea and her new husband were going away, too. Their ship would be sailing from the London dock a bit after nine that evening. As mother and daughter took their leave of one another, Miranda realized that Dorothea was truly starting a new life. She was no longer a Dunham, and for the first time in many years she really had no responsibilities to the Dunhams. Tom was dead, and her girls both well married. Miranda thought her mother looked prettier than she'd ever seen her look. There was a radiance about Doro that her daughter recognized as coming from being well loved. It was strange to think of her mother that way, but Miranda understood that her mother was still a fairly young woman.

"Again, Mama," she said, "I wish you and Mr. Van Notelman happy. Take care of yourself, and when we get back to Wyndsong we will have you all over for a visit."

"Thank you, my dear. You will try to be a good wife to Jared now, won't you? And remember, good manners at all times."

"Yes, Mama," Miranda said demurely.

"Doro." Jared kissed his mother-in-law's cheek.

"Jared, dear." She returned the embrace.

Miranda looked to her new stepfather, somewhat unsure of how to treat him. Pieter Van Notelman saw, and held out his arms to her. "I will be pleased if you'll call me Uncle Pieter. I'm not Tom Dunham, my dear," he said, "but Dorothea's daughters will be as dear to me as my own—and you and Mandy are a whole sight prettier, too! Come on now, and give me a kiss!" And she did, enjoying the tickle of his whiskers and the scent of his bay rum after shave.

"Your girls are most certainly pretty, Pieter," Dorothea protested loyally.

Pieter Van Notelman eyed his new wife with amused affection. "My dear bride," he said, "I love my daughters well, but they're all as plain as bread pudding, and that's the truth. I don't worry about it, though, and neither should you. They've all got sweet natures and fat dowries, and will be proof of the adage that all cats look the same in the dark."

Miranda swallowed her mirth, and tried to look properly shocked, but one look at Dorothea's outraged face and Jared howled with laughter.

"The carriage is ready, m'lady."

"Thank you, Simpson."

Mother and daughter hugged each other a final time. "Good-bye, Mama! Good-bye, Uncle Pieter!"

"I'll go with them to the docks," said Jared softly, "and I may stop at White's on my way back."

"Tonight? Oh, Jared! It is our first night alone."

"I will not be late, and I most assuredly will not be foxed as I was last night." He kissed her mouth lightly. "Foxed, and unable to do my duty by my beautiful wife," he murmured so only she might hear.

"I thought you did your duty admirably, if briefly," she teased in a low whisper.

"I'll be revenged for that slight, m'lady." He grinned rakishly at her, and was gone out the door behind the Van Notelmans.

Alone! For the first time in months she was alone. The well-trained servants moved silently and quickly through the house, restoring order. She moved slowly upstairs to her own empty room, and yanked on the embroidered velvet bellpull. It seemed a very long time before her maid appeared.

"Yes, m'lady?" Perky's cap was askew, and she was flushed from wine or lovemaking, or both.

"Have a hot bath prepared for me," Miranda said, "and I'll want a light supper—perhaps some capon breast, salad, and a fruit tart. Then you may have the evening off, Perky."

Perkins bobbed a lopsided curtsey.

Later, after Miranda had bathed and Perky had brushed her hair, Miranda said kindly, "Go on now, Perky. I shall not need you again tonight. Have a good time with your Martin."

"Oh, m'lady! 'Ow did you know?"

Miranda laughed. "It would be hard not to know, Perky. He's quite calf-eyed about you."

Perkins giggled happily, bobbed a final, wavy curtsey, and was gone. Miranda laughed again and, picking up a small leather-bound volume of Lord Byron's newest poems, sat in the tapestry wing chair by the flickering fire to read while she nibbled on her supper. Mrs. Poultney had prepared her a crispy golden capon wing, and several slices of juicy breast, a light-as-air potato soufflé, tiny, whole baby carrots glazed with honey, and a small salad of tender new lettuce with a delicate tarragon dressing. The woman was a wonder, thought Miranda, finishing everything with a good appetite before turning to the strawberry tart in its flaky crust with the side bowl of clotted Devon cream, and the small porcelain pot of fragrant green China tea. Sated, she sat back in her chair, warm and relaxed, and dozed.

Her book hitting the floor and the clock striking ten woke her. She wasn't sure if it was the good food, the warm fire, Lord Byron's poetry, or a combination of the three that had put her to sleep. She picked the book up, and put it on the table. London's current literary lion bored her silly. She was quite sure Byron had never felt any love for anyone except himself. Standing, Miranda stretched and padded barefooted downstairs to the library in search of another book.

The house was quiet, for the servants, with the exception of the lone footman dozing in the front hall, had long ago sought their beds. A fire lit the dark corners of the library with a warm gold light as Miranda climbed into the small loft to seek one of her favorite histories. Curling up in her chair, she began to read. She had not read long when the library door opened, and she heard many footsteps. Several people were entering the library.

"I think we'll be quite private here," said Jared. "My wife and the servants are long abed."

"By God, Jared," came an elegant London drawl, "if I were married to something as lovely as your lady I'd have been long abed too, not running around London."

There came the laughter of three men, and then Jared said, "I agree with you, Henry, but how can we get together without causing speculation unless our meetings seem to be social ones? Bramwell, pour us some whiskey, will you? Well, Henry, what do you think?"

"I think your people are right. The fly in all our pots of ointment is Boney himself. Parliament has now rescinded the Orders in Council that it was foolish enough to pass. They won't admit to it openly, but we need the American market the same as they need us. Dammit! You people may be running your own show now, but we're branches on the same root stock!"

"Yes, we are," replied Jared quietly, "and still attached enough to England that I can be plain Mr. Dunham in America while still, because of my family's original royal grant, being Lord Dunham here in England."

"Damn, Jared, that's good whiskey!" remarked Henry Temple, Viscount Palmerston.

"I know a Scotsman who keeps a still here in London."

"You would!"

Deep male laughter resounded. Up in the library loft Miranda curled herself into a tight little ball and snuggled deep into her chair. She could not reveal herself, especially dressed in a nightgown. They had assumed the library was empty. She had blushed to the roots of her silver-gilt hair when Lord Palmerston made his remark about her.

"Yes, we know that Gillian Abbott is involved," said Lord Palmerston, "but she is not the ringleader, and he is the one we want. Gillian has had some powerful lovers in the last few years, and she is skillful at getting information from them to pass on to her contact. Why men who are ordinarily prudent, lose all caution in her arms is beyond me."

"You've never enjoyed her favors, then?"

"Good Lord, no! Emily would kill me!" He grinned sheepishly. "But Gillian was your mistress last year, wasn't she?"

"For a brief time," admitted Jared. "She's beautiful and she's sexually insatiable, but Lord, she's boring! I enjoy bedsport, but I like to be able to talk to a woman, too."

"You are a radical fellow," chuckled Henry Temple. "Most men would be delighted—quite delighted—with Gillian as she is." His eyes grew serious as he said, "Mr. Bramwell, have you any idea who Lady Abbott's contact is?"

"I've had her closely watched, m'lord," answered Roger Bramwell, "but she knows so many people and goes so many places. I believe that her contact is someone in society, and that she is passing on information at social gatherings—probably verbally. I can see no other way. I will begin to concentrate on people she sees at social gatherings."

"I cannot understand why she does it," remarked Lord Palmerston, shaking his head.

"Money," said Jared drily. "Gillian is greedy."

"What is your plan, Mr. Bramwell, once we are certain of our man?"

"We will plant information with Lady Abbott. The first piece will be accurate, though of little importance. That will help us identify our quarry. The second piece will be all wrong. Once passed on, it will pinpoint our ringleader, for certain, and you can then make your arrest."

Lord Palmerston nodded and then said slowly, "You realize, Jared, that you must be the one to trap the lady."

"Absolutely not!" exclaimed Jared. "I will not involve myself with Gillian Abbott again."

"Jared, you must! You are under secret presidential orders to help us stop Bonaparte. Madison realized that the French tricked him into that blockade, but he realized it too late. He wants you for this assignment."

"With all due respect, Henry, my orders were to go to St. Petersburg and convince the Tzar that his best interests lie with England and America instead of with France. Nobody said I had to bed Gillian Abbott. And if I do, she will trumpet it all over London, making sure my wife hears it first. Miranda is young and proud, and deucedly independent. She is already aware that I partook of Gillian's favors when I was a bachelor. She will have my hide if I become involved with that bitch again." Miranda nodded vigorously in her hidey-hole. "Besides all that . . . I love Miranda."

"I did not think you were a man to be henpecked," remarked Lord Palmerston smoothly.

"Ouch!" Jared grinned ruefully. "Nice try, Henry, but my wife means more to me than my pride. Why me, anyway?"

"Because we cannot involve anyone else in this, Jared. If we do, we risk the chance of someone finding out. Look, Jared, though Lord Liverpool may be the new Prime Minister, it's Lord Castlereagh, our foreign secretary, who's the real power behind the throne. And God help us, for he's a madman. Poor Prinny may be a connoisseur of fine art, but he don't know how to pick a decent government.

"Lord Castlereagh is a narrow, obstinate man who's never been on the right side of any issue. It's true he hates Boney, and works hard for his downfall, but he does so for all the wrong reasons. I may be a Tory politician, and Secretary of War in a Tory government, but before all else, I'm a loyal Englishman."

"In other words, Henry, what we're doing has no official sanction."

"None."

"And if either side stumbles onto our scheme, the government will fail to acknowledge us."

"Yes."

There was a long deep silence. Miranda heard only the crackling of logs in the hearth. At last Jared said, "I am either a great fool or a great patriot, Henry."

"Then you'll do it?"

"Reluctantly," Jared sighed.

"I suppose I can't go to Russia until our spy is caught. Bram, pour us another tot."

"Not for me," said Palmerston. "I must appear in several other places tonight in order to perfect my alibi. Anyone who saw us leave White's together will hear I was in Watier's afterward, and no suspicion will fall on either of us."

"I'll see you out, then," said Jared, rising and moving to the door.

"No," Lord Palmerston waved him away. "Mr. Bramwell will see me out a side door, Jared. It's best I not be recognized leaving your house." Lord Palmerston held out his hand, and Jared shook it.

"Good night, Henry."

The door closed behind Roger Bramwell and Henry Temple. Left alone, Jared Dunham gazed mournfully into the fire. "Damn!" he said softly. Then he called up into the loft, "Come down, wildcat."

"How did you know I was here?" she cried, making her way down the steps.

"I have very keen hearing, my dear. Why didn't you come down instead of remaining hidden? You heard some rather sensitive matters."

"Come down and greet your guests like this, m'lord?" She twirled, her arms flung wide.

He looked through the sheer silk Circassian wrapper to the pearly sheen of firm thighs, rounded buttocks, and young breasts, their nipples a dark beacon. Then he laughed. "Your point is well taken, wildcat, but now we have a problem. Can you keep all this a secret? For so it must remain." He sounded as serious as Miranda had ever heard him sound.

"Am I some idle London society gossip?" she demanded.

"No, my darling, of course you're not. Don't be insulted. But you have heard things you really shouldn't have."

"Are you a spy?" she asked bluntly.

"No, I'm not, and I never have been, Miranda. I work quietly and behind the scenes for peace with honor. I am first, and always, an American. Napoleon has worked assiduously to destroy relations between America and England, for while we squabble he is free to plunder Europe. He is the real enemy, but politicians often cannot see beyond apparent causes."

"Lord Palmerston said you have a presidential commission."

"Well...not directly. I've never met President Madison. John Quincy Adams is the intermediary in this matter. Soon I will go to Russia to try and convince the Tzar that his best interests lie with the Americans and the English. Tzar Alexander had already been badly misinformed by Boney."

"And where does your friend Lady Abbott figure in all this?"

Jared chose to ignore the bait. "She's part of a French spy ring operating here in London. We need to know who the ringleader is, and put him out of commission. Unless we do, my mission isn't safe. It wouldn't do for Napoleon to know what I was up to in Russia, would it?"

"Do you *have* to make love to her?"

"Probably, yes," he said. He saw no way to deal with this problem except directly.

"I hate her!" Miranda cried.

Jared rose and took his wife in his arms. "Oh, my darling darling," he said softly, "I will not enjoy it. Having known you, how could I enjoy her? She is vulgar and coarse, while you are perfection itself."

Miranda sighed. He was a man of character, and he would do his duty. After some moments she disengaged herself and moved to the other side of the room. She stood facing him and said quietly, "How can I help you?"

"Oh, wildcat," he said hoarsely. "I am beginning to think I am not half as worthy of you as I should be."

"I love you!" she said simply.

"I love you!"

"Then tell me how I may help you, Jared," she repeated.

"By not divulging to anyone the conversation you heard here tonight and by keeping your ears open for any tittle-tattle you think might be of interest to me," he answered her.

"Very well, you have my word on it," she said. "Now can we go to bed?"

Some time later, as they lay together in the heat of passion, she pushed him over onto his back. "Why?" she demanded, straddling him. "Why should the man always ride and the woman be ridden?" Then Miranda impaled herself on his rock-hard shaft. He groaned, and his hands reached up to fondle her breasts. She sought to find the right rhythm, and then rode him like a young Diana. She drove him hard, seeming to take great pleasure from his helplessness. Suddenly his male vanity rebelled and, reaching out, he grasped her round little buttocks in a hard grip. She wiggled wildly to break his hold, but he held her adamantly and then the cresting waves overtook them both at once.

When she had caught her breath she finally rolled away from him and said, "Remember me, when you find yourself *forced* to make love to that female."

"Oh, wildcat, I am hardly likely to forget you," he whispered, and her happy laughter rang in his ears for a long, long time.

Her words came back to haunt him. They went to a ball at Lady Jersey's several nights later, and after greeting their hostess they passed into her crowded, noisy ballroom. Just a shade smaller than

Almack's ballroom, it easily contained a thousand guests. Decorated in white and gold, the ballroom had exquisite plaster designs, and was lit by eight Waterford chandeliers. The long French windows were framed by yellow-sprigged, white satin draperies. Large brass cachepots containing yellow and white rose trees were placed at intervals throughout the ballroom. The musicians had been placed upon a raised dais, which was backed and hemmed slightly on the sides by tall green palms and rose trees. Around the sides of the room were plenty of gilt chairs upholstered in rose silk so that the weary might take their ease while destroying the reputations of their dearest friends.

As Miranda and Jared entered the ballroom the first person to see them was Beau Brummel, and he immediately took it upon himself to further Miranda's career in London society. The Beau was a tall, elegant man with sandy hair, exquisitely styled, and sharp blue eyes with a perpetually amused expression in them, if one were only wise enough to look closely. He had a high forehead and a long nose, and if his lips appeared to sneer, it was only because they were narrow. He had started the fashion of black evening dress, and he wore it well.

Brummel moved to greet Miranda, his cultivated voice deliberately pitched to reach those around him. Catching Miranda's hand, he slowly raised it and brushed it with cool lips.

"Now, madam, I know the Americas are the real home of the gods, for thou art a veritable goddess. I am at your feet, divine one."

"Oh never, Mr. Brummel! Such a posture would ruin the cut of your magnificent coat, and I would never forgive myself," retorted Miranda.

"By God, a wit to match the face! I believe I am in love. Come, goddess, I shall introduce you to all the right *and* wrong people. You do not mind, m'lord? No, of course you don't!" He swept Miranda away, leaving Jared standing alone. But not for long.

"My, my, my," Jared heard the familiar purring voice, "it would seem the Beau is determined to make your little bride a *succès fou*."

Jared forced his face into a smile and turned to face Gillian Abbott. She was dressed in a transparent black silk gown, and was entirely naked beneath it. Around her neck was a diamond necklace that flashed blue fire with her every movement. His eyes raked her coolly and slowly, and he feigned admiration.

"You don't leave anything to the imagination, do you, Gillian?" he drawled.

"But I have managed to get your attention, haven't I, Jared?" she shot back.

"Dear girl, I don't believe for one minute that you wore that gown with only me in mind."

"I did!" she protested. "I had no intention of coming tonight until Lady Jersey told me you would be here. Perhaps now the novelty of that virtuous infant you married has worn off. I am ready to forgive you your conduct toward me, Jared, for I have learned that you were forced into marriage with that child." She leaned forward, pressing against his hard arm. He looked down her gown, as of course he was meant to do. How obvious and how boring she is, thought Jared. "Has the novelty worn off, my darling?" she persisted.

"Perhaps it has, Gillian," he murmured, sliding an arm around her waist.

"I knew it!" Gillian Abbott's voice was triumphant, and she shot him a sultry look from beneath her heavily mascara'd black lashes. "Take me out into the garden, Jared darling."

"In time, Gillian. Firstly you must waltz with me." Taking her in his strong arms, he whirled her off while across the room Miranda watched, heartsick.

"Come now, goddess," chided Beau Brummel softly, "it's not fashionable to love one's husband. The best marriages are generally made in lawyer's rooms, not in Heaven."

"To hell with fashion," muttered Miranda ominously. Then, remembering that she meant to help Jared, she laughed lightly. "I do not begrudge m'lord his toys, Mr. Brummel—I merely question his taste."

"Oh, goddess, what a *very* sharp tongue you have," laughed the Beau. "Look! There's Byron. Would you like to meet him?"

"Not particularly. His poetry bores me silly," she replied.

"Dear girl, you really *do* have taste! Ah, well, we cannot begrudge the ton their season's seven-day wonder, can we?"

"Where is Lady Caroline Lamb?" asked Miranda. "I understand she is his *special* friend?"

"Ah yes, Caro. She was not invited tonight. That was a special favor to Lady Melbourne, her mother-in-law. I understand, however, that she is outside dressed as one of Byron's linkboys. Such a madcap, dear Caro. Come, goddess, and I shall introduce you to Lady Melbourne. She really is quite a marvelous creature."

Jared and Gillian left the lighted ballroom for Lady Jersey's dark garden. The night air was soft and warm, and a million stars glittered. As they strolled through the garden they saw dark, anonymous shapes embracing. Lady Abbott, her sense of direction perfected by familiarity, led Jared to a small, secluded summer house. They no sooner entered it than she was in his arms, her avid red mouth demanding his.

His instinct was to push her away, but his mission drove Miranda from his mind, and he kissed Gillian Abbott as he knew she expected to be kissed. He was savage, almost cruel, which drove her wild. Panting, she pulled away and tore off her gown, laying it over the rail of the summer house. He could see her transluscent body gleaming in the darkness, and in his memory he saw the heavy, cone-shaped breasts, a tiny waist, wide hips, and the full, dark red mound. Reaching out, he pulled her back in his arms, fondling her breasts, pinching the big, brown nipples, making her squeal. "Jesus, you're a hot bitch, Gillian," he whispered.

"And you wouldn't have me any other way, Jared," she murmured huskily.

"How many men have you fucked since we were last together?" he demanded.

"No gentleman would ask a lady such a question," she pouted.

"I'm no gentleman, I'm a Yankee. And you're certainly no lady." His lips came down again on hers, his tongue thrusting into her mouth. She sucked on it hungrily. He pushed her down onto the settee, his hand finding her wet and throbbing sex. He put two fingers into her, moving them quickly until her love juices bedewed his hand.

"Oh, God," she panted, "I do adore you, Jared!"

He laughed, "You adore any stud who scratches that uncontrollable itch of yours, Gillian." He lay back and she knelt alongside the settee. She undid his breeches and released his organ, which she took into her mouth. He was hard within moments and moved over her, forcing her onto her back. He grasped her plump buttocks tightly and jogged her hard and fast. She climaxed half a dozen times before he took his release.

It was over quickly and he said coolly, "Put on your dress, Gillian. Someone may happen along."

"You weren't thinking about that a moment ago," she chortled.

"No, I wasn't," he returned. "I was actually thinking about some news I learned today."

"I expect you to think only of me when we're together," she pouted, smoothing her gown.

He straightened his own clothes. "This was very important. It was something Henry Temple told me."

"What is more important than us?" she demanded.

"I trust you can keep a secret," he said, "though it will soon enough be public knowledge. My country has formally declared war on yours."

"Oh, pooh! England and America are always declaring war on each other," she said.

"Bonaparte should be delighted," remarked Jared casually.

"He should? Why?" Her voice was suddenly sharp.

"He wanted it to happen. I imagine that whoever brings him the news will be well rewarded. Come now, Gillian, we must get back to the ballroom before a prolonged absence makes us a scandal."

"Afraid your milk-and-water wife will find out about us?" she taunted him. "I intend for her to learn that I am your mistress once more, now that you've tired of her. She'll pay for that set-down she gave me at Almack's!"

"Gillian! Gillian!" he lamented. "How many times have I told you not to be obvious? You would have a far sweeter revenge if you kept our relationship to yourself. Then, each time you saw Miranda, you could laugh to yourself, knowing something she did not know. That would be the clever way, but I imagine you will not be content unless you can babble our secret to the ton."

"I can be clever!" she protested, but he laughed mockingly. As they entered the ballroom once again and he bowed over her hand, she demanded, "When will I see you again?"

"Soon," he answered noncommittally, and walked away without another word.

He entered the supper room and sought a glass of champagne. He quaffed it in two gulps, then took another. He stood in a dim corner, staring vacantly, letting his mind wander. He had behaved disgustingly, but, by God, he'd done his job! He shuddered lightly. He was either getting a conscience or getting too old for this sort of game. Then he smiled to himself. The wildcat had certainly spoiled him for other women!

"A penny for them, Jared."

"It's done, Henry."

"During your sojourn in the garden?"

"You don't miss much, do you?"

"Actually I didn't see you go. It was Emily. She was distressed, for she likes your wife."

"I was far more distressed," replied Jared, "for I like my wife, too. Gillian Abbott is a feral animal and she disgusts me. I did my duty by my beliefs and yours, but I hope we can end this thing soon."

"We will, old friend, I promise you," said Lord Palmerston sympathetically, and then walked away.

Jared looked around to see if his wife was in the supper room. His thick, black eyebrows drew together in annoyance as he spotted a cluster of fawning gallants surrounding her. That impudent puppy the Marquis of Wye was leaning over her and grinning. Jared made his way toward her. "Madam," he said firmly, "it is time for us to leave."

A chorus of groans greeted him, but Miranda put her slender hand on her husband's arm, saying, "Fie, gentlemen! It is a wife's duty to accede to her husband's wishes, provided, of course, that his wishes are not unreasonable."

Laughter greeted this witticism, and the young Marquis of Wye said, "But Lord Dunham's request is not at all reasonable, Miranda."

Jared felt a fierce rage rising within him, but Miranda's soft hand closed over one of his, and she laughed lightly. "I bid you all goodnight, gentlemen."

They bid their hostess goodnight as they left. The Prince Regent had already departed, which made their going permissible. Their carriage was brought around, and they were soon home. Not a word had been said between them during the drive, and as they climbed the stairs he said, "Don't wait up for me, Miranda." She nodded. He kissed her perfunctorily, and she smelled the faint fragrance of gardenia on his clothing.

She made herself ready for bed and soon dozed off. She woke suddenly, not quite sure what had roused her. The house was quiet. Damn, she thought! Jared has gone to bed, thinking that I am asleep! She threw back the bedclothes and, without bothering with a robe, hurried through the door connecting their rooms.

He was not asleep, she realized, for though he lay motionless beneath the blankets, his breathing ragged. She moved to the big bed and sat beside him, reaching out to touch his cheek. He turned away. "You did not come to me," she said softly.

"Go to bed, Miranda," he answered sharply.

"If you do not tell me, Jared, it will lie like an ever-widening chasm between us."

"I have done my duty," he said bleakly, "and the whole thing sickens me. I cannot get the stink of that creature out of my nostrils. For the sake of two countries I have betrayed you, Miranda," he finished brokenly.

"You have betrayed me only if you enjoyed coupling with her. Did you?" she asked evenly.

"No!" he spat violently.

"Then you have done your duty and no more, and I love you." She nudged him gently. "Move over, m'lord, I dislike sleeping alone." He had no time for protest before she had snuggled next to him, her loving warmth penetrating his chill.

Miranda felt triumphant. This sophisticated and worldly man was suffering over what he considered a wrong done to her. She knew he wouldn't feel this way if he did not love her, and this especially touched her. "Hold me," she whispered in his ear, licking the inside of it with her pink tongue. Rolling over to face her, he grasped a handful of her soft, gilt hair, breathing in the perfumed sweetness of it. Then his arms went around her, and his mouth was hungrily on hers. He kissed her until she was breathless.

His hands were on her, drawing her silk nightgown away, caressing her slender body with gentle fingers until she ached. His lips explored every inch of her until she thought she'd burst with the desire he was kindling. He covered her body with his, entering her gently, and she sighed deeply, climaxing quickly with him.

"Say it!" he growled, his voice sure once more.

"I love you!" She smiled. "Say it!"

"I love you!" he answered. "Oh, my darling, I love you!" She had cleansed him. He was healed, and whole again.

They lay side by side holding hands, and much later she asked softly, "We will not be able to go home until your secret duties are all over, will we?"

"No," he answered. "We cannot go home, my darling."

Suddenly he realized she was weeping. Raising himself up on one elbow, he looked down into her face and asked, "Do you want to go home on *Dream Witch?* She is still here, and could easily run the English naval blockade."

"No," she sniffed. "My place is with you, Jared, and with you I shall stay. We will go to Russia together. And when there is peace between England and America once more, we will return to Wyndsong. I am homesick, but then my real home is where you are, my love, isn't it?"

"You are becoming an amazing woman, wildcat," he said. But he did not tell her that he intended traveling to Russia alone.

To draw attention to his departure could be fatal to his mission, for Gillian Abbott and her friends were not the only French spies in London. The season was just about at its end, and he and Miranda would travel up to Swynford Hall near Worcester, ostensibly for a summer visit. Adrian would be given a letter of explanation from the Secretary of War, Lord Palmerston, and Jared would depart secretly, leaving his wife in Lord Swynford's care. There would be no fashionable visitors to note his absence, for the newlyweds would not be entertaining this summer. Jared would be back in England by early autumn. It was all perfectly arranged.

❧ Chapter 8 ❧

Jared had an incredible piece of luck—or, rather, Miranda did—and it happened at the last ball of the season, at Almack's. Jared and Miranda circulated together and separately, chattering among their friends. After several hours of gossiping and dancing and innumerable glasses of lukewarm lemonade, Miranda made a trip to the necessary room. Settling herself on the canned commode behind a silk screen, she suddenly heard the door open and then close again.

"I thought we'd never get away." The voice was speaking in French.

"Neither did I," came the voice of Gillian Abbott, also speaking French. "I have some very expensive information for you."

"How expensive?"

"Double what you have paid me to date."

"How do I know it's worth it?"

"Surely I have proved reliable by now," was Gillian's exasperated reply.

"Why this sudden and urgent need?"

"Look," snapped Gillian, "Abbott is on his last legs. When that nephew of his and his horse-faced wife come into the title, I'll have nothing but a dower house in Northumberland to call my own. The whole damned estate is entailed, and I'm not to get a penny! Not a bloody penny! I can't catch myself another rich title in Northumberland, and I don't see the next Lord Abbott giving me living space in the town house. Well," she amended, "he might, but his ugly wife wouldn't, so I must provide my own living quarters. That costs a lot of money."

"I don't know," her companion hesitated.

"I've got an impeccable source," wheedled Gillian. "The American, Lord Dunham, is my lover. He and Henry Temple are very close."

"Lord Dunham is your lover? Very well, madam, I'll pay you double for your information. But if it proves incorrect or of little importance, then you will owe me." There was a rustling noise, and then, the voice said, *"Mon Dieu,* it's not necessary to count it! When did I ever cheat you?"

"Oh, very well."

Miranda leaned forward carefully, and peeped through the crack where the screen was hinged. She saw Gillian Abbott stuff a velvet bag into her cleavage. The other woman was young and pretty, a petite brunette in a fashionable red silk gown.

"Your information, madam?"

"America has declared war on England," said Gillian calmly.

"The Emperor has been waiting for this!" gasped the Frenchwoman.

"I told you the information was valuable," Gillian replied smugly. "You know, it has always amazed me that Napoleon uses a woman to spy."

The Frenchwoman laughed. "There is nothing unusual in women spying. Catherine de'Medici, the wife of Henri II, had a group of women known as the 'Flying Squadron' who gathered information."

"The English would never do such a thing," remarked Gillian.

"No," came the amused reply. "You spy only for others, and for personal gain! We had best go, madam, lest someone come upon us. Adieu."

"Adieu," said Gillian, and Miranda heard the door to the necessary room close. Peeping again through the crack in the screen, she saw that the room was empty.

As quickly as she could, Miranda hurried back to the ballroom to find Jared. He stood talking with Lord Palmerston, who smiled warmly at her.

"As usual, ma'am, your beauty eclipses everyone else's," Henry Temple declared gallantly.

"Even Lady Cowper?" teased Miranda mischievously, knowing that the beauteous Emily was Lord Palmerston's mistress.

"Lord help me, I am Paris with his damned apple," said Palmerston in mock dismay.

"I am the prettiest American in the room, sir, and Lady Cowper is the loveliest Englishwoman," said Miranda.

"Ma'am, you are a born diplomat," chuckled the Secretary of War.

"I am a better spy, sir. Who is the lady in red? The petite brunette dancing with Lord Alvanley?"

Lord Palmerston looked where she pointed. "That is the Comtesse Marianne de Bouche. She is married to the first secretary at the Swiss Embassy."

"She is also the spy to whom Lady Abbott passed on her information. I was in the necessary room just now, and when they came in they believed themselves alone and spoke freely. I am quite fluent in French, my lord, and I understood it all."

"Well, I'll be damned!" said Lord Palmerston. "A woman! No wonder we could never catch our French spy. A woman! All along it was a woman! *Cherchez la femme,* indeed! By God, Lady Dunham, you have rendered us a great service! I shall not forget this, I promise you."

"What will happen to them?"

"The comtesse will be sent home. She is a diplomat's wife and we can do nothing about her except to inform the Swiss Ambassador of the lady's activities."

"And Gillian Abbott?"

"She will be transported."

Miranda whitened. "What will you tell her husband?"

"Old Lord Abbott is dead. He passed away earlier this evening, shortly after his wife left him. After the funeral we will arrest her quietly. Her disappearance from society will be attributed to mourning. She'll soon enough be forgotten. Her own family is dead and she has no children. Frankly, m'dear, the gentlemen who've been her lovers will not be sorry to see her go, and the ladies certainly won't miss her. We will be discreet. No need to embarrass either the new Lord Abbott or the memory of the old Lord Abbott."

"But to be transported!"

"It is either that or hanging, m'dear."

"I should far rather be hanged. And so, I imagine, would Lady Abbott."

"Hanging would make the matter public," replied Lord Palmerston, shaking his head, "and we don't want to do that. No, Lady Abbott will be transported for life—not to a penal colony but to the new Australia territories, where she'll be sold as a bondwoman for seven years. After that, she's on her own, but she'll not be able to leave Australia."

"The poor woman," said Miranda.

"Don't feel sorry for her, m'dear. She really doesn't deserve it. Gillian Abbott betrayed her country for money."

"But she will be virtually a slave for seven years." Miranda shuddered. "I do not approve of slavery."

"Neither do I," replied Lord Palmerston. "But in Lady Abbott's case it is our only solution."

Miranda's fears for Lady Abbott proved unnecessary. Gillian learned of her impending arrest, and fled England. It could only be assumed that one of her lovers had learned of the sentence to be imposed upon her, and felt sorry enough for her to warn her. The King's officers had followed the black-clad Lady Abbott after the funeral, so as to arrest her quietly in her home. But beneath the mourning veils they found a young London actress, not Gillian

Abbott. Horrified by the realization that she was involved in a crime, Miss Millicent Marlowe burst into tears, and told all.

She was a bit player with Mr. Kean's company, and had been hired two days before by a gentleman she'd never seen before. As the poor, frightened girl was obviously telling the truth, she was released and sent on her way. Lady Abbott's maid, Peters, was sent for, but she could not be found. A search revealed that Peters had also fled. The new Lord Abbott wanted an end to the situation. Afraid of a scandal, he gave out that the new dowager had returned to her dower house in Northumberland for a year's mourning.

Jared and Miranda Dunham closed the house on Devon Square and departed for Swynford Hall, outside the town of Worcester.

The trip took several days. They traveled quite comfortably in a large coach made especially for long journeys. There were two extra horses who trotted along with the grooms when Jared and Miranda were not riding them. Roger Bramwell had arranged the stopovers at pleasant, well-run inns. It was a lovely trip, and Miranda enjoyed being with her husband for those few days in the English countryside. She enjoyed it all the more, knowing that they would soon leave England for Russia.

The countryside was lush with midsummer growth, a perfect frame for Swynford Hall, an E-shaped mansion that dated from early Elizabethan times. The bricks were a mellowed rose color, but most of the house was covered in shiny, dark green ivy. The carriage rumbled through gates of brick and iron as the smiling gatekeeper stood by. His plump wife bobbed a friendly curtsey from the gatehouse door as the carriage passed. The driveway was lined by rows of tall oaks, and there was an attractive dower house beyond the drive. Miranda chuckled.

"The dowager Lady Swynford is in residence, I see. I didn't think Mandy could do it."

"I did," replied Jared. "She's as stubborn as you are, my love, but her angelic appearance deceives everyone into believing she is a biddable female."

"Why, sir, am I not the most agreeable of females?"

"Oh very agreeable," he said smoothly, finishing, "when you get your own way!"

"Wretch!" she teased. "You are no better than I!"

"Exactly, m'lady, which is why we suit each other so damnably well!"

They were both still laughing when the carriage stopped in front of the entry to Swynford Hall, where host and hostess were waiting. The two sisters hugged each warmly, and then Miranda stepped back to view her radiant twin. "You seem to be surviving marriage," she smiled.

"I have simply followed your good example," Amanda teased back.

It was the beginning of a wonderful week. They were housed in a beautiful corner apartment that overlooked the gentle hills of Wales to the west and the estate's lake and gardens to the south. Amanda and Adrian were still honeymooning, and were the least demanding of hosts. The two couples met only in the evening for dinner. There were no other guests, and only on their first evening at Swynford Hall did Adrian's mama join them. She left the following day to visit her dear old friend, Lady Tallboys, in Brighton. The simple country life was far too dull and confining for her, she declared.

At the end of a delightful week of riding and long walks in the woods, Miranda entered their apartment to find Mitchum packing her husband's clothing. Startled, she asked what was going on.

"M'lord has said we must depart for Russia tonight, m'lady," answered the tall, austere valet.

"Has Perky been informed? Why is she not packing my things?"

"I was not aware that you were coming with us, m'lady," replied Mitchum, suddenly uncomfortable.

Miranda ran from the room and downstairs to the garden salon, where the others awaited her. Bursting into the room, she shouted at Jared, "When were you going to tell me? Or were you just going to leave me a note? I thought we were going together!"

"I must travel quickly, and it would be impossible for a woman."

"Why?"

"Listen to me, wildcat. Napoleon is about to attack Russia. He believes that England and America are so involved with each other that they will not be able to aid the Tzar. I must get to St. Petersburg to get Alexander's signature on a secret treaty of alliance between America, England, and Russia. We must break Napoleon!"

"But why may I not go?" she demanded.

"Because I must get there and be back before the Russian winter sets in, Miranda. Summer is half gone already and winter comes to the far north long before it comes to the rest of Europe and England. *Dream Witch* is anchored just off the coast. Mitchum and I ride out tonight. We can't wait for a carriage and a lady's maid."

"I'll ride with you! I don't need Perky."

"No, Miranda. You've never spent more than two or three hours in the saddle, and it will be a bone-shattering ride to the sea. You're to stay here with your sister and Adrian until I return. If anyone decides to visit Swynford you can say I'm ill and keeping to my room. I *need* you here, wildcat. If we both disappear for several weeks it could cause talk.

"Oh, my love, I want to go home to Wyndsong! I want to raise our horses, and send my ships to the far corners of the earth in safety. I want to found a dynasty built on the love we have for each other. We can do none of these things while the damned world is upside down!"

"I hate you for this!" she said fiercely. After a moment, she asked, "How long?"

"I should be back by the end of October."

"*Should be?*"

"I *will* be!"

"You had better be, m'lord, or I shall come looking for you!"

"You would too, wouldn't you, wildcat?" He reached out and pulled her roughly against him. She looked up into his face, her sea-green eyes devouring his visage. "I will come home quickly, my love," he said huskily and kissed her hungrily.

Watching them from a corner of the room, Lady Amanda Swynford reflected again that she far preferred the gentle love she had for her Adrian to this savage passion. Her sister and Jared were so intense, and when they became involved in each other the world about them ceased to exist. The blazing love that raged between her twin and Jared was somehow so...so primitive!

Reading her thoughts, Lord Swynford approached quietly and put
a reassuring arm around his bride. "It is just that they are so very
American and you and I are so very English."

"Yes...I suppose that's what it is," answered Amanda slowly.
"How strange that Miranda and I should be so different."

"Yet so alike, for you are, you know. You both possess a strong
sense of right and wrong, and a fierce loyalty to those you love."

"Yes, we do," replied Amanda, "and if I know my sister, she will
be quite impossible once her husband has gone. You and I are going
to have our hands full, Adrian. This is not exactly what I had in mind
for my honeymoon summer."

"No," mused Adrian, "I don't believe we will have any problem
with Miranda."

For several days after Jared's departure, it appeared that he was
right. Miranda kept to herself. Amanda had expected the Miranda of
old, storming and raging. But her twin was quiet and thoughtful. Her
emotions were kept private, and no one knew she wept wild tears
into her pillow in the darkness of night.

August passed, and September. Stranded at the Russian court,
Lord Jared Dunham, the Anglo-American envoy, had yet to see Tzar
Alexander. Napoleon had declared war on Russia, and was marching
on Moscow. The Tzar had not decided whether to side openly with
Bonaparte's avowed enemies. Too, he thought it odd that the English
and Americans, officially at war with each other, should ask him to
sign an alliance with them against the French. He decided to
postpone making a decision. But he did not bother to inform Lord
Dunham of that. So Jared waited, and worried that he might fail his
mission. He fretted over his absence from England.

A message arrived from Lord Palmerston. The Americans and the
English who sought to end the conflict between their countries had
decided that Jared must remain in St. Petersburg until the Tzar made
his decision to join the Anglo-American alliance against Bonaparte.
Realizing, however, that his prolonged absence from London's social
scene would cause comment, his brother, Jonathan, was being
smuggled through the British blockade of the American coast and
brought to England to take Jared's place. The difference in their
appearance was so slight that no one was expected to notice.

Jared smiled ruefully and restlessly paced the small guest house, belonging to a great palace, that had been rented for him. It overlooked the Neva River, which cut through the heart of fashionable St. Petersburg, and was lined on both sides with the opulent homes of the very rich and powerful. The house, a small jewel of a building, had been set in a corner of the garden, and had a fine view of the river. There were only two servants, a cook and a maid. Both old women, their heavily accented French was barely understandable but Jared needed no one besides his own Mitchum. He was not here to socialize. He would not be entertaining.

Jared Dunham suddenly felt very alone, cut off entirely from his world. He wondered if he was not paying too high a price for his ideals. What the hell was he doing in Russia? Away from Miranda, away from Wyndsong. Napoleon was already in Moscow, a wide swath of burnt Russian fields marking his passage through the land, for the fiercely patriotic peasant Russians had fired their own fields rather than allow them to fall into French hands. It would mean famine for them this winter. Jared Dunham sighed, seeing the thin skim of ice on the Neva River glistening in the early-morning sunshine. It would be autumn in England, but here in St. Petersburg early winter was upon them. He shivered. He longed for his wife.

In the early dawn Miranda stood by her bed and looked at the man sleeping there. That it was not her husband she was absolutely positive. She was fairly certain it was her brother-in-law, Jonathan Dunham. Why was he in England? Why was he posing as Jared? A sudden shift in his breathing pattern told her that he was awake.

"Good morning, Jon," she said calmly.

"How did you know?" he replied, not even bothering to open his gray-green eyes.

Sitting on the edge of the bed, she laughed softly. "Jared has never been *that* tired," she said. "Especially after being away from me. You've cut your hair."

"The better to look like Jared Dunham, m'dear."

"Were you planning to tell me, Jon? Or did the clever Lord Palmerston decide I shouldn't know."

"I was to tell you only if you recognized me."

"And if I hadn't?"

"Then I was to say nothing," he replied quietly.

"Just how far were you planning to go, sir?" she demanded and because he knew her so little he didn't recognize the dangerous edge in her voice.

"Frankly I hoped to find you with child," he said. "It would have solved everything."

"Indeed!" she snapped. "Where is Jared?"

"In St. Petersburg, stuck for the winter. The Tzar cannot make up his mind whether to sign the alliance or not. Jared's mission must remain a secret because it hasn't the official sanction of either government. But he is too well known to simply disappear from England and everyone assumes that until this damned war is over the Dunhams cannot leave England and return to Wyndsong. In other words, someone has to be Jared."

"And what of your wife? Does she approve of this masquerade?" Miranda's voice was sharp.

There was a deep silence, and then Jonathan said, "Charity is dead."

"What?!" Her voice was raw with shock.

"My wife was drowned in a boating accident this summer. She was raised on Cape Cod, and adored the sea. It was an eccentricity of hers that she loved to sail her own small boat. She was a good sailor, but she was caught in a sudden violent squall. The boat was destroyed, and Charity's body was washed up on a nearby beach several days later." His voice was harsh.

"It is assumed that I have gone off whaling to ease my sorrow."

"Your children?"

"With my parents."

"Oh, Jon, I am so sorry!" said Miranda, the memory of her friendly sister-in-law filling her mind.

He reached out and took her hand. "The first shock is over, Miranda. I have faced the fact that Charity is gone. I am not sure yet if I can survive without her, but I suppose I must. The children need me." He smiled wryly. "If I could have taken Jared's place in St. Petersburg I would have done so, but I have always been the dutiful son who stayed home while my little brother was the adventurer. I have no experience in diplomacy. The best I can do is hope to fool the ton until by brother returns. You will have to help me."

"You can do it, Jon. I will tell you what you need to know. We do not have to return to London until after the New Year, so you'll be safe here."

"What about your sister and her husband? We can tell them."

"No. The fewer people who know you are taking Jared's place, the safer he will be. Besides, if you can fool Amanda and Adrian, then you'll know you can fool anyone." She cocked her head to one side, then flung herself into his startled arms. "Kiss me! Quickly!" She yanked his dark head down to hers as the bedroom door swung open. Perkins stopped dead, her eyes wide at the intertwined bodies sprawled across the bed. "Oh!" she gasped. "Oh!" The two people moved apart and Perkins sighed with relief. "M'lord! You're back!"

"Indeed, Perky," he drawled lazily, "and I see you've forgotten how to knock. We'll ring when we want you." He turned back to Miranda, his lips taking fierce possession of hers. The door closed, but Jonathan Dunham did not release the woman in his arms. His mouth, gentle now, tasted deeply of hers, and only when he became aware that she was trembling and tasted the salty tears sliding down her cheeks, did he release her. "Dammit, Miranda, I'm sorry. I don't know why I did that."

He saw the sadness in her face, and he gathered her tenderly in his arms. "I have been so wrapped up in my own grief I never stopped to think how terribly you must miss him." He held her close and rocked her as if she were a child.

After a few minutes she said softly, "You kiss differently." Jonathan laughed. "We've been told that before," he said. Then, "This will not happen again, Miranda, I promise you. I apologize for losing my head and offending you. Will you forgive me, my dear?"

"You did not offend me, Jon. I am only sorry I am not Charity. You were not kissing me, but her, and I understand. Had she died of a lingering illness you might have had the opportunity to say good-bye. But she died suddenly, and you had no chance to bid her farewell. It hurts. I know it does."

"You're very wise for one so young. I begin to understand now why Jared loves you so much," he replied.

"I think we should ring for Perky now, Jon. How did you know her nickname?"

"Lord Palmerston told me. Lord Palmerston is always most efficient. By the way, I've brought one of his men along as my valet. We're going to say that Mitchum received a better offer from another gentleman, and that Connors is taking his place."

"Very well." She extricated herself from his arms and drew on the bellpull. "I'll order another down quilt tonight. We'll roll it up into a tube and place it between us for a bundling board."

"I can sleep on your chaise," he said.

"Your feet would hang over," she said, "and the floor is too cold. Don't be afraid, Jon," she teased, "I'll not seduce you." She rose from the bed to sit down at her dressing table and brush her long hair.

There was a knock on the door, and Perkins entered the room again, her tray now set for two. "Good morning, m'lord, m'lady." She set the tray down on the fireside table. "Connors wants to know if you'd like a bath, m'lord. I'm sorry to learn Mitchum has left us."

"Tell Connors I'll have my bath after breakfast."

"Very good, sir," Perkins curtseyed and left the room.

Jonathan went to the tray and began lifting lids from the dishes. "Good Lord, kippers!" he shuddered.

"Jared loves kippers," she said.

"I detest them."

"You'll have to learn to eat them, Jon. Also, you've almost got Jared's voice, but you do have a slight New England twang. Soften it."

She offered him other bits of advice over the next few weeks, and soon he felt his own personality slipping into the background as he became more Jared and less himself.

Amanda and her husband never suspected the deception. Jonathan was uncomfortable with the role at first, but Miranda made it easy for him by treating him with the same mixture of easy affection and spunky independence with which she treated Jared. It was good for him. The pain of Charity's loss began to ease a little. And as it did, the man in him began to awaken again.

Jonathan and Miranda enjoyed themselves. Miranda liked the outdoors, and rode daily except in the vilest weather. Away from

Swynford Hall, free of listening ears, they were able to talk freely. Miranda learned about Jared's unhappy childhood, and how the wisdom and generosity of his Grandmother Lightbody had freed him from their implacable Puritan father. "I have never seen him show any gentle emotion," said Jon, "until her death. At her funeral, he wept like a child."

The dowager Lady Swynford returned from Brighton, and was totally taken in by Jonathan Dunham. "Your husband," she told Miranda, "has the most exquisite manners! But then I've always said so. He's a charming devil, my dear. Simply charming!"

Though the weather was unseasonably mild, Christmas was coming, and Amanda and Adrian had been married nearly six months. On December 6, Lord and Lady Swynford held a dinner in honor of Lord and Lady Dunham's first anniversary. It was the first time they had entertained since their marriage, and there was to be dancing afterward. The premier guest was to be Amanda's rejected suitor, the Duke of Whitley.

Darius Edmund was close to forty. He was tall, with ash-brown hair, fair skin, and bright turquoise eyes. His dress and manner were elegantly subdued. The Duke of Whitley had been quite taken with Amanda, for Darius Edmund collected beautiful things. He had been married twice previously. Both wives, although exquisitely lovely and of flawless lineage, had been fragile and both had died miscarrying his children.

Amanda had taken his fancy, and he had done her the honor of offering for her despite her unfortunate nationality. To his intense mortification, he had been rejected in favor of a minor baronet. He had swallowed his bitter disappointment with as good a grace as he could muster, relieved that no one outside his own family knew of his offer to the little Yankee. Her family were, he sighed with relief, extremely discreet, and had not trumpeted about his acute embarrassment. It was therefore possible for Darius to accept the Swynfords' invitation. This pleased him, for he was frankly curious to see Lady Swynford's twin. For the life of him, he could not remember her, but she had sent his younger brother, Kit, into rhapsodies. "A rare beauty," Kit had said, "and intelligent too!"

As Darius Edmund stood in the receiving line waiting to greet his host and hostess, and their guests of honor, his eyes swept over the lady in question. Why had he not noticed her before? She was absolutely magnificent, and he didn't try to hide his admiration when he raised her gloved hand to his lips. "Lady Dunham," he murmured, "I am devastated to find what a fool I've been. You will, of course, promise me a dance, and be my supper partner."

"You honor me, my lord duke," she said coolly. "A dance, of course, but as for supper, I cannot promise. I have the third waltz free."

"I must be satisfied with that, m'lady, but be warned that I shall try and convince you to sup with me," he replied.

"I shall certainly be on my guard," she smiled.

Darius Edmund took himself off to a corner where he could gaze at Lady Dunham. Her gown had a violet silk underlining, overlaid with sheer lavender shot silk. The hem and the edge of the puffed sleeves were embroidered in a gold classic Greek scroll design. The neckline was quite fashionably low, and the Duke of Whitley admired Lady Dunham's lovely bosom. Fastened around her neck was an ornate necklace of amethysts interspersed with perfect Indian Ocean pearls, all in yellow gold. The stones were oval except for the center one, which was shaped like a star. There were matching earrings and a bracelet and star-shaped ring. The most delightful touch, however, was the two purple amethyst stars in her hair.

Her hair. The duke sighed with pleasure. The pale silver-gilt cap was parted in the center and knotted into a chignon at the nape of her graceful neck. He wondered what it would look like loose and flowing. A woman's hair was indeed her crowning glory, and the duke did not like the short styles currently in vogue.

"Darius, dear boy!"

Annoyed, he turned to face the plump, beaming, turbaned Lady Grantham, a friend of his mother's. He smiled and raised her hand to his lips, murmuring a greeting.

"How fortunate to find you alone," chortled Lady Grantham. "Come along now, dear boy. I want you to meet my niece who's visiting me before her first season in London."

Good God, he thought irritably, a chit from the schoolroom. But there was no help for it. The third waltz could not come quickly enough for him. When it did, he eagerly swept Lady Dunham into his arms and out onto the floor.

Miranda laughed breathlessly. "Heavens, Your Grace! Is such obvious relief polite?"

"I don't have to be polite," he said. "I am Whitley, one of the oldest titles in England. God, madam, but you're ravishing! Why did I not offer for you last year?"

"Probably because you didn't see me," she replied gaily.

"I must have been blind," he said, shaking his head.

They chatted easily and soon, thinking of the man who ought to be dancing with her, self-pity welled up in Miranda. It gave way seconds later to anger. This was her first wedding anniversary, and instead of being at home on Wyndsong celebrating with the man she loved, she was dancing in an English ballroom with an amorous duke while her brother-in-law played her husband. Suddenly she felt wickedly reckless. If Jared felt the damned Anglo-American alliance was more important than their marriage, then why should she be a prim and proper wife? Who knew what Jared was doing at the Russian court?

The dance came to an end and, tucking her hand through the duke's arm, she said, "I have decided to allow you to be my supper partner, Your Grace."

"I am honored," he murmured, kissing her lavender-gloved hand before turning her over to her next partner.

As Miranda's anger increased she became gaily flirtatious. She danced the last dance before supper with Jonathan, and was amused to find him disapproving. "You have practically every young man, married or not, panting after you, madam!"

"You are not my husband," she said low. "What difference should it make to you?"

"As far as everyone is concerned, I am Jared," he hissed at her.

"Go to Hell, darling!"

"By God, Miranda, now I know why Jared calls you wildcat. Behave yourself, or I shall make your excuses."

She glared at him, infuriated, and his arm tightened around her waist. "I hate you!" she said through clenched teeth. "I hate you for not being Jared! Jared should be here with me now, but he is in St. Petersburg."

"Don't," he said, understanding her anger. "Don't, my dear. It cannot be helped, and I know my brother. He is as lonely as you are right now."

The dance ended, and the duke was instantly there to claim her for supper. The two men bowed to one another.

"Your Grace."

"M'lord, I am delighted to have your beautiful wife's company for supper. If only I might find such a lovely lady to make my duchess. Beauty, intelligence, and wit are a rare combination."

"Indeed, Your Grace. I am most fortunate," said Jon, bowing again and walking away.

The Swynford dining room was a temple of gluttony that evening. The long mahogany table was covered by a white Irish damask cloth with a floral basket design. Marching down the table in a neat row were six six-armed silver candelabra with cream-colored beeswax candles. Between the candelabra were five floral arrangements of pink, red, and white hothouse roses with greenery and holly. The center arrangement was a large silver basket. The vast buffet consisted of two great sides of beef roasted in rock salt to keep in all the juices. They were placed at either end of the table. There were four whole legs of lamb stuck with sprigs of rosemary all over, two whole suckling pigs with apples in their mouths, clove-studded pink hams, roast geese stuffed with fruit, huge Scots salmon *en gelée*, sturgeon, oysters, lobsters, and platters of fried sole. There were side dishes of jugged hare, stewed eels, stewed carp, pigeon pâté, oval Wedgwood plates of partridges and quail, marrow pudding, Brussels sprouts, miniature potato soufflés, apple and apricot fritters, and several large silver bowls of lettuce, scallions, and radishes.

On the long, mahogany sideboard were the desserts, footed silver plates of almond cheesecakes, tortes, fruit tarts, great bowls of custard, fruitcakes; pears covered in meringue, baked apples, and layer cakes filled with mocha cream. Tiered silver cake trays held petits fours covered with pink, green, and white sugar icing.

Miranda ate just a slice of rare beef, some salad, and two miniature potato soufflés, but Darius's plate was piled high with beef, suckling pig, a quail, marrow pudding, Brussels sprouts, apricot fritters, and a small lobster. She watched, amazed, as he ate it all, and then sampled three of the desserts to her one. He also drank a great deal of champagne, but here she kept pace with him, for her anger had not abated one whit. The champagne went to her head, and she giggled tipsily as the duke flirted with her. Desire began to inflame him. If he could not have her to wife, what an exquisite mistress she would make!

"Let us walk in the conservatory, my dear," he murmured to her. "I hear your brother-in-law's rose trees are without peer."

"So I am told," she said, rising unsteadily. "Ohh, I'm afraid, sir that I am somewhat tipsy from the champagne."

He bent to kiss her bare shoulder. "Only a little, my angel. Come now, a walk will do you good."

They moved from the dining salon through the grand salon and into the glassed-in conservatory. Miranda's legs were leaden, her head whirling. The warm, humid atmosphere of the conservatory weakened her, but she liked the feel of his arm around her. It had been so long since Jared had left her. Here it was her first wedding anniversary and she had no one!

Darius Edmund led Miranda deep into the miniature jungle, seating her on a delicate white wrought-iron bench. The still air was heavy with the scent of roses, gardenias, and lilies, and she was beginning to feel quite faint.

"I am totally enchanted by you," Darius Edmund said in a deep, intense voice. "You are exquisite, lovelier than any woman I have ever known. I will be frank with you, Miranda, for I understand that Americans prefer directness. I want you to be my mistress." Even before she comprehended, the Duke of Whitley was kissing her. Drawing her lavender silk gown down over her shoulders, his lips eagerly sought her young breasts. "Ah, my darling, I adore you!"

"How unfortunate for you, my lord, since the lady is my wife."

Darius Edmund leaped to his feet. The tall, elegant Lord Dunham faced him imperturbably.

"You will wish satisfaction, of course," said the duke stiffly.

Miranda, half conscious, lolled against the iron bench, her eyes closed. The duke had been holding her, kissing her, and then Jon had spoiled it all. She was sleepy now, and barely aware of the two men.

"I have no wish to involve my good name, nor that of Lord Swynford, in a scandal, Your Grace. Since no one else saw this incident, we will consider the matter closed. However, I would advise you to keep away from my wife in future."

Darius Edmund clicked his heels and, nodding curtly to the American, turned and left the conservatory. Jonathan Dunham looked down on Miranda, aching with need for her. He drew her gown back up, covering her lovely bosom, smelling the champagne on her breath. Shaking his head, he grinned ruefully at the thought of the headache she was going to have in the morning. She protested only slightly when he gently picked her up and carried her swiftly from the conservatory, through the house, and upstairs to their bedroom. Because the guests were involved in dancing and gaming, he encountered no one.

"Gawd, m'lord! Is she all right?" Perkins leaped to her feet as he came through the door.

"I'm afraid your mistress has had an excess of champagne, Perky, and she's not used to it. She'll have quite a head in the morning. Come on, I'll help you get her undressed."

Together they managed to get Miranda undressed, and while Perkins hurried to get Miranda's nightgown, Jonathan sat next to the unconscious woman who was on the bed. He had never seen her nude. In fact, he had never seen any woman totally nude. Charity had always insisted on their making love in total darkness, and she had always clothed herself in the privacy of her dressing room.

His gray-green eyes caressed Miranda. Then his hand reached out to touch her, and he shivered at the contact with her warm silken skin. Night after night in the same bed with her, and he was supposed to remain cool! What was he, a saint?

Realizing suddenly that his hand was resting on her bare thigh, he snatched it away as if the surface of her skin were burning hot.

Damnation, he thought. I cannot go on like this. God, what perfect little breasts she has. He wanted to bury his face in their warmth.

Perky came back with one of Miranda's gossamer nightgowns and they pulled Miranda up and put the silken garment on her. Jonathan picked her up as Perky drew back the covers. After he had her tucked into bed, he stood for a moment gazing down on her and then turned abruptly and left the room as quickly as he could.

Back downstairs in the ballroom, he tried to lose himself in the festivities. He was surrounded by temptation, and the room seemed full of beautiful women with daring décolletage. He was assailed by bosoms. His nostrils were assailed by perfumes of every sort—fresh lavender and spicy gillyflower, exotic rose and tuberrose, elusive moss and fern, heavy musk. He gritted his teeth against the onslaught of dimpled arms, bouncing curls, sparking eyes, lush, ripe mouths.

After an hour of torment, his eye caught a movement by the potted palms near the entry. It was Amanda and Adrian welded together in a torrid embrace. He watched as young Lord Swynford ran his hands down his wife's back to cup her buttocks and draw her closer to him. Tearing his gaze away, Jon flung himself upstairs.

There was no refuge there, however. Miranda lay curled in the very center of the bed, her silken nightgown about her waist, her adorable round bottom bared to him. He fled to the dressing room, disrobed, and lay down on the chaise to doze fitfully for a while. He heard the patter of rain against the leaded windowpanes and the slate roof, beginning softly at first and growing louder. There was a faint rumble of thunder in the distance. Thunder in winter is the Devil's thunder, he thought, remembering an old saying his Grandmother Dunham liked to quote. The thunder boomed nearer now, and the lightning flashed.

"Jared!"

He heard her cry, a cry of stark terror.

"Jared! Jared!" The voice was desperate now.

He rose from the chaise, and went to her, shocked to see her sitting up, her arms outstretched, her eyes tightly closed, tears pouring down her pale cheeks. More thunder elicited another pitiful cry. *"Jared!* Where are you? Oh, please come to me!"

Jonathan sat down on the bed and gathered her into his arms. "I'm here, wildcat. I'm here," he soothed. "Don't cry, my darling. Jared is here."

Wimpering, she pressed her face to his chest. Automatically his hand went to her silvery gold hair, smoothing it. He ached with wanting her. Her voice, softly urgent, said, "Love me, Jared! Oh, God, it's been so long since you've loved me, my darling!" She nuzzled at his nipples, and he shuddered.

"Miranda!" His voice was ragged. The flashing lightning gave the room an eerie gray-blue glow. He could see that her eyes were still closed. The thunder boomed closer this time, peal after peal of it, and she clung to him desperately.

"Oh, Jared! I promise I'll be the kind of wife you want! Don't leave me again! Please love me, Jared. Please!"

She fell back, drawing him with her, and Jonathan Dunham knew that he was going to make love to his brother's wife. Everything fell away except his deep desire for this silvery-gilt-haired nymph. He could no longer fight the hunger within him. He no longer wanted to fight it.

He found her eager mouth and drank from it, tasting the sweetness of her petal-soft lips. He kissed each part of her heart-shaped face, the adorable cleft in her chin, her small, straight nose, the shadowed eyelids, their dark lashes quivering against her pale cheeks like small, black butterflies.

His hands roamed across her beautiful body and he heard her sigh contentedly as bare skin touched bare skin. He wanted time to explore this lovely new land, but she would give him no time. She moved frantically beneath him, and soon her slender fingers sought his sex, touching him with hot little hands that caressed and stroked until he thought he'd burst with passion. He jammed a knee between her soft thighs, parted them, and thrust deeply into her willing body.

"Oh, Jared!" she cried softly. "Oh, my darling, yes!"

About them the thunder crashed and rolled and the lightning crackled violently, illuminating and darkening the room in rapid succession. She was wildfire in his arms. She gave herself to him totally, but of course it was not Jonathan to whom she gave herself, it was Jared.

Jonathan knew that. She had not opened her eyes once and he suddenly realized that she had never been conscious of him at all. Her desperate need for Jared, her fear of the storm, and too much champagne had been responsible. He had taken his brother's wife in adultery, and Jonathan soon felt as low with remorse as he had been giddy with lust.

He would have left the bed, but she curled up next to him, her head on his shoulder. He put an arm around her protectively and drew the quilts over them. Hollow-eyed, he lay and listened to the rain. The thunder had died and with it the lightning. The wind rose, and he knew morning would find the last of the leaves gone. She murmured against him, and his arm tightened around her. Dear heaven, Miranda, Jonathan thought, *What have I done?* He consoled himself with the thought that she probably wouldn't remember this, as she had really been unconscious. The minutes crawled by making an hour, then two. His shoulder was growing stiff, and despite the quilts he was cold. The room began to grow gray with the advent of day, and soon the sparrows set up a mad chattering.

"It was you, not Jared, wasn't it?" Her soft voice cut through his soul.

"Miranda..." He didn't know whether he should lie or admit his crime.

"Thank you, Jon!"

He was astounded. This was hardly what he had expected. Tears, yes! Recriminations, yes! But thanks?

"Yes, Jon, thank you."

"I d-don't understand," he stammered.

"Thank you for making love to me."

"My God, Miranda, what kind of woman are you?!"

"Not really as awful as you are now thinking," she answered softly. "I don't know if this will reassure you or not," she continued, "but I did not know last night. When I awoke this morning in your arms, without my gown, I knew that that marvelous dream I had had was not a dream at all."

He shuddered. "Miranda...dear heaven! How can I ask your

pardon? I took advantage of your terror and the fact that you had had too much champagne. I allowed my ungovernable lust to gain the upper hand!"

"Yes, you certainly did," she replied, and he thought there was a hint of laughter in her voice. "You don't make love at all like your brother does, Jon," she continued, to his acute embarrassment. "Jared is far more skilled and much more patient."

"Dammit, Miranda, this is hardly a thing for us to discuss!"

"Fiddlesticks!" she shot back. "We had best discuss it if we are to continue this masquerade. We can hardly carry on normally if you cannot even look at me. Oh, Jon! Last night was partly my fault, too. I indulged myself in a terrible fit of self-pity, but dear God, I miss Jared so! I drank much too much and I've never had a strong head for champagne. I flirted with Darius Edmund because you were being overbearing with me. I was coiled up tighter than an overwound watch spring."

"Why?" he demanded. "You have everything."

"Not quite everything, Jon, my darling," she laughed softly.

"Miranda!" He was shocked.

"Didn't Charity ever get grumpy when you neglected her? Or perhaps you're not a man to neglect his wife."

"Dammit, Miranda, such talk is unseemly in a woman!"

"We were not married a year when your brother left me!" she snapped angrily. "I care very little for wars or politics or Bonaparte! I want my husband! I want to go home to Wyndsong!"

"If you had not disobeyed Jared by sailing for England without him, he would not have come to England and been forced to take Palmerston's mission."

"He could have said no! I need him, Jon, and last night I needed to be loved."

"What if I have gotten you with child?" he demanded.

"You have not gotten me with child, Jon."

"You cannot be sure, Miranda!"

"I most certainly can. I am already with child."

"What?!"

"I believe it happened our last night together before he left for St. Petersburg," she said. "My baby will be born in the spring. I only hope his father is at home to welcome him to this world. Bonaparte or no Bonaparte, the child will come."

"Dear Lord, this makes it worse," he said hoarsely. "Not only have I forced myself on my brother's wife, I have forced myself on my brother's *pregnant* wife!"

She laughed outright. "You are a strange man, Jon," she teased him. "First you fear you've gotten me pregnant, and now you're upset because you haven't." Understanding his genuine distress, she sobered. "Dearest Jonathan, listen to me. If I was a watch spring ready to snap last night, then so were you. Charity has been dead five months. If I needed to be loved, then so did you. I am not saying that what we did was right, and it will most certainly not happen again, but we needed each other, Jon." She put a gentle hand on his shoulder. "Do you realize what this means, Jon? You have stopped mourning your wife. You are ready to live again."

"But Jared..." he said.

"Jared will never know. Telling him might make us feel better, but would it be fair to Jared? What happened last night will never happen again, will it, Jon?"

"No."

"Then there is no need for Jared to know that the two people he loves best in this world have proved themselves only too human." She took his hand in hers. "You must take a mistress, Jon. No one will think badly of you for it. I shall announce my condition shortly. All gentlemen of fashion keep ladies of the Cyprian persuasion."

"Good Lord, Miranda, do you speak with my brother in such a forward fashion?"

"Yes," she answered, "but I have, of course, never advised him to take a mistress. Should I find he has, I shall cut his heart out."

"I cannot imagine he'll ever find the need for outside entertainments." Mischievously he ran a finger down her bare shoulder.

"I think, Jon, you had best find yourself a companion soon. It is easier to maintain a casual attitude when you do not smolder at me so. No, do not glower at me. Women have their needs, also."

"Close your eyes," he commanded.

"Why?"

"Because I wish to get up and get my clothes."

"You have nothing I haven't seen," she said sweetly.

"Miranda!" he growled.

"Oh, very well," she answered demurely, and he chuckled as he hurried to the dressing room.

Suddenly he realized how much he liked her. For one so young she was amazingly sensible, and he understood how fortunate Jared was. He also felt acute relief over her feelings about last night. Reflecting on her uninhibited passion, he shook his head. It was definitely time that he found a mistress.

❧ Chapter 9 ❧

Miranda Dunham's son was born at six minutes past midnight on April 30, 1813. He was, according to both his mother's and doctor's calculations, two and a half weeks early. Nevertheless he was a lusty, healthy infant. The London season was only two-thirds over, but the current high-waisted fashions had allowed Miranda to be social until her time. In fact it was the doctor's disapproving opinion that Lady Dunham's busy life had been responsible for the slightly premature birth.

"Fiddlesticks!" snapped his patient. "Both the boy and I are in excellent condition."

The doctor had gone his way shaking his head. Young Lady Swynford, he privately declared, was a much better patient than her sister. Although her child was not due until the end of June, she had wisely retired from society at the end of March, a full three months prior to the birth.

Both sisters had giggled behind the good doctor's back, and to the horror of the wet nurse they had undressed the baby in the middle of his mama's bed, exclaiming over his perfection. His toes and fingers, the tiny nails, his thick black hair, his miniature genitals all elicited exclamations of delight.

"What are you going to call him?" asked Amanda one day when her nephew was a week old.

"Would you mind if I named him after Papa?" said Miranda.

"Lord, no! Thomas is a Dunham name. Adrian and I have decided if our baby is a boy we shall call him Edward. If it's a girl, Clarissa. What does Jared say?"

"Jared? Oh! He agrees. The child will be Thomas. I intend asking Adrian to be the baby's godfather, and Jared's older brother, Jonathan, will also be godfather. Jared will have to stand in for his brother at the christening, as Jon cannot possibly come here from America. Will you be my Tom's godmother?"

"Gladly, dearest, and you will be godmama to my child?"

"Of course I will, Mandy," promised Miranda.

Thomas Johnathan Adrian Dunham was christened in mid-May at the small country church in the village belonging to Swynford Hall. If Lord Palmerston had heard from Jared, he had not communicated any message to Miranda. In fact, he had gone out of his way to avoid her at the social gatherings they attended. Not knowing how much he had told his mistress, Lady Cowper, Miranda could not even beg Emily to intercede for her. The situation was becoming intolerable.

Little Tom's birth had been a relatively easy one, and yet Miranda was tired suddenly, and felt more alone than she had in months. Jon, of course, had been with her during her ordeal, sitting by her side wiping her wet brow with a cologne-scented handkerchief, allowing her to squeeze his hands until she thought she was going to crush them, giving her strength. When she thought of Jared, and briefly wanted to give up, looking at Jon had helped. Jon understood the way of a woman in childbirth.

What distressed Miranda most of all was the knowledge that Jared didn't even know there was to be a child. He didn't know she had borne him a strong and fine son. Lacking any real knowledge of her husband, her imagination played havoc with her postpartum nerves. Jared had not been celibate before their marriage, and now, separated from her, what was to prevent him taking a mistress in St. Petersburg? She alternated between tears and fury as she imagined *her* Jared with another woman writhing beneath him. Another woman receiving what should rightfully be hers! She would weep with frustration, hating herself for doubting him, hating him for putting patriotism before his wife.

If Jared had but known her thoughts they would have pleased him immensely, for shortly before the new year he had become a guest of the Tzar. His new home was a spacious two-room apartment in the Fortress of St. Peter and St. Paul. He was currently under the Tzar's protection, and not allowed to leave. He chafed at his imprisonment and another woman was the furthest thought from his mind. The only woman he thought of was Miranda, and he thought of her often. He had made her a woman, his love had given her confidence, and now he imagined her being pursued by every sensible gentleman within the ton, dazzling society with her wit and unusual beauty.

Impotent fury coursed through him. What if that damned royal satyr, Prinny, took it in his head to seduce Miranda? Could she avoid him? Would she want to? Despite his girth, the Prince Regent was a most charming and fascinating man. Jesus! He'd kill the bastard if he had touched Miranda! Oh, Miranda, he thought, for all your intelligence, you are so innocent of the world. You see only what you want to, my darling, and no more. Jared Dunham paced angrily and restlessly back and forth within his quarters, calling himself every kind of a fool for leaving his wife.

As if to mock his black mood, St. Petersburg was experiencing a rare bright and sunshiny winter's day. Beyond the ornate twisted bars and glass on the apartment windows, he could see the blue sky and the bright sunshine. The city was white with snow sparkling brightly from the rooftops and onion-domed churches. Below him the Neva was frozen solid, and the aristocracy amused themselves by holding races, their sleighs racing down the river at breakneck speed. He could imagine the thunder of hooves, and the shouts of participants and spectators alike. Up here in his small world the only sounds were those made by himself or Mitchum.

He thought of London, of the social season now just beginning. He wondered how his brother, that staunch New England Yankee Jonathan, was adjusting to being an Anglo-American lord. He chuckled, tickled at the idea of his sensible, plain-living brother forced to wallow in the lap of luxury, as would be expected of Jared Dunham.

Jonathan had actually settled quite comfortably into his role as the wealthy Yankee lordling. He had his club, and he had a pretty mistress, a little opera dancer, in London. While in London he rode daily with Adrian, gamed quite successfully, visited Gentlemen Jackson's gym to box, and squired his opera dancer to all the places a gentleman might be seen with his light-o'-love. Prior to the Dunhams' and Swynfords' departure to Worcester he had bid the lady farewell and gifted her with a showy necklace, earrings, and bracelet of pale-blue Brazilian aquamarines. He did not expect to see her again, and chuckled with glee at the possibility of Jared running into her someday.

Once again they were to spend the summer and autumn seasons at Swynford Hall. The baby, Tom, was housed in cheerful rooms that had been redecorated in anticipation of his cousin's arrival. They would, Amanda declared, be almost like twins. The nursery staff set about spoiling the new heir to Wyndsong Island, and Miranda hardly saw her child except for a brief time in the morning, and again just before his bedtime.

Jon spent a great deal of time away from her now, and Miranda realized with shock that he genuinely cared for a young widow in the village whom he had met last winter. Mistress Anne Bowen was the daughter of the previous rector of Swynford Church, now deceased. She had been married at eighteen to the younger son of the local squire, but her husband's family had expected their son to marry an heiress, not the daughter of the local minister, and Robert Bowen was cut off without a penny.

Fortunately, he had been a scholar, and his family had educated him. He opened a small penny school to teach the local children their letters. They lived in the vicarage, for his father-in-law was a widower, and with the blessing of a roof over their heads, the kitchen garden that Anne tended, and his small living as schoolmaster they were comfortable.

In the ten years of their marriage, a boy and a girl were born to them. Then two years before both the vicar and his son-in-law had been killed when out walking late one fine autumn afternoon. They had been trampled to death when the London–Worcester mail coach had careened around a bend in the road, completely out of control of its drunken driver. Only the shouts of its terrified passengers had managed to stop the driver, who was pulled from his perch and beaten to a pulp by the angry farm laborers who ran from the nearby fields, outraged at the deaths of both their beloved minister and the kindly schoolmaster.

Anne Bowen was, in an instant, bereft of both her father and her husband and reduced to a state of poverty. Had it not been for the kindness of young Lord Swynford, Mistress Bowen would also have found herself homeless and in the workhouse once the new minister arrived. Adrian saw that she was given a stone cottage in good repair on the edge of the village, rent-free. The young lord of the manor could not afford to pension the widow and her two orphans, but he did see that she had butter and milk daily from his creamery. With her vegetable patch and a small flock of chickens, ducks, and geese, Anne Bowen was assured that she and her children would not starve.

The children were growing fast. Young John Robert needed to be educated, as his father had been. He was already eleven, and should have been at Harrow by then. And what would happen to Mary Anne? She was too well bred to marry a farmer, yet there was no dowry. In desperation Anne appealed to her in-laws, and was firmly rebuffed. Anne Bowen loved her children fiercely, and because she did she humbled herself. "I ask nothing for myself," she pleaded, "only for the children. They are your grandchildren. I can feed and house and clothe them, but I cannot afford to educate the boy or dower the girl. Please help them. They are such good children!"

Brutally they informed her that they did not recognize her alliance with their son, and then she was coldly shown the door. She did not allow herself the luxury of tears until she was near the gates, but then they came, and she stumbled blindly along.

"Pssst! Missus!"

She turned to see a woman in the garb of an upper servant.

"I'm Thatcher, the young missus's maid. She don't approve of how the squire and his wife is treating you. She can't do nothing, but she wanted you to have this." A handkerchief was stuffed into her hand. "She says she wishes it was more." The woman turned and hurried back into the bushes along the edge of the drive.

Slowly Anne Bowen undid the linen square, and found within two gold sovereigns. The kindness of her unknown sister-in-law caused the tears to flow faster during the seven-mile walk back to Swynford village. The next day she let it be known that she was available as a seamstress, and those wishing more elegant garb than they could make themselves availed of her services.

Two years passed. She was so busy keeping her little family that she did not realize how lonely she was. And then one day Mary Anne's new kitten got itself stuck in the apple tree. The kitten was but another mouth to feed, she had thought when her daughter brought it home. But seeing the desperate look in the child's eyes, she sighed and agreed that, yes, the kitten would be a valuable asset to the household. Poor Mary Anne had so little.

"Damnation!" she said softly, staring up at the little gray and white animal. How on earth was she to get him down? Mary Anne wept beside her.

"May I be of some assistance?" Anne whirled around and saw an elegant gentleman dismounting from his horse.

Recognizing Lord Swynford's brother-in-law, she curtseyed. "You are most kind, m'lord, but I would not have you soil your clothes."

"Nonsense!" he replied, swinging into the tree and handing the kitten down to Mary Anne. "There, youngster, keep that imp safe now."

Mary Anne's tears vanished, and she scampered away, the kitten clutched to her little chest.

Jon leaped lightly down from the tree, brushing himself off, and Anne Bowen smiled shyly. "Thank you, m'lord. My daughter would have been devastated if anything had happened to the kitten."

"No trouble at all, ma'am." He inclined his head then mounted his horse and rode off.

For several Sundays he bowed, tipped his hat, and said "Your servant, ma'am," as they left church. His wife had been with him every Sunday and Anne thought how beautiful Lady Dunham was. She envied her the fashionable clothes.

One day, several weeks after their first meeting, he had stopped at the cottage to inquire after the kitten's health. After that he took to coming by at least twice a week, and Anne Bowen found herself looking forward to his visits.

Occasionally he brought sweetmeats for the children who, never having money for such luxuries, devoured them in a twinkling. Then late one afternoon he had appeared with a rabbit, skinned and ready for the pot. She politely asked him to supper, fully expecting him to decline her humble invitation, and was quite surprised when he accepted. She had never entertained in the cottage. Her neighbors held her in awe, for though she was far poorer than they, she was still "vicar's lass." Only occasionally would they even venture over her doorsill.

He sat by the fire in the one good chair, and watched her set the table. She drew from the linen chest a lovely snow-white Irish cloth, which she spread over the oval table. From the Welsh dresser came her mother's bone china, and pale-green glass goblets. The utensils were well polished steel with bone handles, and the candlesticks were pewter. The children brought some greens from the garden to decorate the table. The rabbit stew bubbled, sending a savory odor through the cottage.

The children were ecstatic. They saw meat only rarely. Anne nearly cried at their delight in the fluffy dumplings she made from her precious hoard of white flour. She added a dish of new lettuce and, for dessert, baked an apple tart—thankful that Lord Swynford's generosity made heavy cream possible. Jon noted everything, the children's eagerness over the rabbit stew, Anne's quite pride and soft flushed cheeks. He realized that they did not usually eat this well, silently cursing himself for having accepted her invitation and depriving the children of an extra meal.

She was a marvelous cook, and he couldn't help but eat ravenously, which brought a smile to her lovely face. "It's good to see a man eat again," she said quietly.

"I'll bring you another rabbit tomorrow," he promised, "and I'll not ask to stay to dinner this time."

"You really mustn't. You have been too generous already."

"There are too many rabbits on the estate as it is. After all, my offer is an honest one. I'm not poaching."

"I didn't mean...Oh—" She blushed, realizing he was teasing her. Regaining her composure, she said, "I'd be very pleased to accept another rabbit, m'lord."

The children had gone outside to play, and he offered to help her clear the dishes away, but she refused. "You must go, m'lord, while it is still light enough to see you."

"Why?"

She blushed again. "If the neighbors do not see you leave, they will assume you did not. Forgive my presumption and indelicacy, m'lord, but I must think of my children."

He rose. "No, Mistress Bowen, it is I who should ask your pardon for being so thoughtless. I have enjoyed myself today as I have not in many months. It would ill repay your hospitality if I were to cast doubt upon your reputation." He bowed his way out the door. "Your servant, ma'am."

She stood watching him ride down the road, sighing. If only some good man like that one would come along for her to marry! Anne Bowen knew she would have to remarry if she possibly could. Lord Swynford had been very kind, and the little sewing she could get kept them from starvation, but John Robert must not be allowed to grow up ignorant and Mary Anne must one day make a decent match. Unless some good fairy left her a pot of gold it would be an impossibility for her to do without a man, but who was she likely to meet here in Swynford village? And to leave here would mean the workhouse for certain.

Riding back to the hall in the rose-mauve dusk, Jonathan Dunham found himself unable to get her out of his mind. She was so lovely, and so brave. She reminded him of Charity, and yet she wasn't at all like Charity. Charity had been a big, buxom Cape Cod girl with laughing blue eyes and bouncing ash-brown curls whose complexion was usually tanned because of the amount of time she spent outdoors. She was a strong, practical, sensible, wholesome example of American womanhood. Anne Bowen was an English rose, of medium height, slender with a pale complexion. She had lovely gray eyes and soft, copper curls. She gave the impression of great delicacy although her great strength was obvious. The only true likeness between the two women was in their devotion to their children.

He had been attracted to her from the very beginning. All he heard of her from others and all he saw increased his admiration.

He could not keep himself from seeing her, and soon he came after dark, and to the back door of the cottage. But they remained chaste with each other. He and the family had gone to London after the new year, and it was not until May that he saw Anne again. He had sent the children gifts from London and arranged with Lord Swynford that the Bowen children be allowed to ride the Swynford horses. "Good Lord, Adrian," he chided, "these children are gentry— impoverished, but gentry nonetheless. Until the vicar and their father died they had their own horses. Besides, with both our ladies enceinte, there's no one but the stableboys to exercise the horses. The children would be doing you a favor."

"You've taken a deep interest in the Bowens, Jared. Is the pretty young widow consoling you for Miranda's loss," teased Adrian, and then stepped back at the look of fury on Lord Dunham's face. "Good Lord, Jared! What did I say?"

"Mistress Bowen is not my mistress, Adrian, if that's what you were implying. I am frankly appalled that you would assume such a thing of a lady like Anne Bowen."

Adrian, Lord Swynford, looked at his brother-in-law strangely, but said nothing else. Miranda seemed perfectly happy with her husband, and it was not his place to interfere.

Jonathan saw Anne Bowen again on the first Sunday he was back at Swynford Hall. As he left the church he saw her on the arm of Peter Rogers, the innkeeper. "I thought the innkeeper had a wife," he murmured to Adrian.

"The bailiff tells me Mistress Rogers died last winter, and Peter's been seen in Mistress Bowen's company quite a bit in the last month. He's not such a bad fellow, and she's got to marry again because of the children."

As Jonathan looked at the innkeeper he felt a terrible rage welling up. The man gazed at Anne as if she were a strawberry tart he was going to devour. His small eyes kept darting looks at her full bosom, and each time he did so he licked his lips. Jonathan wanted to smash the man's face. All the rest of that day he thought of Peter Rogers ... Peter Rogers and Anne. By dusk he could stand no more. He rode to her cottage.

Her eyes were wary when she answered his impatient knock. "M'lord?"

"Are you alone?"

"Yes, m'lord."

"The children?"

"Long abed, m'lord. Please come in, for you're quite visible in the light from the door."

He stepped across her threshold and, closing the door behind him, demanded, "Are you going to marry Peter Rogers?"

"If he asks me," she replied quietly.

"Why?"

"M'lord, I have two children. It is difficult at best for a woman alone. I have no money and no family left, and my late husband's family will do nothing to help me. I know that for a certainty because I humbled myself and begged them to help their grandchildren. I *must* remarry, but no one in the village is my social equal, so what am I to do? Mr. Rogers is an ambitious man. If he asks me I will accept him providing he agrees to send my John away to school and to dower Mary Anne."

"You will sell yourself to that swine for money?" He was outraged. "If it's money you want I'll pay more," he snarled. Pulling her roughly against him, he kissed her, kissed her passionately until she stopped struggling, stopped and became a soft, pliant, moaning armful. He picked her up and carried her into her small bedroom. He made love to her, slowly and tenderly, with a gentleness as great as his anger had been great.

Anne could not believe what was happening to her. It had always been pleasant with Robert, but it had never been like this. This was a hot passion that filled her with the most extraordinary feeling she had ever known, and when it was over and she lay spent in his arms, she wept, convinced that anything so wonderful could not be good.

He held her against him, allowing the warm tears to soak his chest. Finally when her sobs became little hiccoughs that gradually died away he said quietly, "If I were free to marry you, would you be my wife, Anne?"

"B-but you are not," she sighed.

"You have not answered my question, love. *If* I were free, would you marry me?"

"Yes, of course."

He smiled in the darkness. "Don't accept Mr. Rogers, Anne. Everything will work out, I promise you. Will you trust me?"

"Are you offering me a carte blanche?" she asked him.

"Good Lord, no!" he whispered fiercely. "I hold you in greater esteem that that."

She didn't understand, but she was far too happy to care. She loved him. She had loved him from the moment she met him. He had not said the words, but she knew that he loved her, too.

He left just before first light, slipping out the back door of the cottage and riding home across the misty fields in the gray world of predawn. At nine that morning Miranda received Jonathan in her bedroom. Sitting up in bed, a rose pink silk bedjacket about her shoulders, her hair in a neat braid, she was an extremely fetching morsel, he thought. He kissed the hand she extended. "Madam."

"Good morning, m'lord. For a gentleman who spent the entire night out, you're looking quite well."

"You're mighty well informed for so early in the morning," he teased.

"Ah," she chuckled, "the stable boy saw you come in and he told the dairymaid who told the kitchenmaid when she brought in the eggs this morning. The kitchenmaid naturally passed it on to the cook who mentioned it to my maid when Perky went for my breakfast tray, and Perky told me. She's quite indignant that you're neglecting me." Here, Miranda skillfully mimicked her loyal servant, "It whats you can expect from a gentleman once he's got what he wants, m'lady."

Jonathan laughed. "I'm delighted to know that I live up to Perky's ideal of a gentleman."

"You're troubled," she said, "I can see it in your eyes. Is there any way in which I can help?"

"I'm not sure," he answered. "You see, I've fallen in love, Miranda. I want to marry, and because I must be Jared, and not Jon, I cannot even tender the lady a respectable offer. And I want to, Miranda. I don't want Anne believing my love a shallow thing. I want to tell her who I really am, but I don't know if I dare. I cannot endanger Jared."

Miranda was thoughtful for a few moments, then she said, "First you must tell me who the lady is, Jon."

"Mistress Anne Bowen."

"A quiet and discreet lady, I have heard. Are you sure she would accept you if you asked?"

"Yes."

"I cannot see that Mistress Bowen's knowledge of our secret would harm Jared," said Miranda slowly. "Surely he will soon be home, and this masquerade can be ended. We are far enough from London, and this is not a fashionable enough place to draw the ton. I would not put Mistress Bowen under a painful strain believing that she is involved in an adulterous situation. I think you had best tell her the truth, Jon. Do you think, however, that she will believe you. This *is* a rather unusual situation."

"She will believe me if you come with me when I tell her."

Miranda's mind began to churn. She had been considering a plan and now she saw that if Jon were occupied with Mistress Bowen she would be free to go her way. "All right, John, I will attest to your honesty with Mistress Bowen."

Elated, he kissed her hand again and left the room whistling. Miranda smiled to herself. She was glad to see him happy, and with Mistress Bowen to soothe him, he should not be too distressed when she disappeared.

She had decided to go to Russia to find Jared. He had been gone almost ten months. Just before they had left London, she had managed to corner Lord Palmerston. The British Secretary of War had been abrupt. "When I know, you'll know, madam," he said.

"He has been gone months, my lord, and I have been allowed no word. I have just borne my child alone. Can you give me no hope? No word at all?"

"I repeat, madam, when I know, you'll know. Your servant, m'lady." He smiled cordially and bowed.

It was all Miranda could do to keep from screaming. Lord Palmerston was the most arrogant man she had ever met, and he was being terribly unfair. She was through with waiting. She could stand no more. If Jared could not come to her, she would go to him.

Of course, she could not discuss this with anyone. She had consulted a map in Adrian's library, and saw that it was well over a hundred miles to the small village on the piece of English coast known as The Wash where Jared's yacht, *Dream Witch,* was moored. She would need a coach, for she could not use a Swynford vehicle. Most of all, she would need help, but whom could she rely on?

Then it came to her that she would have her own coach brought up from London! Amanda and Adrian had insisted it wasn't necessary that they have their own coach here in the country when the Swynford carriage house boasted so many vehicles. She would now need that coach, and Perky could help. Her flirtatious maid was currently enamored of the undercoachman.

Brushing her mistress's hair that evening, Perky sighed quite audibly. Miranda quickly took the advantage. "Poor Perky! That's a lonely lover's sigh if I ever heard one. I imagine you miss your young man."

"Yes, m'lady, I do. He's asked me to marry him, and we thought we'd have this summer to do it in, and be together. Then m'lord left the coach in town."

"Oh, Perky, why didn't you tell me!" Miranda was all sympathy. "We will simply have to get your young man . . . what is his name?"

"Martin, m'lady."

"We will have to find a way to get Martin to Swynford!"

"Oh, m'lady, if you only could!"

Miranda plotted. Adrian and Jon had been invited by Lord Stewart to go fishing on his estates in Scotland. Both she and Amanda had insisted that they go even though the invitation was set for a date immediately after the birth of Amanda's baby.

"I should feel so guilty if I denied Adrian his summer pleasures," said Amanda. "Besides, the christening will not be until Michaelmas. Newborn babies look so odd—not at all at their best, whereas an infant of three months is quite handsome."

"Upon what do you base this conclusion?" teased Miranda gently.

"Old Lady Swynford has assured me it is so. You know, Miranda, I misjudged Adrian's mama. She is quite an amiable female, and we both want what is best for Adrian. I am amazed at how similar many of our opinions are. And she admitted to me only last week that she had been mistaken in her opinion of me. She says that I am the perfect wife for Adrian!"

"How fortunate for you both that you have become friends," remarked Miranda drily. More than likely, Adrian's mama realized that the less she tolerated Amanda, the less she would see of her grandchild, thought Miranda. Well, at least Mandy would not be friendless once she was gone.

Once Jonathan and Adrian were gone off to Scotland, the coach would arrive from London. She had debated what to tell her sister, and finally decided that the truth was best. Poor Jon would be hard pressed to explain her absence to an outraged Amanda and her spouse. Best Mandy know that the man she believed to be Jared Dunham was in reality his brother Jonathan. Better she understand that the reason Miranda must leave her child was to go in search of her husband. But Amanda could not be told until the last minute. She would be horrified and frightened by what Miranda intended to do. No. Amanda should not know until the last minute.

Her own coach, driven by Martin, would take her to the little village of Welland Beach. She would be accompanied by Perky, for no respectable woman would travel without her maid. She would see that Perky and Martin were married before they left. They would wait in Welland Beach with the carriage until Miranda returned with her husband. It was a very sensible plan.

The days passed and spring became early summer. One afternoon Jonathan asked Miranda if she would accompany him in the high perch phaeton. As they drove down the drive he remarked, "You are looking quite fetching today, my dear." Miranda smiled prettily at him. She was wearing a pink muslin dress sprigged in small white apple blossoms with pale green leaves. The dress had short puffed sleeves, and although the back of it was high, the neck was low. Beneath the bustline, the gown was tied with green and white silk ribbons. Miranda wore long green gloves that reached her elbow. Her high-crowned hat was of straw, and tied with ribbons that matched the ones on her gown. As the horses reached the open highway Miranda opened her pink parasol to keep her complexion safe from the sun.

"Where are we going?" she asked.

"I have arranged for us to meet Anne at an inn ten miles from here," he said. "We could hardly meet openly in Swynford village without causing comment, and I want this settled as quickly as possible. I cannot allow Anne to go on believing that I am a married man."

"Ah," she teased him, "it is Anne now, and no longer Mistress Bowen."

"I love her, Miranda!" he said intensely. "She is the dearest, sweetest woman alive, and I want her for my wife. She believes she has gone against everything she believes for love of me. Although she says nothing, I know it hurts her terribly."

"Then why don't you marry her, Jon?"

"What?"

"Why don't you marry her? With our connections it is a simple matter to get a special license. You could be wed in a small parish some miles from here where we are not known." She paused, then had a wicked thought. "Ask Lord Palmerston to help you. I believe he owes us some small courtesy! Mistress Bowen should feel more secure once she is your wife."

"You are marvelous!" he cried.

They drove west to a small whitewashed and half-timbered inn set in the Malvern Hills. The Good Queen had window boxes full of flowers, and was surrounded by a lovely garden. Miranda was puzzled as to how Mistress Bowen would get to such an inaccessible spot.

"I arranged for a closed carriage to meet Anne two miles from the village," Jonathan enlightened her.

"You are most discreet," she replied.

As the phaeton pulled up before the inn, a boy ran out to take the horses and Jonathan leaped down, lifting Miranda to the ground. "Walk those bays till they've cooled down, lad. Then you may water them."

As they entered the building the innkeeper hurried forward. "Good day, sir, madam. Would you be Mr. Jonathan?"

"I am."

"Come this way then, sir. Your guest has already arrived." The innkeeper showed them to a private room and inquired, "When shall I have them serve tea, sir?"

Jonathan turned to Miranda. "My dear?"

"I believe a half-hour should be sufficient, Master Innkeeper."

"Very good, madam," replied the man, closing the door behind him as he withdrew.

A heavy silence hung in the room. Miranda stared openly at Mistress Bowen. She knew the woman was thirty, yet she didn't look past twenty-five. Her gown was white muslin of poor quality, but beautifully made. It was decorated with pale-blue ribbons, and a straw bonnet with matching blue ribbons lay on a nearby table. She was very pretty, Miranda decided, and probably quite the perfect wife for Jon. As he could do nothing but stare like a lovesick calf, Miranda took the initiative.

"How nice to finally meet you, Mistress Bowen. Come, let us sit down, and we shall explain everything to you."

Dazed by Miranda's smile and her kindly attitude, Anne Bowen allowed Jonathan to seat her. The beautiful Lady Dunham enlightened her quickly and without fuss.

"I suspect, Mistress Bowen, that the simplest way to explain this is to be straightforward. This gentleman, whom you and everyone else believes to be Jared Dunham, is actually his brother Jonathan. My husband, Jared, has, since late last summer, been in St. Petersburg on a secret mission for the American and English governments. Since he could not get back to England before the Russian winter set in and it had to appear that he *was* in England, Jon was smuggled through the English blockade of our American coast in order to impersonate Jared.

"No one but a wife or mother can tell the differences between my husband and his brother. They look more like twins than my twin sister and I."

"Wh—what are the differences?" ventured Anne Bowen.

"Jared is taller by about a half-inch, and his eyes are a bottle-green, not the gray-green of Jon's. He has a more elegant hand, and there are other little differences. People here in England do not know Jared well enough to discern those differences. Even my own sister and her husband believe Jon is Jared."

"Jon is a widower. His first wife died a year ago. You shall have three stepchildren, I should warn you. John is twelve, Eliza Anne is nine, and little Henry is three. If you wed Jon you shall have to live in Massachusetts, for my father-in-law owns shipyards, and Jon is his heir.

"Now I suggested to Jon that he go up to London and obtain a special license so you may be wed immediately. It must be secretly, you understand. I should feel guilty if you bore Jon a child without benefit of clergy."

"Miranda!" Jonathan Dunham finally found his voice. "For God's sake, don't be so indelicate!"

"Indelicate? Good heavens, Jon, are you going to deny the fact that Mistress Bowen is your mistress? Poor Mistress Bowen, not you, would be censured if she finds herself with child. I must insist you marry as quickly as possible!"

Anne Bowen had sat almost silent throughout Miranda's whole recitation, her gray eyes occasionally widening in surprise. Now she looked from Miranda to Jonathan, convinced that Lady Dunham was telling the truth.

She placed a gentle hand on Jonathan's arm. "I believe Lady Dunham's point is well taken, m'lord—I mean, Mr. Dunham. Perhaps, however, you do not wish to offer me marriage. A gentleman such as yourself could seek a finer match, I know."

"Oh, Anne, of course I want to offer you marriage! Will you marry me? We have fine schools in America, not as old as Harrow, Oxford, and Cambridge, but very good. I swear I'll educate your son, and I'll dower Mary Anne as well as my own Eliza! Massachusetts is a fine place for children."

"What of the wild Indians there?" she ventured nervously.

"Indians? Well, there are Indians in the Western territories, and some sections of the South, but there are no more wild Indians in Massachusetts."

"What will your family say if you bring home a new wife?"

"They will say that I am the most fortunate of men to have found such a treasure."

"I shall be a good mother to your children, Mr. Dunham."

"Jon. Oh God, Anne! How I long to hear you say my *real* name!"

"Jon," she breathed the word. "I shall be a very good mother to your children. We will, however, have to begin calling my John Robert, plain Robert, so we will not confuse him with your oldest son. How fortunate we are that the children are of like ages."

"You mean you will marry me?"

"Did I not say so?" she said. "No, I didn't, but yes, Jon, I will most certainly marry you. Oh, my darling, I love you so very much!"

"Excellent!" said Miranda as Jonathan took Anne in his arms and kissed her. "Now that that is settled we can have tea. I am famished."

Rosy with kisses, Anne said happily, "How can I thank you, Lady Dunham?"

"You may begin by calling me Miranda," was the sensible reply. "In America there are no titles, and I am plain Mistress Dunham, as you shall soon be!"

It was a lovely afternoon, one that Miranda would remember for a long time. She genuinely liked Anne Bowen, instinctively knowing that despite the difference in their ages they would become good friends. She knew that Anne could be trusted to keep their secret. Mistress Bowen left them immediately after tea to return to Swynford Village. She had left her children in the care of a neighbor, but did not wish to impose.

"I like her," said Miranda, helping herself to another cucumber sandwich and a cream cake. "You are very wise to wed her. I suspect your father has Chastity Brewster in mind for you. Your choice is far more suitable."

"Chastity Brewster! Good Lord, I should never wed that giggling, overstuffed creature. She turned down every eligible bachelor who

ever asked her because she fancied she could catch brother Jared!"
He chuckled. "She's not Jared's type at all. He fancies far more firey
wildcats with sea-green eyes and silver-gilt hair. Thank you, Miranda, for all your help."

"You deserve some consolation for putting up with me, Jon."

He laughed. "You're too much for me to handle, Miranda, and
I'm not ashamed to admit it."

She smiled mischievously at him. "Go up to London tomorrow on
the pretext that Palmerston has sent for you. You will, of course, see
him, and when you do, insist that he arrange for you to have a special
license. If he demurs simply threaten to return to Swynford as
Jonathan Dunham, not Jared. If he still demurs, tell him I shall
scream to high heaven about my missing husband and the nefarious
dealings of England's War Department. Whether people believe me
or not I shall cause a stir and the gossip will last for several months.
Lord Palmerston is not the most popular gentleman in England. I do
not think he can afford the fuss I shall cause."

"You are a very tough opponent, my dear," he said. "May I ask
when you have decided my wedding should be?"

"Oh, yes! Let Adrian go off to Lord Stewart's alone. Promise him
you will follow him in a week. Use our friend Palmerston as an
excuse again—a quick mission perhaps. Then you and Anne can be
wed and have a few days together. She can claim a dying, elderly
relative, and arrange for her neighbor to care for the children during
those few days. It is quite simple if you plan ahead."

"So I see," he remarked. "I begin to think, my dear, that you have
missed your calling. You would make Bonaparte an ideal strategist."

They rode back to Swynford Hall, the bays, fresh and well rested,
stepping smartly along. Upon their arrival they found the Swynford
barony in an uproar. Miranda hurried up the stairs to her sister's
apartment and was greeted by the dowager Lady Swynford, looking
somewhat distraught.

"Oh, Miranda, my dear! Thank heavens you are here! Amanda
will not cooperate with Dr. Blake, and I fear for both her and the
child!"

Miranda went immediately into Amanda's bedroom. "So," she
said cheerfully, "the Swynford heir has finally decided to make an

appearance. Good afternoon, Doctor. Would you like to get a cup of tea while I sit with my twin?"

Dr. Blake looked at Lady Dunham with new respect. "Thank you, m'lady. I shall just be in the anteroom."

As the door closed after the doctor, Miranda looked at her sister. Amanda's golden curls were lank and lackluster. Her pretty face was drawn and frightened, and there were damp spots of perspiration showing through her long white nightgown. "What is the matter, Mandy? You have frightened Adrian's mama to death. This is not at all like you."

"I am going to die," whispered Amanda, turning terror-filled blue eyes on her sister.

"Fiddlesticks, twin! Did I have any great difficulty birthing Thomas? Of course not! Just the usual labor pangs. You were with me the entire time."

"I am like Mama. I know it! You know all the miscarriages she had."

"She had them early, between the second and third months, Mandy, not at full term. You may look like Mama, but you have been disgracefully healthy these whole nine months." Then Miranda gave a deep chuckle. "I received a letter from Mama just last week. She did not want me to tell you this until after you delivered the baby, but I think I had better tell you now if your own child is to be born safely. We have a new half-brother, Mandy."

"What?" The fear drained instantly from Amanda's face and she struggled to sit up. Miranda propped two large down pillows behind her sister's back. *"We have a half-brother?"* repeated Amanda. "How? When?"

"Yes! We have a half-brother. Peter Cornelius Van Notelman, born on March the twenty-second. As to how," giggled Miranda, "I imagine in much the same way as we became enceinte. Did you not tell me the day Mama married that you heard her and Uncle Pieter in their bedchamber? He is obviously quite the vigorous lover. Mama is ecstatic, and sounds as giddy as a young girl."

"She could have died, Miranda! My God, at her age!"

"Yes, perhaps she might have died, but she didn't, and neither will you! Our baby brother is a healthy, plump dumpling of a fellow with a prodigious appetite." Miranda saw the spasm cross her sister's face. "Bear down, Mandy."

For the next few hours Miranda sat chatting by her twin's bedside, and Amanda, her fear vanished, worked hard under her sister's gentle instruction. Finally Miranda summoned Dr. Blake, and within the next hour Amanda successfully bore her child. Joyously the older twin wiped the blood from the squalling infant, cleaned it in warmed oil, and swadled it carefully. All the while the baby howled its outrage at having been thrust from its warm home into a drafty and uncertain world. The bedroom door flew open, and both Adrian and his mother pushed in. Smiling, Miranda handed the squalling bundle to Adrian.

"M'lord, your son!" she said.

Adrian Swynford stared wide-eyed at the red-faced baby. "My son," he repeated softly. *"My son!"*

"Give me my grandson before you mash him," snapped the dowager as she snatched the infant from his father. "Now go thank Amanda for her travail, Adrian!"

Young Lord Swynford stumbled happily across the room to congratulate his wife on their miracle while his mother cradled and cooed at the baby. The head nursery maid arrived flushed with importance, and relieved the reluctant dowager of the child. Agatha Swynford put her arm through Miranda's, and the two women walked from the room.

"Bless you, my dear Miranda! I believe you saved my grandson's life as well as Amanda's. What happened to frighten her so, and how did you calm her fears?"

"For some reason," replied Miranda, "my sister began to see herself as our mama who suffered many miscarriages. I tried explaining to Mandy that just because she *looks* like Mama doesn't mean she *is* like Mama. That didn't help, so I told her the news that Mama sent me in the letter I received last week. Our mother, who was told she must never have another child, gave birth to a son on March twenty-second!"

"Bless my soul!" exclaimed the dowager, and then she chuckled. "Good for your mama, my dear, and good for you, too! You've a good head on your shoulders, my gel, and you're a quick thinker."

Miranda smiled sweetly. Soon they were going to have an excellent sample of her good head. "My sister will not be frightened by childbirth again, ma'am, and I'll wager she will soon feel foolish over her behavior."

Indeed, in the morning Amanda had returned to her even-tempered, sweet-natured self, and thanked her twin for helping to calm her fears the previous night. She was ecstatic over the birth of little Neddie, as Edward Alistair George was to be called. "He is not the least bit wrinkled and red," she enthused. "I'll vow he's the prettiest baby ever born!"

"Except my Thomas, of course," teased Miranda.

"Nonsense!" retorted Amanda. "Neddie is a perfect cherub with his golden curls, and those huge blue eyes. Oh, Miranda! Did you ever see such marvelous curls? I do believe we'll be able to christen him at two months rather than three. Your Tom has lovely coloring, but that straight black hair of his cannot possibly compare with Neddie's curls. My nephew looks like his Papa," she said somewhat smugly, "and Jared is so *American.*"

"So are you, my dear sister, just in case you've forgotten!" snapped Miranda, suddenly angry. "I do believe motherhood has addled your wits, Mandy. I shall leave you to dwell on your son's perfection." She stormed out of Amanda's bedroom, and headed for the nursery. There, to her mounting fury, she found the entire nursery staff clustered about the Swynford heir's lace-dropped bassinet.

"Jester!" she snapped sharply, and her young son's nurse turned. "You are paid to care for my child, not ogle my sister's baby." She picked Tom up, and her rage grew. "He is wet!" she accused, and thrust her now howling son at his nurse. "If this ever happens again I shall turn you out without a reference!"

"Oh, please, m'lady! I didn't neglect Master Thomas! I only just took a moment to look at the new baby." She began changing the baby.

"You have had your warning, Jester," said Miranda ominously. "If this happens again, you will be gone before the sun sets that same day. Remember, though my son must share a nursery with his cousin, it is Dunham money that pays you, not Swynford. My son is heir to a greater fortune and a far greater estate than is my nephew. Were it not for this silly war we should be home on Wyndsong now!"

"Yes, m'lady, it won't happen again," promised Jester, and she lifted little Tom up. "Do you want to hold him now, m'lady?"

Miranda took the baby from his nursemaid, and cradled him a moment. Tom's eyes were beginning to turn green. Looking carefully at his poker-straight black hair and the change in his eyes, she muttered, "You do look like your father, damn him!" The baby gave his mother a lopsided grin, and Miranda's heart contracted painfully. He reminded her so much of Jared. "Oh, my baby," she whispered softly so only he could hear. She kissed his silky little head. "I will bring your daddy home, I promise you!" Giving the child back to Jester, she shook a finger and warned, "Remember, my girl."

"Yes, m'lady." And clutching her charge, the nursemaid curtseyed.

"Wot's gotten into her?" demanded one of the two wet nurses once Miranda was gone.

"Don't know," murmured Jester. "I ain't never knowed her to be mean before. She ain't like the other swells. She's always been more considerate."

"Well, she had some bee in her bonnet today, that's for sure," came the reply.

Miranda stomped downstairs and out of the house. The day was warm and pleasant, and she soon found herself walking beyond the boundaries of the formal garden, past the Grecian temple summer house by the estate lake, and up the green hills. Her anger grew with every step she took. In a nearby tree a lark burst forth in joyous song, and Miranda had the urge to throw a stone at it. Everybody was so blasted happy! Everyone except her!

Jonathan had gone whistling off to London this morning to see Lord Palmerston. Jon was definitely happy. And then there was Adrian, her sweet-natured idiot brother-in-law. He seemed to believe he was the first man in the history of the world to have fathered a son. How many times had he come up to her this morning, wrung her poor hands until they were pulp, and said, "A son, Miranda! Amanda has given me a son!" The last time he did it she had wrenched her bruised fingers from his grasp, and snapped "A son, Adrian? I thought it was a basket of puppies!" The hurt look on his face had made her instantly contrite, of course, and she had excused herself. "I am tired, Adrian."

It was an easy lie, and one readily accepted by the susceptible Lord Swynford, who believed all women were delicate. The truth of the matter was that she was disgracefully healthy, having recovered from her childbirth in a fortnight. Her irritability stemmed from all the happiness about her. She ached for her husband, gone almost ten months now. There had been no word, for how could she explain letters from a husband who was supposedly with her? He didn't even know he'd had a son! She longed for him, for his voice, his touch, the passion he could rouse in her. She sighed. It had been so long!

"Lady!"

Miranda started and looked down at a small boy with a head full of dark curls, and curiously adult sharp black eyes. "Hey, lady, you want your fortune told?"

Within the nearby woods there was a gypsy encampment. There were many bright-colored wagons, and a number of fine-looking horses were tethered in the meadow. "Are you a seer?" she asked the boy, amused.

"Wot's a seer?"

"Someone who tells the future," she answered him.

"Ain't never heard it called that before, lady, but it ain't me who tells the future, it's me grandmother. She's the queen of our tribe, and famous for her predictions. It's only a penny, lady!" He tugged at her hand.

"A penny!?" She pretended to consider the offer carefully.

"Aw, come on, lady, you can spare it," he wheedled.

"How can you be so sure?"

"Yer dress! The fabric's the best quality muslin, the ribbons is real silk, and yer shoes the finest kid!"

Miranda burst out laughing. "What's your name, boy?"

"Charlie," he grinned at her.

"Well, Charlie, my gypsy lad, you're right! I can afford to have my fortune told, and I'd like it if your grandmother would tell mine."

If Miranda expected a sinister, toothless crone she was doomed to disappointment. Charlie's grandmother was a tiny, apple-cheeked woman wearing a full, bright-green skirt with several petticoats beneath, and a yellow blouse embroidered in multicolored threads. On her feet were red leather boots. There was a circle of daisies on her dark, graying curls, and a clay pipe was clenched in her teeth.

"Where you been, you scamp?" she scolded, "and who's this you've brought into camp?"

"Lady to 'ave her fortune told, Grandma."

"You can pay?"

Miranda drew a silver penny from her pocket and handed it to the old woman. The gypsy took the coin, bit it, and said, "Come into my wagon, m'lady." She clambered up the steps of her wagon and Miranda followed her into the cheerfully vulgar interior where plum silks rioted with scarlet, and violet, and mustard, and peacock blue ones. "Sit down, sit down, m'lady." The gypsy reached for Miranda's hand. "Let's 'ave a look now, dearie!"

She looked deeply at her customer for a moment. Miranda expected the usual nonsense about a mysterious stranger and good fortune. Instead, the old woman studied the slim white hand in her own gnarled brown one, and said, "Your home is not here in England, m'lady." It was a statement. Miranda said nothing. "I see water, much water, and in its midst a shining green land. That is where you belong, m'lady. Why have you left it? It will be a long while before you see that land again."

"You mean that the war will go on?" asked Miranda.

"It is you who determine your fate, m'lady. And for some reason you are bent upon your own destruction."

Miranda felt a chill creeping over her, yet she was fascinated. "My husband?" she said.

"You will be reunited, m'lady, never fear. You must be careful, however, for I see danger, great danger! I see in your hand a young golden god, a dark angel, and a dark devil. All three will bring you pain, of a sort, and you might escape them if you only will. It is up to you. I fear you have a stubborn nature that will not be bridled. Your survival will, in the end, be in your own hands. That is all I can see, m'lady." She dropped Miranda's hand.

"One more thing," begged Miranda. "My child?"

"He will be fine, m'lady. You need have no fears for your son."

"I did not say I had a son."

The old gypsy smiled. "Nevertheless," she repeated, *"he* will be fine."

Miranda left the gypsy encampment and walked slowly back toward the hall. If anything, she was even more restless now. In her mind there was but one thought: she had to get to Jared. If she could be with her husband then everything would be all right. She must have her beloved Jared, and nothing was going to stand in her way!

Jonathan arrived back at Swynford Hall several days later, looking as pleased as punch, and Miranda knew immediately that he had been successful in obtaining the special license. She asked him, "When will you wed?"

"We already have," he answered, surprising her greatly. "I had Anne meet me at a small village outside of Oxford two days ago. We were married at the church there, St. Edward's."

"Oh, dearest Jon. I wish you happy, you and Anne both! I truly do! Why, however, did you not wait so I might bridesmaid my new sister?"

"I was afraid of you being recognized, Miranda. When I was in London I bought a pigtail wig to wear so I might look like myself again. Believe me, I enjoyed being Jonathan Dunham again! No one seeing me with Anne would connect the pleasant American gentleman who wed the little English widow with that arrogant Anglo-American milord who is my brother. We were wed quickly and quietly, and Anne returned to Swynford Village the next day."

"You were right, Jon, it was best done that way." Then she chuckled mischievously. "How is our dear friend Lord Palmerston? I must send him a note commending his cooperation."

Jon laughed outright. "Henry's admiration of you is balanced by fury at your cheekiness. He is not used to being blackmailed by, as he so delicately put it, an upstart Yankee wench. Nevertheless he was most cooperative, and sympathetic of my position."

"Did he speak of Jared?" she asked anxiously.

Jonathan shook his head. "He would say nothing."

"Oh, Jon! What have they done with my husband? Why will Palmerston not even offer me a word of comfort? Since the day Jared rode off from Swynford Hall I have heard nothing! Not a word from his mightiness, the Secretary of War! Not a scrap of a note! Nothing! How much longer am I expected to carry on this way? Palmerston is inhuman!"

Jonathan put an arm around her. "Palmerston does not think in terms of you and Jared, of Anne and me. He thinks of England and all of Europe, of the destruction of Napoleon, who is his mortal enemy. What are the lives of four people in light of all that? Lord Palmerston frightens the Regent. He frightens all of his contemporaries. He is a maverick—a brilliant one, but a maverick nonetheless."

Adrian went off to Scotland at week's end. Jonathan bid Miranda a proper farewell, and slipped off to join his new bride. In a few days he would join Adrian in Scotland.

Miranda waited several days after the gentlemen had left before speaking to her twin about her own departure. Everything was arranged. The coach, driven by Martin, the undercoachman, had been brought up from London, and the day after its arrival Perky and Martin were married in the Swynford Village church.

"You are much too indulgent of your servants," scolded Amanda. "It is so American!"

"But I am American," retorted Miranda.

"American-born, living in England, and using your legitimate and rightful English title. When in Rome do as the Romans, my dearest. You would not wish to be censured for conduct unbecoming to a lady of the ton, Miranda."

"How quickly you have changed, little twin. You forget that you too are American."

"Yes, Miranda, I was American-born, and Wyndsong was a lovely place to grow up, but the truth is that I only spent eighteen years of my life there. I am married to an Englishman, and if I live to be as old as Mama I shall have spent most of my life here in England. I know nothing of the politics of governments; nor do I wish to know these things, for I should not understand them if I did. What I do know is that I am an Englishman's wife, and that I prefer living here in England for it's a gentle and civilized land. I am not brave and bold like you, dearest."

They were sitting in Amanda's sunny morning room, which was decorated in yellow and white, and furnished with lovely Queen Anne pieces done in Santo Domingo mahogany. Upon the fireplace mantel and on several tables were arrangements of apricot-colored roses and cream-colored stock in blue and white porcelain bowls. Miranda had been pacing the room. Now she sat down next to her sister on the yellow and white silk sofa.

"I do not know if I am brave, Mandy, but I will admit to a certain boldness. I am going to be bold once more. However, I will need your help, little twin."

"What do you mean, Miranda?" A wariness born of past experience crept into Amanda's cornflower-blue eyes. "Oh, dear, I thought you were over playing tricks."

"I am not going to play any tricks, sister, but I am going away, and I want you to understand why."

"Miranda!"

"Hush, Mandy, and hear me out. Do you remember the reason Jared and I came to Swynford last summer?"

"Yes, Jared had a mission and it could not be known he was out of England so you came here where no one would bother to visit."

"Jared never returned from Russia, Amanda. The man who has been here all these months masquerading as my husband is his older brother, Jonathan."

"No! No!" cried Amanda. "That cannot be!"

"Have I ever lied to you, little sister? Why would I lie about such a thing?"

"Wh-where *is* Jared?" quavered Amanda, stunned.

"To the best of my knowledge he is still in St. Petersburg."

"Don't you *know?*"

"Not really," came the reply. "You see, Mandy, Jared has not been allowed—for security reasons, of course—to write to me. I have not been allowed to communicate with him because, in the eyes of the world, he is here by my side, waiting out this silly war between England and America. Lord Palmerston refuses to give me any information. Do you know what he said to me the last time I saw him? 'When I know, madam, you will know'! He is an unfeeling beast!''

"Miranda!" Amanda's soft blue eyes were round with distress. "Oh, Miranda! You have been sleeping with a man not your husband!"

Miranda's hands clenched into little fists, and her nails dug into her palms. Taking a deep breath to still her irritation, she said, "Mandy dearest, there have been no improprieties between Jon and me. It is true we share the same bed, but there was always a rolled quilt between us, a makeshift bundling board if you will."

"How did Mr. Dunham get here?" questioned Amanda. "The American coast has been blockaded since last June."

"It was arranged by Mr. Adams' people and Lord Palmerston. When it became apparent that Jared would be forced to remain in Russia over the winter, Jon was sent for."

"But how did he explain it to his wife? He could hardly disappear for so long without offering her a reasonable explanation."

"Charity was drowned in a boating accident last summer. Jon left his children with his parents. They know the truth, but as far as the rest of Plymouth is concerned, Jon has gone off whaling to ease his grief."

"The poor man! How brave he is to have put his own grief aside to help his brother," cried Amanda feelingly. "When Jared returns and Jon may be himself again I shall introduce him to a number of fine young women, any of whom will make him a fine second wife."

Miranda giggled. "You are too late, Mandy. Jon wed again by special license several days ago, and who do you think his bride is? Mistress Anne Bowen! The real reason he delayed his fishing trip with Adrian was so that he might have a few days with her."

"Oh! Oh!" Amanda fell back against the soft cushions. "My vinaigrette, Miranda! Oh, I feel faint. This is too shocking! The gossips will have a field day!"

Miranda's patience snapped. "Amanda!" she said, and her voice had a sharp edge to it. "Amanda, stop this missish nonsense at once! I have only told you these things because I am going to St. Petersburg to find Jared, and I will need your help."

"Ohhh!" Amanda's eyes fluttered shut, but Miranda knew she hadn't really fainted, so she continued without a pause.

"I have been without my husband for ten months now, Mandy. He does not even know he has a child! I do not know if Jared is alive or dead, but I will not sit here in England playing Palmerston's game any longer. We are not English, and we owe no loyalties to England. I want my husband back and I intend to go get him!

"You must be responsible for my Tom, dearest, for I cannot possibly take him with me. You do understand that?"

Amanda's eyes flew open. "You can't do this, Miranda! You can't!"

"I can, Mandy, and I will."

"I shall most certainly not aid you in this folly!" Amanda sat up, her curls bouncing indignantly.

"I aided you, Mandy. If I had not gone against my husband's wishes last year you should not be Lady Swynford now, nor have your perfect little Neddie. If I had not aided you last spring, Amanda, I should be safe in my own home on Wyndsong Island with my husband and son, not caught in England, forced to accept your hospitality, *alone,* without Jared.

"I am taking *Dream Witch,* and going to St. Petersburg to find my husband, and you, little sister, are going to cooperate with me! How can you deny me my own happiness when I sacrificed so much to give you yours, Amanda?"

Amanda's firm resolution melted away in the face of her sister's potent argument. She bit her lip anxiously, then looked directly at Miranda. "What must I do?" she whispered.

"Not a great deal really, darling," soothed Miranda. "Your mother-in-law has gone back to her friend in Brighton for the summer, Adrian and Jon will not return from Scotland for at least a month. You will be perfectly safe here, and no one will ask you embarrassing questions. By the time the gentlemen return I shall be in St. Petersburg. You may tell them the truth. I am sure Jared will be ready to return by the time I get there. We will be back quickly and no one else will know. All I ask is that you look after my Tom while I fetch his father."

"You make it sound so simple," said Amanda.

"It *is* simple, Mandy!"

"You make it sound like you are running up to London to pick him up after a minor business trip," remarked Amanda irritably. "How long will it take you to get to St. Petersburg?"

"Probably two weeks, depending on the winds."

"Then you will be gone well over a month! Two weeks there, two weeks back, and however long it will take you to find Jared."

"Oh, I expect the English Ambassador will know where Jared is," said Miranda lightly.

"I have a premonition," said Amanda.

"*You?*" Miranda laughed. "You never have premonitions, dearest, I do."

"I don't want you to go, Miranda! Please! Please! Something is dangerous about this trip," pleaded Amanda.

"Fiddlesticks, twin! You are making a cake of yourself! It is a simple journey, and I shall succeed! I know I shall!"

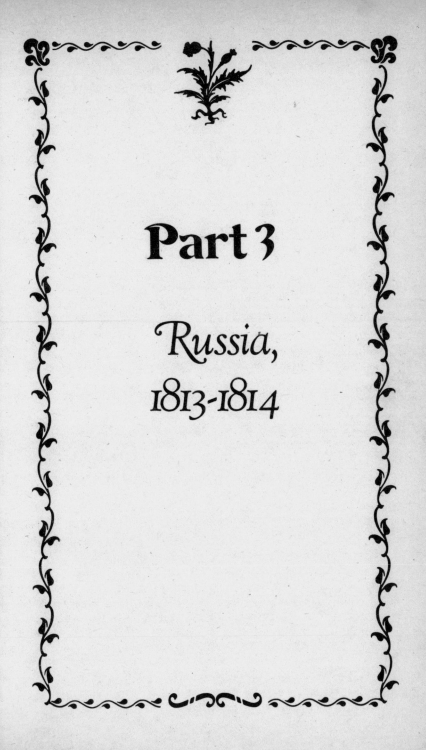

Part 3

Russia,
1813-1814

❧ Chapter 10 ❧

Captain Ephraim Snow looked down at his employer's wife from his six-foot-six-inch height. "Now Miz Dunham," he said slowly. "I ain't letting you go ashore until we find out where Jared is. These Russkies are tricky folk. I've dealt with 'em before."

"I'll send a message to the British Ambassador, Captain," said Miranda. "I expect he'll know where my husband is."

"Very good, ma'am. Willy! Where are you, boy?"

"Here, sir!" A young sailor ran up and saluted.

"Miz Dunham's going to have a note for you to take to the English Embassy in a few minutes. Stand by."

"Aye, sir."

Miranda returned to the salon of the yacht and scribbled a quick message asking for news of her husband. The simple, direct message was then taken to the embassy by young Willy, who was told to wait for a reply. Miranda did not intend being fobbed off by a wily diplomat. Her messenger returned within the hour with an invitation to take supper at the embassy. The ambassador's carriage would be sent for her at seven.

"Oh, Lord! I have nothing to wear," cried Miranda.

Ephraim Snow grinned. "Seems I've heard my Abbie make that same complaint many a time."

Miranda laughed. "In my case it's lamentably true. Not only have I traveled without a maid, I've also traveled without any evening clothes. After all, I didn't come to socialize, Eph. You know the city. Is there someplace I can obtain a decent evening gown and shoes?"

"Levi Bimberg's Emporium is the place, but I'll take you, Miz Dunham. Wouldn't be right for you to go unescorted."

A one-horse carriage was hailed and Miranda and Captain Snow climbed in. He gave directions in careful French, which all the drivers understood, and they headed toward the Nevski Prospeckt, the city's main avenue. Miranda was quite fascinated with St. Petersburg on this beautiful summer day. The boulevards were wide and tree-lined. There were vast green parks, and pretty flower-planted squares. Along the Neva River ran a lovely long promenade where even now in early afternoon well-dressed couples strolled leisurely.

"Why, it's beautiful!" cried Miranda. "St. Petersburg is as fair as Paris or London."

"Aye, it's just what the Tzar wants visitors to see," commented Captain Snow bitterly.

"Why, Eph, what do you mean?"

"It's clear, Miz Dunham, that you don't know much about Russia. There's basically two kinds of people here—the Tzar and his nobles, and the serfs. Serfs is like slaves. They ain't got no rights except what their masters give 'em. They exist for the sole convenience and pleasure of their masters, living in incredible poverty 'cause if one dies it don't matter much since there are so many left to take his place.

"Oh, there's a small middle class. This world just don't work without shopkeepers, and the few free farmers who feed 'em, but if you could see the congestion of the inner-city slums it would make yer blood run cold. They got shipyards here, big metalworks, and textile mills. They pay the workers a pittance, and those who don't live in the slums live in barracks near the factories, which ain't much better."

"That's terrible, Eph!"

"Makes you kinda glad to be an uncivilized American, don't it?" remarked the Yankee captain drily.

"I can't believe in any human being treating another badly. I detest slavery."

"Not all New Englanders feel that way, Miz Dunham. Plenty of 'em running slaves in from Africa to the Southern plantations." Miranda shuddered, and Ephraim Snow immediately felt guilty for having distressed her. "Hey now, ma'am, no need for you to worry about such things. Think about Jared, and how surprised he's gonna be to see you here. Think he'll be at the embassy tonight?"

"No. I'm not certain he's even in St. Petersburg now. I'm sure we would have heard from the embassy if he were."

"Probably. Look, ma'am, there's Levi Bimberg's Emporium now. If you don't find what you're looking for here, then it don't exist. This is one of the finest shops in the city. He has all the latest imports."

The carriage drew to a halt before a large shop as elegant as any Miranda had seen in London. Ephraim Snow stepped down and handed Miranda out. "Wait," he said to the driver, and escorted her into the emporium.

Miranda chose a gown of the finest gold Lyon silk, very, very sheer, and shot through with metallic threads. It was sprinkled with tiny silver stars, and the narrow ribbons that ran beneath the bustline were also silver. It fit as if it had been fashioned for her. She would wear it that evening.

She purchased two other gowns, one of deep rose-pink and silver stripes, and a lavender one tied with gold ribbons. She also bought silk undergarments and stockings, dainty kid slippers in gold and silver, matching ribbons and reticules, and a fringed cream-colored shawl. Miranda had never bought a ready-made gown before; but the shop's seamstress quickly saw to the minor alterations.

The ambassador's carriage was prompt, and Captain Snow escorted her down the gangway and safely into the coach. The gold gown shimmered in the evening sunshine, for St. Petersburg in summer saw only a very brief night. Although she had brought little clothing from England, she had brought her jewelry case, and about her neck was a magnificent necklace of amethysts set in pink gold, with matching oval earrings in her pierced ears. Seated, she smoothed her gown with her gold kid gloves. "I should not be late, Eph," she said as the carriage pulled slowly away.

Across the street from the boat basin, Prince Alexei Cherkessky stood in the upstairs window of an import-export house watching as the English ambassador's carriage drove past below him. "You are absolutely right, Sasha," he said. "The woman appears perfect for my purposes. But before I act I must find out who she is. Follow the ambassador's coach back to the embassy, and learn what you can."

"Yes, master!" replied Sasha. "I knew she would please you! Do I not always know what pleases you?"

"Um, yes," the prince murmured absently, his eyes following the coach. "Hurry along, Sasha!"

Sasha ran from the room, and the prince languidly descended the stairs to the main floor of the business house, staring curiously at the row of clerks high up at their desks, bent over their ledgers. The owner of the warehouse hurried forward eagerly. "I hope we have been of service, Gracious Highness."

"Yes," said the prince shortly as he departed the building and, without even glancing at the man, climbed into his carriage.

Sasha hurried down the Nevski Prospeckt, keeping the English coach in view as he went. He was an extremely pretty young man of medium height and slender build. His dark hair was curly, his face that of a naughty cupid, and he had eyes like black cherries. His clothing—an embroidered open-necked white shirt with wide sleeves, and full black pantaloons—were those of a peasant, but the fabrics were rich, and his boots were of the finest leather. About his neck was a thin jeweled gold collar.

The coach turned off the main avenue, and took several turns down side streets, finally passing through the open iron gate of a large four-storied brick house on the Neva River. Sasha stopped short of the gates, and watched as the carriage drew to a stop. The beautiful lady in the shimmering gold gown was handed from the coach and escorted up the steps and into the embassy.

Sasha watched as the vehicle moved around to the stableyard. Following it, he slipped onto the embassy grounds. "Hey, you!" the ambassador's coachman called to him.

"Good evening," replied Sasha in his best English. The only child of the late Princess Cherkessky's favorite maid, he had been educated with his master, the prince, and spoke several languages fluently. It was unusual treatment for even a privileged serf, but it had amused the princess to educate Sasha and the boy had acted as a spur to her son, who found the peasant boy as intelligent as he himself. Sasha's presence encouraged Prince Alexei to excel at his studies, for it was unthinkable that a mere serf might outdo him.

The coachman eyed Sasha suspiciously. "What do you want?" he demanded rudely. How he hated duty in Russia, but the ambassador paid extra for it.

Sasha smiled up at the burly servant. How he hated these arrogant foreigners. "The pretty lady you just brought here, who is she?" he asked politely.

"Who wants to know?"

"My master, the Prince." Sasha flipped a silver coin upwards. The coachman deftly caught it. In five minutes, Sasha had all the information the coachman possessed.

"Thanks, friend," he said, and walked briskly away from the embassy. Knowing St. Petersburg like the back of his hand, he took several shortcuts in order to reach the Cherkessky palace as quickly as possible. He entered the building through a side door, and hurried upstairs to his master's private apartments, where he found the prince on his bed dallying with his current mistress. Sasha didn't particularly care for the woman, a foreigner, but then he was always jealous of the prince's other lovers, male or female. This one was a particularly irritating bitch, a straw blonde with strange yellow amber eyes. She was wearing a diaphanous negligee, which, thought Sasha sourly, she might as well not have had on at all. The woman lounged against the prince, a smug smile on her lips.

"Well?" demanded Prince Cherkessky. "What have you found out for me?"

"Virtually nothing, Highness. The ambassador's coachman could tell me only the lady's name. He knew nothing more. He was told to fetch her from her yacht, and bring her to the embassy."

The prince's mistress sat up. "Are you considering replacing me, Alexei?" she said sharply.

"I wasn't, my dear," came the smooth reply, "but if you use that tone of voice with me again, I shall."

The woman's face reflected instant distress, and she wove her plump, white arms about his neck, pouting, "Oh, Alexei, I love you! The thought of losing you drives me to behave indiscreetly."

"Give me credit for being a gentleman, my dear. When I tire of you, I shall have the manners to tell you so."

"Then tell me why you have Sasha following women in the streets."

The prince smiled a wolfish smile, his even white teeth bright in his tanned face. He was an attractive man with an elegant figure, broad shoulders and chest, rapier-slim waist and hips, long legs. His straight black hair was cut short. His eyes were also dark and as expressionless as black agate marbles. His nose was classically flawless, his mouth thin, a trifle cruel. He unwound his mistress from his neck, and said, "There is no reason why you should not know, my dear. When Sasha was at Bimberg's Emporium today purchasing those scented kid gloves you set your greedy little heart on, he saw a woman of incredible beauty, the woman I have been seeking for several years now. I have seen the woman. She is just what I want!"

"Want, Alexei?"

"For the farm, my dear. I have long sought the perfect mate for one of my prize studs, Lucas. Lucas throws daughters, unlike his brother, Paulus, who throws sons. I have found Paulus several perfect mates over the past five years, and they have produced eighteen sons already—blond, beautiful little boys who will eventually sell for a fortune in the bazaars of the Mid and Far East. Although Lucas himself has several mates there are no women who look like him, and I have long wanted a woman with his coloring. I want to get a clutch of silver-blond daughters. The Turks will pay a fortune for such little girls, and I can sell them as young as five years old."

He looked back at Sasha. "Who is the woman?"

"All I could learn was her name, Gracious Highness. She is Lady Miranda Dunham."

"*What?!*" The prince's paramour sat up. "What did you say her name was?"

"Lady Miranda Dunham."

"Silver-blond, skinny, green-blue eyes?"

"Yes."

"Do you know this woman?" the prince demanded eagerly.

"Yes, I know the bitch," replied Gillian Abbott venomously. "Thanks to her I can never go home to England. I must wander the earth, an exile, dependent on bastards like you, Alexei. Yes, I know Miranda Dunham!"

Sasha watched as the prince put an arm around the woman. "Tell me, *douceka*," he murmured against her ear, his elegant hand creeping up to fondle one of Gillian's pendulous breasts. "Tell me."

But Gillian was not quite the gullible fool the prince believed. If she told him the whole truth he might be deterred from his purpose, and she would lose her chance for revenge. "Miranda Dunham," she murmured, "is an unimportant little American with no connections at all."

"Unimportant? She travels on her own yacht and has a title, my dear."

"Alexei, you don't understand! She is an *American*."

"Married to an English title."

"No! No! She was the daughter of Thomas Dunham, an American whose holdings were originally a royal grant. The family always kept its English ties, and are entitled to use their title in England. When Miranda Dunham's father died, the title and estate were inherited by a cousin, Jared Dunham. Miss Dunham's sister was shortly to marry and did. Their mother remarried. But unfortunately, Jared had been appointed his cousin's guardian. She tried to force him into marriage, but of course he would not be coerced so she became his mistress instead, and she has been utterly impossible ever since." Gillian congratulated herself on her quick thinking.

"Dare I ask how you know all this, Gillian?"

"I will not be coy with you, Alexei. I, too, was Jared Dunham's mistress at one time. The little chit replaced me in his bed. Jared is a ruthless man. Nevertheless I owe him a favor, for it was he who warned me I was to be arrested as a spy after Abbott's death. What greater favor can I do Jared Dunham than to help in the removal of this annoyance? If you want the girl for your slave-breeding farm in the Crimea, then take her. Lord Dunham will be mightily relieved if she disappears from his life. She has no right to use the title, Alexei. It is mere pretension on her part. As to the yacht, I imagine Lord Dunham allowed her to use it in order to get her out of his hair for a time. If she does not return he will not miss her, I assure you. And neither will anyone else."

"Not her mother or her sister, my dear? Surely they will raise a cry over her disappearance."

"They are both in America," Gillian lied smoothly.

The prince considered the situation thoughtfully.

"Do it tonight, Alexei! Who knows how long she will be in Petersburg," encouraged Gillian urgently. "Think how long you have sought a light-eyed silver blonde for your prize stud. The brats she spawns can make you a fortune!"

Sasha looked closely at his master's woman. He didn't like the eager tone in her voice, and her gaze was too bright. He couldn't help but wonder if she was telling the truth and he seriously suspected she wasn't. "My lord Prince," he said quietly in Russian, a language Gillian Abbott didn't understand, "I am not sure *she* is telling the truth. I know how very much you want the woman, but remember that the Tzar has warned you that if there is one more scandal over the farm, you'll be exiled to your estates."

The prince looked up, then patted the bed. "Come and sit, Sasha," he said. "Tell me your thoughts on this, my love. You have always sought only my best interests. You are the only person in the world I trust completely."

Sasha smiled, relieved, and sprawled himself on the bed next to his master. Propping himself up on his elbow, he continued, "Your mistress seeks revenge."

"She has made no secret of it," replied the prince.

"It is more than that, Highness. Her story is too pat. I do not believe a rich man would allow his mistress the use of his yacht when he is not with her. Now a wife might take her husband's yacht, but never a mistress."

"What husband in his right mind would allow such a beautiful wife to travel without him? Unescorted? Unchaperoned?"

"There are always extenuating circumstances, my Prince."

"I am sure you are right, dear Sasha, but I mean to have the woman, and there will be no scandal. I have the perfect plan. Listen, and tell me what you think. We will snatch the American woman, and of course her servants aboard the yacht will go to the police when she does not return. You, dearest Sasha, will escort her to the farm and oversee her breeding to Lucas. I want you to stay until she is safely delivered of her first child. You need have no fears that anyone will find her, for Lady Miranda Dunham will be assumed dead. The body of a blond woman," and here the prince leaned over and kissed Gillian lightly, "will be found floating in the Neva. She will be wearing Lady Dunham's clothes and some of her jewelry. After several days in the river it will be hard to tell who she really is, but the clothes and jewelry will lead them to think it is Lady Dunham. Well, Sasha, am I not clever?"

"Beloved Prince, I stand in awe of your subtle mind."

"Go back to the English coachman. He will have learned more by now that can aid us in capturing our quarry."

Sasha caught the prince's hand and kissed it. "I am overjoyed to obey you, my master," he said, rising from the bed and leaving the room quickly.

"What was all that gibberish you were gobbling with your toady," asked Gillian in her flawless French.

"Sasha doubts your veracity, my dear," replied the prince.

"The little worm is merely jealous," snapped Gillian. "Surely you don't believe him, Alexei?"

"I have reassured him, my dear," murmured Prince Cherkessky silkenly. "Now, kiss me."

At the British Embassy, Miranda was forced to play a waiting game. She arrived to find herself only one of many guests at a large dinner party where it was totally impossible to talk to the ambassador. Her dinner partner, however, was the ambassador's secretary, who assured her that the ambassador would grant her a private interview on the following day to discuss her husband.

"Only tell me," begged Miranda, "that he is alive."

"Good Lord, yes!" ejaculated the secretary. "Heavens, m'lady, were you in doubt?"

Miranda fought to keep her voice low. "Lord Palmerston would tell me *nothing.*"

"The damned idiot," muttered the ambassador's secretary, realizing what Lady Dunham had been going through for months. "Your pardon, m'lady," he added hastily.

"I have called Lord Palmerston far worse, Mr. Morgan," said Miranda, a twinkle in her eyes, and the secretary laughed.

Outside in the mauve Russian twilight, Sasha had returned to engage the ambassador's coachman in conversation.

"You back?" demanded the Englishman.

Sasha grinned engagingly. "My master gave me a beating for finding out so little about the lovely golden lady. He sent me back to learn more, or he says I can expect another beating."

The coachman nodded sympathetically. "Aye, they're all alike, these rich toffs. They wants what they wants, and don't take no for an answer like the rest of us has to. Well, lad, as it happens I do know more about the lady now. Heard it in the kitchen while I was eating me dinner. She's come to get her husband, who's been here in St. Petersburg on business. The ambassador's a friend of his, so he asked her to dinner. Lord Dunham, however, didn't know his wife was coming so he left the city a week ago for England. I'll bring her back here tomorrow afternoon for tea so the ambassador can tell her."

"Well, now that ought to satisfy my master," said Sasha. He dug into his pocket and produced another silver coin. "Thanks, my friend," he said, pressing the coin into the coachman's hand. Then he sauntered off.

Miranda had been extremely annoyed to find that she must wait for her news of Jared, but at least she now knew he was safe. There had been dancing after the dinner, and she did not find herself shy of partners. Most were members of the diplomatic community, paunchy, overstuffed gentlemen made bold and mellow by the ambassador's good wines. One man, however, stood out. He was Prince Mirza Eddin Khan, the son of a Turkish princess and a Georgian prince. The prince was an unofficial representative to the

Russian court from the Ottoman court, and as far as Miranda was concerned he was the only interesting man in the room that night.

The prince was extremely attractive, standing several inches over six feet. His wavy hair and the thick straight brush mustache above his sensual lips were a lustrous dark brown, his eyes a deep blue, his skin a warm peach tone. Being Moslem, he did not dance, and when Miranda had refused several gentlemen in an effort to catch her breath, he came to stand next to her. "You are far too pretty to frown so," he remarked in amused voice. "I have been led to believe that frowns lead to severe wrinkling."

She turned her face up to him, and at the sight of her marvelous sea-green eyes he felt his breath catch in his throat. "I am not a piece of fluff, Your Highness, but rather a blunt and outspoken American. I would not offend you, but please do not prattle to me like the other gentlemen. I suspect you are far more intelligent than that."

"I stand corrected, m'lady. If it is plain truth you prefer, then let me tell you that I think you are one of the most beautiful women I have ever seen."

"I thank you, Your Highness," she replied, refusing to lower her glance although the rose in her cheeks deepened. He was pleased to see her blush.

They talked of personal matters, finding confidences easy to exchange. At last the prince said, "I have never coveted another man's possession yet I envy your husband one thing."

"What is that?" she asked, genuinely curious.

His deep-blue eyes seemed to devour her, mesmerizing her with a warmth that engulfed her whole body. "I envy him you," Prince Mirza said, and then before she could recover from her surprise he caught her right hand up and pressed a kiss on its back. "Farewell, Lady Dunham." She watched in amazement as he disappeared across the crowded ballroom, his white silk trousers, Persian coat, and turban a vivid contrast to the other gentlemen's black evening attire.

It was then that she decided the time had come for her to return to *Dream Witch*. After all, she had an appointment here tomorrow and she wanted some rest. It was after eleven as the coach lumbered through the quiet streets of St. Petersburg, back to the boat basin. The Russian night was not at all dark. Miranda found twilight at such a late hour rather unnerving. Then, too, there was the memory of Prince Mirza Eddin Khan. She had never felt so attracted to a stranger before, and it distressed her. Why did this Eastern prince with his mysterious eyes fascinate her so?

The London fops who had sought her out had all been firmly rebuffed. Miranda had shocked all of polite society by being openly and passionately in love with her husband and quite unimpressed by other men. The London bucks had retaliated by nicknaming her the Frost Queen. To Mr. Brummel's delight, Miranda considered that a great compliment.

The next morning, after a restless sleep, Miranda went up on deck to enjoy the sun. To her surprise, a small closed coach with the British ambassador's crest on its side was drawing up before *Dream Witch*. On the box sat a handsome young man in Russian peasant's garb. Catching sight of her, he called, "Are you Lady Dunham?"

"Yes, I am," she answered.

"The ambassador's compliments, m'lady. He must change his appointment with you. If you could come now, please."

"Yes, of course," replied Miranda. "I must get my shawl and reticule and then I shall be with you." She quickly ran below to her cabin to fetch the required items, stopping in the main salon on her way out to tell Captain Snow of her departure.

"Good," replied Ephraim Snow. "I hope you find out everything today."

Miranda hurried down the gangway to the waiting carriage, where the driver stood holding the coach door open. He helped her inside, slammed the door behind her, and leaped up onto the box. He whipped the horses up and the vehicle lurched away. She was not alone in the coach. Opposite her sat an extremely elegant gentleman in a white and gold uniform.

"I am Lady Dunham," she said politely in her best French. "May I ask who you are, sir?"

"I am Prince Alexei Cherkessky," was the reply.

"Do you also have an appointment with the ambassador, Prince Cherkessky?"

"No, my dear, I do not," he said.

Miranda found to her shock that he was staring boldly at her. His gaze was quite unlike anything she'd ever experienced, and she did not like it. There seemed to be no life in his eyes. "If you do not have an appointment with the ambassador, then why are you in his coach?" she demanded.

"This is not the ambassador's coach, my dear, it is mine," he said evenly.

Miranda was suddenly aware that she was in terrible danger. "Prince Cherkessky, I must demand that you return me to my yacht at once!" she said in a firm tone that belied her thundering pulse and trembling knees.

The prince laughed. "Brava, my dear! Your spirit is quite commendable. You are indeed everything I had hoped for, and I have not been mistaken in my judgment of you."

"What is it you want of me, sir, and why have you resorted to subterfuge in order to get me into your carriage?"

Prince Cherkessky moved across the coach to seat himself next to her. "Actually I want nothing *personally* of you, my dear. You need have no fear of me. I don't intend to rape or murder you. I do, however, want you. I have long sought an exquisite woman with your silver-gilt hair." He took her chin in a firm grasp and looked intensely at her. "Your eyes are like emeralds, yet there is the tiniest hint of a blue flame in them. Perfect!"

Miranda yanked her head away. "You babble, sir!" she said sharply. "Why have you lured me into your coach? I demand an answer!"

"You demand?" said the prince. "Demand? I think, my dear, you had best understand your new place in life very quickly. You do not have the right to demand anything. You now have no rights at all. You are now my property. From the moment you stepped into my coach you became my property, but you needn't fear that I shall mistreat you. I am sending you to my slave-breeding farm in the Crimea where you will become the foremost mate of one of my two best stud slaves. I expect you to produce some beautiful children for me."

More angry than frightened, Miranda burst out, "Are you mad?! I am Lady Miranda Dunham, wife of Jared Dunham and Mistress of Wyndsong Manor! Do you know who I am? Return me at once to my

yacht! I shall make no mention of this, for surely you are drunk, sir."
She cried out with shock and pain as cruel fingers closed about her
wrist.

Pinioning her with one arm, the prince clapped a sweet-scented
cloth over her nose and mouth. Miranda struggled wildly, opening
her mouth to scream. But she was unable to scream because her
lungs were filled with the burning, sickening sweetness. The
prince's grip was unbreakable, and though she fought madly to
escape the engulfing blackness, it reached up with unrelenting
fingers and pulled her down into its dark whirlpool.

The coach picked up speed as it left the main part of the city and
entered the suburbs. Soon the prince's carriage entered a forest and
traveled a little-used road until it finally stopped before a small
house. Sasha carried the unconscious woman into the house. The
prince followed him, and stared with genuine pleasure at his victim,
now motionless on the bed.

"St. Basil!" he swore. "She's even lovelier than we could see
from a distance. Look at that coloring, Sasha! The rose in her
cheeks, the faint violet shadows above her eyes." He bent, gently
drew the pins from Miranda's hair, and pulled her pale-gold mane
down, fingering its texture. "Feel it, Sasha! It is like thistledown."

Sasha bent to take a handful of Miranda's hair between his fingers,
marveling at its softness. "She is a true aristocrat, master. What did
she say when you told her her fate?"

Prince Cherkessky shrugged. "Some nonsense about being the
wife of Jared Dunham. It matters not."

Sasha looked troubled. "Beloved Highness," he said, "I think I
would believe her. Look at her! She is an angel, and your mistress is
the Devil's daughter herself. I think the Lady Gillian revenges herself
on Lord Dunham for having married this beauty rather than her. Let
us return the lady to her people. It can be done discreetly."

"*No!* Dammit, Sasha. I have sought a woman like this for three
years now, and she is more perfect than I dared to hope! I will not
return her. I am denying even myself the pleasure of her body in
order to breed her with Lucas as quickly as possible. Here now, help
me undress her. I will need her clothes to take back with me."

Together the two men stripped off Miranda's fashionable green-and-white-striped muslin morning gown, her petticoat, vest, and lace-trimmed drawers. The prince removed her black slippers while Sasha rolled off her white silk stockings. For a moment they stared at their nude victim, and Sasha said softly, "How very beautiful she is. Look how fine her bone structure is, master. Though her legs are long they are perfectly proportioned."

The prince reached out and cupped one of Miranda's breasts, sighing, "Oh, how I deny myself, Sasha! You know that I always sample the merchandise for the farm, but I must not contaminate this particular slave's womb with my dark seed."

"You are a good master," murmured Sasha, falling lightly on his knees, putting his arms about the prince and nuzzling at his distended groin. "Give me your permission, oh beloved Highness," he begged. "Let Sasha please you. Was I not born and raised to do so? Have I not always been your one true love?"

Prince Alexei Cherkessky gently stroked the dark curly head. "You have permission, my darling Sasha," he murmured as he abandoned himself to the sweet pleasure his serf always gave him. Several minutes later, the sexual tension gone from his body, he was all business again. They dressed Miranda in the skirt, petticoats, blouse, and felt boots of a well-cared-for serf. Silently Sasha braided her long hair, tying the ends with bits of colored wool. Then they carried her back outside and settled her in the coach. The prince caught a glimpse of gold on Miranda's hand, and swore lightly. "St. Basil! Her jewelry! I almost forgot." He pulled the rings from her fingers, and the earrings from her ears. "Anything else?" he questioned Sasha.

"There was a cameo pin on her gown, but that's all," came the reply.

"Get some water from the well, Sasha," commanded the prince. "If we are going to keep your passenger quiet it is time we administered the first dose of tincture of opium. She is beginning to stir." The prince mixed the water and the brownish tincture in a small silver cup. Then the two men climbed into the coach, and while Sasha helped the barely conscious Miranda to a half-sitting position the prince carefully forced the liquid down her throat. She gulped the cold liquid eagerly, soothing her throat. Her brain was fuzzy, and before she could piece things together she was sinking back into the comforting darkness.

Down the narrow forest road came an elegant phaeton. "Good!" said the prince. "Boris Ivanovich is right on time. Now listen to me, Sasha. I want you to drive straight through to the Crimea without any layovers. Do whatever you have to do to relieve yourself, eat while the horses are being changed. I want her on the farm within two weeks. Rest her up a few days after you arrive, and then breed her. Remember, the longer it takes, the longer we will be separated, my dearest Sasha."

"Must I stay until she delivers a child? Can I not come back while she is pregnant as long as I'm back for her confinement."

"No," said the prince firmly. "I do not want to take any chances with her. She is much too valuable a slave, Sasha. Keep her in the house with you, for I don't want her in the quarters with the other women. She is not like them, and those damned peasant sows could hurt her. Give her whatever she wants—within reason—to keep her happy."

Sasha gazed lovingly at his prince, then catching his master's hands up he covered them with kisses. "We have never before been separated, my beloved master. Each day away from you shall be an eternity."

"You are the only one I can trust to do this for me, dearest Sasha," said the prince.

Sasha kissed the prince's hands once more and then climbed out and carried Miranda into the other coach. It began moving as soon as he had closed the door.

Prince Alexei Cherkessky drove himself back to his palace in the city, where Gillian was waiting for him.

"Where have you been?" she pouted. As usual she was wearing a sheer silk gown that left nothing to the imagination.

In answer he pulled her into her arms and kissed her, his cruel mouth forcing hers open. Quickly inflamed, she responded ardently, pressing her voluptuous body against him, taking pleasure from the pain the gold buttons of his uniform inflicted on her soft flesh, from the pain his hands inflicted as they crushed her buttocks. He pushed her onto a settee and, kneeling before her, sought the sweetness between her open legs, his knowledgeable tongue wreaking havoc, biting at her little love button until she screamed with delight. Then as swiftly as he had begun his attack he stopped, standing up and straightening his tunic.

For a moment she lay panting with disbelief, then she swore at him, "You bastard! Don't leave me hanging!"

He laughed cruelly. "Tonight, *douceka*. I'm saving myself for tonight. I have a special treat for you, one you've never experienced, and will never, I promise you, experience again. You can finish yourself now. Go ahead. I like watching you when you do it to yourself."

"Rotten bastard!" she snarled, but her fingers were already busily working her aching flesh. It was never the same as with a real man, but she had to do something or explode with the longing.

Prince Cherkessky lit a thin black cheroot, and sat back to watch his mistress as she writhed before him. She was probably the most insatiable female he'd ever met. She would do anything he wanted, and always with gusto. He would miss that, but she was too dangerous to keep around any longer. He knew she hoped to blackmail him into marriage, but he had no intention of making a highbred English whore who spied for Napoleon against her own country the next Princess Cheressky. That honor was being reserved for a young cousin of the Tzar's, Princess Tatiana Romanova, and unknown to everyone in St. Petersburg society except his future in-laws, the engagement would be announced next month on Tatiania's seventeenth birthday, the wedding to take place the following month.

Of course, he had to tie up some loose ends. Sasha was one, but he was safely on his way to the farm. Eventually, thought the prince, I will write him about Tatiania, but I cannot allow him to come back until she has given me several children. Sasha may be the only person I truly care for, but he cannot give me children to insure the continuation of my family.

A moan from Gillian penetrated his thoughts, and he focused his glance on her again, watching her face with interest as she climaxed. "Very nice, my dear!" he said. "Now I shall reward you by telling you where I have been today. I arranged for your former rival to travel south with Sasha. They are already well on their way."

"Alexei!" Gillian flung herself into her arms. "Oh, I do adore you!"

He smiled thinly. "I am pleased to make you so happy so easily," the prince said. "Go and bathe yourself in preparation for our evening together, my dear."

Gillian scrambled to her feet and hurried to her own rooms. She wondered what wonderful surprise he had in store for her. Would it be the sapphire necklace and earrings she had admired last week at the jeweler's? It was too soon for a marriage proposal. Now that they shared the secret of Miranda Dunham, however, he would marry her to keep her silent. It was only logical, and in the event that it did not occur to him, she would suggest it. He was not a stupid man. He would see the advantage of her being his wife.

In his own apartments the prince prepared, ordering iced champagne and fine black caviar. He bathed, and then surprised his servants by giving them the evening off. By nine o'clock all was in readiness. The draperies were drawn and his bedchamber was lit by shimmering candlelight.

Gillian's hair had been red and short in London. In St. Petersburg it was long, wavy, and blond, an effective disguise. Tonight she wore it loose, and she was totally nude except for a necklace of diamonds and pink satin slippers. The prince wore only a silk robe.

Gillian's color was high. She had spent her few hours away from the prince dwelling on Miranda's fate. Having drunk two glasses of champagne, she grew bold. "Tell me what it will be like for her, Alexei?" she begged him.

"Who?"

"Miranda Dunham. What will it be like for her on your farm?"

"I am sorry to disappoint you, my dear, but it should be quite comfortable for her. Do not your English horsebreeders take especial care of their prize brood mares? Well, I too take excellent care of my breeding stock."

"What if she refuses to cooperate," urged Gillian. "What if she fights your attempts to mate her with Lucas? A woman can fight, you know."

"If she will not cooperate, Gillian, she will be forced."

How?"

"She will be tied down so Lucas may complete his duties," said the prince drily. "Does it please you to know that, Gillian?"

"Yes," she breathed huskily. "Oh, God, how I wish Jared Dunham could know her fate! Know that another man is using what he considered his!"

The prince's eyes narrowed. So, Sasha had been right after all. Not that it mattered. The silver-blond beauty was on her way to the farm. Stupid Gillian didn't even realize that, in her eagerness for revenge, she had exposed her lie about Miranda not being married. "Let us not dwell on the functions of serfs, my dear," he said. "There are far more pleasant ways in which we may amuse ourselves." Removing his silk dressing gown, he then removed her necklace and took her hand to lead her toward his bed. "I was cruel to you this afternoon, *douceka,* but tonight I promise to give you your heart's desire."

Gillian's heart skipped a beat. Had she misjudged him? Was he going to propose tonight, after all?

The prince pulled her to him. "Ah, *douceka,* what pleasure you give me," he said, tracing the line of her jaw with his supple fingers. She shivered with delight, and his slanted eyes narrowed. They fell back together on the bed, Gillian atop the prince, and his strong arms lifted her slightly to seat her on his already strong lance. She squealed with pleasure and wiggled her plump bottom provocatively on his thighs. His hands reached out to play with her breasts, rolling the cherrylike nipples between his thumb and forefinger.

"What a sensuous little cossack you are, my dear," he said as she rode him. "But you are too anxious for your pleasures. Tonight you will have to wait a bit." He lifted her off him.

"No!" she protested. "Damn you, Alexei, I can climax a hundred times for you, and I want to!"

"No, no, *douceka,*" he scolded. "This night we will come close several times, but I will allow you only one pleasure. However, it will be greater than any you've ever known or will know again. I promise you perfection, my dear."

He turned her over onto her stomach and, without her seeing it, reached for the riding crop he had placed conveniently near the bed. Seating himself on her shoulders facing her feet, he applied the crop viciously to her bottom. Gillian screamed and tried to buck him off, but she could not, and he did not stop beating her until her buttocks were a mass of dark pink weals. Then as she lay weeping and helpless he entered her as he would one of his male lovers, using her skillfully until her sobs of pain began to turn into moans of an entirely different nature. When she was quite close to fulfillment, he withdrew from her and rolled her onto her back. Pulling her legs over his shoulders, he buried his face in her, tonguing her with marvelous deftness, then withdrawing with incredible instinct only a moment before she slipped over the edge.

She cursed him again and again, using every foul word she could think of in at least three languages, and he laughed delightedly. Finally Alexei Cherkessky believed his mistress ready for the final pleasure. She was whimpering and clawing at his groin now, so he murmured "All right, *douceka*, I'll fuck you now," and pushed his swollen organ into her. She sighed as he entered her, thrusting her fevered body upward to meet him. He smiled down at the look of pure pleasure on her face; her eyes were closed, the lids trembling.

Expertly he drove her toward a perfect orgasm, his slim hips thrusting downward in rhythm with her movements. His hands slipped around her white throat with its madly jumping pulse, and he began to speak softly to her. "I am granting you your greatest desire, Gillian, *ma douceka*. I have allowed you your revenge on Lord Dunham for preferring his exquisite Miranda to you." The prince's fingers began to tighten about Gillian's neck. "Lord Dunham, will, I fear, seek her unless there is nothing to seek. You wanted to be Lady Dunham in life, Gillian, but that was not to be. You shall, however, be Lady Dunham in death."

Gillian's eyes flew open as sudden sickening realization of his intent penetrated her mind. Her hands flew to his in an effort to release his hold. She opened her mouth, desperately seeking air, trying to scream, but his grip was relentless. Gillian knew she was going to die. His hands began to squeeze the life from her at the very moment she began to experience the greatest climax she ever had known. Survival struggled with sensual pleasure, and she found her strength to fight him gone as her eyes closed.

"They will find your body in the Neva, *douceka,* dressed in Lady Dunham's clothes and jewelry. You will be identified as her, and buried in her grave, with her name on your tombstone. Have you no thanks for me, *douceka?"*

Gillian Abbott's body shuddered in a combination of orgasm and death throes, and then she was still. Prince Alexei continued to fuck her until he attained his own pleasure a few moments later. Then he withdrew from her and rose from the bed to wash himself in his dressing room. He drank down a full glass of champagne to steady his nerves. He was shaken from what he considered the most exhilarating experience he had ever had.

He felt he had been more magnificent than he had dared to hope, her orgasm and her death all tangled into one mass of passion. He sighed sadly, realizing it was not likely to happen again. No woman he'd ever known had been as primitively sexual as Gillian. She was unique, and he would miss her. But nothing must endanger his marriage to the Tzar's young cousin. Slowly he dressed himself, and then he dressed Gillian's fast-cooling body in Miranda Dunham's clothing. He could not fit the vest over Gillian's overgenerous breasts so he discarded it. The drawers were skintight, for Gillian had a plumper bottom than Miranda, but he managed to squeeze her into them. He solved the problem of a too-tight dress bodice by ripping the front of the gown to make it look as if the cameo brooch had been torn off by thieves. After fastening the garters about her legs to hold up the white stockings he discarded the black slippers, for Gillian's feet could not fit Miranda's slender shoes. Lastly the prince jammed the wedding ring onto his dead paramour's finger and, picking up her lifeless body, he carried her from his apartments downstairs and out onto the palace terrace, which faced the river Neva.

The palace was quite deserted. No one saw him. At the terrace edge he paused to lift Gillian over the balustrade, and then he lowered her body by her own arms down into the river where the current quickly caught at it and sucked it away. Alexei Cherkessky watched with great satisfaction. Everything had gone as perfectly as he had planned it. In the morning he would have Marya, his old nurse, clear Gillian's apartment out. There would be no need for an explanation. Mistresses came and went. Well-trained serfs did not ask questions, and his serfs were as well trained as physical violence and pure fear could make them.

Reaching into his tunic, he drew out a thin black cheroot, and lit it from one of the garden lanterns. Then, slowly inhaling the rich tobacco smoke, he wiped Gillian Abbott from his brain, and began to contemplate Princess Tatiana Romanova, his innocent bride-to-be. He held no hope that a well-brought-up seventeen-year-old virgin would be as interesting as Gillian. Still, if she were not prejudiced against bedsport and was an apt pupil, he could school her, and they would get on quite well. All in all, it was an encouraging thought.

❧ Chapter 11 ❧

Jared Dunham galloped up the drive of Swynford Hall, his heart hammering a joyous refrain: *Miranda! Miranda! Miranda!* The green English countryside looked marvelous to him after his stay in gray-brown Russia. Eleven months! He'd been gone almost a full year! What had ever possessed him to take on the mission? What had ever possessed him to leave Miranda?

A stableboy ran out to take his horse as he arrived at the front entrance to the hall, and a footman hurried down the building's steps to greet him.

"We thought you were still in Scotland, m'lord," he said. "We weren't expecting you till next week."

"Where is Lady Dunham?" Jared asked.

A strange look passed briefly over the footman's face, but before he could answer, Amanda and a lovely young woman with copper-colored hair appeared and hurried to his side. "Thank you, William," Amanda dismissed the servant, then turned to her companion. "Which one of them is it?" she asked.

There was not a moment's hesitation. "It is Lord Dunham, Amanda, not Jon."

"Jared! Oh thank God! You have Miranda with you?"

Jared thought he'd entered a madhouse. "What do you mean, Amanda? I do not understand you."

"My lord," said the other young woman, "I think it would be best to go into the house. Mandy dear, come along. I believe the library will do nicely."

Once in the library, Jared roared at his pretty sister-in-law, "What the hell do you mean, do I have Miranda with me? Where is my wife?!" Amanda burst into tears, and Jared swore angrily. "Dammit, kitten, this is not the time for weeping! I want an explanation!" But Mandy only wept harder. Defeated, Jared turned to the other woman. "Madam?"

"I am Anne Bowen Dunham, m'lord, your new sister-in-law."

"What!?"

"Please sit down, m'lord. I'm afraid my explanation is lengthy. Would you like a sherry perhaps?"

Jared looked at her shrewdly. "I have a feeling, Mistress Anne, that I'm going to need something stronger. A whiskey, I think."

Anne moved serenely to the table where all the decanters and glasses were set up. Carefully choosing a short cut-crystal tumbler, she poured a generous dollop of smoky Scots whisky into it and handed it to him. Amanda was sniffling on a nearby settee.

He took a deep swallow of the whiskey, and looked levelly at Anne. "Mistress?" he said.

"Were you aware, m'lord, that Lord Palmerston brought your brother Jonathan to England late last autumn to impersonate you?" Jared strongly nodded his head, and Anne continued. "Lord Palmerston felt that your absence should not be a public fact, and as your sister-in-law Charity had been lost in a boating accident, Jon was free and willing to come, and masquerade as you all last winter."

"Did my wife know?" asked Jared.

"Of course. It was very hard for her, m'lord. She loves you terribly, you know. Being alone during her confinement was especially difficult for her." His face registered complete amazement at these words. "M'lord!" Anne caught at his hands. "Oh, heavens! Did you not know that, either?" He shook his head weakly.

"M'lord," she said softly, "you are a father. Your son was born on April thirtieth. He's a lovely, healthy little lad."

"What is his name?" Jared asked.

"Thomas," she said.

Jared nodded. "Yes, I would have agreed to that," he said, and she hid a smile. "Where *is* Miranda, Mistress Anne?"

"She went to St. Petersburg to fetch you, sir."

"What?"

"Hear me out, please," said Anne, and then she continued. "Your brother and I met, and fell in love. Miranda arranged for us to wed in secret. She wanted us happy, bless her. But she herself was wretchedly unhappy, far more unhappy than anyone knew. Or so I believe."

"It's true, Jared!" broke in Amanda. "She begged Lord Palmerston for word of you, but he would tell her nothing. He kept saying, 'When I hear, madam, you'll hear.' You know that icy, awful tone of voice he uses when he doesn't want to be bothered. If he'd only taken the time to reassure her, Jared! Where *were* you that it took you so long to return?"

"I was in prison, kitten. Had I not been I would have returned months ago."

"Prison? Why on earth were you in prison? Who put you there?" gasped Amanda.

"The Tzar, kitten, but don't fret. I was treated quite well. I was confined within the Fortress of St. Peter and St. Paul, and lived in a comfortable two-room apartment with a fine view of the Neva River. My valet, Mitchum, was with me, and other than the lack of freedom we were quite comfortable."

"But why?" Amanda demanded again.

"When Napoleon took Moscow, the Tzar became frightened. He was fearful of many things—that the French would continue on to St. Petersburg, that the Emperor would discover Alexander was contemplating an alliance against the French. I believe the shock of Moscow's fall drove him to panic. He ordered me imprisoned in the Fortress of St. Peter and St. Paul, but I was not to be mistreated. I was to be given comfortable rooms above ground. I was to have my servant with me, and food, wine, and a fire, as well as any small comforts such as books and a chess set. Since only a few people at the British Embassy even knew I was in St. Petersburg my disappearance from the scene was no problem. The ambassador, of course, did what he could, but he could do little as he himself was in a tenuous position."

"Did Lord Palmerston know?" asked Amanda.

"Of course," came the reply.

"Then why didn't he tell Miranda?"

"He probably felt he might endanger her health, and the baby's."

"Then why didn't he say something after little Tom was born?"

Jared shook his head. "I don't know, Amanda. I simply don't know."

"Well I do!" replied Amanda, now recovered and warming to her subject. "Lord Palmerston believes he is a law unto himself! Your mission had been sidetracked, and he no longer wished to be reminded of it. Then, too, he holds that most women are of little other than decorative use. Considering his admiration of the dowager Lady Melbourne, and his close association with her daughter, Lady Cowper, I am surprised he did not see Miranda's intelligence and confide in her.

"His attitude drove Miranda to desperation. If he had offered her one crumb of hope, one word of encouragement, she would have never left little Tom and gone sailing off to St. Petersburg to find you. This is all his fault!" Once more she burst into tears.

Anne rose quickly and put a comforting arm around Amanda. "Mandy, you cannot give way like this. I am distressed to see you so. Go to the nursery and have the children made ready to see Lord Dunham. I shall finish explaining to him." She helped Amanda to the door, gently shoving her from the room. Turning back to face Jared, she was disconcerted to see him watching her with a look akin to amusement. "Do you find something funny, m'lord?" she asked more sharply than she had intended.

"You, my pretty English rose! I wonder if brother Jon is fully aware of the treasure he has."

She colored becomingly. "Fie, sir, I see that your reputation is well earned."

He laughed, "I am going to call you Anne, and you are going to call me Jared." Suddenly he stiffened and said, *"What children?* You said *children."*

"Amanda became a mama just a bit over a month and a half ago. Your Tom has a cousin, Edward, or Neddie as he's called."

Jared nodded, dazed. "Why did I go to Scotland?"

"A fishing party on Lord Stewart's estate."

"Good Lord, Jon hates to fish! He hasn't the patience. Says there is something demeaning in having an air of pride over outwitting a fish."

Anne laughed. "Yes, he is ever practical, my Jon. By the way, m'lord—Jared—since he is you, in public I am still Mistress Bowen. Only Amanda knows our secret, no one else. Not Lord Swynford, not the servants, nor even my own two children. In his role as Jared, Jon pretended to be called away by Lord Palmerston so that we might have a brief honeymoon. Then he went on up to Scotland to join the others."

"When are they due back? I seem to recall the footman who greeted me saying something about next week."

"Yes, midweek," replied Anne.

"No need to send a messenger then. They'll be back just as quickly. Perhaps, however, I might meet them before they get here. Be easier to exchange identities away from Swynford. I assume you and my brother are then going to meet publicly, fall in love, and elope."

"It seems the simplest way," admitted Anne.

He smiled, "Does anyone know by which roads they're traveling?"

"Amanda would know, but I am quite sure they'll be staying at the Brindled Cow in Shrewsbury the night before they get home."

"Then Jon and I will switch identities in Shrewsbury," said Jared. "Tell me, how did my wife travel to St. Petersburg?"

"You need have no fear, Jared. Miranda traveled on *Dream Witch.*"

"Good! My captain's a sensible man who'll take good care of her. She'll get to St. Petersburg, find out I've returned home, and come back to England."

"How did you get home?" queried Anne.

Jared grinned. "Well," he said, "as you've undoubtedly heard, Napoleon's retreat from Moscow was a disaster. He kept waiting there for Alexander to offer him terms of surrender, and Alexander kept waiting in St. Petersburg for Napoleon to go away. The French, of course, delayed too long and got themselves caught in a particularly bad Russian winter. Not the most ideal conditions for a retreat. Still, the Tzar worried that the French might return. It wasn't until this past June that he was convinced that he and St. Petersburg were safe. It was then that I was finally released. As compensation for my incarceration I was sent along with two shiploads of the finest Baltic timber and timbermasts. One ship was to go to my father's yards in Plymouth, the other was to be a gift to Lord Palmerston. The English Ambassador in St. Petersburg, however, let slip how badly things were between the United States and England, so I had the ship originally bound for England drop me off on the English coast near Welland Beach, and then I sent it along with its sister across the Atlantic to Massachusetts. I feel Lord Palmerston owes me that gift of wood, and now that I hear how badly he handled Miranda's anxieties I feel entirely justified."

Anne nodded. "You can be proud of her, Jared. She has been very brave, but it was finally just too much for her. As I am now your brother's wife, I cannot say I blame her. You Dunhams have a way of binding your ladies to you." She stood up. "I think, sir, that it might be a good time to see your son."

"I have not kissed the bride yet," he said as he rose, towering over her. Anne froze, but Jared bent and gently brushed her mouth with his. "Welcome to the family, Anne," he said. "I suspect you are going to be a valuable asset."

"Th-thank you," she stammered. She felt very foolish, but he did look so much like Jon.

Jared chuckled. "I wonder," he remarked mischievously, "if Miranda had the same problem."

Anne had to laugh. "What a villain you are, Jared Dunham! I suspect you are a naughty little boy at heart. Come along now to the nursery and see Master Thomas."

He steeled himself. He had to remember that the nursery staff would be present, and as far as they were concerned Lord Dunham had seen his son a hundred times. But Amanda, recovered from her emotions, had thoughtfully dismissed the staff and was alone with the two babies. She held up a tiny blond and blue-eyed cherub with a fat face whose rosebud mouth was now blowing bubbles. "This is my Neddie, Jared. Is he not perfection?"

Anne laughed softly. Dear, sometimes silly Amanda. Hurrying across the room to a lace-draped cradle, she tenderly lifted out another child. "Here is your son, Jared," she said.

He came slowly across the nursery, his eyes rapt on the baby. Wordlessly he took the boy from her, and his eyes devoured the child, the thistle-soft black hair, the eyes that he could see were going to be green. The infant had Miranda's rose and cream coloring, but otherwise it was like looking in a mirror. "Hello, young Tom," he said softly. "I am your papa, and I must say on first sight you seem to be everything I would want in a son." The baby stared unsmiling at his father. Recognizing the expression as his own, Jared grinned delightedly and extended a finger, which the baby eagerly grasped. "He's certainly a big strong fellow compared to Amanda's boy," remarked Jared.

"He is two months older," replied Anne. "Your Tom is three and a half months old; Neddie is but six weeks. Still, I believe this young gentleman is going to be every bit as big as his papa."

"Do you know what this is like for me?" Jared said softly. "I never even knew she was with child. I have lost almost a year of my married life, and for what? I will never know the joy other men experience upon learning that they are to be fathers for the first time. I have never seen her full with my child. I have thrown these pleasures wantonly aside to play at a game of war." He cradled the child in the crook of his arm. "Ah, my son, I ask your pardon. Now if I may ask it of your mother, perhaps I will be able to redeem myself somewhat."

Anne put a comforting hand on her brother-in-law's arm. "You have not played at war," she said gently. "You have but attempted to make peace, and I was always taught, Jared, that blessed are the peacemakers."

He handed her the baby, and said intensely, "If my brother doesn't treat you like the queen you are, I shall personally throttle him." Then he stomped from the room.

"Gracious," said Anne, somewhat taken aback, "what a fierce man he is."

Amanda looked up from tucking Neddie back into his cradle. "They are both like that," she said, "and when you see Miranda and Jared together there is something about them—an aura . . . a power— as if together they could do anything."

"And apart?" asked Anne.

Amanda sighed. "Together," she said, "they can be dangerous, but apart they tend to be destructive, and that destruction is usually directed toward themselves. They become ingrown, and secretive. I only hope Miranda hurries back from St. Petersburg."

Jared fussed restlessly about Swynford Hall for the next few days, riding recklessly about the estate on a big black stallion that Adrian had bought for stud, visiting Anne and her children at their cottage, playing with his baby son. Finally word of Jonathan and Adrian came early one afternoon. He packed some of Jonathan's distinctly American clothes in a saddlebag and rode off to the Brindled Cow in Shrewsbury. The trip took him several hours, and when he finally arrived in early evening he was pleased to see that the inn was a well-run prosperous-looking establishment. The rambling two-story half-timbered building probably dated back to the Elizabethan period, Jared thought, noting the charming diamond-paned casement windows with their red window boxes full of bright summer flowers. In fact there were flowers everywhere about the Brindled Cow, and there was a garden scented with lemon verbena and sweet lavender.

As he rode into the inn yard a stableboy hurried up to take the horse. "Staying the night, sir?"

Jared nodded and flipped the boy a silver penny. "His name is Ebony, and he's a bit high-strung, but a good fellow and not at all vicious. Walk him well before you water him, lad."

"Yes, sir!"

"Has Lord Swynford arrived yet?"

"Yes, sir; 'bout an hour ago."

Jared hurried into the inn and was shown to a private room. He instructed the landlord to show Jonathan and Adrian to the room when they came downstairs to dine. Soon the door opened, and Adrian and Jonathan entered the room, chatting amiably. They stopped short, and then Adrian said, "I beg your pardon, sir, but this room is already taken. There must be some mistake."

"No mistake," replied Jared, turning to face the two men. "Hello, brother Jonathan."

"Jared!" Jonathan's face registered surprise and delight. "God, man! It's good to see you! Thank heavens you're safely home."

"Yes, I understand your joy quite well, Jon," remarked Jared wryly. "I have met Mistress Anne. She is, of course, far better than you deserve."

The two men hugged warmly while Adrian Swynford glanced from one to the other, a look of total confusion on his handsome face. When they finally took notice of him, the two brothers laughed, and Jared pressed his sherry glass into young Lord Swynford's hand. "No, Adrian," he said, "you've not gone mad. The gentleman you've been entertaining these last months is my older brother, Jonathan. I have only just returned from Russia a few days ago."

Adrian Swynford gulped the sherry down. "Well, damme if I ain't totally confused. You mean you've been in Russia almost a year?"

"Yes," smiled Jared.

"Then when you came back early last winter it wasn't you?"

"No, it was Jon who took my place so it would not be known that I was gone."

Adrian flushed. "Did Miranda know?" he said.

"Indeed she did!" said Jonathan quickly, and Lord Dunham forced back a chuckle. "I'll bet you got a warm welcome from your wife, eh, Jared!"

"No, Jon, I did not. My wife, it seems, waited until you and Adrian were safely out of the way. Then she hied herself off to St. Petersburg to bring me home. It was my bad fortune that I left St. Petersburg the very same day Miranda left Swynford. I expect, however, that having found me already gone from Russia, Miranda turned around and is now on her way home. I think she'll reach

England sometime between the sixth and eighth of August. At any rate I'll be at Welland Beach to greet her. I always seem to be waiting for Miranda to come home from the sea," he chuckled. "I don't imagine, Jon, that you want to wait with me."

"No, thank you, m'lord Dunham. I am very happy to have my own identity back. The quicker Anne and I can have a public courtship, the quicker our marriage can be announced. You do understand, Jared?"

"Yes, Jon."

"Anne?" queried a totally confused Adrian. "Who is Anne?"

"Mistress Anne Bowen."

"The vicar's daughter? Do you know her?"

"Quite well, Adrian. In fact we were married a month ago by a special license. Since, however, Jonathan Dunham was not officially in England a month ago, let alone personally acquainted with Mistress Anne Bowen, we must begin at the beginning for public observation."

At that moment Captain Ephraim Snow was ushering into the main salon of the *Dream Witch* the English Ambassador's secretary, Mr. Morgan, and an official in the Tzar's police. "Brandy, gentlemen?" Both men nodded. Captain Snow filled the snifters full, and passed them around. "Well," he said, "what word do you have for me? Have you found her?"

"Possibly," replied Mr. Morgan, "but the news, Captain, is not good." Reaching into his pocket, he drew out something and proffered it. "Do you recognize this, Captain?" he asked.

Shocked, Ephraim Snow stared at Miranda's wedding band. There was simply no mistaking the delicate rose-gold band with its tiny diamond-chip stars. Still, he had to be sure, and so he took the ring from Mr. Morgan's hand. Inside it was engraved. *Jared to Miranda December 6, 1812.* "It is *her* ring," he breathed. "No doubt about it."

Mr. Morgan turned to the burly police official. "This is Nicolai Ivanovich, Captain. He speaks quite good English, and he has questions for you."

"Please," the Russian said, reaching into a small leather bag at his side and drawing out a garment, "you recognize this?"

Horrified, Ephraim Snow took the sodden, discolored garment

from the man. It was the green-and-white-striped muslin dress Miranda had been wearing several days earlier when she had disappeared. He had had enough suspense, and he was no fool. The news was bad and he wanted it now. "Tell me the truth, Nicolai Ivanovich," he said.

The Russian looked at him sadly. "One more question, Captain. Is your mistress a blond lady?" Ephraim Snow nodded. "Then our identification is complete. The body of a blond woman wearing this garment and this ring was pulled from the Neva this morning. Lady Dunham, I regret to tell you, is dead. The unfortunate victim, obviously, of robbery. Was she wearing any other jewelry at the time she left?"

"Yes, yes, of course! She had diamond and pearl earbobs on, and a gold bracelet, her cameo brooch with the diamond, and at least two other rings. I'm not certain what pieces they were, but I am sure she was wearing jewelry."

"There, Mr. Morgan, I thought so!" said Nicolai Ivanovich with grim satisfaction.

"No," snapped Captain Snow, "it ain't simple at all! How the hell do you explain that coach that came for her?"

"I can't," said the policeman, "but obviously someone saw her and her jewelry, and made it their business to find out that she was a foreigner, deduced how best to lure her away, and did. This is a painfully unpleasant incident, Captain, but I can only offer the most abject apologies of my government to you."

Ephraim Snow had dealt with Russians before. They were an obdurate people. They had stated their position on the matter, and not even an act of God would force them to change their mind. Tight-lipped, he asked, "May I see the body?"

"I'm afraid not," came the answer. "We were forced to bury it quite quickly, Captain. It had been in the water several days, and was horribly bloated. Then, too, portions of it, including the face, were eaten away by the fish. We tentatively identified it, and buried it in the English cemetery. I brought the ring and the dress so we might have final identification."

Sickened, Ephraim Snow nodded his understanding. "Jesus Christ! How am I going to tell this to Master Jared? My God, what kind of animal would murder such a beautiful woman?"

"The Tzar's government is deeply distressed by this incident, Captain Snow," said Nicolai Ivanovich sympathetically.

"Perhaps we had best go now, Nicolai Ivanovich," said Mr. Morgan gently.

"Da! You are right!"

Ephraim Snow called out to them as they reached the door. "I want to up anchor right now. Will you see I ain't stopped, Nicolai Ivanovich?"

"Da, my friend, and go in safety with the God who watches over all of us."

On August tenth, *Dream Witch* arrived back at the village of Welland Beach on the English coast. She had encountered heavy seas almost from the moment she had left St. Petersburg, and until she got into the North Sea it had been slow going. For some reason Captain Snow was not surprised to see a familiar figure waiting on the stone quay as he brought the yacht into the safety of her dockage. He sighed, and took a quick swig of black Jamaican rum from the flask in his pocket. It didn't help. *Dream Witch* was made fast, and Jared Dunham came briskly aboard.

"Hey there, Eph, you're two days later than I thought you'd be! Where's that wildcat wife of mine?"

Unable to meet his employer's gaze, Captain Snow said, "Come on into the main salon, Master Jared." Not even bothering to wait for a reply, he walked into the ship's interior. There just wasn't any easy way to do this, so he turned to face Jared and the words came quickly, tumbling out with brutal force. He ended by shoving Miranda's wedding ring into Jared's hand, and then bursting into unashamed sobs. The tears poured down his weathered face into his salt-and-pepper beard while Jared, rigid with shock, stood staring at the gold band, its tiny stars twinkling mockingly at him. Then to Captain Snow's immense horror Jared Dunham cried, "Damn her! Damn her to *hell* for the wayward bitch she is! Any other woman would have stayed put, but not her! *Not her!*" Violently he jammed the ring into his pocket. "I don't hold you responsible, Eph," he said a little more quietly, and then stormed from the yacht.

Striding purposefully down the quay, Jared headed to the Mermaid. Slamming into the inn's taproom, he called for a bottle of brandy and proceeded to get drunk. Ephraim Snow discreetly followed his employer, sick with worry, but the innkeeper knew a desperate man when he saw one, and had already called Lord Dunham's servants. When Ephraim Snow entered the inn he saw them: Jared's valet, Mr. Mitchum; Martin the coachman; and Miranda's maid, Perky. Ephraim signaled to the three to join him, and then tersely told them of the tragedy.

"God have mercy on her," sobbed Perky. "She was a good mistress, she was. She wanted everyone about her to be happy."

"I think," said Mr. Mitchum, who was the senior servant, "that we had best let his lordship get good and drunk. When he finally collapses we will load him into the coach, and proceed back to Swynford Hall. Lord Dunham's brother and brother-in-law will know how to handle the situation from there."

Ephraim Snow nodded. "Sounds like a good idea to me," he said. "I'll tag along with you, if you don't mind, Mr. M."

"I should be obliged to you for your help, Captain," came the reply. "It may be a difficult trip back."

Alfred Mitchum had no idea how really terrible a coach trip could be. Miranda did. During the first few days after her abduction Sasha kept her in a drug-induced sleep. Occasionally she would become aware of the movement of the coach, but the second he caught her returning to consciousness he would force the bitter-tasting water down her throat, and she would tumble back into the dreamless darkness. After some days, in the few moments of lucidity she had, she realized she must stop him from drugging her further. She needed to think out her situation.

The next time she began her perilous return to consciousness she was careful to not alter the rhythm of her breathing, or open her eyes. Gradually her thoughts began to focus, but she had a dreadful headache. Finally, after several hours, she could no longer hold her cramped position, and to Sasha's surprise she sat up. He quickly reached for the silver flask, but she stayed his hand.

"Please, no more of whatever it is you've been giving me. I am your prisoner. I don't even know where I am." He looked at her closely. "Please," she begged softly. "My head is simply throbbing. I promise I'll give you no trouble."

"All right," he said finally. "But a wrong move on your part, and I'll pour the whole damn flask down your throat."

"Thank you," she said.

"Don't thank me. I'm just tired of playing nursemaid to you. Now I won't have to diaper you, either. You can take care of your own needs."

"Oh!" Miranda blushed beet-red.

"Well, hell," he muttered a little less sharply, "the coach would've stunk if I hadn't taken proper care of you."

"Please, sir."

He laughed. "Quite the lady, aren't you? Call me Sasha. Actually I'm Pieter Vladimirnovich, but I've always been called Sasha. Your first name is Miranda, I know, but what was your papa's name?"

"Thomas."

"Then your proper name is Miranda Thomasova, but I'm going to call you Mirushka."

"No," she said, "I am Miranda Dunham, wife to Jared Dunham, the lord of Wyndsong Manor."

"Were you really his wife? She said you were only his mistress."

"Who said?"

"Prince Alexei's mistress, Gillian."

"Gillian Abbott?"

"Yes. She was an appalling bitch. She said you had stolen Lord Dunham from her, and that he'd be grateful to be rid of you. She said she owed him a favor."

"Then I have *her* to thank for my current predicament! God, I'll throttle the bitch myself when I get my hands on her!"

"Easy, easy, Mirushka," cautioned Sasha, his hand on the silver flask.

For a moment her sea-green eyes flashed angrily, but then she said, "I'm not angry at you, Sasha, but your prince has been very badly misled. Lady Abbott's reputation in London was not of the best. She always went to the highest bidder, even when poor old

Lord Abbott was still alive. Please, Sasha, turn the coach back to St. Petersburg. My husband will reward you for my return."

"No," he said. "I saw you first, you know, in the Jew's store. Jews aren't usually allowed in St. Petersburg, but this one has the Tzar's patronage. Besides, they're good at running shops, and if they didn't, who would?" He chuckled. "Anyway, I saw you in Bimberg's. I was there purchasing a pair of lavender kid gloves for the prince's woman, and you came in with a sea captain."

"Captain Snow," she said.

"Alexei Vladimirnovich has been looking for several years for a woman with your coloring. Lucas has the same coloring. The moment I saw you I hurried to tell the prince. He might not have taken you if his woman hadn't convinced him that you were an unimportant creature."

"But in my world I *am* important," said Miranda, desperately trying to convince him to turn back. "I am a great heiress, I am married to a very important American!"

"America is a long, long way from Russia, Mirushka, and it is a savage, unimportant backwater. America doesn't matter."

"My husband's title is English, Sasha, and my sister is married to a *very* important English milord."

"Gillian said your sister was in America with your mother."

"She lied to you, Sasha! Our mama is in America, the wife of a rich and powerful man, but my sister is the Duchess of Swynford and her husband is quite close to the Prince Regent." As she spoke she wondered if Amanda would appreciate her elevation in rank.

"I suspected she might not be telling the whole truth," replied Sasha, nodding proudly. "I told the prince so, and on the chance that she was lying he devised a plan so that your disappearance would not be questioned. No matter who you really are, you will not be missed. Your life is now here in Russia on Alexei Vladimirnovich's slave-breeding farm. You will be very well taken care of, Mirushka. All you must do is have babies."

I am having some awful kind of nightmare, Mrianda thought.

"Why will my disappearance not be questioned, Sasha?"

"Because you are dead," was the calm reply.

Miranda shuddered, but her voice held not the faintest hint of the panic she was feeling. "I do not understand, Sasha."

"The prince's woman, Gillian, let her hair grow and dyed it blond when she escaped from England," Sasha began. He explained everything to her. When he was through, Miranda sat very still, listening to the rhythmic gall-op, gall-op of the horses as their hooves hit the road. *Dead! Dead! Dead!* went the mocking refrain. *Jared!* she cried out in her mind. *Don't believe them! Oh, my love, don't believe them! Don't believe them! I am alive! I am alive!*

"Mirushka, are you all right?" His voice was anxious.

"I am Miranda Dunham, wife to the lord of Wyndsong Manor," she said. "I am not dead! No one will believe it! Gillian Abbott doesn't look anything like me!"

"Do you know what a body looks like after several days in the water with the fish nibbling on it, Mirushka?" She blanched, and he continued. "Besides who is to connect Alexei Vladimirnovich with your disappearance? You never met except when he took you in his coach, and no one could identify the coach as his. It isn't like the time with Princess Tumanova's governess."

"What do you mean, Sasha?"

"Two years ago," began Sasha, "my master became quite intrigued with a little French girl who had come to be governess to Princess Tumanova's children. She was really an exquisite creature, with silky yellow-gold hair and gray eyes. Alexei Vladimirnovich wanted her for Lucas, and so he lured her from St. Petersburg. Unfortunately, the silly girl left her mistress a note. The princess was quite furious, and complained bitterly to the Tzar, who warned the prince that there could be no more scandals concerning the farm. Of course, he didn't scold my master too harshly, as Alexei Vladimirnovich pays the Romanovs handsome revenues each year. Revenues that come from the farm's operation."

"What happened to the French girl?" asked Miranda.

"She's still at the farm, of course. She fell in love with Lucas, and has borne him two children already. You will love Lucas, too. All his women do. He is a bit simple, but quite sweet-natured."

"I will not love Lucas, Sasha. I will not be mated like some pedigreed animal. I will not produce children for a slave market. I hate slavery! I would rather be dead!"

"Do not be foolish, Mirushka. You have no choice in this matter. You must do as you're told. We all must."

"You cannot make me, Sasha," she said grimly.

"Yes, Mirushka, we can. If you do not cooperate you will be forced. Come now, lovely one, do not make it painful. Lucas is not some ravening beast. He will do his duty as he knows the master expects him to do, but he would sooner be kind to you, I know."

"Where are we?" she asked, pretending only to want a change of subject.

"South of Kiev," he said, unaware that he should not tell her. "We will be in Odessa late this afternoon, and at the farm tonight. It is located about twenty miles from Odessa."

Miranda's mind quickly pictured the map of Russia. Thank God, she had paid attention to those dull geography lessons their governess had forced on them. "Good heavens!" she gasped. "How long have we been traveling?"

"Almost six days."

"Six days! That's impossible!"

"Not really. We have traveled around the clock. Are you hungry, Mirushka? We will be stopping to change horses again soon. Perhaps some soup, a bit of chicken, and fruit?"

She nodded. Then, huddling in a corner of the coach, she lapsed into silence. Odessa was on the Black Sea. The Ottoman Empire was nearby, and the Turks were allies of the English. She would need time to get her bearings. Could she hold off Sasha and this Lucas until she had formulated a plan? She must not panic. Above all, she must not panic.

The coach rambled on across the countryside. She wondered how far it was to the Turkish border and then how far to Constantinople from there. If Prince Cherkessky's farm was on the sea perhaps she could steal a boat. It would probably be safer to flee by water. No farmhouses, people, or dogs to question her. If she hid her hair—no, she would have to cut it short, probably dye it too, but if she did and then stuffed it beneath a cap and dressed like a boy...She glanced ruefully at her breasts, no longer petite, but round and full since little Tom's birth. Well, she would need a tight band to flatten them. In a small boat, and from a distance, who would know she was a woman?

A compass! She would need a compass. Did they have such things in this part of the world? It would hardly do to escape in the wrong direction. How Jared would tease her about that! *Jared*. She felt the tears spill from her eyes. Would he believe she was dead? Dear heaven, what other choice would he have in the face ·of such overwhelming evidence? I love you, Jared, her mind repeated over and over again. I love you! I love you!

Sasha left her to her feelings. He did not particularly care for women, never having received kindness from one. His unmarried mother had been chief maid to Alexei Vladimirnovich's mother, and although no one had ever told him, he knew that his father had been the late Prince Vladimir Cherkessky himself. He had been born seven months after his master's youngest sister. Sasha had been lucky. He might have been dumped onto one of the Cherkessky estates to be raised an uneducated serf, but Princess Alexandra had found him a pretty baby, and wanted to honor her favorite servant. He had been placed in the family nursery, and at the breast of the family wet nurse. When he was five, and Alexei Vladimirnovich eight, he had joined the boy who was to be his master in the family schoolroom. He was actually there as the prince's whipping boy. If Alexei Vladimirnovich was careless in his lessons, it was little Sasha who received the beating, for it was unthinkable that the prince's person be touched by a humble governess or tutor.

During his first six months in the schoolroom there was rarely a day he wasn't whipped thoroughly by the governess, an embittered French émigrée noblewoman who had just escaped the Revolution in her native land. Impoverished, she was forced to earn her living. Sasha represented to her the peasants of her own country who had dared to rebel so violently against their masters, against the natural order of things. She vented her fury on the helpless child. Unfortunately for Sasha, the prince was a lazy student.

The younger boy, however, had a phenomenal memory, and quickly caught up with the older one. Soon, to Alexei Vladimirnovich's acute embarrassment, he was surpassing his master. The prince began to learn his lessons, and Mademoiselle was forced to curtail her abuse of Sasha. When the prince was twelve she was replaced by an English tutor, Mr. Bradbury, whose British sense of fair play caused him to treat the boys as equals. Alexei Vladimirnovich tolerated this, for it made his body servant a far more interesting companion and confidant, and he was now *the* Prince Cherkessky, his father having died in a wild race down the frozen Neva. Five noblemen had taken part in the sled race that had left Prince Vladimir Cherkessky and his current mistress dead, three others injured, and one woman crippled for life.

The prince had only been fourteen, and though haughtily aware of his position, he needed the friendship of a grown man. Mr. Bradbury had willingly supplied that friendship, and soon he had affectionately introduced the boy to his first sexual experience. A year later Sasha was initiated into their pleasure. The Englishman and the prince also enjoyed ladies. Sasha, however, did not. He had learned young not to trust women. His own mother had never even held him, let alone given him a hug or a kiss.

No, Sasha didn't particularly care for women, but this one he was traveling with didn't seem a bad sort at all. He had expected hysteria, even an attempt at physical violence, when she regained consciousness. He had fully expected he would have to keep her drugged the entire trip, perhaps even the first few days at the farm, but here she was this last day of the trip fully conscious, and quiet. She had asked him relatively intelligent questions, knew enough to keep quiet, and did not talk all the time.

For the briefest moment he stared at her and was sad. The story she had told him of her background was obviously the truth. He hadn't for a moment believed that bitch Gillian.

The coach rumbled on down the badly paved and rutted road across the high central plateau that led to the city of Odessa. The city, which descended in terraces from its heights, had originally been the site of an ancient Greek settlement. The first city was gone by the

fourth century A.D. In the fourteenth century a Tatar chief built a fort
on the site, which was captured two centuries later by the Ottoman
Turks. Then, seventeen years before Miranda was to visit the city,
the Russians had captured it and built a fort and a naval base.

It was a lovely city, its streets laid out in sections of tree-lined
rectangles. The coach slowed to accommodate itself to the city
traffic, but neither of its inhabitants woke. Miranda's young and
healthy body was quickly throwing off the effects of several days of
the opium elixir, and she slept a deep and restful sleep, sure she
would find a way out of this. Next to her, Sasha, certain that his
charge would behave sensibly, snored lightly. They were roused
simultaneously when the coach stopped at the gates of Prince
Cherkessky's huge estate.

"Hey, Sasha, wake up!" The Russian dialect penetrated their
consciousnesses, and both awoke.

"Hello, Misha, open up. I've a precious new cargo for the farm."

"Who's this one for?"

"Lucas. Alexei Vladimirnovich finally found him the perfect
mate."

The gatekeeper leered in at Miranda, making smacking noises.
"Whew! That's a tasty morsel. Lucas is a lucky bastard, all right,
and I know he'll enjoy fucking this one, but I don't think the little
French girl will be too happy. She's been his favorite for quite a
while."

"Too bad about her! Open up now. We've had a long trip, and the
quicker I get Mirushka settled the faster we can get down to
business."

"What was he saying," she asked, flushing, not quite sure she
needed a translation.

"He was admiring you and envying Lucas," came the reply.

"Oh." She was silent a moment, and then said, "How can I speak
to your Lucas? I don't know Russian."

"You'll have to learn then, won't you," he said, but seeing the
stricken look on her face, relented. After all the prince wanted her
happy. "Lucas has a natural flair for languages, Mirushka. He knows
God knows how many Russian dialects; some German, for two of his
women are from the Rhine valley; and his French is excellent thanks

to the French girl, Mignon. I don't think you'll be doing too much talking though," he finished.

"You're horrid!" she declared angrily. "If, however, your Lucas does speak French I shall explain my situation to him. Surely he will not rape another man's lawful wife. I'm afraid your prince's plans for me will be foiled, and you will have to let me go. You could tell the prince I died, and then go back to St. Petersburg to be with him. You miss him already, I can tell."

He ignored the first part of her speech. Why bother to explain to her that Lucas would do what he was told because he was a dutiful slave? "If I returned to St. Petersburg and told the prince you'd died, he'd kill me," he said simply. "And he would be justified, for you are a very precious possession of his, and I have been entrusted with your care. I have served Alexei Vladimirnovich since I was five years old, and *never* have I disappointed him!"

She turned away from him, and looked out the coach window. It had been worth the try. Now she knew his loyalty couldn't be subverted. She gazed at the estate. It was partly wooded, and partly open rolling fields, and ahead she could see the main villa nestled on a green hillside above the sea. There were golden wheatfields, vineyards heavy with purple and green grapes, and orchards. She saw cattle, sheep, and goats grazing in lush pastures. It was a lovely picture, seemingly innocent of its true purpose.

As if anticipating her thoughts, he spoke. "The farm is almost totally self-sufficient. Everything needed is grown, or else we barter for it. The farm is divided into several sections. The children, for instance, live the farthest away from the main section, as we don't want them disturbing the women. Newborns are taken from their mothers immediately after birth, and removed to the nurseries. We have five nurseries, each staffed and capable of caring for up to ten babies. There is one nursemaid for every two children, and they remain in the nursery until the age of three, when they are transferred to the children's quarters.

"Here the children are separated by sex, ten to a building overseen by two older women. Each group sleeps in one room, but all the children eat together in a common dining hall. They are happy, active, well-fed youngsters. We cannot sell unattractive, poor-spirited children. The boys are all gelded quite young, for most are quite beautiful, and will be very successful as eunuchs. Most of the girls, of course, are meant for harems, although occasionally we keep some for fresh breeding stock. But we're very careful not to breed them with their own sires. Once we were not so careful, and then we got malformed or idiot children. The prince is very wise, and when we were more careful in our cross-matching we eliminated our problems."

He spoke with obvious pride as he detailed the operation of the estate, explaining how and what the children were taught so they might increase their value and please their future masters. Miranda almost laughed aloud at the ludicrous obscenity of it all. Two years ago at this very time, she was more innocent than an average ten-year-old on Prince Cherkessky's slave-breeding farm.

"Now the breeding women—we have almost a hundred—live ten to each quarters. Each building consists of five-bedroom cubicles sleeping two each and a common room for eating and recreation. They are cared for by two older women. Their only job is to breed healthy, beautiful babies.

"We have ten studs whose living arrangements are the same as the women. By the way you won't be living in the quarters for a while, but staying in Alexei Vladimirnovich's villa with me. He thought you might be more comfortable there until you've accustomed yourself to your new surroundings. Your happiness is important to the prince."

"He is kindness personified," she murmured sweetly. He ignored her obvious sarcasm.

"There are breeding huts and baths too in the quarters, and we have several midwives. In a difficult case there is a doctor on the estate, but he mostly cares for the children."

Curious in spite of herself, Miranda asked, "How long has Prince Cherkessky had this estate?"

"The farm has belonged to the prince for twelve years now, but it has been in his family for close to two hundred years. The prince's maternal grandfather was the Tatar overlord of this region, Prince Batu. When Russia won the area, the old man's Tatar sons and grandsons were killed or executed. The Tzar, of course, was happy to see that the estates passed to Alexei Vladimirnovich when Prince Batu died, thus keeping them in the family. Slaves from this farm have been justly famous, and highly prized in Constantinople's best slave markets for over a hundred and fifty years now."

While Miranda was digesting all of this information the coach swept up the gravel drive of the white stone villa and came to a stop. Two young men ran up to hold the horses' heads, and another hurried out of the house to open the coach door. "Welcome, Pieter Vladimirnovich. We had a pigeon two days ago foretelling your arrival. Everything is prepared for you."

Sasha climbed down from the coach, and offered his hand to Miranda. She took it, stood up, and promptly fell back. "Sasha, my legs are too weak to stand," she cried, frightened.

"It's all right, Mirushka, it's only a temporary thing." He turned to the footman. "Help her! Take her to her room."

The man reached in and picked her out of the coach as if she was a bouquet of flowers. She was overcome by an unpleasant odor that she soon realized came from her. Flushing with shame, she remembered Sasha's remark about diapers. "I want a bath immediately," she said.

"Rest assured it's already drawn and waiting for you," he laughed, realizing her discomfort. "Your legs will begin to work after a good hot soak. I will see you later, Mirushka."

The footman hurried into the house, moving so quickly she had no time to get her bearings. He carried her into a steamy square tiled room where they were greeted by half a dozen pretty young women who immediately took over, cooing and clucking at her as they stripped off her clothing, and, to her mortification, the foul-smelling diaper. She couldn't understand a word they were saying. They motioned her down two steps into a lovely warm square pool that obviously served as a bath. Two of the girls were by her side, and they gently drew her through the water to a corner of the pool where an array of crystal bottles sat neatly in a row. Quickly they uncorked them, and presented them individually so she might choose the scent she preferred. She waved away the attar of roses, the gardenia, the jasmine, the lily of the valley, the musk, and gillyflower. There were three bottles left. The first was a violet fragrance, the second orange blossoms. Sighing, she sniffed the last, and a smile lit her face. "Sweet stock!" she said, and nodded at her escorts. Smiling back, they generously poured the scented oil into the pool, and each took a bar of matching soap preparatory to washing her. Miranda snatched up her own soap and, shaking her head, began to wash herself. They nodded their understanding, but then handed her a bristled brush.

"No," she said, thinking it would ruin her skin.

She was grasped and held firmly by two girls while the others leaped into the tub. While she protested noisily they went about the task of vigorously scrubbing her. Next her hair was thoroughly washed, and then she was hurried from the water to be gently dried. Her protests were ignored again as her entire body was massaged with a thick stock-scented cream by four of the girls while the other two toweled and brushed her long hair until it was soft and fluffy and it gleamed silvery-gold in the candlelight that lit the room.

It was then that one of them pointed to her eyes and hair, and said something excitedly. The only word she could understand, however, was "Lucas." The others nodded vigorously, then they led her naked from the steamy bath into a delightful room with a view of the sea. One of the girls handed her a filmy rose-colored robe to put on, and as she helped Miranda into bed, the others left the room. The girl curtseyed brightly and then departed, closing the door behind her.

Miranda sighed, and wiggled her toes delightedly. She felt better than she had in weeks. She hadn't had a real bath since she had left England several weeks ago. Suddenly two things dawned on her. Her legs had actually worked! They were a bit weak from her enforced inactivity of the last few days, but they worked! The other unusual thing was the girls who had waited on her. They were all blondes, blondes of varying shades, but blondes nonetheless. She must remember to ask Sasha about that, and as if in answer to her thought he came into the room without knocking.

"Do you feel better?" he asked pleasantly.

"Yes, thank you, but I'm hungry."

"Marya will bring your supper shortly. She's an upper house servant, by the way, and can speak French, so if you need anything you have but to ask her."

"The servant girls who bathed me...why were they all blondes? They could almost be sisters."

"Some of them probably were—half-sisters at any rate. They're from the farm. Being able to bathe a person properly is an important skill in Mideastern life. They usually practice on each other. The reason they were all blondes is because we raise blondes. Fair-skinned, preferably light-eyed blondes are the most valuable slaves sold. Oh, occasionally one of the women whelps a redhead, and they bring a great deal of money too, but it's the blondes that the pashas and the sheikhs want the most. What the hell difference it makes in the dark I'll never know, but how those golden heads sell!"

Before she could reply the door opened again, and an old woman entered carrying a tray. "Good evening, Miranda Tomasova. I have brought your supper," she said. "Plump those pillows up, Sasha! How can she eat on her back?"

Sasha grinned at the old woman, but hurried to do her bidding. "Marya is the real ruler at the farm," he said. "Even Alexei Vladimirnovich obeys when she scolds." He fluffed the pillows, and helped Miranda to sit up.

Marya gently set the tray on Miranda's lap. "Can you eat by yourself, dearie, or shall I feed you?" she asked in French.

"I can manage, thank you."

"Very well then, I will leave you. If you need me, just pull the bell cord by your bed." She shuffled out, and Sasha pulled a chair up to the bedside.

"I'll keep you company while you eat, Mirushka," he said. "Then a good night's sleep will help you to feel more yourself."

Miranda began to lift the covers on the dishes. Absolutely tantalizing odors were issuing from the tray. There was a bowl of red soup with a blob of something thick and white in it. "What is that?" she asked.

"Borscht—beet soup," he said. "The topping is sour cream. Taste it! It's good!"

She did, and it was. The borscht quickly disappeared. The next dish she lifted contained two flaky pastries stuffed with a spicy chopped meat, sweet onions, and a grain. It was kasha, he told her, and was buckwheat that grew on the estate. There was a small dish of peas, and a tiny peach tart with cream. The entire meal was delicious, and as she licked the last crumb from the corner of her mouth she sighed with regret.

"You have a good appetite, Mirushka," he approved. "In a few days you will be recovered from your trip. The prince suggested that you have time to acclimate yourself. You will rest, and perhaps we will walk in the gardens and on the beach."

"And then?" Dear Lord, why had she asked that question?

"Then you will begin your visits to the breeding hut with Lucas." He stood up. "I will take your tray now. You must rest. I will see you tomorrow."

He was gone, and she lay alone and quiet. She was warm and well fed, but not one bit lulled by the kind treatment. Of course, they were all being kind. She was a valuable commodity, but she was not going to sit meekly by and cooperate, be led to the slaughter like an innocent lamb. She needed time to get her bearings. He had said they would walk on the beach tomorrow, and that would give her an opportunity to see the harbor and the coastline. Perhaps if she could trick him into pointing the way to Turkey she could simply follow the coastline in that direction when she made good her escape. Trying to obtain a compass might prove dangerous.

She was going to be a terrible disappointment to Sasha, but then he and his master had obviously never come up against an American before. They were unimportant, the prince said. Obviously the Russian understood nothing of the world outside his own rather backward country. America is simply young, she thought, but someday we will be a power to be reckoned with, for our people are vital and ambitious, and it is these things that make a great nation.

She was beginning to relax, and she glanced about the room curiously. It was medium-sized with wide casement windows to her right and a small tiled fireplace opposite the bed. The walls were rough plaster, whitewashed. The ceiling had dark open beams, and the floor was of red tile. There were only three pieces of real furniture, a tall painted oak wardrobe, its matching bed, and a chair with a woven seat. There was a candlestand with a chamberstick and flint on it. Over the bed was a wooden crucifix that seemed totally out of place, Miranda thought, considering where she was.

The windows, which were hung with simple, natural-colored cotton curtains embroidered in gaily colored threads, had been left slightly open, and she could smell the garden flowers. The bed was marvelously comfortable, with a good mattress topped with a featherbed. The sheets, cool and scented with lavender, were topped by a lovely red satin quilt, an oddity in the rustic room. She was grateful for the warmth of the quilt, however, as the evening was becoming quite cool. Outside her window she saw the twinkling of courting fireflies, and heard the chirrup of an early chorus of crickets. It seems like home on Wyndsong, she thought, and a tear slipped down her face, quickly followed by a minor flood that soaked her pillow. Angrily she scolded herself for this indulgent weakness, but she felt strangely stronger, relieved of her tensions, and quickly fell into a dreamless sleep.

The fireflies scattered to the woods to play their games of hide and seek among the trees and brush; the cricket chorus gave way to the soft and sibilant sounds of night wind; and a late moon rose to silver the fields, the beaches, the woods, and the sea. Miranda slept peacefully, not stirring when the casements creaked wide to admit the figure of a large man into the room. The bright moonlight made a candle unnecessary, and the man walked to the bed to stare down at Miranda.

She lay on her back like a child, her legs half drawn up, one arm straight, the other flung over her head. She had thrown the covers off, and he reached down to draw her sheer robe open, his breath hissing sharply at the sight of her full, round, moon-silvered breasts and long torso. She stirred slightly, and he carefully drew the covers over her. Noting the tear stains on her face, he tenderly touched her cheek in a sympathetic gesture, gently fingered her soft gilt-colored hair, and then, turning, left the way he had come.

Miranda was awakened by Marya the following morning. "Arise, dearie, the sun is up these past two hours."

Slowly she opened her sea-green eyes and, for the briefest moment, she imagined herself back on Wyndsong. Jemima was calling to her to get up. But as her vision cleared she saw the tiny, white-haired woman. Her heart sank. "Good morning," she murmured.

The old lady smiled. "Good, you are awake. Today I am going to pamper you, dearie, and let Marfa bring you breakfast in bed. Tomorrow, however, you must rise and breakfast with our Sasha. He

would not tell you himself, but he likes your company." She drew on
the bellpull. "Did you like your supper last night?"

"Yes, it was delicious!" complimented Miranda.

"You must tell me the foods you like, Miranda Tomasova, for it is
my duty to help make you happy. If there is a special dish you want
prepared, you have but to ask. If I do not know the dish I shall learn
it."

Marfa entered with the breakfast tray and Miranda sat up, eager to
see what delicacies Marya's kitchen had contrived this time. The
white wicker tray was set with delicate porcelain sprigged with pink
rosebuds. "What is this, Marya?" Miranda pointed to a little round
bowl filled with a creamy pale-gold substance the top of which was
dotted with a few fat green grapes.

"Yogurt flavored with fresh honey, and just a touch of cinnamon," was the reply.

"What is yogurt?"

"It's made from milk, dearie. Try it. I think you will like it."

The tangy sweet flavor at first surprised Miranda and she wasn't
sure she was going to like this yogurt, but before she realized it the
dish was empty. A small plate of fluffy scrambled eggs and two flaky
croissants followed the yogurt. There was a pot of delicate pale-
green tea that she drank greedily from an eggshell-thin cup.

Chuckling her approval, Marya removed the tray while Marfa
aided Miranda in dressing. She was given several white petticoats, a
black skirt, a short-sleeved white peasant's blouse, and a pair of
simple black slippers for her feet. The skirt came to just below her
knee, which seemed dreadfully immodest. She had been given no
stockings, so her legs were bare. She had also been given no
drawers, but when she protested this omission in sign language to
Marfa the girl raised her own skirt to reveal a bare bottom. Miranda
was horrified, but Marfa just giggled.

Miranda plaited her long hair into one braid and, moving on
stronger, surer legs, went off to join Sasha, little Marfa showing her
the way. He waited for her in a comfortable sunny room of painted
tables and overstuffed chairs and settees. There was a short, spare
man with him.

"Come in, Mirushka," he said genially to her. "Did you sleep well? You have had breakfast?"

"Yes, and yes," she said. "Are we to go for a walk now? My legs are much stronger and I am not used to inactivity, Sasha."

"We will walk, but first you must meet Dimitri Gregorivich, the overseer of the prince's farm."

"Miranda Tomasova, I bid you welcome," said the overseer in careful French. "You are going to be a valuable asset to us."

"I am not here willingly," she answered him shortly.

"But you are here," he said, "and so like the rest of us you will do your duty by our master." He turned to Sasha, and spoke again as if she weren't even there. "If she were in my charge a good beating would cure her impudence. There are ways it can be done without leaving a mark on the skin. But Alexei Vladimirnovich has put this in your hands."

"Mirushka simply needs time to adjust, Dimitri Gregorivich," soothed Sasha. "She is quite different from any of our other women. She is a real lady."

"She will be trouble for us, Pieter Vladimirnovich. If she is really a lady how can she possibly adjust to such a life as we offer? Look at her! Educated, I will wager! Proud and," here he looked at her again, "rich! You are rich, aren't you, Miranda Tomasova?"

She nodded. "I am an heiress, and my husband is also quite wealthy."

"A poor girl would accept her fate, but she will not adjust," the overseer said flatly. "Alexei Vladimirnovich has made a mistake. He saw only her coloring."

"He is right, Sasha," taunted Miranda. "Let me go! Say that I took my own life rather than face the kind of life you offered me."

"You will accept everything," said Sasha positively. "How long," he taunted back, "how long, Mirushka, since you last made love to a man? You told me your husband had been away for several months, and you had just had a child. You have not known a man in a long, long while, Mirushka. Do you not desire to make love with a strong, passionate man? I have stood outside the breeding hut with the prince many times, and heard the cries of rapture that Lucas's mastery of the sensual arts can wring from a woman. Unless you are cold—and I do not for a moment believe you are—you too will soon cry out your joy. Come now, let us go for a walk."

Furious, she wanted to refuse him and return to her room, but instead she meekly followed him, much to Dimitri Gregorivich's surprise. She had to see the beach, ascertain the way to freedom, escape at all costs. She kept her temper in check and chatted with Sasha about the flora and fauna of the Crimean area, a subject on which he was quite knowledgeable. Finally they stood on the beach gazing out at the Black Sea.

"My home is an island," she said. "I do so love the sea!"

He was lulled. Good, he thought, she can accustom herself to being here because it is like her home. Next Lucas will make her forget her husband.

"Which way did we come from," she queried. "I mean, where is Odessa? I am so sorry we slept going through it."

"Odessa is a bit over twenty miles back up the coast," he replied, pointing to the left. "We are about six miles from the border with Bessarabia in the other direction. The few bands of Tatars still left occasionally raid the small farms around here, carrying off the livestock and an occasional girl or two. Then they scuttle back over the border to Bessarabia, and we can't touch them."

"Have they ever raided this farm?"

"Bless me, no! Remember Prince Cherkessky is half Tatar himself. They have never dared to come here. Besides, we are too big for a little band of raiders to deal with."

They turned to walk back toward the villa, and Miranda's spirits were soaring. She had her information. If Odessa was to the left, then freedom was to the right. She had seen an elegant sailing yacht moored in the cove. She assumed it belonged to the prince. She could not steal it, but drawn up along the beach had been several boats similar to the dories with which she was familiar. The difference was that these boats had a mast and a single sail. She smiled to herself. No one can sail a small boat like I can, she thought. Just a few days to gather her strength, and she would be gone. She had already observed that there were no guards of any sort protecting the estate. Obviously no one had ever considered escaping. Why would they? Most of the inhabitants of Prince Cherkessky's farm probably knew no other life. And compared to the serfs and even the small Russian middle class, the slave population of the prince's farm lived lives of comfort and luxury. Why would they want to leave?

It would be easy to slip out from her ground-floor room at night. First, however, she must become familiar with the villa's kitchen, for she would need food and vessels for fresh water. Lack of proper preparation could cost her her life.

The next two days passed pleasantly enough with Marya stuffing her full of marvelous food and Sasha offering her pleasant companionship between their walks and games of chess. Her peasant dress had been replaced on the second day by a long loose-fitting gown that Sasha told her was called a caftan. It was a Middle Eastern garment, quite comfortable, and she felt less on display than in the short skirts and low-cut blouses.

On her third evening they walked a different route, not on the beach but through a nearby orchard. The fruit trees were heavy with ripening apples, and she could smell their faint perfume. She sighed. "Autumn is coming," she said, almost to herself, and thought of Wyndsong. Sasha said nothing. Before them stretched a field of wild flowers. They walked on toward it, and then she saw on the edge of the field a small, low building. "What is that?" she asked him.

"Come, and I'll show you," he said as they reached it. He opened the door, and stepped back politely so she might see inside. The cabinlike structure consisted of one room with a fireplace, and in the dimness was a piece of furniture she couldn't quite make out. Stepping inside to investigate further, she turned to question him as the door behind her swung shut and a long bolt slammed into its iron holder.

"*Sasha!*" Her heart began to thump wildly.

"I am sorry, Mirushka, but if I had told you that tonight was to be your first visit to the breeding hut, you would not have come willingly."

Anger replaced fear. "You're damned right I wouldn't have!" she shouted. "Open this door, you little bastard!"

"No, Mirushka, I will not. You are more than recovered from your trip, and the sooner we get down to business, the sooner I can leave this damned bucolic countryside, and return to Alexei Vladimirnovich. I am forbidden his presence until you are delivered of your first child. At the least it will be nine months before I can return to St. Petersburg.''

"I will not be violated by your damned slave stud!" she yelled. "If he tries to touch me I'll fight! I'll claw his eyes out! I'll kick and scratch whatever I can! I warn you, Sasha, that I'll ruin him for future service if you try and force him on me.''

"Mirushka, Lucas is big and strong and you cannot hurt him. Please cooperate.''

She began to bang frantically against the thick door, her fists beating a futile tattoo. She hammered and hammered until her knuckles were raw and bleeding, her face wet with tears. Suddenly she swung about, frightened and wondering if she were actually alone. She held her breath, listening for a moment to see if she might hear the sound of another's breathing, but the room was silent and as her eyes grew used to the dimness she could see that she was indeed alone. She called out, "Sasha?" and heard only silence. He had left her.

Miranda could make out the piece of furniture now. It was a low bed with rope springs, a thin pallet thrown over the ropes. She sat down on it wearily. The thing was hardly made for comfort, but then that wasn't the bed's function. She shivered. There were no windows in the room, but a little twilight came through the uneven boards. As night fell the room became darker and darker, and her fears intensified. She wept, crying harder and harder until she fell into an exhausted, nervous sleep.

She woke with a start. Through a chink in the boards she could just make out the rising moon. Suddenly she knew she was not alone. Her breath caught in her throat as she strained to listen, but all she could hear was the frantic beating of her own heart. She lay rigid. Perhaps if he believed her asleep he would leave her alone. She was very frightened and, despite her courage, unable to keep from trembling. Finally Miranda could no longer stand the tense waiting and a strangled sob escaped her.

"Are you frightened?" said a deep, warm voice. "I was told you were not a virgin. Why are you afraid? I will not hurt you.''

She saw a dark form in the corner by the door. It rose to an enormous height, and started toward the bed. *"No!"* Her voice was sharp with hysteria. "Stay where you are! Don't come any nearer."

He stopped. "My name is Lucas," he said. "Tell me why you are afraid."

"I cannot do what they want us to do," she said, low. "I was stolen from my husband. *Please* understand. I am not a slave."

"You *were* not a slave," he corrected her gently, "but I'm afraid you are now. It will take some getting used to, I know." His French was quite cultivated.

"Weren't you born a slave?" she asked, curious despite her fear. He stayed where he was and explained.

"No. I was not born a slave. My brother Paulus and I come from the north of Greece. Our father was a Greek Orthodox priest. Our mother died when we were twelve and fourteen, and father then married a woman in the village who had one daughter. Mara was the most beautiful woman in our town, and unknown to Father, the most corrupt. She had not been in the house a year when she bedded us both. Then father began to sicken, and soon he died. I imagine she was poisoning him, but I didn't know it then. Our loving stepmother quickly arranged a match between her ugly daughter and the eldest son of the richest man in the village. We kept hearing talk in the village of an enormous dowry for Daphne, but we could not understand where Mara was going to get such a dowry. In the meantime she kept us content, and happy in her bed.

"Our stepsister's wedding day was a week away when a mounted troop of men arrived in our village. They were slave traders. As our 'mother' it was her right to sell us, and she received a large sum. The money, of course, was for our stepsister's dowry. Without it, our stepsister Mara wouldn't have gotten any husband, let alone a rich one! I overheard Mara haggling our price with the leader of the troop, and believe me, she got every penny she could from him and more." He chuckled. "What a woman she was! 'They can both fuck like stallions,' she told the slaver. 'I've taught them myself, and they're both potent as hell. I've aborted myself seven times in the last year!'"

"That's horrible!" Miranda cried. "What an evil woman she was to sell you into slavery."

"She did us a kindness," was his surprising reply. "Our village was poor, and our father had been the priest. We were the poorest of all. When Mara sold us she knew we would be sent to a breeding farm as we were too old to be successfully gelded. That is why she told the slave merchant that our seed was so potent. The farms are always looking for fresh stock, and the slaves on the farms are very well treated.

"Paulus and I were brought to Constantinople, and there we were both bought by Dimitri Gregorivich. He was on a buying trip for Prince Cherkessky, who had just come into the estate. We have been happy here, and you will be too, I promise you. Just give it time."

"My story is not like yours," Miranda said. "You were a peasant, and slavery has improved your life. You left nothing behind when you were brought here. Both your parents were dead, your step-mother and her child meant little to you, you had nothing. I had everything.

"I am wealthy in my own right. I have a husband and a child I love, a mother, a sister, a home! I do not belong here."

"Then why are you here?" he asked, moving just a bit closer.

"Your prince kidnapped me from my yacht in St. Petersburg because, it seems, my coloring matches yours. I am told you father daughters, and Prince Cherkessky believes a race of our daughters will make him richer. But if you touch me I will kill myself!

"I am not a brood mare! I am Miranda Dunham of Wyndsong Island, wife to Jared Dunham, the lord of the manor."

He sighed. "Poor little bird," he said. "Whatever was is no longer. You are here now, and this is your life. I don't want you unhappy, for I am a softhearted man and a sad woman pains me." He moved closer.

"No!" She backed herself into the farthest corner of the bed.

"Miranda, Miranda," he said chidingly, tasting her name for the first time. "I have never taken a woman by force, and I promise you that I will not force you. Trust me, little bird. All I want to do is sit by you, and hold your hand. I will court you as the boys in my village used to court the pretty maidens."

"It will be no use," she said. "I will never yield to you, and when they find out that you have not done what you should they will force us. Sasha warned me."

"*Sasha!*" Lucas's voice dripped scorn. "The prince's little pretty-boy lover! What can he know of a man and a woman? Dimitri Gregorivich knows that I will do my duty, and he trusts my judgment in these matters. Eventually we will make love, Miranda, and with God's blessing you will conceive my child, but you need have no fear that I will rape you. You will come to me willingly, little bird."

"N-no!"

He sat down on the edge of the bed. "Give me your hand, little bird. You will see that you can trust me."

"It's too dark. I can't see you," she said.

"Just place your hand in the center of the bed," he said. "I will find it."

She hesitantly slid her small cold hand across the mattress. Instantly his big hand covered it, and she started, frightened by the contact.

"No, Miranda, it's all right. I will not hurt you," he reassured her.

For a few moments they sat in silence, and she could hear his calm, even breathing. It was odd to sit here almost peacefully with this stranger and talk of lovemaking. "Your French is excellent," she said finally, in an effort to ease the awkward silence.

He chuckled as if understanding her thoughts, and the sound was somehow comforting. "One of my women is French. She came here over two years ago, and we could not understand each other. So, having been a teacher, she set about teaching me her language, and I taught her some of the Russian dialects I know."

"She adjusted to this...this way of life after having been free?" Miranda asked.

"Yes," he answered.

"I will not, Lucas," she said.

"Yes, you will, Miranda. You tell me you had a husband and son. If he loved you as you loved him, why didn't he come after you?"

"Because the prince convinced him that I drowned in the Neva River," she cried.

"So as far as your family is concerned you are dead. Eventually your husband will marry again, for that is a man's way. He will have other children, and your own child will forget you. In the meantime you will sit here lonely and unloved. Is this the kind of life you want? If your husband can make himself a new life, why can't you?"

"Jared honestly believes I am dead, but I know I am not! If he marries his mistake will be an honest one; but if I yield my body to you I am an adulteress, a whore! I will not do it!"

"Because you love your husband, Miranda, or because your proud spirit cannot violate the morals which you were taught as a child? You must think about this carefully, for Dimitri Gregorivich is only so patient, and the prince is not patient at all."

"I would sooner be dead than a slave!" she said fervently.

"Little bird, they will not let you die. Eventually they will demand I force you. And then I will be ashamed, for I have never forced a woman. Or else the prince will give you to the others to play with as a lesson to those who might be tempted to follow your example. "But I will love you, and be good to you. You are very beautiful."

"How can you know that? You can't see me here in the dark."

"I have seen you before tonight."

"Out walking with Sasha?"

"No."

"Wh-when?"

"I have come to your room each night when you were asleep, and watched you. They do not know."

There was nothing she could say. He was not at all what she had imagined. She had expected a brute, and he was gentle and understanding. She wished she could see what he looked like. It was growing chilly, and she shivered in her light cotton caftan.

"Are you cold?" he asked solicitously. "Come, let me hold you, little bird."

"No!"

"Miranda, it's damp and cool in here," he said patiently, as if reasoning with a child. "Only in winter is a blanket or a fire supplied. The rest of the time we are supposed to make our own heat. Let me hold you and warm you. It cannot be disloyal to your husband if I keep you from pneumonia." His voice held a hint of laughter.

"No!" she repeated, and then she sneezed, not once but three times.

Without another word he reached over in the blackness and yanked her back across the bed into his bearlike embrace. She started to struggle, but he tightened his grip. "Easy, little bird, I told you I would not force you. Now, be quiet, and let me warm you."

"You're naked!" she protested.

"Yes," he answered simply.

Her cheek, against his furred chest, grew hot with embarrassment. She was settled quite comfortably into his lap, and although at first she was rigidly resistant, she gradually began to relax. He was a very big man. Shyly she moved her arm into a more comfortable position, and felt the muscles of his upper chest rippling beneath her hand. He smelled clean, yet definitely masculine, and she felt quick tears prick her eyelids as a hundred sweet memories assailed her.

"I am a very patient man, little bird," he said quietly, as if reading her thoughts.

"Why do you call me 'little bird'?" she asked, trying to change the subject.

"Because you are graceful and golden, and soft, like a canary my mother once had. It lived in a little willow cage in our house window. When she died, it died."

"You are very big," she said.

"I am six feet six inches tall," he said. "My brother is taller by a half-inch."

She could feel his heart beating evenly beneath her cheek. He was so sure of himself. Suddenly she realized how fortunate she was. He was kind. He had said he would be patient, and it occurred to her that she might very well hold him off long enough to make good her escape. Her heart quickened at the thought. Outside, the night creatures hummed and sang in the moonlight, and as his body heat began to penetrate her she grew sleepy again. It wasn't half bad here in this windowless place, safe and warm in this gentle giant's arms. Instinctively she cuddled nearer, and his big hand began stroking her head gently.

"Good morning, Miranda Tomasova!" came Marya's cheerful voice, and the sun was bright in Miranda's confused eyes. She was back in her room! "Get up, dearie. Sasha and your breakfast are both waiting. I have brought you a pitcher of warm water to bathe with, although perhaps later you will want a real bath. The girls all say

Lucas is an insatiable bull, but then I'm too old to know, more's the pity!" Cackling merrily at her wit, she left the room.

How on earth did she get back from the breeding hut? He must have carried her. She swung her feet over the bed and got up, removing the wrinkled caftan. Washing her face and hands, and cleaning her teeth with a mint leaf, she went to the wardrobe, picked out a new caftan, and put it on. She brushed her hair fiercely. She had a bone to pick with Sasha!

"You worm!" she hissed at him as she entered the small dining room. "You lied to me!"

"I did not lie," he protested.

"You didn't tell me what you were going to do last night, you worm! You tricked me!"

"If I had told you, would you have cooperated?"

"*No!*"

"Didn't Lucas *please* you," he said slyly. "I have been told that he always leaves his women begging for more."

She laughed mockingly. "I am untouched!" she said triumphantly.

His face darkened. Leaping across the space between them, he grasped her by her pale-gold hair. "You bitch! What have you done?" he shrieked into her face. "Every time you refuse to cooperate I am forced to remain here another day!"

"I warned you!" she shouted, pulling away from him. "I will not be treated like an animal! I am Miranda Dunham, wife to Jared Dunham, lord of Wyndsong Manor."

The first blow caught her unaware. "You bitch! Miranda Dunham is *dead!* You are Mirushka, a slave woman belonging to Prince Cherkessky." He hit her again. "Your function is to breed, and if you don't cooperate I swear to God I'll stand over that peasant giant and make him do his duty!"

She saw the third blow coming, and raised her hands to defend herself.

"Pieter Vladimirnovich! Don't injure her! Remember the prince!"

Dimitri Gregorivich placed himself between them. Sasha's cupid face was almost purple in his rage. The overseer turned to Miranda, and spoke quietly. "You little fool! Go to your room before he loses control entirely." She fled gratefully, and he turned back to Sasha, who was now simpering to himself.

"I have never been away from Alexei Vladimirnovich. I cannot bear it, Dimi. 'I can trust no one else but you, Sasha.' That's what he told me, Dimi. Now I am exiled from his sweet presence until that bitch whelps her firstborn!" His black cherry eyes glittered with self-pity and malicious anger. "Is it true? Is it?! Why didn't he fuck her? Why!"

"Calm yourself, Sasha, calm yourself. You yourself said that Miranda Tomasova must acclimate herself to her new life. Lucas agrees with you. He did not force her because he wishes to earn her trust. He is a gentle man."

"I don't care if he earns her trust or not! He was supposed to fuck her! He didn't! There is, therefore, no chance of her being pregnant, which means I am exiled here an even longer time. I want him whipped!"

"No," said Dimitri Gregorivich. "Alexei Vladimirnovich sent the woman especially for Lucas, and although I have my reservations yet, she *is* perfect for him. If he forces her she will be unhappy. Unhappy women make trouble. We have never had trouble here, and the prince would not like it if there was trouble. You are hardly an expert in relations between a man and a woman. I will let Lucas handle her in his own time, and in his own fashion. If you try to interfere I will complain to Alexei Vladimirnovich."

"I hate it here!"

"You only hate it here because you are lonely and you miss St. Petersburg. I would not offend you, dear Sasha, but among our youth is a most charming and affectionate lad whom I know would be a great consolation to you. Let me bring Vanya to you. Lucas will do his duty as he always has done it, but he must do it in his own time. If you are less concerned with the timing it will happen more quickly. Diverted, you will be happier."

"I don't know," demured Sasha.

"Let me show you the boy," tempted Dimitri Gregorivich. "He is a delight."

"I can't promise I'll like him, but I suppose I can look. How old is he?"

"Twelve," was the smooth reply, and Dimitri Gregorivich knew he had won. That night it was he who escorted Miranda to the breeding hut, for Sasha was involved with his new young friend.

Miranda was feeling rather pleased with herself for, after having fled the infuriated Sasha, she had found the kitchens. Playing on old Marya's sympathies, she had eaten her breakfast there, which gave her plenty of time to look around. She had seen where the bread and fruit were kept, and where the waterbags were hung. Yes, she was pleased with herself.

"Where is Lucas?" she asked the overseer.

"He will be waiting for you," came the reply.

"I can go from here without you," she said.

"Are you anxious to see Lucas?" he asked. She ignored him, but then he said, "Remove your caftan."

"What?" Miranda was shocked.

"Remove your caftan," he repeated.

"Please, Dimitri Gregorivich, I was cold enough last night with it."

"If you do your duty, Miranda Tomasova, you will not need the gown." He held out his hand, and she knew there was nothing she could do. Shrugging fatalistically, she complied with his request and entered the small structure, leaving him behind. As the door shut she saw Lucas's bulk in the dimness, but the room darkened too quickly for her to make out his features.

"I see you are no longer frightened of me," he said teasingly.

"You were very kind to me last night," she said.

"I should like to be kinder to you tonight," he replied.

Suddenly she felt shy. "Please..."

He laughed ruefully. "My brother says I am being too easy with you; nevertheless, I don't want you hating me. We will share a bed tonight, Miranda, but we will do nothing more than sleep the sleep of the innocent." He reached out and found her hand. "Come, little bird."

She lay down, and felt the rope bed supports give as he joined her.

"Tonight you are also naked," he remarked. "You made a delectable sight in the doorway, the setting sun behind you, little bird. One kind word, and I would be your slave instead of the prince's," he teased.

"Please, you will make me shy again."

"I would like to put my arm around you," he said as he did so.

She stiffened at his touch, but gradually relaxed. "Tell me what you look like?" she asked.

"I am just a man," he said modestly. "My hair is the same gilt color as yours, my eyes are blue like the Persian turquoise. I prefer to be clean-shaven, while my brother wears a beard. Paulus is a golden blond with light blue eyes."

He drew her closer, and they were hip to hip now. She was glad he could not see her embarrassment. "I am sleepy," she said. "Good night."

"Good night," he answered pleasantly.

Shortly he was snoring lightly while she lay chilled and wakeful. God, his legs were so long, and they were as furred with soft downy hair as his chest was. She dozed briefly only to awaken when he pulled her closer and began fondling her breasts. She was about to protest when he murmured, "Mignon, sweetheart," and she realized he must be dreaming. As his thumb rubbed insistently at her nipple she grew more tense. A corresponding ache began to build between her legs, and she realized with horror that she was experiencing desire. But how could this be? How could she feel anything having to do with love for a man whose face she'd never even seen, a man who was not Jared? Pulling away from him, she moved to the farthest corner of the bed. Confused and shivering, she softly cried herself to sleep.

Miranda awoke in her own bed. She could hear the sound of an insistent rain. She rose, dressed herself, and went to the kitchens, where old Marya was grumbling. "Rain, rain, rain!" she said irritably. "It makes my old bones ache. I hope the rainy season is not beginning early this year." She filled a small bowl with kasha, and slammed it on the table before Miranda. "Eat up, dearie. Its warmth will help keep out the chill." She filled a mug with steaming tea, and lacing it heavily with honey shoved it across next to the bowl. "I apologize for such simple fare this morning, Miranda Tomasova, but everyone has overslept because we were kept so late last night by Pieter Vladimirnovich. He had us prepare a banquet for two, the likes of which I have never seen before." Her tone, her entire body registered extreme disapproval.

Miranda swallowed her laughter. So it was Pieter Vladimirnovich this morning, was it? Sasha must really be in disfavor with Marya. Miranda ate her breakfast and, seeing a row of capes of various sizes hanging by the back door, she snatched one up and hurried out into the wet morning. With Sasha well occupied and everyone else keeping indoors she had a chance to inspect the boats on the beach. Unless the rain turned into a really bad storm, she intended escaping tonight.

She knew she would not be sent to the breeding hut tonight. Farm policy for women was two nights, then a night of full rest. Dimitri Gregorivich had told her so last night. Tonight would be her night of rest, and she would certainly make the most of it. If the rain continued there would be virtually no chance of anyone being out, and her escape was assured. Sasha was nicely entangled with his new friend, and probably would be for the rest of the day and night. Yesterday afternoon, when he and the boy had been frolicking naked in the sea, she had crept into his room to steal a pair of breeches, a shirt, and a cap. Sasha was so involved with the lad that he seemed not to have missed the garments at all.

The wet salt wind teased at her long hair, whipping it wildly about as she reached the beach. The sea was running a trifle higher than normal, with an occasional two-foot swell, but the rain was soft. Though gusty, the wind was not a sustained one. Experience told her that by evening it would be an even, low gale. She suspected the rain would go through the night before it wore itself out. Nothing could be better, she thought with satisfaction.

There were four boats drawn up on the damp sand. Carefully she inspected them for soundness, and immediately discovered that two of them would not be seaworthy at all, for they were too old and their floorboards were loose. They might be fine for a day's fishing within the safety of the cove, but not for a trip of several hundred miles down the Black Sea. The last two boats were practically brand new, and would be tight and safe. Unfortunately, only one of them had a good sail. The sail in the other was ripped. This, then, would be her boat. The tide was out, but she could see the high-water mark that ended just beyond the stony part of the beach. Bending, she pushed at the boat, but it was stuck in the sand. For several minutes she shoved at the boat until it finally gave and slid forward. She moved it back and forth several times, smoothing the sandy groove until the little vessel moved easily. God, she wished she might go now, but it was too risky. She had to wait. Her worst mistakes had always been made because was was impatient, and galloped precipitously into situations without stopping to think things out.

Reluctantly, she turned away from the boats and made her way back across the beach and up the hill to the villa. Tonight! She was going to escape. It would be a long time before Prince Alexei Cherkessky tangled with an American again!

"Oh, Jared!" she whispered aloud. "I am coming home to you, my darling! I am coming home!"

ᵔᵔ *Chapter* 12 ᵔᵔ

S he was brought supper in her room. "Sasha's orders," said old Marya disapprovingly. "He and that wicked little scamp, Vanya, are lording it in the dining room. When the boy heard you ate with Sasha he had a tantrum, and so you are banished until further notice."

Miranda laughed. "I would sooner eat alone than listen to another recitation of Alexei Vladimirnovich's virtues. Besides, this is my night of rest, Marya. I shall go to sleep immediately after I've eaten. Would you think me lazy if I asked to sleep late tomorrow? Sasha won't care."

"Why not, dearie? Lucas can exhaust the strongest girl, I am told." She patted Miranda's cheek fondly. "What a good girl you are," she said. "Once I had a pretty little girl child like you, but she died..." The old woman's voice trailed off sadly for a moment then, catching herself, she smiled. "Sweet dreams to you, Miranda Tomasova. Good night."

Alone, Miranda ate slowly of the delicious capon breast Marya had brought. Would there be some left in the kitchen, some she could take with her? Maybe a ham. Salted meat lasted longer at sea.

Bread? Yes. Fruit. A knife. Lord, yes! She couldn't go without a
knife. Perhaps there would be a fishing line in the boat. She realized
that the trip would take her close to a month providing she
encountered no severe difficulties. Why hadn't she looked for a
fishing line?

Her supper finished, she lay on her bed. She dared not attempt
leaving yet. It was far too early, and she could hear the servants
moving about, while from the dining room came the sound of high-
pitched laughter. The tiny mantel clock chimed seven, and she
dozed, waking a little after eleven. Now all was quiet but for the
insistent patter of rain of the red roof tiles.

She rose. Shedding her caftan, she put on Sasha's breeches. They
were a good fit. A linen towel served to bind her breasts, and then
came the shirt. She retained her little black slippers, for no one
would see her feet in the boat, and if she had to run she couldn't be
bothered with shoes that didn't fit. She had decided not to cut her
beautiful pale-gold hair. Instead, she plaited it into a thick braid,
which she tucked beneath Sasha's cap. She was ready.

Snatching a pillowcase from her bed, she carefully crept from her
room and hurried to the kitchen. The goatskin water bags hung full,
and she quickly went about the task of stuffing food into the
pillowcase. *The knife!* Don't forget the knife! She chose one from the
rack near old Marya's claw-footed chopping block. Then, taking a
thick cloak from one of the hooks near the back door, she quietly let
herself outside into the night.

She moved slowly, the water bags weighing her down and the
darkness confusing her somewhat. She stopped and recalled the way
as she had traveled it in daylight. Feeling more confident, she
hurried purposefully forward. Soon she could hear the sound of the
sea, and it was all she could do not to run to it.

The rain was coming in torrents now and she could hardly see.
The wind had not come about quite as she had anticipated. It blew in
off the sea in fierce gusts, and she again began to have doubts about
leaving in this wild weather. She reached the boat and, dropping the
pillowcase of food into it, began to unload her waterbags.

"Miranda, where are you going?" Lucas asked gently.

She nearly fainted. She couldn't see him, but he was obviously nearby. Stealthily she began to shove at the boat, and it slipped easily down toward the wildly pounding surf. She felt the tide catch at the boat, and she quickly scrambled into it.

"Miranda!"

Frantically she sought for the sail to raise it, but it was gone! Desperately she sought for the oars, but there were none. She knew that there had been oars. Where were they? Sobbing, she tried paddling with her hands, but the winds blew the boat back to shore, and then he was looming over her, dragging it back onto the beach.

"No!" she shrieked at him. "No! No! No!" In violent desperation she flung herself into the churning sea. Better death than this! Jared! Jared! her mind cried out to him. Oh my love, help me! Help me!

He saw her dark shape poised for a brief moment before she leaped into the water, and letting the boat go he dove in after her, catching at the sodden, heavy cloak to pull her back to safety. He dragged her onto the beach. She was coughing, sobbing, and screaming at him in a language he couldn't understand. He tore the cape from her, and attempted to get a firmer grasp on her, but she fought him like one demented, clawing, hitting, biting. For several minutes she battled him wildly, and he was astounded by her strength. But then he felt her weaken until finally she collapsed against him, weeping piteously.

Lucas carried her up the beach and toward the nearest shelter, the breeding hut. He used his foot to open the door, and set her down on the bed. She was sobbing bitterly. He closed the door and then gathered wood from a small bin where he had put it earlier. He started a fire, stripped off his own wet clothes, and, pulling her to her feet, stripped her soaking garments off of her. He then carefully spread them on the floor near the fire to dry. She had lost her cap and her hair was sopping wet. He unplaited the braid, and loosened her hair. It tumbled damply down her back.

Miranda stood shivering and naked, in shock, unable to stop crying. He put his arms around her and held her close to him. Finally, as her sobs subsided, he began to speak softly. "There is never any going back in life, Miranda. We can only go forward. I

love you. I have loved you from the moment I first saw you those few
nights ago. I will not allow you to destroy yourself hungering for a
life that is no longer yours. You are my woman now. The prince gave
you to me, and I will never let you go!"

"*No!*" she whispered hoarsely.

"Yes!" he answered firmly, and then he was raising her head up to
face him. A warm, demanding mouth descended on hers. He kissed
her slowly, thoroughly, savoring her, tasting the salt taste of her lips.
He kissed her shut and quivering eyelids, her nose, her high
cheekbones, her cleft chin, and then kissed her soft lips again. His
tongue sought hers, but she pulled her head free.

"You promised you would not force m-me!" she sobbed.

"I am not forcing you," he said.

"Then release me!"

"No," he said, continuing to hold her close.

"H-how did you know?"

"I watched you this morning as you looked over the boats. Then I
waited for you tonight. You are very brave, Miranda, and clever and
resourceful and foolish."

"Why did you stop me?" Her voice was anguished.

"You would have died out there, Miranda. I could not let you
die."

"If you really cared for me," she whispered low, "you would have
let me go."

"No," he replied. "I am not that unselfish, Miranda. A gentleman
might have been that self-sacrificing, but I am a simple peasant, and
could not be." He paused, then said, "Any man who would be that
noble does not deserve you. Peasants learn not to be wasteful of
anything, and that includes people." He gently trailed a finger from
her shoulder down her bare arm, and she shivered.

"Don't," she said sharply.

His laughter was soft and insinuating. "Why not?" he persisted,
and she tried to pull away from him, suddenly aware that their naked
bodies were touching from breast to thigh. His free hand pushed her
long gold hair aside, and he gently squeezed first her right buttock
and then her left. He felt the nipples of her breasts hard and thrusting
against his chest, and although she was trying very hard to hide it,
her breathing was suddenly short and ragged.

"Please...please...stop," she whispered. "You promised not to force me! You promised."

He pulled her down on the bed. "I am not forcing you, Miranda. Have you never experienced desire, little bird?"

"With Jared! But I love Jared!"

"Never with the other young men who courted you? I find that hard to believe."

"No one else ever courted me," she said, and suddenly he understood what he had not understood before. Though she had been married and had had a child, she had been very, very sheltered. No man but her husband had ever touched her. She didn't understand that a body could experience desire for another even without love. If he told her that, she would fight him even harder, for she was not the kind of woman to accept plain lust. It would be better for her to believe that she was falling in love with him. The quicker she accepted her fate the easier it would be for her.

Lucas had not lied when he told Miranda that he loved her. He fully believed he did. That first glimpse of her, sleeping so innocently in the silvery moonlight, had caught at his heart. She was like none of his other women—the two plump and stolid German girls, the half-dozen women who had been born here at the farm, or the intense Frenchwoman, Mignon, who was several years his senior. The prince had given him Mignon because she was intelligent, and the prince believed she might breed intelligent children.

Intelligent women, said Alexei Vladimirnovich, if placed strategically, could be of immense value to Mother Russia. Lucas had been both amused and amazed by this confidence. Prince Cherkessky had deigned to speak to him only once before. At that time his master had congratulated him on the quality of the children he sired, and his rate of productivity. He had thanked the prince civilly. Then Alexei Vladimirnovich had promised him a silver-blond mate to match his own coloring. The promise had taken five years to fulfill.

He put an arm around her, drawing her near. His hand found her breasts, and he touched them gently. She trembled as he bent his head and his tongue flickered over first one nipple then the other. His mouth sucked hungrily at her right breast, and she whimpered, frightened.

Her body was growing feverish, and she was confused by the feelings assailing her. The feelings were wrong! They had to be wrong, and yet she was beginning to want him! He wasn't Jared! Yet his lips on her body were tenderly insistent, sweet and somehow... somehow... oh God, she didn't understand herself, but she didn't want him to stop. To her shame, she didn't want him to stop!

"Little bird," he murmured, his warm breath assaulting her ear, "your breasts are like small summer melons, tender and sweet." Again his fingers gently caressed the round, tight globes, and he buried his face between them, inhaling her scent.

His hands moved all over her body and his head moved down to her navel. She knew as he kissed it that it would just be a second longer before his eager, seeking mouth would taste of her. She cried out in despair at the very moment, her hands reaching out to catch at his thick hair, to draw him away, but she could not move him. His skilled tongue seemed to know the exact spot that would rouse her to a frenzied passion, when she thought she could bear no more, his big hungry body covered her burning one. He caught at her reluctant little hand, and drew it down to touch his aching manhood.

"I will give you such pleasure, little bird," his deep warm voice soothed. "I will give you such pleasure," and then his hand was gently spreading her thighs, and he was slowly, tenderly entering her.

Miranda turned her head to one side, and the tears trickled down her face. He had said he would not force her, and he had not. She had not really given herself, but neither had she successfully prevented him from taking her, for the truth was that she did not want to stop him. He rode her forcefully, driving her up passion's peaks, yet always holding her back from sweet fulfillment. Miranda began to lose the little control she had held on to, clawing at his back with desperate fingers. She lay breathless, helpless beneath this great man who was loving her so expertly, and his triumphant laughter rumbled about the small room.

"Ah, little bird, little bird, you are a fit mate for me! What beautiful, wonderful daughters we shall make together!"

Then he thrust hard and deep within her, over and over and over until she climaxed with a wild, angry cry, and his potent seed overflowed her womb. His lips carved a fiery trail down her throat, and he murmured love words in French and another language she didn't understand. As she floated back to earth she realized with a shock that she had not yet seen his face! Once he had tasted of her body he was insatiable. In all he took her five times that night, and she was barely aware of the last time because she was so exhausted.

She awoke once more in her own room. Not only had he returned her safely, but he had taken the time to dress her love-bruised body in a soft gauze gown. She lay on her back silently watching the dawn unfold. There were no more tears left. She had nothing left. Her body had betrayed her in a way she hadn't believed possible.

Once Jared had told her she had many things to learn about love, and he had promised to teach her. He hadn't taught her all, though. There hadn't been time. He had deserted her for his mission. And now he believed her dead. But she was not dead. She was instead another man's possession, and last night that man had taught her that passion and love were not necessarily intertwined. It had been a bittersweet lesson, a lesson she would never forget.

Though Lucas had prevented her escape last night, she would not give up. Her life as Jared Dunham's wife seemed over. He would not want her now, for what respectable man would want her now. But there was her son, little Tom, and there was Wyndsong. The worst was behind her now, and she no longer felt quite so frightened or desperate. She felt a strange calm.

Later, in the kitchen, she asked old Marya where the men lived. She intended satisfying her curiosity. She could not go on making love with a faceless stranger. The old woman cackled delightedly, saying, "So, you are anxious to be with your lover, Mirushka. Well, that is no crime, dearie, and here it is not forbidden, but encouraged. I will tell you where the men's quarters are, and if you would not mind you can run an errand there for me. My two sisters care for the men, and I promised them some of my plum preserves. I was going to send Marfa with it, but you may go if you like."

"I will go," Miranda replied, and a few minutes later she was on her way. She understood now how Lucas had seen her yesterday by the boats. The men's quarters were located on a hilltop near the beachfront. As she walked along she realized that she felt almost happy. It was a perfect September day, warm and bright with only the hint of a breeze to blow against her Persian blue caftan and disarrange her long loose hair.

There were six stone crocks in the basket she carried, and she hummed a little snatch of tune as she moved briskly along. She chuckled to herself. It was "Yankee Doodle"! Lucas was going to be very surprised to see her. She wondered again what he looked like. Was he handsome? Were his features fine, or those of a large peasant? Would it make any difference to the way she felt. What *did* she feel? She simply hadn't sorted all that out yet. Somehow she believed that she had to feel something for a man who made love to her, but then she realized that her experience didn't offer answers. She was still learning, and she seemed to understand so little.

There ahead were the men's quarters, a one-story whitewashed wooden building. Outside were several attractive young men kicking a ball around. Her cheeks grew pink when she saw that they wore only loincloths. They reminded her of a painting of a group of young athletes in ancient Greece that hung in Amanda's London town house. Every one of them was a light-eyed blond!

When they saw her they began dancing around her, making kissing noises with their lips and suggestive gestures. One managed a quick kiss to her cheek. Swinging around, Miranda slapped his face hard, to the delighted guffaws of the others. She was glad that she could not understand what they were saying, for she would have been twice as embarrassed as she already was. Eyes straight ahead, she walked determinedly toward the building while they continued to tease her.

"Christos, what a beauty!"

"Who is she?"

"With that coloring? She has to be Lucas's new woman."

"The lucky bastard! God, I'm getting hard just looking at her! How come he always gets the best piece to fuck?"

"Probably because he does his job better than any of the rest of us. Lucky devil!"

"Do you think he'd share her?"

"Would you?"

"Hell, no!"

Miranda went inside the building. She was sure that none of the men outside was Lucas. Entering the kitchen, she immediately bumped into a huge man. She gazed up at him, her heart hammering, wondering whether the man with the golden beard was Paulus, Lucas' brother.

He tipped her face up, looked boldly down at her, and fingered her silken hair. "As always," he said roughly, "my little brother has had incredible good fortune."

She couldn't understand what he said, but she didn't particularly like the look in his eye. Quickly his hands moved over her body, lingering a moment on her breasts. Angrily she pulled away and walked across the room to where two older women sat shelling peas. She addressed the two women in her excellent French. "I have brought the plum preserves from Marya."

"Thank you, child. Will you sit and take a glass of tea with us?"

"No, thank you," she answered, feeling foolish and out of place. "Please thank our sister."

"I shall." Miranda practically ran from the kitchen and out of the building. The young men did not bother her now, and she quickly made her way across the grassy yard, fleeing down to the beach.

The light breeze brushed against her hot cheeks. How silly she had been to go there. She wasn't really interested in what he looked like. It didn't matter at all, and it was probably better she not know. She would endure his attentions as long as she had to before she could make good her escape.

"Miranda!" He was suddenly behind her.

She began to run, but he caught her easily, and pulled her back tightly against him. "No," she said.

He laughed softly. "If you want to see what I look like you have but to turn around, little bird."

"How did you know I was here?"

"My brother came and woke me. He admires you tremendously, but then he always wants what I have." He nuzzled at her neck, gently biting it. "I can't get enough of you, little bird. You are in my blood now."

She pulled free, took a hesitant step away from him, and then turned quickly around. Her breath caught in her throat and her sea-

green eyes widened in amazement. Before her stood the most
incredibly beautiful human being she had ever seen in her life. His
oval face was classic, with high, sculpted cheekbones, a high, broad
forehead, and a firm, square chin with a deep cleft in it that matched
hers. His nose was long, narrow, and straight. His blazing turquoise-
blue eyes were set well apart and heavily fringed with dark, thick
lashes. His mouth was generous without the disadvantage of thick
lips. His blond hair was short and waved, and his big body was
perfectly proportioned. Miranda could not help but think how
wonderful he would look in elegant London fashions. Women would
beg for this man's attentions. He was magnificent, standing here
almost naked, the sun lighting his bronzed chest and thighs and
muscled arms.

"You are beautiful," she said, finally finding her voice.

His deep laughter rumbled. "Then you are not disappointed in me,
little bird?"

"No," she said slowly. "I am amazed that anyone could be so ...
so perfect in both face and form. However, I am afraid I shall
disappoint you when I tell you it would not have mattered to me if
you had been as ugly as you are fair."

"Why not?" he demanded, puzzled.

"Because in the dark hut, when I was frightened, you were kind to
me, and patient. You cared more for how I felt than for your own
wants."

"Any man—" he began, but she cut him short.

"No! Another man would have raped me. Your brother would
have taken me instantly to satisfy his own lust. You are special,
Lucas." Then without another word she turned and ran back up the
beach toward the villa. He did not follow her. He stood on the beach
watching her hurry up the hill.

He had best be careful not to fall in love with her. But then, he was
already in love with her, Lucas thought ruefully. His trick had always
been to make his women feel loved, for a loved woman was a happier
creature. But now...

He hoped he could help her adjust to her life. For the first time in
years he wondered what it would be like to live as an ordinary man.
How wonderful to have a house of his own, where Miranda would

live by his side and bear his children, children they would raise together. Then Lucas laughed at himself. He remembered the glorious days of his freedom, days of bitter poverty, with never enough to eat. In the winter rainy season they had always been cold, for there was never enough fuel. As Prince Cherkessky's slave he had a warm home and all his wants taken care of. It was better this way. He did not choose to share Miranda with anyone, even their child. He wondered how Miranda's husband had felt about sharing her with their son.

At that moment, Jared Dunham was feeling nothing. Drunk and unconscious, he was returned to Swynford Hall by his three anxious servants and Captain Ephraim Snow. At the sound of the carriage in the drive, Amanda, Lady Swynford, had hurried outside to greet her sister and Jared. Instead, she found herself facing a nightmare. Her gentle world had been invaded by horror. She watched as Jared was removed from the coach and wrinkled her nose in distaste as Martin and Mitchum carried him past her, for he smelled simply dreadful! Whiskey! He stank to high heaven of whiskey!

Sobbing, Perky stumbled down from the vehicle, her pretty face red and swollen with weeping. She took one look at Amanda, and began wailing. "Oh, milady! Oh! Oh! Oh!"

"Where is Miranda?" demanded Amanda, her heart hammering. "Where is my sister, Perkins?"

Perky wailed, "She's gone, milady! She's gone!"

Amanda fainted. When she was revived by means of aromatic spirits and a burnt feather waved beneath her nose, both Adrian and Jonathan were by her side. Gently they told her Captain Snow's tale, and she listened, unaware that tears were pouring down her little face. When they had finished and a heavy silence filled the air, Amanda wept in her husband's arms but found no comfort. Finally, after several moments, she said, "She is not dead. My sister is not dead!"

"Sweetheart," begged Adrian, "I know how painful this is for you, but you must not delude yourself. You must not!"

"Oh Adrian, you don't understand! If Miranda were really dead I would know it. I would know! Twins are different from just sisters,

Adrian. If Miranda were really dead I would feel it, and I just don't!"

"She is in shock," said Jonathan.

"I most certainly am not in shock!"

"Eventually she will come to accept it," continued Jonathan.

"I am not in shock!" repeated Amanda, but they paid no attention to her. Instead they fed her tea laced with laudanum so she would sleep.

A day later, Amanda awoke with a pounding headache and a firmer conviction that her twin was not dead. She tried to explain it again to Adrian, but he only looked distressed and called for his mama to come up from the dower house to reason with his wife whom, he was sure, teetered on the brink of insanity.

"I am not mad," Amanda said to Agatha Swynford.

"I know that, my gel," came the reply.

"Then why will Adrian not listen to me?"

The dowager chuckled. "Amanda, you know as well as I do that as dear a man as Adrian is, he lacks imagination. For my son the world must be either black or white, fish or fowl. He cannot accept anything in between. For him the evidence of Miranda's death is unassailable, therefore she is dead."

"No!"

"Why do you feel so strongly she is not?" asked the dowager.

"I told Adrian that twins are different, but I cannot make him understand it. Miranda and I look different, our personalities are certainly different, yet there is something between us, some awareness we have always shared. I have no name for it, but Miranda and I have always known when the other was in trouble. We have even been able to speak to each other without words. If she were gone from this earth I should know because I would feel it. But I don't."

"Is it possible, my gel," said the woman quietly, "that you do not sense the loss of this feeling between Miranda and yourself because you do not wish to sense it? Death is a closed door, impossible to reopen. I understand how close you two were."

"Miranda is not dead," said Amanda firmly.

"Then where the hell is she?" demanded Jonathan angrily six weeks later when Amanda persisted in her belief. "My brother has been drunk for over a month now, and if there is to be any chance of his recovering then he must face the truth. *Miranda is dead!* I won't allow you to give Jared false hopes!"

"Captain Snow never saw a body!" gentle Amanda shouted back at Jonathan. "The Russian official only said that the body was that of a blond woman. Miranda isn't a true blond, and when her hair is wet it is more silver than pale-gilt gold."

"What of the ring? The dress?"

"Someone could have dressed another woman in Miranda's things. How do we even know there was a body?"

"My God, Amanda, are you mad? You make it sound like a plot! Miranda was the unfortunate victim of a robbery."

"A robbery committed by someone arriving in a coach bearing the British Ambassador's crest. Doesn't that seem strange to you, Jon. Even Captain Snow has his doubts."

"All right, I cannot explain the carriage, but whatever the truth, one thing is certain. Miranda Dunham is dead!"

"No!" Amanda had never felt so frustrated or so angry in her entire life. Why did they not understand? "No, Jon, my sister is not dead. Whatever you tell me, she is not dead!" She turned her back on him so he might not see the tears filling her blue eyes. She jumped, startled, as surprisingly strong hands grasped at her shoulders and spun her around.

"Miranda is dead, kitten," said Jared Dunham. He was unshaven, gaunt, and hollow-eyed. But he was sober. "I have spent over a month trying to hide from that truth, Amanda. I am sure I have half-emptied Adrian's fine cellars. But eventually there is no escaping it. My wife is dead. My beautiful wildcat is gone, and part of the blame for it must rest with me."

"Jared—" Jonathan and Amanda spoke simultaneously.

"No," he answered them, a sad little smile briefly crossing his face. "That is another truth I have faced. I did not value my wife enough. If I had I would have told Mr. Adams and Lord Palmerston no. Instead I selfishly mounted my noble charger and self-righteously galloped off to help right the world's wrongs. My first duty was to Miranda. I failed in that duty, but I will not fail the magnificent legacy she has left me—our son. I am taking him up to my house in London where we will wait out the war. I don't believe I could face Wyndsong quite yet."

Amanda was deeply troubled by this. "Please," she said, "please leave little Tom with us here at Swynford, Jared. At least for a little while. The air in town is so bad for a child. I know Miranda would agree. Go to London if you must, and mourn my sister in private, but leave little Tom with us."

"I will mourn Miranda for the rest of my life," declared Jared grimly, but no more was said about taking the young Dunham heir to London.

Jonathan Dunham and Anne Bowen, now publicly acquainted for almost two months, announced that they had eloped. Amanda thought perhaps they ought to plan a ball to celebrate the joyful news, but Adrian wouldn't hear of it. They were all in mourning for Miranda. According to the story they circulated to explain her disappearance, Miranda had been swept overboard from her yacht in a sudden squall. Local society chattered enthusiastically. The Dunhams and the Swynfords had provided them with enough gossip to gnaw on during this dull time between seasons.

How fortunate Mistress Bowen was to have snared the Yankee. He was handsome and rich to boot—and her with two children—but then it was said that he had three! Then there was the deliciously macabre coincidence of both the Dunham brothers' first wives dying in boating accidents. Best of all was the fact that that elegant devil Lord Dunham would soon be back on the marriage market. He would not, he had announced, mourn a full year for his beautiful wife. At the end of three months he would re-enter society.

Although the season did not officially begin until after the new year, Jared Dunham went up to London in early December. He had no desire to be at Swynford on St. Nicholas Day. They would have been married for two years, and on that sad evening he sat alone in his study before a big crackling fire sipping smuggled French brandy. In his hand he held a small miniature of Miranda painted by Thomas Lawrence, England's most prominent portrait painter.

The famous artist had actually done a marvelous painting of Miranda and Amanda when they returned to England for Mandy's wedding. Jared had commissioned the portrait for his mother-in-law, and she had carried it with her when she had returned to America. Dorothea had been ecstatic over her gift. It showed Amanda in a blossom-pink gown seated on a Chippendale side chair and Miranda in a deep blue gown standing behind her twin. She was smiling down at her sister whose head was half in profile and tilted just slightly up, gazing back at Miranda.

Lawrence had caught the girls perfectly. Amanda was sweet in her blue-eyed, blond beauty, with just a hint of steel at the corners of that little rosebud mouth. Miranda was an unconquered spirit with a proud and defiant look in her sea-green eyes. Jared had arranged with the artist to paint the sisters' heads in miniature also. He then had each of the two pictures framed in oval silver frames decorated with raised silver grapes and vine leaves. He had presented Amanda's miniature to Adrian on their wedding day. He had kept Miranda's, taking it with him to St. Petersburg. Dear heaven, how many times had he held the miniature in his hand last winter? How many times had he stared down at her face as he was staring now? Her sweetly haunting, heart-shaped face with its lush mouth, that determined chin with its little cleft, her sea-green eyes? Miranda! Miranda! They had wed two years ago, and in those twenty-four months he had lived with her only seven months. God! He must have been mad!

Two years ago this day he had married her. Two years ago tonight she had faced him, frightened but defiant, across their bed. He remembered how she had clutched the coverlet to her sweet breasts, and then he had taken her in his arms and kissed her and soon the world exploded into passion. Now she was dead, and it was his fault, his fault for having left her for so long.

Her love for him had obviously been greater than his, which amazed him. She had borne with him even to having his child alone, and when she could finally bear no more she had come after him. In the first shock of her death he had damned her to hell and back for not staying in England, but what had he expected? She was his wildcat, purring at him one moment, hissing and clawing at him the next. Suddenly overwhelmed by fury and grief, Jared threw his brandy snifter into the fireplace, where it shattered into a thousand shards and the liquid flamed blue for a moment. Jared's face was wet with tears. "Oh, wildcat," he spoke into the silent room. "Why were you taken away?" For the only time in his life, Jared Dunham sounded like a lost little boy.

If Jared Dunham's reputation in his bachelor days had been low key it was no longer so in the days of his widowerhood. Without Miranda, he became, as Amanda had once said, destructive to himself. His bout with alcohol following Miranda's death taught him that drink did not help one forget, and gave him a bad headache besides. He had to find something to relieve his terrible anguish.

His stable increased to overflowing as he began to frequent the horse auctions at Tattersall's. He bought whatever caught his fancy, easing his conscience by telling himself that he would bring the excellent new stock with him to Wyndsong, to introduce new blood into the island breed. Some of his horses were racers, and he soon found a trainer and two jockeys. He took to racing his high-perch phaeton on the Brighton road with the other young men, but the amusement faded when he discovered that no other horses could beat his.

Gambling was boring for the same reason. Jared Dunham never seemed to lose, whether it was cards, or a boxer at Gentleman Jackson's gym, or something as simple as which raindrop would reach the bottom of the windowpane first. The irony amused him. He was lucky in everything except love.

Jared did not, however, forsake the ladies. On the contrary, his appetite was unquenchable. Among the beauties who accepted a gentleman's protection it was quickly acknowledged that Jared Dunham was a magnificent lover, a generous lover, but a short-term lover. No one woman could seem to keep him for more than a few weeks.

Married women of his class gazed at him with open interest. Ambitious mamas made certain that he was aware of their fresh and nubile daughters. Miranda Dunham was dead, and that handsome Lord Dunham needed a wife to set him straight. Why not their Charlotte? Or Emily? Or Drusilla?

Most of the maidens thrust at him were terrified of the tall, dark-browed, forbidding Lord Dunham. He seemed always to be glowering, and most were not quite sure he was not laughing at them, his narrow lips twisted into a sarcastic smile. This was hardly the sort of treatment they were used to!

One of the season's incomparables, however, did not quail from Jared Dunham. Lady Belinda de Winter was the Duchess of Northampton's godchild. Petite, with a pink and white complexion, dark ringlets, and deep blue eyes, Belinda gave the impression of purity, innocence, and goodness. Nothing could have been further from the truth. The daughter of an impoverished baronet, Belinda de Winter would stop at nothing to get what she wanted. She wanted Jared Dunham.

Belinda had come to London for her season courtesy of her godmama, who had been her late mother's best friend. Aunt Sophia's husband, the Duke of Northampton, had three daughters of his own to launch, so he had not been enthusiastic about sponsoring a fourth girl. Though one of the richest men in England, he was not a man to waste money on someone else's child. Knowledgeable beyond her years, Belinda had sensed his reluctance. But she desperately needed a London season.

Her own home, the Priory, was near the Northampton holding, Rose Hill Court, and Belinda was a frequent visitor. Biding her time, Belinda waited until one afternoon when she knew that Rose Hill Court would be empty of all but the duke and the servants. Catching her uncle in his library, she had cooly seduced him. Then she left him before he had a chance to recover. She had made damned sure he didn't get the chance to be alone with her again before they went to London.

The duke had been shocked by her behavior, shocked and fascinated. He had never known a woman as aggressive as that slip of a girl with her angel's face. He ached to have her again, but she avoided him and laughed at him from behind her little hands, her blue eyes dancing wickedly. He had finally succeeded in cornering her at a musicale, and heard himself sounding like a green boy.

"I want to see you again," he had said.

"If you take me to London you can see me every day," she had replied.

"You know what I mean, Belinda!"

"And you know what I mean, *uncle* dear."

"If I take you to London you will be nice to me?"

"Yes," she said, and brushed past him.

Belinda de Winter had gotten her season in London, and a magnificent wardrobe as well. But the Duke of Northampton never seemed to be able to find his godchild alone again. She was far too busy leading the exciting life of a London debutante. He continued to watch her, though. Eventually his time would come.

Jared Dunham, the American lordling whose beautiful wife had been swept overboard from their yacht in rough seas, was the subject of endless gossip that season. Belinda watched as other women sought to attract his attention. She listened silently to the talk that surrounded the incredibly attractive man, and she vowed to become his second wife. He was perfect—wealthy, handsome, and he would take her away from England, away from her damned father and brother!

Their behavior and reputations were an albatross around her pretty neck. Although men desired her, and she had had several proposals since bursting upon the London social scene, none of the gentlemen wanted Baron Chauncey de Winter and his son, Maurice, as relations. Belinda couldn't blame them.

The weather that winter was very bad all over Europe, and Miranda had been confined to the house for several days because of rain. Sasha had quickly tired of Vanya's jealousy and beaten the boy one day in October. After that, Vanya no longer complained if Sasha chose to play chess or talk with Miranda. And Miranda, feeling sorry for the child, was teaching him French. He was surprisingly good at it, and she suspected that Vanya was one of Lucas's offspring. She never asked, however. It was better not to know.

She was setting up the chessboard one evening when Sasha entered the room, wineglass in hand. "I've just been talking with Dimitri Gregorivich. You won't have to go to the breeding hut any longer, Mirushka."

Miranda looked up, surprised. "Why not?" she asked.

He gaped at her. "Why not? Come now, Mirushka, don't be coy with me. You know you are with child."

"What?" She looked stunned. "No!" she said. "I can't be!"

"Mirushka, since we have arrived here you have not had one show of blood, Marya tells me. When was your last cycle with the moon? I know. It was those first days on the road when you were unconscious. You began your flow the day after we left St. Petersburg. I made and changed the pads for you. And before that? Do you remember?"

She was white-faced. The last moon cycle she could remember had happened in England a week before she had left. He was right, she had had no flow in months, but she had simply put it down to shock. But she hadn't had any other symptoms! At least she didn't think she'd had any symptoms. Oh God! To return to Jared a soiled dove was bad enough, but to return with another man's child would be unforgivable.

Sasha's hand covered hers. "Are you all right, Mirushka?" His voice was kind, genuinely concerned.

"I'm all right," she said slowly. "Well, Sasha, this means you will be able to return to St. Petersburg in the summer. You must be happy."

"Yes!" he answered excitedly. Then seeing her sad look, he said, "This doesn't mean you can't see Lucas, Mirushka. You can, but there can be no more love between you until six weeks after the child is born."

"There is no love between us now, Sasha. There never has been."

"Oh, you know what I meant, Mirushka. I meant lovemaking."

"Making love, Sasha, is not love. It is copulation, and animals do it that way. Without caring."

He looked at her strangely. She was a curious woman, and he didn't understand her, but then who could really understand a woman? "Let us play chess," he said, and they sat down facing each other over the table.

Miranda played badly that evening. Her mind was elsewhere. She could not escape the farm now. She would be forced to remain here until the child was born. Of course, as soon as she was able she would get away—before he impregnated her again. She would leave the child behind. It would be taken from her at birth, anyway. How could she have any feeling for it? It was an alien being, forced upon her, and she meant for Jared never to know of her shame. No, she could not love this baby now growing within her. Why should she?

Lucas. Poor Lucas. She had been a great disappointment to him, for after that first night she had never again reached that peak of passion. Although it frustrated him, angered him, and confused him, she had not been disturbed by it. She had been distressed instead at actually enjoying relations with a man other than her husband. Her body had betrayed her, but her prayers had been answered and now she felt nothing. She had willed it so, and if she had to endure his touch, at least she would not allow her body any pleasure while her spirit was being so heinously violated.

Lucas had been kind to her, though, and for his sake she had pretended, but after a week or so he had stopped in the middle of his rutting, and said, "Why do you pretend?"

"To make you happy," she answered him. "You are good to me, and I would have you happy."

He immediately withdrew from her. "My God, Miranda, why do I not give you pleasure any longer?"

"It is not you," she said.

"I know that!" came the proud, quick reply.

"I warned you in the beginning, Lucas. I am Jared Dunham's wife. The prince cannot change that. All Prince Cherkessky has done is to remove me from my world and place me here, but my world is still there in my heart and mind. The first night you took me my body did indeed respond to yours. I will not deny it. I do not know why it happened, but I prayed it would not happen again and it has not. I am sorry if I have hurt you, for I would not do so deliberately. You are my friend."

He was silent for a few moments, and then he said quietly, "You are still hoping to go back, little bird, but that will not happen. In time you will come to accept that fact, but meanwhile I want you to know that you have not lost my love. I am a patient man, and I adore you, little bird. But please do not pretend. I will continue to make love to you, and eventually I will melt the ice in which you have encased your heart."

"Check, and mate!" came Sasha's triumphant cry. "Mirushka! Mirushka! Whatever is the matter with you? I have taken your queen with a pawn!"

"I am sorry, Sasha. I am simply not in the mood tonight, I am tired."

"Well, I hope that you're not going to turn into a dull companion just because you are breeding," he pouted.

"You must bear with me, Sasha," she mocked. "After all, I have only done what Alexei Vladimirnovich wanted me to do."

"Indeed," he brightened. "I shall write him tomorrow with the good news."

"Be sure to include my felicitations," she said sarcastically. She rose. "I am going to my chaste bed. Good night, Sasha."

In the morning she put on a woolen cloak and walked to the men's quarters to find Lucas.

"Miranda, my love!" he called to her from across the kitchen.

"I am with child," she said.

"I am glad."

She almost screamed at him. She turned to go, but he caught her and drew her back. "I must return to the villa," she said.

"Stay with me," he answered. "Let us talk. Sonya, some tea, my darling, and some of that good apple cake of yours."

"There is nothing to talk about, Lucas. I am with child, as everyone has planned. In mid-June I will give birth to a beautiful silver-blond slave, who in five to ten years can be sold in Istanbul for a small fortune. Perhaps she will even become a sultan's favorite. What a credit she will be to the Cherkessky slave-breeding farm! It is just what I have always wished for a child of mine!"

"Little bird, don't!" He put his arms around her and held her close.

To her chagrin she burst into tears, and he soothed her until her sobbing stopped. "Damnation," she hiccoughed in English, and he laughed. She was teaching him English, and he had understood her. "Why are you laughing?" she demanded.

"You are adorable," he chuckled, "and I love you."

She sighed with exasperation. He would never understand.

But over the next few months she had to admit that he was most attentive and loving. She had carried little Tom alone, without her husband's love and support, but it had not mattered for she had wanted Jared's child. She did not want the baby now moving so actively within her, yet this child's father was with her every chance he had, and strangely, she found his presence helped. As she grew bigger and bigger, and the painful reality of her situation bore down on her, she needed his honest kindness. She believed she would have gone mad without it. She was having another man's child while, far away, her dear husband believed himself a widower!

Spring arrived in late March, and with it a letter for Sasha from Prince Cherkessky. Miranda was seated in the sunny salon with him, and she was startled by his moan.

"Sasha, what is it?"

"Oh God!" he cried, and his voice rose to a keening wail of anguish. "He has left me, Mirushka! I am alone! Alone! Ohh!" And he fell to his knees, sobbing bitterly.

Miranda rose and, crossing the room, bent awkwardly to retrive the prince's letter from Sasha's grasp. Quickly she read the elegant French script.

Alexei Vladimirnovich had been married on the eve of the Russian Christmas to Princess Romanova, and she had instantly proved fertile. The new Princess Cherkessky was expecting the heir to the family fortunes in very early autumn. Alexei Vladimirnovich believed it better that Sasha remain at the farm in the position of manager. His presence in St. Petersburg could easily upset the princess, and in her delicate condition that was unthinkable. After she had put two or three children in the nursery and Cherkessky's line was assured, then Sasha might return to his master in St. Petersburg. In the meantime he was to remain in the Crimea. It would be only four or five years at the most.

The prince expressed pleasure at the impending arrival of Miranda Tomasova's child, and reminded Sasha to be sure and inform him immediately when his beautiful slave woman whelped her first baby for him. She was to be returned to the breeding hut within three months rather than the usual six, and put to stud with Lucas again. With luck they could have another child by her the same time next year.

Miranda shuddered. The prince was certainly an unfeeling brute. The man obviously cared for nothing except money.

The letter closed with the prince wishing Sasha well, and reminding him that if he disobeyed his master's orders, whatever had once been between them would be forgotten in the prince's anger and the punishment would be the most painful and severe that could be devised.

Miranda put the letter down and looked at Sasha. The man was now huddled in a heap on the floor, weeping piteously. She narrowed her gaze dispassionately. Perhaps in losing the one person he loved, Sasha would now understand her feelings.

Then a marvelous thought began to take form. If she could use the prince's cruelty to turn Sasha against him, then maybe, just maybe, she could convince Sasha to retaliate against Alexei Cherkessky! What greater revenge could Sasha take than to free the long-sought breeder?

She smiled to herself. She would convince him to take her and Vanya to Istanbul on the prince's yacht. He would also take the money the farm would receive in late June, when the farm would host buyers from all over the world at its annual sale. Her smile widened. What a sweet revenge! The prince would be robbed of the fattest part of his yearly revenues as well as her, his prize mare! First, however, she must win Sasha to her side. She bent over and put motherly arms around him.

"Sasha, Sasha, do not grieve," she soothed. "Please, dear friend, come and sit on the settee with me. Please, I cannot lift you."

Her gentle, sympathetic tone penetrated, and he stumbled to his feet and crossed the room with her, falling on the settee. "Oh, Mirushka, how could he do this to me? I knew he must marry for the family's sake. I would have behaved properly. I have always behaved well. I never embarrassed him. I am, after all, also a Cherkessky by blood."

"Dear Sasha, what can I say to you?" she murmured. "Now you have been torn from the one person you love in this world. Believe me, I understand. Oh, I understand!"

He raised his tear-streaked face and gazed sorrowfully at her. "And now I understand you, Mirushka. I do, and I beg your forgiveness!"

She cradled him in her arms as if he were a child.

"Poor Sasha, poor Sasha," she crooned sadly. But there was a triumphant smile on her face.

During the next month she subtly played with him, and upon him, as on a fine instrument. She went along with his moods, loved him, was properly indignant for him. Gradually he began to lean on her and to trust her. Soon she felt safe enough to suggest revenge. Given a few well-chosen words, he would come up with the right solution all by himself.

She had to be careful. If Lucas discovered what she was planning, he would try to stop her again. He was extremely attentive to her these days, taking her for long walks on the beach, holding her little hand in his big paw as any loving young husband might do. Once he had said, "I am going to ask Dimitri Gregorivich if I may suckle upon your breasts before they give you the herb that stops your milk. I shall be your only child, Miranda, and finally you will love me—as I love you." No, Lucas must not suspect that she had found an escape plan.

The boy Vanya was another concern. His round, childish face contrasted with his sharp little dark blue eyes. He watched her with Sasha for several weeks, finally daring to accost her one afternoon when she was alone.

"Why are you being so kind to Sasha?" he demanded boldly.

She eyed him with amusement, for she had every right to slap him and order him away. She asked him, "Do you love Sasha?"

"Of course! He is the only person who has ever really loved me. I am not just one of the slave children to him. I am special."

"Would you like to remain with Sasha always?"

"Oh yes, Mirushka!"

"Then trust me as Sasha does. Ask me no more questions. Keep your agile little mind on other things, and speak to no one about your curiosity. If you do these things I can promise you a long and lovely life with Sasha."

"What if I speak with Lucas?" the boy demanded slyly.

"Then none of your dreams will come true, Vanya. Though you do not understand it now, believe me when I say that I am the key to your happiness. Betray me, and you will be sold off this very year."

"Can you really do all that, Mirushka?" His childish voice held a note of fear.

"Yes, Vanushka, I can," she answered him in a voice so confident that he believed her.

"I will be loyal to you," he promised fervently.

She smiled sweetly at him. "I know you will," she said, and patting his plump, rosy cheek with one hand, she popped a chocolate into his mouth with the other. "Run along, and play now, Vanushka. I want to take a nap."

May came, and the pastures were filled with lambs and kids and colts and calves, all gamboling in the bright green grass. The children frolicked in the warm sea, and Miranda was within six weeks of giving birth to *the child* as she called the unwanted growth within her. She had no feelings for it. She longed only to be rid of it. The quicker she gave birth, the quicker she could leave this place.

She had eased back on poor Sasha. Letting him come up with her escape plan too soon would give him too much time to think about it seriously. Too much thought could change his mind because, deep down, his love and loyalty to Prince Cherkessky were still there.

She smiled to herself, watching the children playing in the sea. "Freedom!" she whispered to herself. She was Miranda Dunham of Wyndsong Island, and she was born to freedom. She would not stop fighting for freedom until death stilled her heartbeat.

❧ Chapter 13 ❧

The Tatars struck at dawn. Sweeping across the Bessarabian border to the west, they surprised the helpless inhabitants of Prince Alexei Cherkessky's slave-breeding farm. The Tatar raiders encountered no resistance, for no one here was foolish enough to resist the Devil's Horsemen, as they had always been called. Hearing the commotion, Miranda rose as quickly as her condition allowed. Sasha was rushing into her room.

"Tatars!" he gasped. "I don't understand! The prince is half-Tatar. They have never bothered us before."

Miranda didn't bother to mention that the other half of the prince was Russian, and that the Russians had been the ones to murder all of old Prince Batu's direct male descendants. "What will they do?" she asked.

"The slave markets in 'Stanbul," was the chilling reply, sobbed by terrified Sasha.

Damnation! Just when it had all been going so well. "Sasha, you must help me!" she said.

"How, Mirushka? How?" he gasped.

"Since I don't live in the quarters they will not know my situation. Say that I am the married sister of the English Ambassador in St. Petersburg, offered the prince's hospitality because I could not face another winter in St. Petersburg in my delicate condition. Tell them they can get a fine ransom for me from the British."

"But who will pay it?"

"The English Ambassador in 'Stanbul will pay. I have told you that my husband is very wealthy, but what I did not tell you is that he is also very good friends with Lord Palmerston, the Minister of War. Please, Sasha! Your loyalty to Alexei Vladimirnovich at this moment would be misplaced! Did he not betray you and exile you with no thought of your love?"

The pain leaped into his dark eyes, and he looked at her closely.

"Please!" she begged him. "Please!" She could hear the Tatars moving toward the villa. It was the longest moment of her life.

"I will do it, Mirushka!" he said. "I owe you at least a chance. But remember, it may not help."

"I understand," she said. "Hurry, we must tell old Marya!"

Together they hurried to the salon. Marya was already there, surrounded by Vanya and the housemaids. Quickly Sasha explained the plan to save Miranda. "She is a great lady in her own land, and the prince was wrong to steal her from her family. We must try to make it right for her now," he finished, and the frightened group all nodded eagerly, happy that one of them might be spared, glad it was to be Miranda, who had always been kind to them.

The main door to the house was suddenly kicked in, an unnecessary gesture since it had not been locked. The room filled with Tatar warriors. The terrified servant girls shrieked in fright, for the Tatars were a fearsome sight. Their skin had a yellow tone, which contrasted dramatically with their short black hair and slanted dark eyes. Dressed in dark baggy pants that ended at the knee where their boots began, they wore colorful shirts belted in the middle with metal links, and pillbox-shaped dark felt hats with long side flaps.

The raiders were extremely well organized, quickly separating the young servant girls and Vanya, stripping the girls naked and hustling them from the room. Old Marya refused to budge from Miranda's side, which seemed to amuse them. They ignored Sasha for the moment, scornfully eying his red silk dressing gown. But they were extremely solicitous of Miranda, insisting she sit down, patting her belly with broad grins and murmurs of approval.

They all snapped to attention as a slim, fierce-looking man entered the room. Walking up to Sasha, the man spoke in guttural but understandable French. "I am Prince Arik, last surviving grandson of Prince Batu. Who are you, and who is the woman?"

Sasha drew himself up proudly. He knew his fate even if Miranda didn't. "I am Pieter Vladimirnovich Cherkessky, called Sasha, son of the late Prince Vladimir Cherkessky."

"You are the current prince?"

"No, my mother was only a serf. I was raised, however, with my half-brother, Prince Alexei."

"Is the woman his wife? His mistress?"

"No, Prince Arik. This woman is Lady Miranda Dunham, sister to the English Ambassador in St. Petersburg."

"What is she doing here?" demanded the Tatar chief.

"Her husband, who now fights a war for his king across the great western ocean, left her with her brother. Her doctor in St. Petersburg believed she could not take the severe winter there, and so Prince Cherkessky, my master, offered her the hospitality of this estate. He is a great good friend of the ambassador."

Prince Arik whirled on Miranda. "When is your child due, madam?"

"A week or two," Miranda lied.

"When did you come here?"

"November. A month after my husband left for the Americas, and I was lucky to get here with all the snow in the north. It was terrible!"

"Why were you in St. Petersburg in the first place?"

"We were visiting my brother before Jared was due to depart," Miranda answered, and then she drew herself up as haughtily as her pregnancy would allow. "How dare you question me, Prince Arik! I was under the impression that Prince Alexei was the late Prince Batu's only grandson. Sasha, are you sure this man is not a fraud?"

Prince Arik laughed. "Yes," he said, "this lady is most definitely English. They are always so arrogant. In answer to your question, my fine lady, Prince Batu had five sons who lived here on this estate. His only daughter wed a Russian. He had thirty grandchildren. Three were his daughters' half-breeds. There were twenty-two other grandsons and five granddaughters—all pure Tatar.

"He was dying, and the Russian soldiers came and massacred the entire family. No one was spared. I saw my mother and my aunts raped over and over again. In the end I think the soldiers coupled with dead bodies, for they all died under the assault. I was just ten, and knocked out by a blow on my head. I was covered over by the bodies of my brothers and cousins. They thought me dead too, but I was determined to survive.

"After the slaughter they all repaired to my grandfather's wine cellar to get drunk. When I was sure it was safe I escaped to my mother's family in Bessarabia. I have waited a long time for the chance to revenge myself on the Russians. Today, I shall!" He stopped and looked closely at Miranda. "The question is, my fine lady, what to do with you?"

"I assume you will go to 'Stanbul to sell Alexei Vladimirnovich's slaves, Prince Arik." When he nodded, she continued, "Then take me with you."

"Why?"

"Because I will bring you a fat ransom. The English in 'Stanbul will pay very well for my safe return."

"You cannot travel in your condition, my fine lady."

"Of course I can," she quickly answered. "Don't tell me you're leaving the pregnant slaves behind?"

"No," he said.

"Do you think that breeders in a place like this are any less pampered than I am, Prince Arik? I most certainly can travel!"

He pretended to consider the matter, although he had every intention of taking her. "Very well," he finally agreed. "I will take you to 'Stanbul."

Prince Arik's second-in-command asked in the raiders' dialect, "Will you ransom her?"

"Of course not," chuckled the prince, "but let her believe that, so there will be no trouble on the journey. She will bring a hell of a lot more on the block than the English can pay, Buri, my friend. Look at that hair! Those eyes! With a child to prove her fertility she will make us a fortune. Take her outside while we dispatch these two." He turned to Miranda. "Go with Buri, my fine lady. He will take care of you."

"Prince Arik!" Sasha's voice was sharp with urgency. "It has been my duty to care for this lady while she was under Prince Cherkessky's protection. May I bid her farewell?" The prince nodded, and Sasha moved close to Miranda. To her amazement, he spoke in swift, clear English. "Don't trust the Tatars! They mean to sell you in 'Stanbul. The English Embassy is at the end of a small street called Many Flowers near the Sultan Ahmet Mosque, which is by the old Hippodrome. God go with you, Miranda Tomasova. I ask your forgiveness for the suffering I have caused you." He raised her hand and kissed it. "For your own safety, show no closeness to me."

"I forgive you, Pieter Vladimirnovich," she said. "What will happen to you?"

"Go now," he said, switching to French.

She gazed at him closely, and suddenly she knew. "Oh God!" she whispered, horror dawning.

"Get her out of here!" Sasha appealed to Prince Arik, and the Tatar captain Buri took Miranda firmly by the arm and led her from the room.

"Please," she cried, "I want to get my boots," and she pointed to her bare feet.

He understood and followed her back to her room, but he refused to give her any privacy, standing in the open door watching her. She took two caftans from the wardrobe, and put them both on over her thin gauze sleeping gown. She had managed to wheedle a decent pair of boots out of Sasha several months before, explaining that the dainty house slippers they had given her were too flimsy for her long walks. Since the prince had said she might have anything within reason, Sasha had had the farm's elderly cobbler fashion her a pair of red leather boots. They came to her knees, and were lined in soft lambswool. She pulled them on and took up her dark brown light-wool cloak. Taking a small carved bone hairbrush from the dressing table, she stuffed it into the inside pocket of the cape. "I am ready," she said. Buri quickly took her from the house.

The spectacle that assailed her outside made her blood run cold. The half-grown fields had been fired and the vineyards trampled beyond redemption. Where orchards had once stood were piles of newly felled trees. Every building except the villa was in flames. She could see bands of riders driving off the livestock and squawking poultry hanging from saddles. But most terrifying of all were the sobbing women and children, every one of them naked, huddling in frightened groups. She scanned them, but she could not see Lucas. She saw none of the men.

"Where are the men?" she asked. Buri looked blankly at her and she realized she had spoken French. She tried the local dialect that Lucas had taught her. "Where are the men?"

"Dead," he answered.

"Dead? Why?"

"What would we do with them? We couldn't sell them anywhere, for Prince Cherkessky's studs are too well known. Even in 'Stanbul they are known. Prince Arik wants this land totally destroyed. It is cursed, and only when what once was is no more can the souls of the Batu family rest, fully avenged." He asked slyly, "Why should you care about the men?"

"Because they were beautiful animals," she answered quickly, lest she betray herself. "I dislike waste, especially of good blood-stock."

"Ah, you English," he laughed. "So bloody cold, except with your animals."

Prince Arik and the rest of his men emerged from the villa carrying all the valuables they had found. They were piled into a two-wheeled cart. Behind them she could see fire beginning to spread through the villa, and she shuddered.

"Get into the cart, woman," he commanded.

"I can walk," she said, "and with your permission I would like to do so."

He nodded curtly. Grasping the mane of a black and white pony, he pulled himself into the saddle.

"Please, Prince Arik, must the women and children go naked?"

"Yes," was the curt reply. Then, kicking his pony, he was off.

"Why must they be naked?" she demanded of Buri.

"To instill fear, so they will quickly accept Prince Arik as their new owner and not even consider escape." He leaped lightly into his own saddle. "Stay by the wagon with old Alghu. I'll be watching you even if you don't see me."

The large procession began to move away. It was now two hours before midday, and the orderly, well-run farm that had seen a glorious May dawn was now entirely gone. As she walked along, Miranda saw sights she had never expected to see even in nightmares. The prince's serfs, with the exception of the pretty girls and the children, lay slaughtered. Every woman lay on her back with her skirts up, legs spread, throat cut. The men and the old people had all been shot or decapitated. As they passed by the men's quarters, now a smoldering ruin, the air heavy with the stench of burned flesh, she saw that several of the men had died fighting for their survival, Paulus among them. She did not see Lucas, but knew he was there. She said a silent prayer in memory of the gentle giant whose child was in her womb. Suddenly her eyes widened with fresh horror.

The Tatars had been doubly cruel. The genitals of the men who had chosen to defend themselves had been cut off and stuffed into their mouths. The Tatars had taken these gallant defenders alive, though wounded. They had performed the terrible mutilation and left the men to die either from blood loss or from choking to death on their own flesh.

She felt her kidneys empty themselves, her legs grew weak, and she vomited the scant contents of her stomach until she was retching only bitter bile. She fought fiercely to regain self-control, forcing herself to breathe deep, long breaths until she steadied herself. Looking away from the awful sight, she focused her vision straight ahead and moved steadily forward, placing one foot before the other, one foot before the other, one foot before the other. Her body was wet with clammy, cold perspiration, and her head ached terribly, but she moved onward.

They walked all day long without stopping, crossing over the border into Bessarabia late in the afternoon, long before the Russian authorities in Odessa could possibly know about the raid on the Cherkessky estate. Finally, at dusk, they stopped near a stream, and within a short time the campfires were blazing and the smell of roasting meat permeated the air. Numb, Miranda was sitting alone by the cart when Buri approached and shoved a tin plate into her hand.

"There's a slave woman who wants to stay with you. Says she was your maidservant."

"Of course," Miranda replied. Marfa! A friendly face! However, the naked woman with the slightly protruding belly who appeared in Buri's custody was not Marfa, but a sweet-faced petite blond with corn-colored braids and desperate, begging, light-blue eyes. Although she had never seen her before, Miranda knew instantly who she was. "Mignon, my dear, thank heavens you are safe! Here, sit by me." She patted her cloak, looked to the Tatar, and said, "Would you ask Prince Arik if my servant may stay with me and have her gown back? She will not run away."

He grunted and went off.

"You knew me? How?" asked Mignon in beautiful French.

"Lucas spoke of you, and of course, Sasha told me your story."

"Why do these animals treat you well?" Mignon asked.

Miranda explained, and Mignon nodded. "You are fortunate," she sighed.

"They have no intention of ransoming me," Miranda said quietly. "Sasha warned me before we were separated, but he told me where the English Embassy is. I plan to escape when we get to Istanbul. Do you want to come with me? We'll show these barbarians what it is to deal with a free American and a Frenchwoman!"

Mignon smiled suddenly. *"Mon Dieu,* yes! I will have a chance to return to France, and believe me, madame, if I ever get there I shall never stir from Paris again!"

"What of your children?"

"I have no idea which ones they are," she said matter-of-factly. "I birthed them, but I never saw them afterward until it was too late to know. I am four months pregnant. I will have to keep the one I carry now."

Buri returned and tossed a caftan at Mignon, who looked gratefully at Miranda. *"Merci, madame!"* she said.

Miranda nodded and then turned to the Tatar. "What did the prince say?"

"You may keep your servant with you. He also told me to say that you two are to sleep beneath the cart tonight. Old Alghu will guard you, and the prince has already given orders you are not to be touched. Still, our men are celebrating, and there is no reasoning with a drunken man, so be warned." Then he disappeared into the darkness.

Miranda offered to share the haunch of meat on her plate, but Mignon declined saying, "I've already eaten, but you eat. It's baby lamb, and very good."

Miranda followed the Frenchwoman's advice, knowing that she must keep her strength up and her wits sharp. She ate the lamb right down to the bone, even sucking the marrow from the bone's end. "Do you think we dare get some water from the stream?" she queried Mignon.

Mignon looked about. "Why not?" she answered. "They're too busy stuffing themselves and getting drunk to bother us."

The two women stood up, and Miranda spoke to Alghu in the local dialect. "We want water." She pointed to the stream. "Is it permitted?"

He lumbered to his feet, nodding, and escorted them to the stream, chuckling as they squatted modestly behind the bushes to relieve themselves before drinking. Once back at the cart, they sat on the end of it comparing the events that had brought them to Prince Cherkessky's farm, and telling of their lives before being kidnaped.

Mignon had been born the year the Bastille fell. Her father was a duke, her mother a farmer's daughter. They were not married. Raised by her mother in the Normandy countryside, she and her peasant relatives escaped the worst of the terror accompanying the Revolution. Her father had escaped to England where his title and sexual prowess had gotten him an heiress wife. When Napoleon came to power he returned to France and, by loyal service to the emperor, won back his estates.

Ten years after Mignon's birth her mother received a letter from her former lover. The letter was read to her by the disapproving village priest. His bastard daughter, the duke stated, was to be educated. He enclosed money, and Mignon's mother obediently complied with his request. Each year from then on a letter with money arrived right after the new year. Mignon met her father for the first time when she was fifteen.

"Why have you educated me?" was her greeting.

"Because there will be one less peasant to turn on her master next time," he growled back at her.

They both laughed. The two became good friends. She was brought to Paris and sent to an excellent convent school, which filled in the gaps in her education and taught her how to be a lady. She had left the convent at eighteen to become a teacher in a fine Paris boarding school. At twenty she obtained an excellent position as governess in the household of Princess Tumanova in St. Petersburg. Miranda knew the rest of her story.

Miranda outlined her own history and downfall. "Thanks to Sasha, however, I shall escape, and you will come with me, Mignon," she said confidently.

"Did you love Lucas?" the Frenchwoman asked suddenly.

"No," said Miranda candidly. "He was a good man, but the only man I have ever loved is my husband, Jared."

"I loved him," Mignon whispered low, "but until you came I didn't believe his heart could be touched at all."

"He was not like us," said Miranda. "His life as a slave was better than his early years. It was different for us. Did you ever go hungry? Were you ever cold?" Mignon shook her head. "I thought not," Miranda continued, "and though you were not your father's legitimate daughter, he loved you and he saw to your welfare."

Miranda shifted her position, for the baby was making her uncomfortable. "I lacked for nothing. But poor Lucas had none of these things, nor did he understand what freedom really was. Neither do the rest of the poor souls captured at the farm. But we do, Mignon. Trust me, we will be free."

"You will have your baby soon. It will not be easy, Miranda."

"We will succeed!" came the confident reply.

The two women sat companionably for several more minutes, and then they retired beneath the cart to sleep under the warmth of Miranda's wide wool cape. They had barely dozed off when a shriek tore into the night. They woke together, and both realized what was happening. The women who were not virgins were being raped by their captors. The two women huddled close together, hands over their ears, attempting to blot out the cries, and as the noise gradually died they dozed nervously until dawn, when Alghu shook them awake. He had brought them mugs of steaming sweet black tea and cold meat.

Miranda took out her brush, and brushed both her own and Mignon's hair. Then they both rebraided neatly, and washed their faces and hands in the cold stream nearby. The journey began again.

"Keep your eyes out for early strawberries," said Mignon. "I suspect they mean to walk us all day again without any real rest or food."

"But why?"

"Tired and beaten prisoners don't run away. They'll feed us well at night so we'll arrive in 'Stanbul in fairly good condition, but they want the journey to wear us down. Look for the strawberries, Miranda. Their sweetness will help keep us going."

"I don't need another day's trek to be too tired to run away," replied Miranda wryly. "I'm exhausted. But I told Prince Arik I could keep up, and I will."

Their lives took on a monotonous pattern: up at dawn, hot tea and cold meat, walk all day except for a few minutes' rest around noon when the Tatars watered their ponies, stop for the night, broiled meat to eat and water to drink, exhausted sleep. They supplemented their diet with the strawberries Mignon found, and one day as they marched by the sea Miranda captured several large crabs, which they wrapped in seaweed and cooked that night in the hot coals of Alghu's little fire. Nothing had ever tasted so good, Miranda thought, as she picked the hot, sweet meat from a claw.

The warm Black Sea spring weather held for almost two weeks, and then one day they awoke to a steady downpour. The word was passed through the camp that they would rest all day in shallow caves that would protect them from the rain. The slave women were grateful for the rest, for they were all exhausted. They slept while the children played games. Their captors, however, preferred to drink and gamble, and by midafternoon had become unusually surly. Old Alghu had fallen into a drunken sleep. A couple of the Tatars wandered over to the cart where Mignon and Miranda were talking quietly.

"What a shame the silver blond is so far gone with child," remarked one of them. "She looks like she could fuck a man into paradise."

"Too thin for me, Kuyuk. Now this plump little quail is more to my taste," the second Tatar said, dragging Mignon onto her feet, and pinioning her against his body with one hand while the other hand fumbled with her breasts.

"Please," Miranda cried, struggling to her feet, "my servant is with child. Prince Arik promised me she would not be touched!"

The men stopped. But when they realized Alghu's drunken condition, they resumed their abuse. "On your back, slave!" snapped the second man, and Mignon complied without a word.

"No!" screamed Miranda. "I will report you to Prince Arik!"

"Gag her!" came the command, and Miranda found a dirty rag stuffed into her mouth. "She can watch, Kuyuk, and though she is about to whelp, her tits aren't off limits!"

"By God, you're right, Nogai!" He sat down on his haunches and dragged Miranda with him. He placed her firmly on her knees between his spread legs and, sliding his hands around, he grasped her swollen breasts and squeezed. She gasped with pain, but bit her lip. She would not give this Tatar the satisfaction of knowing he had hurt her.

Miranda could feel the child within her moving restlessly, trying to escape her cramped position, and a sudden great anger welled up within her. Mignon was submitting in order to save her baby possible harm, and also to save Miranda. Furiously she jammed both her elbows into Kuyuk, taking him by surprise and knocking the wind from him. She scrambled clumsily to her feet and ran, tearing away the gag as she went. The Tatar thundered after her.

"Prince Arik!" she screamed. "Prince Arik! Prince Arik!"

Kuyuk caught up with her and slapped her several times. Her head reeled, but she shrieked nonetheless. Her cries brought slaves and Tatars running. "Pig of a Tatar! Your mother was born of a pile of dog droppings, and coupled with an ape in order to beget you!"

He delivered a brutal blow to her belly. "Bitch!" he roared. "Pregnant or not, I am going to take you like a stallion takes a fractious mare! Your belly isn't going to protect you any longer! On your knees before the whole camp, woman!"

Waves of pain overcame her, and she vomited. Gathering her last ounce of strength, she shouted, "Prince Arik! Is this how the word of a Tatar is kept? Your word has no value!"

Suddenly the crowd surrounding them parted, and the Tatar chief was there. His blazing eyes flicked from the disheveled Kuyuk to Miranda, now on her knees clutching her belly. The prince knelt, and with surprisingly gentle hands brushed the hair from her face. A sharp command brought a flask, and he forced a potent fiery liquid between her lips. She gagged, but managed to keep it down. "Take deep breaths," he commanded her, and when the color returned to her face he commanded quietly, "Explain!"

"Two of your men, this one and his friend, Nogai, came to where Mignon and I were resting. They have raped Mignon despite her pregnancy. I have been subjected to their abuse as well. I think," here Miranda's voice caught and tears rolled down her cheeks, "I think they have killed her."

"Where was Alghu?"

"Drunk," she answered.

Prince Arik turned to Buri. "Find out!"

For several minutes they all waited in deathly silence. The crowd of Tatar warriors and their captives stood quietly, and then Buri returned with both Alghu and Nogai. "She's right," he said. "The Frenchwoman's dead, and her baby with her. What a waste!"

The Tatar prince stood very still and looked around at his warriors. "I put this woman and her servant off limits to you all," he said. "You have not only violated my word, but you have wantonly murdered two expensive slaves, the woman and her unborn child. The punishment is death. As for you, Alghu, you seem to love wine more than you love your duty. You are no longer fit to be called a Tatar warrior. You will lose your sword hand, and if you don't bleed to death, you may follow us to Istanbul, but you are exiled from Tatar life forever. Temur!"

A young warrior leaped forward. "Temur, I am placing this woman in your keeping. I know you will do your duty better than Alghu did his." He looked to the captives. "I want another house servant," he said, and Marfa quickly stepped forward. "See to the lady, girl, until you are told otherwise."

"Yes, master!" Marfa leaned down and helped her mistress rise. Miranda swayed dangerously. Temur picked her up and carried her back to the cart, Marfa hurrying behind. Temur set Miranda gently down. Hurrying off, he returned a few moments later with a huge armful of fresh-cut pine boughs, which he placed near the fire. Rummaging in the treasure cart, he pulled out a sheepskin rug and tossed it over the pile of pine boughs. Over this he placed a simple woven wool hanging that Miranda recognized as having come from the dining room of the villa.

Picking her up again, he set her gently on this comfortable bed and covered her with a cape. "We are not all beasts," he said. "I am ashamed for Kuyuk and Nogai, and I am sorry about your friend. Rest now. No harm will come to you while I guard you." He fumbled in a pouch of his belt. "Here, girl, make your mistress some tea," and he handed her a small packet of leaves.

Miranda lay very still, gazing at the place where Mignon had lain. The body had been removed, and a dark patch of her blood was all that remained of the horrible death Mignon had known. Miranda wept softly. Perhaps now she was with Lucas and their child, but she would never see her beloved Paris again.

"Tea, Miranda Tomasova. Drink." Marfa helped her sit up, and put the mug of boiling sweet liquid to her lips. Miranda sipped at it, and soon she became very sleepy. The child was quiet now too, and the pain in her belly was gone. She fell asleep, a sleep so sound that she did not hear Alghu's cry of anguish when his sword hand was severed, and the stump stuck in boiling pitch to prevent his bleeding to death. Nor did she hear the hissing "Ahhhhh" of the spectators at the swift executions of Kuyuk and Nogai.

The rain grew worse during the night, and in the morning Prince Arik made the decision to remain camped in the caves. After the previous day's tragedy, the mood of the camp was deeply subdued.

Miranda awoke to a terrible, wracking pain that tore from her back through to her belly. She was in labor. It was too soon. The baby wasn't due for three or four weeks, but it was coming now. She grit her teeth and groaned. The young Tatar was immediately by her side, his eyes sympathetic.

"My baby is coming," she whispered hoarsely. "There are midwives among the slave women. Get me one!"

"I'll go!" volunteered Marfa. "You'll want Tasha. She is the best," and she ran off.

"I'm here," the Tatar soothed Miranda, then stated proudly, "and I can help if necessary. I've helped my ponies foal many times."

She almost laughed, but he meant to be kind. "Please," she begged him, "just a little sweet tea. I am so thirsty."

He got to his feet as another sharp pain knifed through her. Marfa returned with a stocky, capable-looking woman who said briskly, "I'm Tasha. Is this your first?" Miranda shook her head and held up two fingers. Tasha nodded. Kneeling, she drew the cape back to examine her patient. "Your waters must have broken while you slept," she observed. "It will be a dry birth." She probed her patient gently, finally announcing, "The baby's head is down in position. It is just a matter of your pushing."

Temur brought her a tiny bit of tea, which she drank greedily. Her lips were dry and cracked. He moved behind her and, kneeling, propped her body up with his. Tasha nodded approval. "At the next pain, I want you to push," she said. Miranda thought back to her son's birth, and was barely conscious of the pain of this one. She followed Tasha's instructions and after a while heard her calling, "It's a girl!" Then Miranda heard one weak cry, but nothing more. She slid in and out of consciousness until, finally, she fell into a restful sleep.

When she awoke again it was with a feeling of great relief. She was free again, and now she must gather her strength, for they would reach Istanbul in several more weeks. She would escape. She would be free.

A whimper by her side made Miranda turn her head. With a shock she saw a small, swaddled bundle tucked in next to her. *The child!*

Why had they not removed it? Then her mind began to clear. Only on the farm would they have taken the child away. Here in the Tatar camp the child was believed to be the offspring of her lawful husband, and she could hardly reject it. Damn! The brat would slow her up. Oh well, she could always leave it behind with Marfa when she fled into the city.

The baby whimpered again. Rolling onto her side, she drew the infant closer, gently loosening the swaddling clothes around it, remembering as she did her first inspection of little Tom. This child was beautiful—tiny, so very tiny, but beautiful. Her downy hair, barely visible, was Miranda's own silver gilt—or was it Lucas's? Her eyes were violet, but Miranda immediately noticed something strange about those lovely eyes. She passed her hand across the child's face, but the baby didn't react at all. Was the baby blind? The child had a tiny cleft in her chin, as both her parents had. Miranda touched the soft rose-tinted cheek so like her own, and the infant turned its small head, revealing an enormous dark purple bruise.

Miranda sighed. Kuyuk's vicious blow had found its mark after all, injuring her child. As she rewrapped the baby securely she suddenly realized what she had been thinking. Her child? Yes, it was *her* child, and she couldn't deny it any longer. It had been forced upon her in a frightening, degrading way, but the baby was just as much a victim as she had been.

Miranda struggled to a sitting position and, unbuttoning the front of her caftan, put the baby to her breast. Although the child seemed to nuzzle at her, it made no attempt to take the breast and suck. Gently Miranda forced her nipple into the baby's little mouth, and then began to milk herself. Suddenly the infant understood, and began to suck weakly. A smile lit Miranda's face. "There, my little one," she cooed at the child. She spoke in English. Her daughter was an American. Yes, she realized again, *her* daughter.

Prince Arik came into the light of her campfire and squatted next to her. His eyes moved admiringly over her. By God, he thought, this is a real woman! She looks as fragile as an early rose, but she is as tough as iron. He motioned toward the baby. "Let me see her," he said.

Miranda turned the child from her breast for a moment.

"She is beautiful," he said, "but the midwife says she won't live. You shouldn't waste your strength nursing her. Let us leave her on the hillside when we leave this place. It is more merciful."

Her sea-green eyes blazed furiously. "My daughter may also be blind. Blind from a Tatar blow. But she will live, Prince Arik. She will live!"

He stood up, shrugging. "The weather is clearing," he said, "and we will leave tomorrow. I have told Temur you are to ride in the cart for a few days until your strength returns." Then he turned abruptly.

"Thank you," she called as he left.

She spent the rest of the day dozing and feeding the baby. Marfa brought her a mug of rich beef broth. "Temur gave me a piece of meat from a heifer they slaughtered. I've boiled it for several hours with some greens and wild onions," she said proudly.

Miranda sipped the broth. "It's delicious, Marfa, thank you. I'm hungry, too. Will you get me several slices of that beef, the rarest you can find, and some of the juices if you can?"

Marfa was able to do just that, even bringing Miranda a full cup of the beef juice. She also found a small patch of wild strawberries to bring to her mistress. Miranda stuffed herself shamelessly. She was already feeling stronger, and twice rose to move around their shelter, leaning on Temur's shoulder.

In the hour just before the dawn she awoke to feed her child. The infant's skin was so very pale, and she seemed barely to be breathing. All Miranda's mother instinct welled up, and she cradled the baby protectively. "I won't let you die!" she said fiercely. "I won't!"

Temur reloaded the cart, leaving enough room for her to ride comfortably. Cutting more pine boughs, he made her a fresh new bed and settled her. Once again, the days took on a pattern.

One thing Miranda had done since the Tatars had captured them was to keep close track of the days. The farm had been raided on the fifth of May, and her baby was born thirteen days later, on the eighteen of May. Ten days after the baby's birth, she guessed they were still two weeks from Istanbul. Miranda grew stronger, and soon she was even walking all day, carrying the baby daughter in a sling that nestled her close to her heart. She worried constantly. The little one didn't seem to gain weight, and was really too quiet.

Strangely it made her think of her son. Little Tom was now thirteen months old, and she had missed his babyhood. She was, she decided, no more mature than Jared, who had missed the early months of their marriage. Perhaps now they had both finally grown up, and when they began anew, they would behave in a more sensible manner. *If* they began again, she reminded herself.

Excitement began to build as they neared the Turkish capital. Finally they came in sight of the great and ancient city of Constantine, the Rome of the East captured by the Turks in 1453 and held by them ever since. The Tatars camped that night by the ancient walls of the city which were locked for the night. They would enter the city the next day, and their captives would be taken to one of the best slave merchants there.

The days of wandering and raiding were just about over, and Prince Arik was wise enough to see it. His tribe needed money to purchase land so they might settle somewhere permanently. Some of them, he knew, would return to Asia, and align themselves with other wandering bands of Tatars, but as leader of the Batu clan he had made a decision for his people. The great days were over, and would never return. They were now stories to be retold about the campfires, but nothing more.

"My lord?"

Prince Arik looked up. "Yes, Buri?"

"The fine lady, my lord. Do you want a guard on her now?" Buri asked.

"It is not necessary. Her ladyship has stated her case and, being a noblewoman, is used to being listened to. She assumes that I will do her bidding, and we will allow her to continue believing that. We will take the others into the city first, and arrange with Mohammed Zadi for their disposition. I will explain to him about our fine lady, and he will arrange a private auction for discriminating buyers. When the time is arranged we will get her to the baths on a pretext, drug her there so she will be docile, and it will be over quickly. I expect such a beautiful woman, with an infant at her breast to attest to her fertility, should bring us a fine price."

Buri nodded in agreement.

The two men continued to talk while deep in the shadows Miranda slipped silently away. Thank heavens she had learned their dialect! She had waited in the darkness for several hours after sunset, hoping to learn their plans, and she had certainly gotten more than she had bargained for! She decided it would be better to leave immediately. Tonight the Tatars were still concerned with their camp full of captives. Yes, tonight was her best chance.

She reached her small campfire. Just beyond its shadows she could see Temur and Marfa entwined in an embrace. To her good fortune, they had become enchanted with each other in the last several days. She suspected the young Tatar would buy the plain, sweet Marfa for a wife. At least they would keep each other busy tonight.

Miranda sat down by the campfire and nursed the child. Another good thing was that the baby hardly ever cried. It would make escape easier. Miranda was beginning to suspect that she was deaf as well as blind, but she couldn't let herself think about that now. Perhaps the baby was simply weak.

Finished with the feeding, she quickly changed the baby's napkin and, reswaddling it, rebound the sling tightly against her chest. Then she carefully scanned the camp. All was quiet, but she forced herself to wait seated by the fire for another hour to be absolutely sure.

A waning moon was half risen, and offered her just enough light to see her way. She cut a wide swath around the camp in order to avoid detection by anyone who might be awake, and it took her time to work her way back onto the well-worn path. Once there, she quickly covered the final distance. Reaching the gate, she sat down with her back against the wall, pulling her dark cape around her to camouflage them so she might doze in relative safety.

The noise of carts arriving early the next morning awoke Miranda, just as she had intended. Feeding and changing the child, she then joined the crowd waiting for the gates to open. She could see the name "Charisius" carved deeply into the marble at the top of the ancient gate.

The new sun climbed over the eastern hills with slender, golden fingers, and from the heights of every mosque in the city the muzzins sang praise to God and the new day in a wailing chorus. About her, all fell to their knees, and Miranda followed suit, anxious not to be singled out. Then the gates creaked open, and Miranda hurried through with the rest of the crowd, eyes lowered as befit a modest, lowly woman. She had cut a rectangle of cloth from one of her caftans, and this was fixed in place across her face by her hair ornaments. With the hood of her cape pulled low to her eyebrows, she appeared a respectable woman garbed in the traditional black yashmak of the poor. She was no different than a hundred other women, their yashmaks making them anonymous to curious eyes.

She had no idea where she was, but she realized that she must reach the English Embassy as quickly as possible, for as soon as her captors knew she was gone, Prince Arik would realize where she was fleeing to and hurry to head her off.

Miranda looked around for a shop, not one catering only to neighborhood trade, but a shop that would be attractive to a visitor, whose owners would probably speak French. Her eye lit upon a jeweler, and she boldly entered the shop.

"You, woman! Begone! Begone before I call the sultan's police! This is no place for beggars."

"Please, sir, I am a respectable woman." Miranda imitated the whining cry she had so frequently heard from her elegant carriage in London. She spoke a crude French, badly accented. "I merely seek direction. I am not of this city. Your fine shop obviously caters to the *ferangi* infidels so I assumed you could direct me safely."

The jeweler stared at her with a little less hostility. "Where are you going, woman?"

"I must find the embassy of the English. My cousin, Ali, is their doorkeeper, and I have been sent to fetch him. Our grandfather is dying." She paused as if thinking, and then said, "No one else could be spared from the farm to come."

The jeweler nodded. It was the growing season, and no man could be spared even in an emergency. "You came in through Charisius, eh?"

"Yes, sir, and I know the English Embassy is located at the end of the Street of Many Flowers near the old Hippodrome, but I do not know how to get to this Hippodrome."

The jeweler smiled a superior smile. "The street outside this shop is called the Mese, woman. It is the old commercial avenue of this city. I know that because I am Greek, and my family has lived in this city for a thousand years."

He paused. Knowing what the pompous fool expected, she widened her eyes and said, "Ohhh!" Gratified, the jeweler continued.

"You have but to follow the Mese across the city, and at its end are the ruins of the old Hippodrome. The avenue goes right at the Church of the Holy Apostles, so don't be fooled and go to the left or you will be lost. A pleasant neighborhood has been built up around the ruins. One street before you reach these ruins is a small street to the right. That is the street you seek. The embassy is at its end. It is quite near the sultan's palace."

"Thank you, sir," Miranda said politely as she left the shop, trying not to run. Now she knew! Across the city, he had said.

She glanced fearfully toward the gates but there was no sign of unusual activity. Miranda began walking, reassuring herself as she went of her safety. Every woman on the street was as muffled as she was, and they were all quite indistinguishable. If the Tatars sought a woman with a baby she was also safe, for the child slept peacefully in its sling beneath her enveloping cloak, out of sight.

Behind her she heard a troup of horsemen coming up, and her heart seemed to swell painfully in her throat, almost stop, then thump violently. She somehow managed to scramble frantically to the side of the avenue with the rest of the pedestrians as a group of men in red and green cloaks cantered past on their dark brown horses.

"Damned, arrogant Yeni-cheri," muttered the man next to her, and she almost laughed aloud in her relief. She felt the chilly perspiration of fright rolling down her back. God, how she longed for a bath! It had been five-and-a-half weeks since her capture, and in all that time she hadn't been able to bathe. Her hair was also filthy, and she wasn't totally sure it wasn't lice-ridden at this point. She walked doggedly on, fascinated in spite of her fear, and the need to hurry, in this marvelous city about her.

The street noise was incredible, a mad cacophony of loud voices, each shouting in a different language, each with something very important to say. The shops were just as varied and fascinating. She passed a street where the shops were all tanners and shoemakers and leatherworkers. Then, farther along, there were linen drapers, men who sold only the finest silks, goldsmiths, silversmiths, jewelers. The open-air bazaars were a wonder, offering everything from fish to figs to old icons. It was growing hot now, and odors rose from everywhere. There were the pungent smells of cinnamon, cloves, nutmegs, and other spices, melons, cherries, bread and honeycakes, gillyflowers, lilacs, lilies, and roses.

She walked on, and the establishments began to lose their big-city elegance and become shops of a residential neighborhood. She was getting closer. Dear God, let the Tatars not be there before her! Up ahead she could see the old chariot racetrack of the Hippodrome now made into a small neighborhood open-air market. She began to check the street signs at each crossing. They were done in both flowing Arabic script and French. There it was! *La Rue des Beaucoup Fleurs*. The Mese was empty here, and cautiously she approached her destination, peering down the narrow little street for any sign of an ambush. But the small birds in the flowering vines that hung over the blank walls on either side of the street were active and noisy, a sure sign of safety.

Miranda turned and looked back down the Mese for signs of pursuit, but there were none. She hurried down the Street of Many Flowers toward her destination—a black iron gate set in a white wall. As she neared it she could see the shining bronze plaques on either side of the gates. In three languages, they announced His Majesty's Embassy.

Reaching the gates, she pulled boldly on the bellcord, and was instantly greeted by the gatekeeper, who popped like a jack-in-the-box from his little gatehouse. One look at her set him to shout "Begone, misbegotten daughter of a she-camel! No beggars! No beggars!"

Miranda didn't understand his words, but she understood his meaning well enough. Tearing the veil from her face she threw back her hood, and shouted back at him in English, "I am Lady Miranda Dunham. I am English. Let me in quickly! I am being pursued by Tatar slavers!"

The gatekeeper looked stunned, then frightened.

"Please," pleaded Miranda. "I am being pursued! My family is wealthy. You will be well rewarded!"

"You have not escaped from the seraglio?" demanded the gatekeeper, half fearfully.

"The what?"

"The sultan's harem."

"No! No! I have told you the truth! For God's sake, man, do women come to your gate each day looking as I look, speaking correct English? Let me in before my captors catch me! I swear you will be well rewarded!"

Slowly, the gatekeeper began unwrapping the chain that held the gates together.

"Achmet! What are you doing?" An English naval officer strode down the gravel-lined embassy driveway.

"This lady claims she is English, my lord."

Miranda looked up and suddenly recognition made her legs give way. She grabbed at the gatekeeper for support. "Kit!" she called out. "Kit Edmund! It is Miranda Dunham!"

He stared hard at the woman on the other side of the gate. "Lady Dunham is dead," he said stiffly. "Lady Miranda Dunham is dead."

"Christopher Edmund, Marquis of Wye!" she shouted at him. "Brother of Darius, who loved my twin sister, Amanda. *I am not dead!* The body in St. Petersburg was someone else. Kit," she begged, "for God's sake let me in! I am pursued by my captors! Do you remember how you brought Mama and Mandy and me to England from Wyndsong so Mandy wouldn't miss her wedding to Adrian?"

He stared past her, his face whitening. "Jesus," he swore, then turning shouted, "Mirza! To me! Hurry!"

Miranda felt her arm grasped in an iron grip. "So, my fine lady," hissed Prince Arik, "I suspected we would find you here." He began to pull her away, back down the street. She could see horses waiting. "You'll go on the block tonight, my fine lady, make no mistake about it!"

"Kit!" she screamed in English. "Kit, help me!" Then she switched to French, and turned to her captor. "Stop, Prince Arik! The British naval officer is a personal friend of my husband's. He knows me! He will pay your ransom."

The prince whirled Miranda around to face him, and slapped her across her face. "Bitch! Understand me well. I can get more for you on the block, and I damned well intend to! Buri, block their pursuit!" He yanked her down the street, but Miranda struggled fiercely, managing to escape his grip by shedding her cloak, and ducking past Buri and his startled men. She ran as if pursued by the devil himself, flying through the embassy gates, now open, which Achmet quickly slammed shut and rechained.

The Tatars howled their outrage, shaking their weapons. "The woman is a lawful captive," cried out Prince Arik. "I will go to the sultan's magistrate!"

It was then that a tall, dark-haired man in a flowing white cloak stepped forward and, undoing the gates, moved out into the street.

The Tatars surrounded him. "This woman is a noblewoman of England," he said quietly. "You could have obtained her only by dishonest means."

"There is no shame in raiding the Russians, and we found her among the Russians," Prince Arik shot back.

The tall man smiled, his blue eyes flashing. "There is no shame whatsoever, my friend, in raiding the Russians. I sometimes think that Allah created the Russians solely for the purpose of being our victims. Nonetheless, the lady is not a Russian, she is English."

"I can sell her for a fortune," whined Prince Arik. "If I let you simply take her I have lost money. It is not fair!" The prince was ready to bargain.

The tall man laughed pleasantly. "Hold out both your hands, Tatar. I will pay you a king's ransom. It will be more than you could get for her on the block, I promise, and no greedy slave merchant to take her commission, eh?"

Prince Arik held out his hand. The tall man pulled a chamois bag from his white robes. Loosening the ties on it, he tipped the bag and a stream of brightly colored gemstones poured into the startled hetman's hands. There were diamonds, rubies, amethysts, sapphires, emeralds, topazes, and pearls. The tall man poured until the treasure overflowed the Tatar's hands. Some of the jewels spilled onto the street and the other Tatars scrambled for them.

The tall man retied his bag, which was still quite full. "There, Tatar! I imagine you won't get as much for all your other captives as you have gotten for this one woman. Are you content now?"

"More than content, sire. Who are you?"

"I am Prince Mirza Eddin Khan," came the reply.

"The sultan's cousin?"

"Yes. Now begone, Tatar, before these misguided infidels misunderstand and set their dogs on you!"

The Tatars backed down the street and, mounting their ponies, galloped off. The tall man turned around and said, "Kit, send my palanquin down here. I will take Lady Dunham to my home. I think she will be better able to answer questions after she has bathed, and is dressed properly."

Kit Edmund saluted neatly and ran back up the driveway.

The large palanquin came down the drive, and was set down by its slave bearers. Mirza Khan helped Miranda into it, and then settling himself opposite her gave the signal to depart. He drew the vehicle's curtains.

"You don't think the Tatars will be waiting to ambush us, do you?" she said worriedly.

"No," he answered. "They were more than content. You are safe now."

After a silence she said, "I imagine this sounds woefully indelicate of me, but, oh lord, how I long for hot water and soap!"

"Sweet stock," he said.

"What?"

"Your scent is sweet stock, isn't it?"

"Yes," she answered slowly, amazed. How could he remember
such a trifle from their very brief previous acquaintance? She fell
silent, a little embarrassed, and finally he said quietly. "The child?
Is it yours?"

For a moment her sea-green eyes were wet. "Yes, she is my
child."

"Perhaps if you would tell me about it I might help. You were
reported murdered in a robbery, your body tossed into the Neva
River. That was a year ago. Believe me, Lady Dunham, you may
trust me."

She looked into his dark blue eyes and knew with a deep certainty
that she could indeed trust him. She needed someone to help her
through what she knew was going to be a very difficult period. "Do
you know who Prince Alexei Cherkessky is?" she asked.

"I never met him, but I know of him. His money comes from a
famous slave-breeding farm in the Crimean area. The slaves from the
Cherkessky estate are quite sought after here in Istanbul." The blue
eyes suddenly widened. "Allah! Do you mean to tell me—?" he
stopped as her level gaze met his, and she nodded solemnly. "The
swine!" said Mirza Khan.

Miranda told him her story, finishing "The child was born before
its time on the journey to Istanbul. She is beautiful, but probably
blind and even deaf."

In the awkward silence, he asked, "What gate did you enter
through?"

"Charisius."

He looked at her with open admiration. "You walked across the
city! You are an amazing woman, Lady Dunham."

"Walking across the city was a mere stretch of the legs, my lord.
You must not forget that I walked all the way from Prince
Cherkessky's farm in the Crimea."

"You walked?"

"Of course. We all did. I did ride in a cart for several days after the child was born," she said, "but mostly I walked."

"You *are* amazing," he said softly.

"No," she said softly. "I am not amazing. I have survived. I vowed I would return to my husband and son, and I will! Jared, of course, may choose to divorce me. I have borne someone else's child, and he will have every right to rid himself of me."

"You love him deeply, don't you?"

"Yes," she sighed. "I love him." Then she fell silent, lost in her thoughts.

He studied her discreetly. A year ago in imperial St. Petersburg he had been overwhelmed by the exquisitely beautiful woman in the shimmering gold gown that he had met at the English ambassador's soirée. She had surprised him with her sharp mind, her quick wit.

Occasionally, after being told of her death he had dreamed of that evening, seeing her beautiful face again. Awakening suddenly, he was filled with a deep, terrible sadness. He wondered now if death wouldn't have been a better fate for her than the bleak, loveless future she was expecting. She was much too young and far too beautiful and sensitive to live without love. The horrors she had seen had, of course, changed her. They had not broken her magnificent spirit, but something was not right. First things first, however. She needed to be made comfortable, to be free of fear, to sleep and to eat. She was quite thin and there were purple shadows beneath her eyes.

"I live in the Eastern manner, Lady Dunham. I hope you will not be shocked by the fact that I possess a harem."

She shook her head. "It is your way," she said. "Do you have any children?"

"No," he said, and she heard the sadness in his voice.

"Have I offended you, Mirza Khan?"

"No," he said hastily. "There is no reason you should not know what everyone else does. When I was a young boy I spent some time in the palace of the late sultan, Abdulhamit, who was my maternal grandfather. In the Ottoman family the eldest living male inherits the throne, not necessarily the eldest son. I was not, praise Allah, the eldest! I had several cousins in line for the throne. There was Selim, who was my best friend and nearest to me in age, and then there was Mustafa, and finally little Mahmud.

"Mustafa's mother was a very ambitious woman, and not just for her son, but for herself. She managed to poison Selim and me, but we were saved by Selim's marvelous mother, the bas-kadin, Mihri-chan. Unfortunately the poison rendered my seed lifeless. Poor Selim only managed to produce two daughters before his death.

"My father was, of course, very angry, for I was his heir, but then my own mother is an admirable wife. I have four younger brothers, the eldest of whom is now our father's heir, and I, thank heavens, do not have to live in the Georgian mountains, but can instead live here in the civilized and beautiful city. There are compensations for everything, Lady Dunham."

"I think I would like it if you called me Miranda, Mirza Khan," and she smiled the first real smile she had smiled since he had rescued her.

"Miranda," he smiled back, "from the Greek, meaning *admirable,* and by Allah, you are! What you have suffered would have broken most women."

"I am not like most women, Mirza Khan," she said, and her sea-green eyes flashed. "I will not be beaten!"

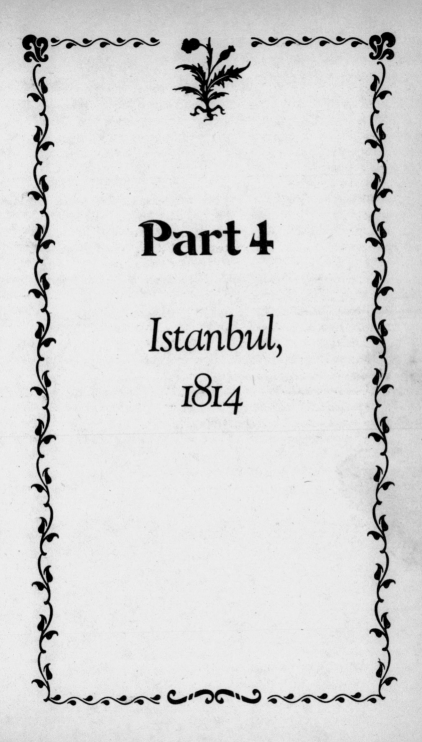

Part 4

Istanbul,
1814

✤ Chapter 14 ✤

Mirza Khan's small palace was outside the city on the shores of the Bosphorus, with a stunning view of both Asia across the waters and of the minarets of Istanbul. The original foundations of the building dated back several hundred years to when the Greeks ruled the city, and it was said that a Byzantine princess and her husband had once lived there. The house had been rebuilt several times, the last time being when Mirza Khan bought it fifteen years before.

The three buildings that comprised the current villa were a cream-colored marble, with red-tile roofs. Across the front of the center building facing the sea, ran a classic portico, its creamy pillars veined in dark red. Standing on this porch and looking toward the sea, the haremlik, or women's quarters, was to the right. The building housing the public rooms of the villa was to the left. Mirza Khan's apartments were in the center building.

The three buildings were separated by lovely large gardens. The main entry to the estate was through a gate in the garden wall outside the public rooms, thereby preserving the privacy of the rest of the household, for Mirza Khan was an easy, though firm master and his women were allowed the freedom of the villa provided they preserved their modesty.

When they arrived Mirza Khan had taken Miranda directly to the women's quarters and introduced her to a small, plump brown man with eyes like two black raisins. "Miranda, this is Ali-Ali, my chief eunuch. He will see that you have all you desire."

Mirza Khan then switched to rapid Turkish and swiftly explained Miranda's history to the eunuch.

"The child's existence is not to be known, Ali-Ali, even to Captain Edmund. In this lady's land it is considered immoral for a woman to bear a child not her husband's, even if it is not the woman's fault."

"But she is not responsible for the fate that befell her," protested Ali-Ali.

"Nevertheless she will be blamed," was the reply.

"Westerners," mused the eunuch, "are a strange and confused people. Their men are openly wanton with other men's wives and women of questionable morals. Yet let a virtuous woman be taken forceably, and they scorn her. I do not understand them at all."

"Neither do I, old friend."

"You like this woman," stated the eunuch.

"Yes," smiled Mirza Khan, "I like her." He turned back to Miranda and spoke to her in English. "I have explained everything to Ali-Ali. I think your daughter's existence should be kept from Captain Edmund, Miranda. The gossips in London will have a field day when you turn up alive. We will think what to do. But for now, only the harem women and Ali-Ali must know of the baby. Captain Edmund did not notice her, I believe, and we will not tell him."

"What shall I say to Kit then?"

"Merely that you were kidnaped by Prince Cherkessky, and sent to his villa in the Crimea to await his pleasure. Fortunately he never came, and the Tatars who raided his villa brought you to Istanbul to sell you, but you escaped them. It is simple, and it is reasonable. Go now with Ali-Ali, and I will see you later when Kit arrives."

Miranda followed the eunuch across the peaceful garden to the women's quarters, and into a light and lovely salon. The walls of the room were covered in silk fabric with a multicolored floral silk on a pearl gray background. The walnut parquet floors were covered with thick blue, rose, and gold carpets, and in the very center of the room a three-tiered shell fountain tinkled merrily in a refreshing glazed light blue tile pool.

There were several women in the room, all stunningly beautiful. Two were working at embroidery frames, one was strumming on a musical instrument, one was reading, and another was painting her toenails. As Miranda entered the room with Ali-Ali they gave her friendly though curious looks.

"Ladies, ladies," called the eunuch in his high-pitched voice.

The woman reading looked up, rose, and came forward smiling. "What have we here, Ali-Ali?" she asked in a cultured voice.

Miranda almost gaped foolishly, she was so surprised by the woman's incredible beauty. Her long blue-black hair floated about her like a storm cloud, her skin was the color of a creamy gardenia, her eyes were emerald green. She had to be at least thirty, thought Miranda, and yet she was absolutely stunning. Not only was her face flawless, but her figure was perfect, too.

The woman's eyes twinkled. "I am Turkhan," she said.

"She is Mirza Khan's favorite," explained Ali-Ali. "She has been with him for many years. The others come and go, but Turkhan remains."

"I am like an old slipper to my lord," laughed Turkhan. "Comfortable and predictable."

The old eunuch smiled fondly at the woman. "He loves you. You make him happy." Then catching himself, Ali-Ali said, "This lady is to be Lord Mirza's guest. She has suffered greatly. She is to remain with us until she can be safely transported back to her own people."

"How are you called?" asked Turkhan.

"Miranda, and if it is possible, my lady, I should dearly love a bath. A hot, hot bath! I have not had one since the Tatars captured me six weeks ago."

Turkhan's emerald eyes widened, and filled with sympathy. "Heavens, you poor child!" she said. "Safiye, Guzel. Help our guest, and take her to the baths." She reached out for the cloak that

Mirza Khan had placed about Miranda's shoulders earlier. Whisking it off, she stared at the infant in its sling next to Miranda's breasts. *"A baby!"* Her voice softened. "A baby," she repeated.

Suddenly the other women were all clustering around Miranda, chattering and smiling, reaching out to touch the baby, making soft cooing noises at her. "Oh, how beautiful she is!" cried one. "What is her name?"

"She has none," said Miranda quietly, and then her sea-green eyes met Turkhan's, and the compassion she saw there almost made her cry. She hadn't really cried through any of this.

Turkhan lifted the baby from the sling and looked down at her.

"Go and have your bath, Miranda. I will care for the little one."

"I had best nurse her first. She never complains, but she has not eaten since dawn."

Turkhan nodded in agreement, and waited until the baby had been fed. Then, taking the child from her mother, she hurried off with her while Miranda followed Safiye and Guzel to the baths.

"Burn those clothes," Miranda said as she stripped them off. "I should sooner be stark naked than ever wear them again. The boots, too. I have worn them thin."

She was bathed and then dressed in pale-green harem trousers with a matching slash-skirted, long-sleeved dress trimmed with narrow gold braid, its low neck made more modest by a delicately sheer cream-colored chemise beneath. A slave tied a finely embroidered shawl around her hips, and over all of this was a sleeveless forest-green robe edged in wide velvet ribbon and embroidered with seed pearls. Her beautiful pale gilt hair was brushed out until it gleamed with silvery-gold lights. It was banded by a dark green velvet ribbon with pearls, but otherwise left free.

"How beautiful you are!" exclaimed Turkhan, coming into the room. "Captain Edmund is here, and I am to take you to the main salon."

The young Marquis of Wye was standing, elegant in his blue and gold naval uniform, talking with the white-robed Mirza Khan. He turned as the women entered the room, his baby-blue eyes sweeping over the women. "Miranda! My God, Miranda, it really is you!"

"Yes, Kit, it really is me." She settled herself comfortably on a silk divan and they talked. Turkhan stayed in the background, not wishing to intrude.

"Your sister kept insisting that you were alive. But your family believed the shock of your death was too much for her. They said she could not face it," he explained.

Miranda smiled. "Mandy and I have always known if the other was in trouble," she said. "It is a difficult thing to explain to other people." Then she grew more serious. "Jared? Our son? Are they all right?"

"I don't know a great deal about your little boy, Miranda, except that he is with your sister's son at Swynford. Lord Dunham...is well." Kit used every shred of his self-control to keep his voice neutral. How could he tell her that Jared Dunham had, in his grief, become a rake among the ton's fastest set?

How could he explain about Lady Belinda de Winter? Kit's older sister, Augusta, the Countess of Dee, had a daughter who had made her debut this year and was in on all the latest gossip. Livia had told her mother that Belinda de Winter was already enjoying wifely favors from Jared Dunham. Good heavens, thought Kit, what a coil! Miranda's voice brought him back.

"Will you take me back to England on your ship, Kit?"

"I cannot, Miranda. You see I am no longer a private citizen, but the captain of *H.M.S. Notorious,* and I am unable to take civilians aboard my vessel without official permission. We leave for England tonight. I will, of course, carry word of your rescue to Lord Dunham immediately."

"I must remain here?"

"I think," said Mirza Khan gently, "that it would be best after your great ordeal if you spent some time resting."

"Perhaps," she said softly, looking from one to the other.

"What happened, Miranda?" asked Kit. He blushed and looked embarrassed.

She touched his hand in a gentle gesture. "It is really quite simple, Kit," she said, deciding to try Mirza Khan's story for the first time. "I went to St. Petersburg to meet Jared. We had planned to

sail home together, a second honeymoon, you know. I was barely
there when I was seen by Prince Cherkessky. He must surely be mad.
He had me kidnaped and taken to his estates in the Crimean area. I
was drugged. I went in the custody of the prince's own body serf, a
man named Sasha. When I asked this man why the prince had
kidnaped me I was told that I had been taken to await the prince's
pleasure.

"I must tell you I was never mistreated; rather, I was quite
cosseted. I never saw Prince Cherkessky again, for he never came to
his estates in the Crimea while I was there. Then, several weeks ago,
the Tatars attacked the prince's estate and took all the women and
children to sell as slaves here in Istanbul. Now all I want to do is get
home to my husband and our son. Oh Kit, are you certain you cannot
take me with you? Couldn't you get permission?"

"I only wish I could."

"Then I really have no choice but to remain here," she said.
Then, realizing how that had sounded, she quickly added, "I shall be
delighted to accept your hospitality, Mirza Khan."

"May I carry a personal message to your husband, Miranda?"

She thought a moment. What could she say? How could she
explain? By the time Kit arrived she would have been gone a year,
and by the time she finally got home they would have been separated
for over two years. Suddenly she felt shy. Surely it would be easier
when she saw Jared. "Just tell him I love him," Miranda said softly.

Then she stood up. "I am really suddenly very exhausted, Kit.
Mirza Khan was quite surprised that I walked all the way from the
Crimea."

"Walked?!" He was astounded. "Your poor feet!"

"At least a full size larger," she teased, and then she bent and
kissed him in a sisterly fashion. "Hurry, Kit! Please hurry! I want to
go home to Jared and to my baby. I want to go home to Wyndsong."

That night, Kit Edmund stood on his quarterdeck watching the
twinkling lights of Istanbul recede in the distance, wondering how he
was going to tell Jared Dunham that his beautiful wife was still alive.
Perhaps he ought to approach Lord Swynford. No! Lady Swynford!
Amanda had, in the face of devastating evidence, refused to believe
that her twin was dead. She had steadfastly refused to wear mourning

for Miranda. Kit himself had been witness to a scene at Almack's when a crusty dowager had taken it upon herself to criticize not only Amanda's colorful gown, but the fact that Amanda was appearing in public at all.

Young Lady Swynford had listened politely, and then replied in her clear, sweet voice, "I do not believe that my sister is dead, madam. And she would be the first to insist I wear no mourning. Miranda knows how sallow my skin looks when I wear black or violet."

The old dowager had gasped. "Mad as a hatter!" she pronounced. "Well, at least Swynford's got an heir on her, and that's a mercy!"

Adrian Swynford had been furious with his wife, one of the few times Christopher Edmund had ever seen the mild young nobleman angry. "Why can you not accept the truth?" he demanded.

"Because," said Amanda stubbornly, "I know Miranda is alive. I feel it. Miranda is out there somewhere. *And*," her voice became crystal clear as she looked directly toward Jared, who was with Lady Belinda de Winter again, "any respectable young woman seen in the company of a married man surely risks her reputation."

Adrian Swynford grasped his wife by the arm and practically dragged her from Almack's ballroom. As they went, Amanda's voice was again heard quite clearly as she said, "Go gently, my lord. I am breeding again, you know!"

Princess Dariya de Lieven and Lady Emily Cowper collapsed in each other's arms, laughing so hard that tears rolled down their cheeks. No one had ever seen the two proper matrons—the backbone of Almack's group of patronesses and the social arbiters of all the ton—so overcome with hilarity.

"Oh! Oh!" gasped Emily Cowper, wiping her eyes with a delicate scrap of fine, lace-edged white lawn, "it is almost as good as having dear Miranda herself back." Then she lowered her voice. "Do you really think there is anything to what Amanda Swynford says, Dariya?"

The princess shrugged elegantly. "You English are so reluctant to credit feelings, yet many people do. I have known stranger things, Emily, than a twin who insists her other half is still alive. It is possible that Miranda Dunham survived."

"Then where is she?" came the exasperated reply.

Again the princess shrugged. "I don't know, but if I were she I should hurry home. Belinda de Winter is zeroing in on Lord Dunham like a robin on a fat worm."

Belinda was so certain that Jared would declare himself by the end of the current season that she was emboldened to do something she would not otherwise have done because it put her reputation at risk. She seduced him, letting him believe, of course, that it was he who had done the seducing.

She had planned it carefully, for it had to appear to be happening spontaneously. He had refused to accompany her on a picnic being planned by a group of young people, claiming that he was too old for such childish nonsense. She pouted prettily, and he laughed.

"Come now, Belinda, does it really mean that much to you? Do you really want to go out to the country and sit in the damp May grass?"

She sighed. "I expect you think me childish, but I am not really a city girl, m'lord. London is wonderful, and quite exciting, but I do miss my home. This is the first year in my entire life I have not gathered primroses and bluebells still wet with the dew on May Day morning. I love the countryside!"

"Then I am sorry, my dear, to have disappointed you."

"Could we not have our own picnic?" she suggested daringly.

"My dear girl!" Jared protested.

"Oh, Jared! Who would know?" Catching his hands, she looked up at him eagerly. "Please! You are permitted to take me driving. Your cook could prepare the basket, and I could tell my aunt that you had offered to accompany me shopping, and then were taking me for a drive."

A sane voice warned him against such folly, but she pleaded so adorably, and he was feeling reckless and bored. He had never even kissed her, but now he leaned forward and touched her lips with his. "You are a persuasive minx, Belinda," he said. "Very well, we will have your picnic."

They departed one bright May morning for what he promised was a perfect spot six miles from the city. A wicker basket was tucked carefully beneath the seat of the high-perch phaeton, which was being pulled by the smartest stepping ebony team she had ever seen. She knew that he had paid a fortune for them only last week at Tattersall's, boldly outbidding a representative of the Prince Regent himself.

She chattered lightly about nothing of importance, maintaining the illusion of girlish exuberance. Who would ever doubt her innocence? Belinda had been sexually active since eleven, losing her virginity at twelve, but her indiscretions had always been discreet. She had never involved herself with people of her own class, preferring the lower classes, who dared not brag of their conquest with the young miss lest they be charged with a crime. Men had been transported for less. The Duke of Northampton was the only man of her own social class with whom she had involved herself even briefly, and he would certainly say nothing. No, Belinda smiled smugly to herself, her reputation was spotless.

The picnic spot Jared had selected was secluded and charming. On the far side of a daisy-filled meadow, it was bordered by a stream, which was edged with soft green willow trees. Securing the horses to a tree, Jared lifted Belinda down and, taking the basket out, walked to a grassy spot by the water. Belinda took the carriage robe, and spread it on the wet grass with a little flourish.

"Oh, Jared," she sighed. "It is simply too lovely."

What a dear girl she was, he thought, smiling down at her. She was so petite—an inch shorter than Amanda—that he sometimes felt foolish standing next to her. "I am glad I have pleased you so easily, Belinda," he said.

"Everything you do pleases me," she said softly, lowering her dark blue eyes shyly.

"Thank you, my dear," he answered sincerely, touched by her girlish confession.

Belinda blushed. Attempting to change the subject, she asked, "Shall we eat, m'lord?" She sat down on the robe and began to spread the contents of the basket out on it, exclaiming with delight at the goodies she found. There were tiny sandwiches of cucumber and

watercress, miniature meat pastries, chicken wings encased in puff
pastry, little strawberry tarts, early cherries from France, and a glass
container of lemonade.

"It is perfect except for one thing," said Belinda.

"And what is that?" Jared asked, wondering what he could have
possibly forgotten.

"The desserts will stay cooler if we have some ferns to shade
them. I believe there must be some by the water, perhaps around the
bend in the stream beneath those trees. Will you fetch some for me,
Jared?"

"Of course."

No sooner had he gone than Belinda reached for the lemonade
container. Uncorking it, she poured equal portions into the two silver
cups he had packed. Into one of the silver cups she carefully emptied
a paper of white powder she had had secreted in her bosom. The
powder dissolved almost instantly. Belinda looked carefully around
to be sure she had not been observed, and smiled to herself. The
silver cup of lemonade now contained a powerful aphrodisiac, and
once Jared drank it his senses would be so fired that he would have to
be a saint to resist her. He would seduce her, and she would allow it
to happen. Within the pocket of her gown was a membrane of
chicken's blood which she would smear on her thighs at the
appropriate moment in order that her virginity might be attested to.

Belinda did not expect Jared Dunham to propose marriage directly
after the seduction. He was no green boy. He would think about what
had happened between them, and she would accept the blame for
their actions and be sure he was allowed no further liberties lest he
think her a wanton. Just a taste of the fruit to whet his appetite, but
no more. By the end of the season he would propose.

"What are you smiling at?" he asked, sitting next to her and
handing her a bunch of cool green ferns.

"At how very happy I am this minute," she said.

Jared was touched. How charming she was, how innocent, how
very different from Miranda. Belinda was all sweetness and softness.
She would never leave her child to go tearing off in search of a
husband who had expressly forbidden her to leave England. No,

Belinda would be obedient and predictable. She would never break a man's heart. She was a real woman.

"A sandwich, m'lord?" She held the bone-china plate out to him.

They ate slowly. Jared was more relaxed that he had been in months. She was really quite lovely. Her full, young breasts swelled enticingly above her scooped neckline, contrasting with the girlish white muslin dress with its pink sprigs of apple blossom. Those round, smooth fruits beckoned him, and when she leaned forward to refill his lemonade cup he felt himself looking down her gown at her large, pink nipples. The sight sent an ache into his groin. Jared was appalled. He didn't lack for women. Why should this young girl excite him so much?

"It is really quite warm for May," she commented. "I am quite faint with the heat." And she leaned back against him, her snow-white shoulders and chest his for the taking. His arm slipped around her waist and, dipping his dark head, he placed a kiss on her plump shoulder. "Oh!" she cried out softly. Turning in his arms, she said, "You must not be so bold, m'lord."

"Would you deny me a little kiss, Belinda?" he teased her.

"You may kiss me only on the lips, m'lord," she said solemnly. "I do not believe it is quite proper that you kiss me at all, let alone on my shoulder. But if you do not think me bold, I should like it if you kissed me as you did the other day."

My God, she was innocent! He thought. He pulled her into his grasp and kissed her mouth. Belinda melted against him triumphantly, accepting kiss after kiss, pretending to let him guide her, shivering with genuine pleasure when his velvet tongue touched hers. She felt his hands seeking her breasts, and protested faintly although the truth of the matter was that she was reveling in his touch. Her potion had obviously worked, for he was hot with his lust for her, and she almost laughed aloud with victory.

He freed her full breasts from her bodice, crushing them, kissing them, enjoying their softness, their lily-of-the-valley-perfume scent. Boldly he sucked on her nipples while she protested with mewling little cries and pretended to push him away, but there was no stopping him now. Impassioned, he pushed her gown up, drawing her undergarments down, all the while murmuring at her as a drunken man does.

"Let me, Belinda. Let me love you, my darling. Ah, God, you're too sweet!"

"Oh, Jared, you mustn't! I don't think you really should! Oh! I shall be ruined!"

She barely had time to get the blood-filled membrane from her pocket before he was thrusting into her. She gave a little shriek which he muffled with his mouth, and struggled against him. Jared assumed she was merely attempting to protect her virtue, but Belinda was fighting to get her hand between her legs so she could crush the pouch and bloody her thighs. Finally she succeeded, and then she burst into tears, sobbing piteously. He attempted to soothe her with kisses, apologizing for his behavior. Taking up her cue, Belinda nobly assumed full responsibility for his actions.

"It is all my fault, Jared," she wept daintily. "I should not have suggested that we picnic alone. Oh, I am so ashamed! What must you think of me?"

"I think that you are a dear and trusting girl, Belinda. I can only apologize for my behavior."

"You do not think badly of me?" She put on her best woebegone face.

"No, I do not, and I hope you do not think badly of me."

"Oh, no, Jared! I could *never* think badly of you!"

The innocent declaration only made him feel worse. Damn! He had behaved badly, very badly. He had seen blood on her thighs, too, which meant that he had taken her precious virginity. He had not, however, forced his way through her maidenhead, which seemed odd. It hadn't been like that first night with Miranda. Miranda! Oh my darling, he agonized, why did you leave me? Making love to Belinda only reminded him of his beloved Miranda.

Belinda de Winter was certain that Jared would declare himself shortly, by season's end at the latest. So she was not surprised when, one day, her maid brought word that Lord Dunham was waiting to see her in the morning room, along with her guardians, the duke and the duchess. This is it, she thought, coolly triumphant, pinching her cheeks as she peered into her dressing table mirror before hurrying downstairs. The duke and duchess would be so proud of her!

"Oh, miss, it's so exciting!" bubbled her maid, and in a rare show of generosity Belinda de Winter gifted her maid with one of her lace handkerchiefs. "Oh, milady, thank you!" the woman cried.

"To remind you always of my good fortune," she said archly, and hurried downstairs to receive the reward of all her labors.

Her godmother and the duke were both looking rather grim, which seemed odd. She curtseyed politely and prettily, and sat down next to the duchess.

"Belinda, dear," said her godmother, "Lord Dunham has asked our permission to speak with you on a certain matter."

Belinda looked suitably coy, casting her eyes downward in a show of modesty, and murmuring, "Yes, Aunt Sophia." Lord! Weren't they going to leave them alone? No one moved. Obviously not. Oh well, thought Belinda, the more witnesses the better!

Jared Dunham sat down on the other side of her, and began to speak words she had never expected to hear. "Lady de Winter— Belinda—before the gossips begin, before you can be injured, I must tell you that my wife, Miranda, has been found alive. I know that you will rejoice with me. It is indeed a miracle, and yet my miracle is apt to jeopardize your reputation. You must now understand that anything I might have said must now be forgotten. I regret any pain or embarrassment I may have unwittingly caused you."

She was stunned, infuriated, outraged, but her saner self held her in check. "How happy you must be, my lord," she said, forcing a smile. "I, of course, fully understand your position, and you must have no concern for me now that your dear wife is so fortuitously restored to you."

Jared Dunham stood, looking much relieved, and bowed to the duke and duchess and then to Belinda. He left the room. Only when they heard the front door close did the duke say, "Bad luck, my gel! Well, the season's not over by a long shot. If you took my advice you'd settle for something less showy with a good income."

Belinda's face blotched most unattractively, and her blue eyes bugged. "Shut up, you old fool!" she snarled. "The American was

my ace in the hole, and I bloody well mean to have him! I won't be
the laughing stock of the ton! I won't! Without a penny to my name,
and with my charming relations, who else will have me!"

"Belinda! Apologize to your Uncle Algernon at once!" scolded
the duchess. "Lord Dunham's wife is alive and that is the end of it. It
is unfortunate, but there it is."

"You've had other respectable offers, my gel," said the duke,
totally unperturbed by Belinda's show of temper. "What the hell's
the matter with young Lord Arden that you sent him packing? Boy's
one of the best judges of horseflesh I've ever met."

"Two thousand a year, and a moldy, tumbledown mansion in
Sussex?" scoffed Belinda. "Be serious, uncle. I could spend two
thousand a year on negligees alone."

"Plenty of people have lived well on less, miss. Reconsider young
Arden, and I'll restore his mansion as a wedding gift to you both.
You could do a hell of a lot worse. At least he's young and virile."

"I could do better!" Belinda snapped back.

"I'll not pay for you to have another season in London, miss,"
warned the duke. "I've three gels of me own in the nursery almost
ready to be fledged. Forget the Yankee, and find yourself a decent
husband quick, or it's back to Hereford at season's end for you, an
old maid. Think of that, my gel!"

Lady Belinda de Winter picked up a valuable Chinese vase.
Looking straight at her uncle, she hurled it across the morning room.
Then she stormed out.

Jared, driving his phaeton back to his Devon Square house, was a
rolling sea of confused feelings. He had been on the point of leaving
his home last night for a few hours of gambling at White's, when
Amanda had arrived, flushed and triumphant, Adrian and young Kit
Edmund trailing in her wake.

"She is not dead! She is not dead! I told you! *I told you!* Miranda
is alive, and Kit has spoken to her!" Then she had collasped into a
nearby chair, weeping and laughing at the same time.

He had gone white, believing her finally gone mad, but Adrian
had quickly confirmed Amanda's tale, and the Marquis of Wye had

asked to speak with him. The four of them had gone into the library, and after Jared had, with surprisingly steady hands, poured everyone a brandy, Kit told his tale.

When he had finished Jared asked quietly, "You are sure she is not an impostor?"

"My lord," said Kit Edmund with great dignity, "it is no secret that I have long admired Lady Dunham. Even if I were blind I would recognize that not quite English lilt in her voice. It is your wife."

Jared nodded. "Did my wife have any message for me?" he asked.

"Her exact words, my lord, were *'just tell him I love him.'*"

Lord Dunham swerved his matched bays just in time to avoid a mail coach pulling out of an inn yard.

She was alive! Alive after the most incredible series of adventures. He suspected Kit Edmund's tale was not the full story, but she would not confide that in anyone but him.

He pulled up before his house, and the groom was there to lead the horses around to the carriage house. Should he go for her himself? He couldn't bear to wait any longer before seeing her. He would go to Istanbul on *Dream Witch*. He would ask Ephraim Snow to be his captain. He would take Perky, too. Although married for two years now, the little maid had no children and would be delighted to resume her former position.

That evening, still in profound shock, Jared spent an hour with his old friend and sometime lover, Sabrina Elliot. A retired actress, she was an attractive, elegant, warm woman who enjoyed gentlemen very much. She conducted her affairs with the utmost discretion, but the truth was that her lovers enjoyed talking with Sabrina as much as they enjoyed making love to her.

When Sabrina had heard Jared's astounding news, she cried, "How soon will you be leaving?"

"Sabrina, I am not sure yet," he replied, running a long hand through his dark hair. "The truth is that I have had a most awkward day. I had to explain...these new circumstances to the Lady de Winter, whom I had planned to marry."

"God forbid!" muttered Sabrina.

"What?"

"Nothing, darling. But surely your heart does not belong to Belinda de Winter?" she asked, amused.

"No," he admitted, "but she seemed a suitable candidate for a wife."

"Hmm...unlike your wayward Miranda. Is that it, Jared? Belinda de Winter would never do anything improper, isn't that right? Oh, Jared! To compare the two is like comparing oatmeal to champagne."

"Sabrina," Jared began, grateful for her directness and insight, "the fact is, of course, that I cannot wait to be with Miranda again, and I am leaving tomorrow. But somehow I think you already knew that."

Sabrina laughed. *This* was a man who knew his own heart! "When you catch her, Jared, hold on to her this time. You have been given a second chance, and you must know how miraculous that is."

Jared Dunham nodded slowly. Suddenly realizing all he had to do before *Dream Witch* could sail, he bid his friend a hasty goodnight, kissing her hand with warmth, lingering over it a shade longer than necessary. As he took his leave, however, Sabrina was no longer in his mind. His thoughts were with Miranda, as hers were with him.

Miranda leaned her elbows on the cool marble balustrade and stared at the flat sea just a few feet beneath her. The water was a clear, deep blue, and she could see its sandy white bottom where the tiny minnows scuttled to and fro in the last of the sunlight. The thoughts racing back and forth in her mind were very much like the tiny, dark fish. They touched on her consciousness only briefly before hurrying away. Sighing, she wondered whether Jared would want her back at all. Would he send for her? Would he come himself? Dear God, she hoped he would not come himself! She needed time. How was she going to explain the child?

"You are looking very fierce," said Mirza Khan. "I hope that I am not the object of your thoughts."

She looked up, and laughed softly. "No, I was thinking that I am very well revenged on the Russian. Although I am sure that the Tzar won't let his cousin and her husband starve, it will never be the same for him again. From now on Prince Alexei Cherkessky will probably be only an unimportant pensioner, and I imagine this will eventually kill him."

An admiring look came into his eyes. "How magnificently you hate, Miranda," he said. He wondered, as Jared had once wondered, if she loved as fiercely.

"Yes, I hate him!" she cried. "In my world, Mirza Khan, women are born free, and raised that way. My land is a young one yet, women are needed as much as men are. Just over sixty years ago the women in my home state of New York stood shoulder to shoulder with their men on the palisades of every frontier fort, and battled the Indians for possession of the land. That is my heritage. My family came from England almost two hundred years ago to carve a small empire of their own from Wyndsong Island. I am a free woman!

"Think on it, Mirza Khan. Think what it is like to be a slave. You are forced to remain where the master chooses, do what the master says, eat what is given you, sleep when you are allowed, and make love when permitted or even on command."

He gazed levelly at her. "Oh, Miranda, how I wish you weren't so intent on returning home to your husband."

Her sea-green eyes widened in surprise at this candid declaration, and to his intense delight she blushed. "I had best see to my child," she said, and hastily fled across the garden.

He watched her go. Why did the mention of what was natural between a man and a woman seem to distress her? Surely her experience had not flawed her. He wondered if he might find out without breaking the laws of hospitality. He called down to his boatman, who lay dozing in the sunset.

"Abdul, I will want the caique later. Be ready!"

"Yes, master," came the reply, though the lazy Abdul never even opened his eyes. Mirza Khan laughed indulgently. Slavery in his house was an easy thing. He admitted to himself that she had spoken the truth. Still, how could one exist without slaves?

Returning to his own quarters, he bathed and then ate a simple meal alone, as was his custom. Then he paid a visit to the women's quarters. To his amusement, his women were all busy fussing over Miranda's child. The baby had begun to gain a bit of weight, but she was still quite tiny, and a quiet little thing. He winced at the sightless violet eyes. If anything, she reminded him of a newborn kitten. She responded to touch, seeming to crave the kisses and cuddling she received from his women. He looked at the baby's perfect little features, thinking sadly that had she been a normal child she would have grown into a fantastic beauty. He frankly didn't think she would live to see her first birthday, and glanced toward Miranda. All that pain and horror, he thought once more.

"Miranda," he said, "come and cruise with me on the sea. My barge awaits, and it is a lovely night. Turkhan, my dove, will you join us, too?"

"Thank you, my lord, but no. My head has been aching all day. I shall retire early." Turkhan had been with her lord long enough to know her presence wasn't really wanted. "Do go, Miranda," she encouraged. "The weather is perfect, and there is a moon tonight. Is it not lovely out on the water, ladies?"

A chorus of agreement rose, and Miranda accepted, leaving the child in Safiye's care. Mirza Khan noted that of all his women Safiye seemed the most motherly. Perhaps he would marry her off so she might have children of her own.

The air heavy with the scent of flowers, Miranda found drifting lazily on the flat sea quite relaxing. They talked of many things, of his youth in Georgia before he was invited by the sultan's bas-kadin, Mihri-chan, to spend some time with his cousin, Prince Selim, of her growing up on Wyndsong, her kingdom which nestled between the two fishtails of the much larger Long Island. She told him of her twin sister, and of her husband. Her voice grew sad.

"It will never be the same for us again," she said. "How could it be? I shall be fortunate if he does not choose to divorce me."

"Why should he divorce you?"

"Have you ever visited London?" she asked.

"Yes."

"If you mingled in fashionable society then you know the meaning of the term 'soiled dove.' I believe you understand what I am saying, for did you not hurry me from the embassy so no one would see my daughter? So that my shame might not be exposed to the world? You sought to preserve my reputation, Mirza Khan, and I thank you.

"It may be that, after hearing of my misadventures, Jared will chose to divorce me in order to marry again and have other children. At least I have the satisfaction of knowing that I have given him his heir, and that the direct line of the family will continue through me."

"I cannot understand," he said. "One moment you tell me of the great love you and Jared have for each other, and then you say he will cast you aside to satisfy convention. I do not believe it!"

"If I were your wife, Mirza Khan, would you want me back in your bed dishonored by another man?"

"Yes," he said quietly. "It is not as if you ran away with the gentleman and submitted willingly."

"I have borne another man's child. Another has used what was my husband's alone."

"You tell me you are a free woman, Miranda. If this is so then no man, even your Jared, owns you. Your body is yours, my love. It is yours to share with whom you choose. I do not advocate promiscuity, Miranda, but you can belong only to you. If your husband is the man you tell me then all will be well between the two of you when you return."

"Perhaps Jared will forgive me and remain my husband for the family's sake," she mused, "but there can never be any question of a physical relationship between us again. Honor must be satisfied."

He was astounded by her calm and horrified to realize that she meant what she said.

"Jared will be quite discreet about his mistresses, I know, for he is that kind of gentleman," she said.

"What of your needs?" he burst out.

"My needs?"

"How will you satisfy your desires, Miranda?"

"I have no desires," she said. "Not anymore."

He was thunderstruck, and then suddenly very angry. What the hell had they done to her? The woman he had met in St. Petersburg had been a beautiful, sensual creature, full of life. Who was this sexless woman who sat next to him? He wanted desperately to prove her wrong, show her that desire had not fled.

Turning smoothly, he pulled her into his embarce and his mouth came down on hers. Mirza Khan's head whirled. The lips beneath his were petal-soft. Reining in his passion, he became tender, tasting her mouth as a bee seeking nectar deep within the heart of a flower. Sweet stock assaulted his senses with its provocative innocence. Suddenly he realized that she was lying quietly in his arms. His own desire was soaring wildly, but she felt nothing at all.

Holding her in the curve of his arm, he gazed down into her face and said, "Has it always been like this for you?"

"No," she answered slowly. "When Jared made love to me I died a little each time. It was magnificent. He is magnificent." She smiled sadly. "I was a true virgin when we married. I don't just mean that I had never lain with a man, I mean I had never even kissed another man. I knew nothing of what happens between a man and a woman." She chuckled softly. "There were times when it was downright embarrassing, but he was wonderfully patient, and I grew to love him more each day. He is the only man I have ever loved, Mirza Khan, and the only one I shall ever love.

"From the moment I was kidnaped I vowed that I would return to him, that nothing would keep me from my husband. That night when Lucas finally took me I responded to his lovemaking with an ardor that shocked me. I had believed that only the man I loved was capable of rousing those feelings in me. I did not understand then that my body could respond to lust just as it had once responded to true love. My body could detach itself from feelings."

"But having discovered these things," he finished for her, "you then discovered that you could control your body through a supreme effort of your mind."

"Yes," she said grimly. "After that, whatever he did to me evoked no feeling in me at all. I regretted hurting him, for he was a kind man."

Mirza Khan felt a stab of sympathy for the unfortunate Lucas. How maddening it must be to have driven this exquisite woman to passion once, to have had her hot with desire beneath him once, and then never again to be able to arouse her. "Tell me, Miranda, do you think you can awaken yourself on command? It is dangerous to play the game you have played."

"I have told you, Mirza Khan, that my husband and I will probably never be able to resume lovemaking."

"I see," he said gravely. "And so you will spend the rest of your life unloved, in punishment for the sin of being kidnaped and raped. Your husband, however, will be permitted his mistresses, or possibly a divorce and a new wife as compensation for your behavior. I dislike your appalling Western morality, Miranda. It lacks logic, to say nothing of compassion."

"You are laughing at me," she accused.

"No, my little puritan, I am not laughing. I weep for you, and for a morality that punishes an innocent victim. Is your husband really that rigid a man that he would cast you out so cruelly?" She turned her head away, pressing it against his shoulder in grief, and he put his arms around her. "Oh, Miranda, if what you tell me is the truth, then let me send word to England that you have sickened and died with a fever, for the life you propose to return to really will kill you.

"Stay with me and be my love. A good Muslim is permitted four wives, yet I have never cared enough for anyone to marry. I care for you. I would make you my wife."

Her slender shoulders shook with the force of her sobs, and he held her as his elegant hand smoothed her beautiful head. The caique bobbed gently on the silvery sea now, and the world about them was silent but for the soft gurgle of the waves beneath the boat and the sound of her weeping. Then he said in a quiet, firm voice, "I am going to make love to you, Miranda, and there will be no shame involved. You will respond to me, my darling, because I will not allow you to shut yourself away from life, and making love is an important part of life."

"No," she said weakly, "it would be wrong."

"It will be right!" he countered, signaling his rower to return to shore. "If, on your return home, your life is to be the loveless hell you describe then I will give you sweet memories to feast upon in the long, dark nights ahead, memories to soften the pain you suffered in Russia."

"My husband..." she began faintly, confused.

He took her heart-shaped face in his two hands. "Look at me and tell me that you do not want to know the sweet pleasures of passion again." In her sea-green eyes, in those bottomless emerald depths, he saw the answer she could not say, and the corners of his mouth lifted in a triumphant smile before his lips took possession of hers once again.

She began to warm with his embrace. She tried to struggle free, to escape long enough to clear her mind, but he pinioned her against the bright satin pillows, never letting her free of the sensuous kisses he pressed upon her. His dark, brushlike mustache was soft, and tickled her delightfully.

Suddenly she felt all the terrible tension that had built up within her over the last year flowing away from her body. *I love my husband,* she thought, *but I want this man to make love to me.* And with that silent admission she began to return his kiss.

Her lips softened and parted, allowing his velvet tongue into her mouth where it expertly caressed hers, sending a molten fire pouring through her veins. He rained kisses all over her beautiful face and throat, murmuring huskily against her ear, "I adore you, Miranda! Trust me, my darling, and I promise to give you only pleasure."

Sweetness engulfed her, cradling her. She became oblivious to everything but him.

The caique bumped the quay, and he reluctantly broke away. Gazing down at her with undisguised longing, he cupped her face in his hands and whispered, "Only pleasure, my darling." Then he stood, leaped lightly from the caique and picked her up in his arms. He carried her swiftly toward the house. Seeing him arrive, his slaves opened all the doors leading to his bedroom so that his passage would be smooth and uninterrupted. The unseen hands quietly shut the doors behind them. Miranda would always remember the wonderful silence in the little palace that night, a silence broken only occasionally by the murmuring of the night wind.

Mirza Khan's bedchamber was lit softly by hanging crystal lamps that cast a warm golden glow over the entire room. The lamps burned with fragrant oils that scented the room. The walls were paneled in ivory silk sprigged with green, the moldings were of a golden poplar, and the ceiling done in recessed squares of the same wood. Thick wool carpets of an ivory color with gold and green designs covered the floors. The large bed was hung with green silks.

The furniture was walnut and gilt, styled in the French manner of the Louis XV period. Scattered throughout were rare Chinese vases,

Venetian crystal, gold and silver pieces. Never before had Miranda seen such opulent luxury in one room. Though it was an odd assortment, it all came together beautifully.

In a corner of the room stood a full-length Venetian mirror set into an ornate gold baroque frame. He set her down before the glass, facing it, and slowly began to undress her. She watched, mesmerized, as his beautiful hands removed the deep-mauve sleeveless robe edged on each side of its opening with a three-inch band of tiny crystal beads and then the belt of the same beads that sat upon her hips. His slender fingers quickly unfastened the pearl buttons of her soft rose tunic dress at the sleeves and the neck. Beneath the tunic dress she wore only sheer pale-pink harem pants and a little gauze blouse of the same pale pink.

He moved to draw the blouse open, and she caught at his hands. Their eyes met in the mirror. She could hear the beat of her heart, and wondered if he could hear it, too. He waited, intuitively knowing there would be no need to force her. Suddenly her hands fell back to her sides. Baring her beautiful breasts, he gently cupped them in his palms as if making an offering to a god. The intensity of his gaze sent a weakening warmth through her body, and her large nipples tightened like frosted flower buds.

" 'Behold thou art fair, my love,' " he said. " 'Behold thou art fair. Thy two breasts are like two young roes that are twins, which feed upon the lilies.' " Mirza Khan's deep voice was filled with such passion that she came close to tears.

"I quote to you from 'The Song of Solomon,' Miranda," he said softly, smiling at her in the mirror. "I speak only the bits and pieces that come to my mind. 'Thy navel is like a round goblet, which wanteth not liquor,' " he murmured into her neck, his hands moving from her breasts to loosen her harem trousers. " 'Thy belly is like a heap of wheat set about with lilies.' " He smoothed the roundness with teasing fingers.

"These words are written in your own holy book, but I don't imagine that little puritan girls are taught them. It is said that they were composed by the great Hebrew king, Solomon, son of David. It tells of the delights experienced by a bride and her bridegroom in each other." He lifted her gently from the jumble of silken fabrics at her feet and moved her so they stood sideways to the mirror, facing each other.

She began to undress him, removing his long white silk robe to bare a wide, muscled bronze chest. Placing her palms flat against his warm skin, she looked up at him shyly, and said, "You have told me what he says to her, Mirza Khan, but does she not speak to him?"

" 'My beloved is white and ruddy,' " he answered. " 'His locks are bushy and black as a raven, his lips like lilies dropping sweet-smelling myrrh. His belly is as bright ivory overlaid with sapphires. His mouth is most sweet, yea he is altogether lovely. This is my beloved, and this is my friend,' " said Mirza Khan softly, his deep vibrant voice sending shivers through her. She didn't notice that he had kicked off his slippers, stepped from his baggy white trousers, and was now as naked as she.

"And then?" she whispered, blushing as she realized his state. "What does he say to her then?"

Mirza Khan wrapped his strong arms around Miranda, their naked bodies touching from breast to belly to thigh. Softly he brushed her lips. " 'Let him kiss me with the kisses of his mouth, for thy love is better than wine. I am my beloved's,' " he murmured against her lips. " 'I am my beloved's, and his desire is toward me.' "

Their mouths met in a passionate kiss, her arms slipping up around his neck to draw his mouth closer down to hers. Lifting her into his arms, he carried her slowly across the room and gently placed her on the bed. Her pale-gold hair fanned out onto the plump pillows. Tenderly Mirza Khan took a foot in his hand.

" 'How beautiful art thy feet, o prince's daughter!' " He kissed the arch of it, then the ankle, his mouth moving slowly up her leg as he crooned, " 'The joints of thy thighs are like jewels, the work of the hands of a cunning craftsman.' " He lay his dark head upon her white thighs, and her hands tenderly caressed his dark hair.

He took nothing she was not willing to give him, and she could not, it seemed, give him enough. This was confusing. His wonderful voice pierced her to the heart and she grew warm with his words, and helpless to the sweet desire he roused in her.

"'My beloved spake, and said unto me, Rise up my love, my fair one, and come away. For lo, the winter is past, the rain is over, and gone; the flowers appear on the earth; the time of the singing of birds is come, and the voice of the turtle is heard in our land. Arise, my love, my fair one, and come away.'"

Mirza Khan sought the secret sweetness of her. Her legs fell apart and a violent shudder tore through her as he found her treasure. She cried aloud her deep passion. His tongue was wildfire, touching her here and there until the pleasure was so great it poured over her like molten gold, and her breath came in short, painful gasps.

Oh God, it had never been like this before! *Not like this!* "Mirza!" she cried, not even aware that she had spoken.

When he raised his head she saw that his deep-blue eyes were blazing. Slowly, slowly, he pulled himself up until his lean, masculine body covered hers. "'As the apple tree among the trees of the wood, so is my beloved.'" She felt his pulsing shaft seeking entry, and reached down to guide him. "Then, Miranda, my darling, the bride said, 'I sat down under his shadow with great delight, and his fruit was sweet to my taste.'" She felt him thrusting within her as he continued to speak. "He brought me to the banqueting house, and his banner over me was love."

Miranda wept silently, her face wet with salty tears, but they were tears of joy.

Taking her face in his hands, he kissed her again and again, his shaft pulsing within her, until she shuddered with the force of her ecstasy and floated away into a honeyed, spiraling world, knowing that he had joined her.

When she came to herself again he was lying with his dark head on her breasts, but she knew he was not asleep. "I understand now," she said softly, with a touch of wonder.

"Tell me..." She heard the smile in his voice.

"You have shown me love in another form. I love my husband, and when we made love the desire to do so came from our mutual love, and from our passion as well. Lucas loved me too, but I had no choice. I was resentful and I wanted to punish him for making me respond to his lust that first time. I wanted to punish myself for what I considered my body's betrayal of me as well as my husband's honor."

"And what have I taught you, my darling, that your voice is now so filled with laughter instead of tears?" he asked.

"That lovers should be friends, Mirza Khan, even a husband and a wife." He raised his head and she took his face into her hands and kissed his mouth. "We are friends. We have been since we met in St. Petersburg."

They sat facing one another upon the large bed, and he asked her, "Will your husband really repudiate you, Miranda?"

She sighed. "By our code he has every right to do so." Then she smiled ruefully. "The upper-class gentleman in England is expected, even encouraged, to keep some bit o' muslin, as mistresses are referred to in polite society. I even know of certain upper-class women who are unfaithful to their husbands. But, although their behavior is suspected, it is permitted because they are discreet. You know what London is like."

"Indeed I do!"

"Appearance is everything to the ton. Society will say that I did something to bring my woes down upon my head, and my husband will be thought quite correct to rid himself of me if he chooses."

"I think you misjudge your husband, Miranda. If he is the man you say he is, he will love you more for your bravery."

She reached out and took his hand. "Do you remember what you said to me earlier this evening in your caique? You said that if my life was to be loveless then you would give me sweet memories to feast upon in the long dark nights ahead. I need those memories, Mirza, for whether Jared casts me aside or not there will be many lonely dark nights ahead for me. Will you love me while I remain here in your house enjoying your hospitality? I have never even believed that I could ask such a thing of a man not my husband, but you are my friend, Mirza Khan, and in a strange way I care for you."

His startled look surprised her, and she said quickly, "I have shocked you! Oh Mirza, forgive me! It was a foolish request."

"*No!*" His voice was husky with emotion. "I adore you, my Miranda! I think I fell under your spell the moment we met last year in St. Petersburg. When I heard you had been killed on the streets of that barbaric place I left it as soon as I could, for I could not stay in a city so savage as to murder you.

"Then when I saw you again I believed in miracles. Not only were you alive, but you were unbeaten. I have never known a woman like you!

"Will I love you while you remain in my house? Miranda my darling, I will love you forever if you will but let me!"

"Thank you, Mirza, but I must go back when Jared sends for me. I have a son. Wyndsong will be his one day."

"You worry about your son, Miranda, but what of your daughter?"

"I have decided that Jared will never know of the child's existence if I can prevent it. I am a wealthy woman and I will see that the child is placed with a good foster mother. She will want for nothing, and I will see her regularly."

"And when you return to America? What of your daughter, then?"

"I will not leave her behind, Mirza. She is my child for all the shame of her conception. But Jared must not know, and neither must anyone else. As long as no one knows the child is mine, there can be only speculation about what happened to me this past year."

"You must give her a name," he said quietly. "You call her 'the child' as if she had no real identity, and as long as she is nameless she doesn't."

"I can't," Miranda said sadly.

"Yes, you can!" he answered. "She is such a beautiful, dainty little creature. She is like a delicate little flower. Think, my darling! What is her name?"

"I. . .I don't know!"

"Come, Miranda," he urged her.

"Fleur!" she said suddenly. "You said she looks like a flower and she does. I'll call her Fleur! Are you satisfied now, Mirza Khan?"

"Not entirely," he said lazily, reaching out to catch at her pale-gilt hair and draw her closer to him. She was in his arms once more, and his mouth was teasing hers again.

She stopped his lips with her fingers, and began to recite softly, " 'My beloved is mine, and I am his: he feedeth among the lilies until the day break, and the shadows flee away. Turn, my beloved, and be thou like a roe, or a young hart upon the mountains of Bether.' "

"You vixen!" he chuckled, delighted. "You know 'The Song of Solomon'!"

"I'm afraid I was a *curious* little puritan girl, Mirza Khan, and Papa never discouraged a study of the Bible," she finished demurely. Her sea-green eyes were dancing with delight at having surprised him.

"Oh, Miranda," he said seriously, "I am not sure I am ever going to let you go."

"There will come a time, my dearest friend, when you will have no choice but to let me go. Until then I am yours if you will have me."

"And afterward?"

"Afterward I shall have sweet memories to feast upon in the long dark nights," she answered. Pulling his dark head back down, her mouth scorched his, and together they entered paradise once again.

❧ Chapter 15 ❧

Miranda looked into her mirror. She had changed, and she liked the change. She was twenty years old and, at last, the girl she had been was gone. A woman stared back at her from the Venetian glass, a woman whose bittersweet experiences of the last year had served only to increase her beauty, refine it as one would refine gold.

Her skin was as translucent as the finest porcelain. Her cheeks, washed with pale rose, stretched tight over her high, fine bones. The sea-green eyes never wavered in their direct gaze. If she had been a beautiful young girl, she was now an incredibly stunning young woman.

There were deeper changes as well. Where once she had been quick to act and ruled by her heart, she now considered carefully and thoughtfully.

Mirza Khan, her tender lover these few months, had begged her to remain with him, or at least to return to him if Jared repudiated her. She cared deeply for him, yet she knew she would never love him as she loved Jared Dunham, and Mirza Khan deserved all of her heart.

She sighed, allowing herself a moment to think back over the terrible things she had seen in the last year. Perhaps the most painful was the death of little Fleur. The day of her death, which was the day after Mirza Khan had insisted that Miranda name her, seemed to mark the closing of one door and the opening of another. The child's quiet and apparently painless death had been no surprise at all to Miranda and had been, of course, something of a relief. What kind of life would she have had, blind and probably deaf as well?

Miranda would always be grateful to the prince for insisting on a name. How awful if the baby had gone to her grave nameless! She was buried in a secluded part of the garden, and Mirza Khan had held Miranda while she wept and wept. There were no longer any tears for the child. Perhaps there would be again one day, but for now Miranda intended to walk through the new door, into a new life. She could not, just now, allow herself to dwell on the past.

Rising, she left her room and sought Mirza Khan. Walking alone in the selamlik garden when she found him, the prince's face lit up at sight of her, and she walked proudly into his outstretched arms. "Thank you, Mirza," she said. "Thank you. I have suddenly realized that I am whole again, and it is you who have created this miracle."

He held her against him, aching with need for her. "We are friends, and so it was written before either of us was even born. It is what we call *kismet,* a preordained fate." His hand lightly touched her soft hair. How long? he wondered. How long before I must let her go, and then spend the rest of the years apportioned to me wondering what I ever did that I must bear such pain, such loss.

"You love me," she said quietly, knowing his thoughts so clearly that it startled her. She had never been able to play that particular trick with anyone else but Amanda.

"Of course I love you," he said with false heartiness.

"No!" Her voice was sharp, and demanded his attention. "You really love me. Oh, Mirza, have I brought you pain? You don't deserve that, darling."

"Walk with me, Miranda," was his reply. They strolled the smooth marble paths of the garden. "Do you know how old I am?" he asked her, and then without waiting for her answer said, "I am forty-five years old, Miranda, a full twenty-five years your senior. I might be your father."

"No, Mirza, you could never be my papa." To his surprise he heard laughter in her voice.

"What I am trying to say to you, Miranda, is yes, I really do love you, but had we never become lovers I would still love you because it is my fate to do so. It is also my fate to see you returned safely to your world. If you remain there with your husband then I must accept that bitter portion of my fate as I have so joyously accepted the sweet portion of it. My years have taught me not to rail against Allah's plan for me, though I may sometimes feel that I know better than God himself. If I have given you sweet memories to feast upon in the long dark nights ahead, then so have you given me sweet memories in return." Turning, he tipped her face up to him, his deep-blue eyes locking onto hers with such tenderness that she felt the tears pricking, and blinked them fiercely back. "Into each man's life, if he is lucky, comes one very special love. There will never be another, but my dearest little puritan, my life is so much richer for loving you. I regret nothing, and neither must you, for regret would lessen what has passed between us, and make it only ordinary."

Reaching up, she took his head in her hands and, pulling it down, kissed him a tender, sweet kiss. "I have become a woman with you," she said. "Never have I felt so strong, so sure, and it is your love that has done this. It will envelop me when I leave you, an invisible, protective armor."

She slipped her hand into his, and they strolled wordlessly, enjoying the beauties of the garden with its tinkling, blue-tiled fountains, its fish pools whose swift golden inhabitants darted to and fro amid the water lilies. The yellow rose trees were in full bloom amid beds of fluffy white gypsophila, tall spikes of purple lavender, lemon balm, and other sweet herbs.

The sunlight caressed her long hair while a soft wind teasingly played with it. Soon he led her into his dimly lit bedchamber. She shed her peacock-blue caftan, he his long white robe, and they came together in an embrace. His body, lean, warm, and hard, felt good against hers. Her lips parted to receive his tongue into her mouth, a tongue that loved hers with tender familiarity. Her hands smoothed down the long line of his back, cupped his buttocks, and moved back upward, her nails gently raking his skin. He bore her backward onto the bed, his passionate mouth never leaving hers, and her arms slipped up around his neck. Her pale-gold hair billowed outward, and he tangled his hands in its soft thickness as he covered her face with a thousand kisses.

Rolling to one side, he cradled her within the shelter of his arm while his other hand gently caressed her breasts, his fingers touching her skin slowly as if committing its texture to memory. Watching him through half-closed eyes, she said softly, "This is the last time for us, isn't it, Mirza?"

"How did you know?"

"I saw *Dream Witch* anchor off your beach earlier this afternoon," she replied.

"You will sail with the evening tide, Miranda, my love. Your Captain Snow has brought your maid. She will come ashore later with your clothes."

"Oh, Mirza, I am suddenly afraid!" she cried.

"No!" His deep voice was fierce. "You must *never* show fear, my darling, for if you exhibit any sign of weakness you will be overcome. Your world is full of people who have never faced a decision more serious than having to choose between two invitations. They believe that the correct thing in your situation would have been suicide. However, if in your shoes, would they have killed themselves? Of course not!

"Live, Miranda. Apologize to no one, not even to yourself!"

Then Mirza Khan sealed her mouth with a burning kiss, and continued to make tender, passionate love to her. He kissed every inch of her, slipping down the silk sheets to begin with her pretty pink toes. His tongue flicked at the arch of each foot, and she giggled. He worshiped at each long leg, nuzzling, then playfully nipping at the soft skin on the insides of her thighs.

Her nipples grew high and tight with longing, and she gasped when his mouth closed over first one and then the other. She held his head close to her breasts. Slowly he lifted himself so as to face her, and as their eyes met hers filled with tears. It was so unfair that he loved her like this, and that she must leave him.

He kissed her belly, and said, "I have tasted of your milk, my darling, now will I taste of your honey," and his dark head dipped down to that secret grotto of love. Tauntingly his tongue flicked at the sweet flesh, and she moaned low, a sound that came from deep, deep back in her throat. Her body began to shudder.

"I...I want to love you...that way, too," she managed to gasp, but he didn't stop. "Please, Mirza!" He stopped and swung his body sideways so she might taste of him as he had tasted of her.

She took him gently into her mouth, her naughty tongue teasing the crimson head of his manhood. He sobbed, and his mouth reciprocated her loving until she thought she would go mad with the pleasure. Playfully, she nipped at him.

"Oh, bitch, to do this to me now!" he groaned. Then, disengaging her grip on him, he pulled her beneath him and thrust into her, pushing his shaft as deep as he could. She thrust herself up to meet him, pulling his head to hers, kissing him hungrily, tasting herself in his mouth. Together they reached the final peak, and then together they tumbled whirling through timelessness until reaching earth once more to cling together in a last sweet embrace before sleep overtook them.

When Miranda awoke he was gone. Slowly she rose, donned her caftan, and made her way back across the harem garden to her room in the women's quarters. Turkhan awaited her, and the two women embraced in sisterly fashion.

"Will he see me before I go?" Miranda said. "I cannot leave without seeing him once more."

"He will see you."

"You love him, Turkhan." It was a statement, and the reply was not surprising.

"Yes, I love him, and in his fashion he cares for me. I have been with him for fifteen years, since I was fourteen. Others come and go, but I always remain, as I will remain to comfort him after you have gone."

"He is fortunate to have you," replied Miranda sincerely.

Turkhan smiled, and put an arm around the younger woman. "Miranda, little sister, how very Western you are! I do not mind that my lord Mirza loves you, for you have made him happy, and we all

knew that you would have to leave us one day. When you have gone
we will have the pleasurable task of soothing our lord's pain. The
other butterflies of his harem believe they will succeed, and he will
kindly tell them they have, but I know better. You will always be
with him, hidden in a dark, secret place deep within his heart. I
cannot change that, nor would I. Every experience we face in this life
is for a purpose, even the bittersweet ones."

"I might return," Miranda said softly.

"No," Turkhan shook her lovely head. "You care for my lord
Mirza, but your heart is with the man to whom you return. Even if he
casts you off, you will remain near him as I remain near Mirza
Khan—because you love him, as I love my lord."

"Yes," came the reply. "I love Jared, and no matter what happens
I will want to be near him."

"I understand," said Turkhan, and then she said in a lighter tone,
"Let us go to the baths. Your people will be here soon."

Miranda luxuriated in the lovely harem baths a last time. After a
massage, she dozed and was awakened by an elderly woman slave
offering sweet, boiling Turkish coffee. Drinking the coffee quickly,
she was wrapped in a large, fluffy towel and left the baths. Miranda
opened the door to her room and entered it. She heard a gasp, and
then a joyful cry.

"Milady! It really is you!"

She swallowed. The transition had begun. "Yes, Perky. It really is
me."

Perkins burst into tears. "Oh, milady, we was so heartbroken.
Milord was wild with grief. He was drunk for close to two months."

"Was he?" Miranda smiled, quite pleased. "What happened after
he sobered up, Perky?"

Perkins' plain, girlish face became tight with disapproval. "It ain't
my place to criticize, m'lady, but after he sobered up he became the
biggest rake in London. Thank God you weren't really dead, and
you're coming home. I shudder to think of that Lady de Winter being
little Tom's mama!"

"What?!" Miranda felt her temper rising. He certainly hadn't put
himself out with a long mourning period, had he?

"Oh m'lady, forgive me for upsetting you! I'll tell you true. The
gossip was that he was planning to offer for her, but he didn't. They

say all he wanted was a mama for little Master Tom, for the child's been with Lady Swynford ever since you left. She wouldn't let him go from the hall, but kept him with Master Neddie. Now, however, she's breeding again. And besides, m'lord wants the boy. He loves the child so much. I never heard that he loved Lady de Winter, m'lady. There's never been the slightest gossip of that! I swear it!"

Miranda put out a gentle hand and patted Perkins' cheek. "It's all right, Perky. I think it's better that I know exactly what has been happening. Come now, help me dress." She needed to change the subject, and grasped the opportunity. "Have fashions changed very much in the year I've been away?"

"Oh yes, m'lady! The bodices are tighter, the skirts a little fuller, and the hems come just to the ankle. Wait till you see the cabin full of lovely gowns his lordship's brought for you."

Very slowly, Miranda began to lose her color. She swayed and Perky reached out to steady her.

"He's here?!" Miranda whispered. "Is Lord Dunham aboard the ship?"

"Why, yes, of course," Perky replied.

Miranda grew silent. So there was to be little time to plan what she would say to Jared, little time to prepare herself? Miranda dropped her towel, and Perky, blushing, handed her a pair of fine muslin drawers and white silk stockings with embroidered gold clocks on them. There were braided gold silk garters to hold the stockings up. "Oh, this is new!" Miranda noted as her maid dropped a quilted white silk petticoat with its own attached bodice over her head. The bodice was sleeveless, and had wide straps.

The dress Perky had brought her was of coral and apricot muslin in alternating stripes. The scooped neckline was low, the sleeves short puffs, the bodice indeed quite tight. The skirt belled out gently over her petticoat, ending just at the ankle. Miranda slipped into a pair of black slippers.

"The dress is a bit tight in the bodice, m'lady, but I can let it out later. I'd have thought you'd be a bit less in the bustline what with not nursing all these months."

Miranda nodded, sat, and watched quietly as her maid parted her hair in the center. Perky braided it and then arranged the braid in a round knot at the back of her head. "Lord Dunham sent your jewel case along, m'lady," said Perky, and she opened the top tray in the red Morocco leather case.

Miranda first removed a strand of pearls on a gold chain with a diamond clasp, and fastened them about her neck. Then she took the matching pearl-and-diamond earrings, and secured them in her ears. The fashionable London woman in the mirror stared at her cooly, and Miranda knew it was time to go. She stood. "Take the case, Perky, and go to the barge. I must bid Prince Mirza farewell and thank him for his hospitality."

She took a final look around the small bedroom with its yellow-and white-tiled corner stove, its built-in single bed, and the small dressing table with the Venetian glass mirror. She had been happy here, and though her heart longed for Jared, she was afraid of what awaited her and reluctant to leave the safety of Mirza Khan's sure love. "You must never show fear," he had said. "Never apologize, even to yourself."

"Come, Perky," she said brightly, and the two women left the room. The harem women were waiting in the salon. The little English maid stood back shyly, her eyes wide at the sight of the beautiful women in lavish, colorful costumes. Perky did not understand any language other than English, and could not understand what was said, but she knew that the women were sad to see her mistress leave.

Having bid a warm good-bye to the women of the harem, Miranda turned back to Guzel and Safiye, and asked, "Will you show my maidservant the way to the quay?"

Miranda then spoke to Perkins. "I will be with you shortly. These ladies will show you to the barge."

Perky curtseyed. "Very good, m'lady," she said, and followed Safiye and Guzel from the room.

"He awaits you in the main salon," said Turkhan. Giving Miranda a farewell kiss on the cheek, she finished, "I will take good care of him."

"I know you will. I only hope he knows how fortunate he is to have you," said Miranda sincerely. "Men can sometimes be such damned fools!"

"In his own way he appreciates me," was the contented reply. "Go now, Miranda. May you find true happiness again with your husband."

Miranda walked to the main salon in the public rooms of the small palace. He was waiting, dressed as he had been the first time she had seen him in St. Petersburg, in white trousers, a white Persian coat, and a small white turban.

"We end as we began," he said quietly, taking her hand and kissing it in the Western fashion. "How beautiful you look, Lady Dunham, the picture of the fashionable European woman!"

"I love you," she said softly. "Not in the way in which I love Jared, but I do love you, Mirza. I didn't know a woman could care so deeply, in such different ways, for two men at the same time."

"I wondered if you would ever understand that," he smiled, holding out his arms to her.

With a little cry she buried herself in his embrace. "Mirza, I am so confused!"

"No, Miranda, you are not really confused, you are simply reluctant to exchange my love for the uncertainty of what awaits you. I will not deny my love for you or my need for you, but neither will I accept second best, for I am a proud man. Your love for Jared Dunham is far greater than your love for me could ever be. Return to him, little puritan, and fight for him!

"I don't give a damn what polite society in England says. When a woman is forced, the shame is *not* on her but on the man who forces her. Your Jared has had more than his share of ladies, I will wager, and if he is the man you claim then he will not hold you responsible for something you could not help. Remember what I have told you. *Never* apologize!"

"And what shall I tell him of you, Mirza Eddin Khan? You did not force me."

"What do you want to tell him, Miranda?"

She moved out of his embrace just enough to look up into his handsome face. His deep-blue eyes challenged her. "I think, Mirza Khan, that there are certain things in this world a wife must keep to herself," she answered, and her sea-green eyes were laughing.

"I have taught you well, oh daughter of Eve," he said softly.

"I have been an apt pupil, my dearest friend."

He smiled his oddly roguish smile, and then pulling her back into his embrace, he kissed her deeply and tenderly. She melted back against him, tasting him one last time, enjoying the tickly softness of his mustache one last time, feeling so loved that when he finally released her she lay in his arms for a moment or two more, her eyes closed. Finally she sighed deeply, regretfully, and, opening her eyes, stepped away from him. Neither of them said anything, the time for words being long past. He took her hand in his, and they walked from the salon across the portico, across the green lawn, and down to the marble quay.

Perky, who was on the barge approaching *Dream Witch*, saw them and caught her breath in surprise. When she had been told her mistress was staying at the palace of a cousin of the sultan, she had envisioned a kindly, white-haired patriarch, and she assumed that Lord Dunham had, too. This very tall, handsome gentleman was not at all what she had expected. "Coo," she whispered to herself, "ain't he gorgeous!" They held hands, too. Well, it wasn't her business, and heaven only knew Lord Dunham had chased every lightskirt in London, and lifted them, too! These last months hadn't been easy on any of them.

The couple walked out onto the quay. The barge would return for Miranda in a very few minutes.

"Allah go with you, my darling. I shall think of you each day for the rest of my life and count the time well spent."

"I will not forget you, Mirza. I only wish I were as deserving of your love as I should be. Turkhan loves you, you know. She would make you a very good wife."

He laughed. Catching her hand, he kissed the palm in a teasing gesture. "Farewell, my little puritan! When you write me that you have made your own happy ending, then I will consider your advice!" He helped her down into the barge.

"Consider my advice well, my proud prince," she teased. "Have you not taught me that true love is a rare thing, to be prized above all else?"

"I bow before your wisdom, Miranda," he answered. Though he laughed, his eyes were sad, so sad she almost cried with his pain.

"Farewell, Mirza Eddin Khan," she said softly, "and thank you, my love."

For the briefest moment he gazed raptly at her. Then speaking curtly to his boatman, he gave orders and the barge bobbed out onto the gentle evening seas. She watched the shore recede, looking for a last time at the lovely little palace where she had been so happy, so safe.

From the building on the hill emerged a regal female figure in flowing ruby-red robes. The woman made her way to Mirza Khan's side and stood silently next to him. Wordlessly he put his arm about her, and Miranda smiled, pleased. Turkhan will surely win him over, she thought.

Jared Dunham stood on the deck of *Dream Witch,* watching as the barge moved slowly across the water toward him. Thoughtfully he lowered his spyglass and stared at the man in white who was standing on the quay. The prince was certainly not what he'd expected. Jared had seen clearly the way Miranda had looked at him and also the way the prince had looked at Miranda. Jared felt extremely uncomfortable, as if he'd been spying on a private meeting. Cold anger welled up in him. She was his *wife!* Why should he feel like an outsider? Jared had been advised by many people in England that Miranda would need him desperately, that she would need all the love and understanding he could give her. But the elegant woman walking hand in hand with the handsome prince did not look in need of anything at all.

Suddenly Jared felt that he was being watched, and he put the spyglass to his eye once more. Prince Mirza stood staring directly at him and his look carried this message: *Take care of her,* it said, *for I want her too!* Jared was astounded. It was as if the man had spoken clearly in his ear. With an angry oath, he slammed the spyglass shut and stormed from the deck.

Perky had arrived some time before, with the jewel case, and was below. Ephraim Snow, alone on deck, awaited Miranda. As she was hoisted up in the bosun's chair, the old captain was suddenly overcome. Helping her from the chair with trembling fingers, he sobbed, "Oh, my lady!"

Miranda reached over and touched his cheek, knowing that to kiss him would be wrong.

"Hello, Eph," she said softly. "I'm so glad to see you again."

The sound of Miranda's voice made her presence a firm reality, and helped the old man to recover. Wiping his eyes, he said gruffly, "Worst time of my whole life was telling Master Jared that you'd been killed."

"I didn't do it deliberately," she sighed. Damn! Was it going to be like this with all of them? Was she to be held accountable for her abduction? *Never apologize!* She heard Mirza Khan's voice as clearly as if he were standing beside her. Miranda turned away from Eph and walked swiftly to the stern of the ship. She raised her hand in a farewell gesture. The gesture was quickly answered by a red arm and a white arm waving back from the quay.

The anchor was raised, and *Dream Witch* slipped down the Bosphorus into the Sea of Marmara. The evening sky had darkened to a deep lavender, and on the far western horizon was the thinnest slash of scarlet. Miranda gazed intently at the disappearing coastline. It was over. The nightmare was over, and she was going home. Home!

Wait, said a small voice. You may not have won yet. You have yet to see Jared.

Ephraim Snow's voice cut into her thoughts. "You gonna stay out here all night, Mistress Miranda?"

She turned to face him. "Where is my husband, Eph? I was told that he came to Istanbul. He was not on deck to greet me when I came aboard."

Je-sus! Something sure as hell was eating at her. "He was up on deck, with his spyglass, watchin' as you said your good-byes. Somethin' sure as hell riled him cause when you were halfway between us and the shore, he went below lookin' madder than a boiled owl."

"Where is he now?"

"In his cabin."

"Tell my husband I am in the main salon, Eph," she said, and she left him.

Lord, she'd changed. He'd understood the enthusiastic girl-woman he'd brought to Russia those long months ago. But she was as gone as if she really had been murdered. The woman who had given him that cool, sharp order looked at him with eyes that never wavered. In fact it had been he who had looked away first. Praise the Lord she wasn't his problem! Let Jared Dunham handle her...if he could! The Captain went to fetch the gentleman.

Jared looked somewhat chagrined by the message Ephraim Snow brought. He had a question:

"Has she changed?"

"Aye."

He had known it! "Very much?" he asked.

"You'll judge for yourself, Master Jared."

He nodded, swallowing hard, and, brushing past, the captain walked to the main salon. Opening the door, he entered it. Her back was to him. He couldn't fathom the set of it and that annoyed him. She didn't appear the broken reed he had been told she would be. The words were out of his mouth before he could stop them. "So, madam, you are back at long last!"

She turned. Her new beauty stunned him. "Indeed, m'lord, I am most certainly back." The mouth mocked him, as did the knowing sea-green eyes.

He didn't remember her mouth so lush, and the last time he had looked into those eyes they had been innocent. He stared angrily back at her. The dress had too low a neckline, and her breasts swelled far too provocatively above it. "I trust, madam," he said coldly, "that you have a good explanation for your conduct."

"I merely sought my husband," she said in a syrupy sweet voice that was belied by the stormy look in her eyes, "my husband, who left me to play at a game of intrigue while I carried and bore our first child alone."

"A child you cared so little about that you left him when he was barely two months old!" he retorted.

"I love little Tom!" she shouted furiously at him. "I expected to

find you, and bring you home immediately. My son was safer in
England with Amanda. Would you rather I had exposed him to the
rigors of the journey to Russia?

"I could bear it no longer without you! Your beastly friend,
Palmerston, would tell me nothing! *Nothing!* He behaved as if you
did not even exist."

"Touching, madam, but tell me, how did you attract Prince
Cherkessky's attention?"

"What?"

"Alexei Cherkessky, the man who abducted you. Ephraim Snow
told me you attended a party at the English Embassy the night before
you disappeared. Did you meet the prince there? Did you flirt with
him and bring the situation on yourself, Miranda?"

She threw the nearest thing at hand, a heavy crystal inkwell. It
dented the door behind his head, the black ink running down the
paneling onto the deck, where it sank slowly into the wide boards.
"So, m'lord, I am to be held accountable for this situation, am I? Oh
God, how little you know me to believe such a thing! When did I, in
the few short months of our marriage, *ever* give you cause for doubt?
Never! But you, m'lord! First there was Gillian Abbott, then who
knows how many women in St. Petersburg, and you mourned me but
a few months before you were back in the social swing. So now there
is Lady de Winter."

She turned away furiously, hiding her face from his angry gaze,
blinking back the tears fast filling her eyes. She would not let him
see her weakness. He would only use it against her.

"Did Cherkessky rape you?" His voice was ragged.

She turned back to face him, and he thought he had never seen her
so angry. "No," came the short, sharp reply, and then she swept past
him and left the room.

Tears nearly blinding her, she made her way to her spacious cabin
by memory, ordering a startled Perky from the room as she flung
herself on the bed.

He had looked so handsome! But they were at odds, and her heart
was breaking again. She had noticed just the faintest touch of silver
at his temples, and wondered if her disappearance were responsible

for it. At least *her* scars didn't show. What a terrible beginning it had been!

He came into the room now and, kneeling by the bed, said quietly, "We did not make a good new beginning, did we, Miranda? I am glad to have you back." He cautiously placed his arm around her.

"I have been coming back to you ever since Prince Cherkessky had me abducted," she said. "I attempted to escape his villa within a month of my arrival."

"You did?!" This was the Miranda he knew. "How?"

"By sea. I thought if I could sail to Istanbul I could go to the English Embassy. But I was caught, and until the Tatars came I was too closely watched." She shrugged off his arm, not seeing the spasm of pain that crossed his face. "I walked practically all the way to 'Stanbul," she said proudly. "Oh, sometimes I'd ride a few miles on one of their booty carts, but mostly I walked. The prince's servants told the Tatars that I was a rich Englishwoman who could be ransomed in 'Stanbul, but they also warned me to beware the savages, and how right they were. The bastards intended to sell me right along with the rest of the poor souls they'd captured, but I overheard them plotting the night before we entered the city.

"We were camped outside the wall. I waited until they were all sleeping, then walked to the nearest gate, and when it was opened at dawn I walked across the entire city to the English Embassy. I had a hell of a time convincing the idiot gatekeeper who I was; but by wildest coincidence Kit Edmund appeared, and I was saved!" She rose and began pacing the cabin. Her look was very far away.

"The Tatars were behind me. Kit and his friend, Mirza Eddin Khan, were ahead of me, and there I was in the middle. The Tatars were screaming that I was honest booty from a raid and Kit was shouting that I was protected under British law."

"How did you get out of it?"

"Mirza Khan poured half a pouch of unset gemstones into the Tatar hetman's hands. It was a fortune, and really quite gallant of him! The Tatars were more than satisfied with the price, and they finally left me alone.

"May we eat now? I am really quite famished."

She brushed past Jared and entered their private day cabin, where a small feast had been laid out for them. The cook had taken the trouble, while waiting for her to board the ship, to shop the bazaars of the waterfront for fresh food. Here was the delectable result of his labors.

There was a joint of rare beef, a plump brown capon stuffed with rice, dried peaches and apricots, and a platter of mussels cooked in herbs and wine. Miranda paused over a large bowl of tomato and eggplant, and decided it looked too much like what she'd been eating for a year. She moved on to a bowl of green beans and then to one of carrots and celery in sherried cream sauce. There was rice pilaf and kasha, and she passed up the latter without a second thought. Next to a crock of sweet butter was a large loaf of fresh hot bread. She cut herself a large slice and slathered it shamelessly with butter. It had been over a year since she had seen white bread. Quickly deciding on the rest of her meal, she took several slices of beef, a little rice, and some creamed carrots and celery. She eyed the sideboard, covered with berry tarts smothered in cream, a wedge of Stilton cheese, the makings of tea, and bottles of both red and white wine.

She seated herself and instantly popped a slice of beef in her mouth.

"How I missed rare beef," she giggled. "The Russians overcook it."

"And the Turks?"

"They eat a lot of lamb," she replied. "Pass me the salt, please."

He handed her the round pewter dish, and taking up a plate helped himself to some supper. He would have to be satisfied for the time being because she was going to tell him only what she chose to, and no more. Probing would only drive her away.

They ate in silence, Miranda quickly finishing and going to the sideboard to brew a pot of black China tea. Then, cutting two generous wedges of the berry tart, she placed them on the table.

"Your appetite is as magnificent as ever, m'lady," he said.

"There were times on the journey to Istanbul when I was very hungry," she replied. "Mignon and I tried to supplement our diet with seafood when we marched near the sea, and we picked greens and wild strawberries."

"Who is Mignon?"

"She was the illegitimate daughter of a French nobleman. She had been a governess in St. Petersburg when the prince lured her to his Crimean estates. Two Tatars raped her and killed her when we were halfway to 'Stanbul. All she wanted was to get back to Paris."

My God, he thought, how she has suffered! Remembering her former innocence, her uncertainty, he was truly admiring of the strong woman she had become...and a little jealous not to have had a part in the transformation.

She stood up. "I am going to bed now, and I would like to be alone."

He protested. "We have been separated for over two years."

She heard the soft plea in his voice. How she wanted to answer that plea! How she longed to have his strong arms around her, comforting her, telling her it was all going to be all right. She took a deep breath and said, "Before we resume our life together I want to tell you what happened to me in Russia. Earlier you suggested that I might have been responsible for my own predicament. That is not so. I was not responsible in any way. I do not, however, choose to tell the story over and over. I will tell it once to you and our family. After that I will speak of it no more. When you have heard my tale you may not choose to resume our marriage. I cannot be dishonest with you. You know that is not my way. We have waited all this time. A few more weeks should not make any difference." She turned away, unable to bear the look on his face.

"Do you know, Miranda," he said quietly, "that you have not once said my name today."

"I did not realize it."

"Say my name!" He gripped her shoulders, and spun her around to face him. "Say my name, dammit!"

"J-Jared! Oh, Jared, I have missed you so much!" and his mouth swooped fiercely down on hers before she could pull away. She reveled in the kiss, the familiar taste and touch of him rising up to assault her. For the briefest time madness overtook her, urging her to let the kiss take them to its natural conclusion.

Let him pick her up and carry her tenderly to her bed. Let him undress her and kiss away all the shame. Let him learn the truth and, revolted, hate her!

She pulled away. "Please, Jared! Please wait for my sake until we are back in England!"

He was shocked by her desperation, by the fact that she was both trembling and crying, yet didn't seem to be aware of it. *What had happened to her?* He wasn't sure he wanted to know. "I don't care what happened in Russia," he said hoarsely. "I love you, Miranda, and we have been given a second chance!"

"But I care!" came the harsh reply. "I care because it happened to me! It weighs on me terribly. Now let me be! You will know all soon enough, but I will not willingly sleep with you until you do, and if you force me I will never forgive you!" Then she turned and fled into her cabin, slamming the door behind her.

Jared stood a moment, looking at the closed door. Then he walked to the sideboard, and picked up a snifter and the brandy bottle. Uncorking the bottle, he poured himself a generous drink, and then sat leaning forward, the crystal glass cupped in his big hands.

She had said the prince hadn't touched her, and he believed her. Then what was so terrible that she could not resume their marriage immediately?

Jared got up and entered her bedchamber. Her even breathing told him that she was asleep. He stayed there for a long time, sitting in the dark. Occasionally she shivered and whimpered. Once he thought she cried out a name, but he couldn't make it out. Finally, after she was quiet for a long while, he gently tucked her beneath the quilts.

In the morning she was paler than she had been the day before. Jared was forced to accept her silence until she could talk to the family, at Swynford Hall, but it was not easy for him. Being so close to her, caught within the confines of the ship with no way of escaping her tantalizing presence, was difficult for him. Only the pain in her face stopped him from pressing her.

The voyage was idyllic, with gentle breezes and bright blue skies during the day and starry nights. As the ship passed the Greek isles and the Mediterranean coast, Jared was ironically reminded of a honeymoon voyage.

Dream Witch slipped past Gibraltar, past Cape St. Vincent, past Cape Finisterre and into the Bay of Biscay, where the weather took a sudden turn and they rode through a fierce late-summer storm. In the midst of it he could not find her, and his heart leaped wildly until he saw her standing at the ship's rail, her knuckles white with her iron grip, her face wet with tears or rain, he did not know which. Leaning into the wind, he fought his way across the deck to her, and put his arm tightly around her.

He could feel her trembling through the thin fabric of her swirling cloak, and he bent so that she might hear him. "If this has been hard on me, it has been harder on you, Miranda. Frankly I do not know how you have borne it, and you have borne it alone. For God's sweet sake, wildcat, I am your husband! Lean on me! I am here! Do not shut me out! There is nothing in this world that could stop me from loving you!"

She looked up at him, the pain in her eyes searing him, but she would say nothing. What was her secret? What was so terrible that it was tearing her apart? "Come inside with me, my love," he said gently, and she nodded, loosening her grip on the rail and allowing him to lead her back into the shelter of the main salon.

The storm was gone the following morning, and a steady south wind pushed the sleek vessel along into the English Channel. A few days later they docked at Welland Beach.

At last she was back in England! Miranda endured the stuffy carriage and the tension between Jared and herself for a day. They spent the night at an inn, and when they set off the next morning, Jared smiled at her, and said, "I ordered the two extra horses so we might ride instead of sitting all day in the coach. Would you like to ride, Miranda? I didn't bring your breeches," he teased her, "but I think you can manage a sidesaddle."

They rode together across the October landscape to Swynford, stopping to rest their horses and to eat picnics prepared for them by innkeepers. At last they came within sight of Swynford Hall, the sunset crowning the manor house and its dark gray roof.

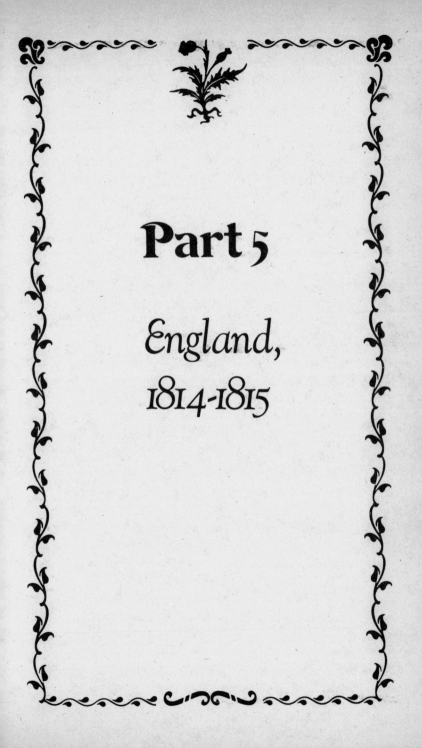

Part 5

England,
1814-1815

❧ Chapter 16 ❧

Miranda and Jared cantered down the hills toward Swynford Hall, the two coaches lumbering behind them. They
passed through the gates and the gatekeeper, his weathered
face wreathed in smiles, began tolling the rarely used welcoming
bell. They rode up the drive to the house, the bell ringing, and then a
petite round figure in a pink gown was flying out the front door past
the liveried footman. Jared saw the first real smile he had seen on
Miranda's face since their reunion. Her eyes crinkled. Putting spurs
to her horse, she galloped the rest of the way.

"Miranda! Miranda!" Amanda, Lady Swynford, pregnant with
her second child, bounced excitedly up and down as her sister flung
herself from her horse and into her younger twin's open arms. "Oh,
Miranda! I told them you weren't dead! I *told* them, but they
wouldn't listen. They thought I was mad!"

Miranda stepped back and gazed down at her sister. "No," she
said, "they wouldn't understand. How could they? Oh, Mandy, I've
missed you terribly! And I owe you a great debt. Perky says you've
had my Tom with you all this time. Oh, Mandy, bless you!"

They hugged again, wiping the happy tears from each other's faces. Entwining their arms, they went into the house. Jared had stayed back, allowing them their reunion, but now he hurried to join them, for he wanted to see her face when she saw little Tom.

"Where is my son?" were Miranda's first words as they came into the paneled entry hall. Amanda pointed to the stairs where Jester stood, a small, black-haired boy in a white dress in her arms. The nursemaid advanced slowly, releasing the squirming child at the bottom step.

"Papa!" Little Tom raced straight for Jared who, smiling broadly, swooped the youngster up into his arms and kissed him.

Miranda stood rooted to the spot. She had left an infant, a baby just learning to raise his head. This was a boy! A little boy, but nonetheless a boy. Her baby was gone, and she had barely known him. Suddenly the enormity of what she had missed hit her and, looking directly at Jared, she said softly, "I am not sure I will ever forgive you for this."

"I am not sure I will ever forgive myself," he answered her. "We have a great deal to make up to each other, Miranda."

She shook her head wearily. "It may not be possible, Jared."

"Do you think you might now greet your son, m'lady? He has the attention span of a naughty flea at this stage in his life." Indeed, the child was beginning to grow restless in his father's arms. "Thomas, my son, this pretty lady is your mama come home to us. What do you say to her?"

Miranda looked into the little face with its bottle-green eyes, so like Jared's, and held out her arms to him. The little boy grinned rakishly at her, holding his own arms out in response. Jared handed him to Miranda, and she cradled him close, tears spilling down her cheeks.

"Mama cry?" said little Tom, puzzled, and then he hugged her. "Mama no cry!"

Miranda had to laugh. The imperious tone was so like Jared's. She kissed the soft back of his neck, and then looked at his little face, also the image of his father's. "Mama will not cry, Tom," she said. She could barely stand to give him up, but she reluctantly handed him back to Jester. "Good night, my little love," she said. "Mama will see you in the morning." She looked at the nursemaid. "You have taken good care of him, Jester. Thank you."

Jester beamed. "It's so wonderful to have you back, m'lady," she said, flushing, and then turned back upstairs with her little charge.

"I've arranged a wonderful welcome-home dinner, Miranda," Amanda smiled.

Miranda turned slowly away from the stairs. "We cannot possibly sit down and eat a normal meal until I have answered all the questions I know you have. I would not speak of it to Jared until we were all together. I will tell my tale once, no more."

"Jon and Anne are coming for dinner," said Amanda.

"They have not gone back to Massachusetts?" Miranda queried.

"The war between England and America has been mostly a sea war," Jared answered, "and travel has been next to impossible. They could not go safely."

"It is not over then?" she said, and for a moment he saw the angry mockery in her eyes.

"It will be soon, and we'll all go home in the spring. They are negotiating a treaty now."

"You are not involved?" Again that mockery.

"I have given up politics—all politics," came the reply.

"What will you do then, m'lord?"

"I will take care of you and our son properly," he answered her.

"It is too late," she said, so softly that only Amanda heard her. Then, "Jon and Anne must hear, too. I trust there are no other guests?"

"No, dearest."

"I will rest until dinner then," Miranda said. "I assume we have the same rooms, twin."

"Yes," said Amanda, entirely subdued now.

Miranda disappeared up the staircase. Her younger sister said quietly, "She is so changed, Jared. What happened?"

"I do not know, kitten. It is as she said. She will tell the tale."

"I am afraid, Jared."

"So am I," he replied.

Miranda lay down to rest until dinner. Waking two hours later, she chose a dinner gown of soft black silk with long fitted sleeves and a deep, low V neckline. The ankle-length hem was edged in black-dyed swansdown. Miranda's stockings were ribbed black silk and her black point-toed heel-less shoes had star-shaped silver buckles. However had Jared gotten all these gowns before she arrived? As she sat debating her jewelry Jared stole up behind her and placed around her neck a long, thin gold chain at the end of which was a very large tear-shaped diamond. She stared at the stone, nestling sensuously between her breasts.

"Welcome back, Miranda," he said quietly.

"Had we lived a normal married life these last few years," she quipped, "I believe I should have to ask you what sins you are expiating with this magnificent jewel."

"You still have a sharp tongue," he answered drily.

She chuckled softly. "Some things never change, m'lord."

Downstairs they found Amanda, Adrian, Jon, and Anne waiting for them. Anne Dunham flew to embrace Miranda. "Mandy was right," she wept. "Thank God! You are responsible for my happiness, and I am so happy you are back safe. You will be godmother to my next child! Promise me, Miranda!"

"Heavens, Anne! I am told you have just recovered from a birth. Surely you are not breeding again?"

"Not from lack of effort on my part, I assure you, Miranda! Welcome home, sister!"

She smiled. "Thank you, Jon."

"Will everyone have sherry?" Amanda asked brightly.

Miranda laughed. "Little sister, you are ever the good and proper hostess." She turned to Adrian. "Will you see we are not disturbed until I have finished talking to you all?"

"The servants have been told, and I've put the mastiffs outside the door so no one may listen."

Miranda nodded. "I know that you are all curious as to what really happened to me, and I will tell you now. The story is a terrible one. Mandy, Anne, I know that you will be horrified by what I have to say, so decide now if you wish to hear it. Be warned that if you go, your husbands may repeat nothing of what I say. If you decide to stay, prepare to be shocked."

"If it is so terrible, Miranda," said Jonathan Dunham, "then why must you tell us at all?"

"For two reasons, Jon. I must answer all the questions I see in your eyes and in the eyes of my family. Then, too, because it is possible that when my tale is told my husband may wish to end our marriage, and I will not have Jared misunderstood. This story will hurt him. We women have our honor too, Jon."

"Oh, Miranda, what have you done?" Amanda's cornflower-blue eyes were wide with worry.

"Hush, Mandy," scolded Anne gently. "Miranda has committed no sins. I suspect the sins have been committed against her."

"Dear, wise Anne," Miranda said quietly. "Sit down, everyone, please. I would like to begin." She stood with the fireplace behind her and looked out over her audience. Her sister, her sister-in-law, her two brothers-in-law, her husband. The gentlemen in their severe black and white evening dress. The sweet-faced Anne with her pretty copper-colored curls and serious gray eyes in a lime-green gown. Dear Amanda in lilac, her late pregnancy very visible, as visible as the concern in her eyes.

"You all know of the deception played by Lord Palmerston with Jared and Jonathan Dunham. Jared had been gone close to a full year, and Jon, having fallen in love with Anne, had secretly married her. I had borne my son alone. Oh, I know, Mandy, that you, Adrian, and Jon were with me, but I was still alone. I wanted Jared, and Palmerston simply refused to tell me anything. I was beginning to wonder if my husband was even alive. My nights were terrifying.

"I decided that I must go to St. Petersburg. Looking back, I realize how naive it all was, and yet at the time it seemed so simple. I was traveling on my own yacht with a trusted captain and crew. I would go to St. Petersburg, demand my husband's whereabouts from the British Ambassador, and then Jared and I would return to England. Even I had figured out that if his mission hadn't been successful by then—and it obviously hadn't—it wasn't likely ever to be."

She explained about the brief time she had spent in St. Petersburg.

"Now I must digress from the story a moment to explain that the Cherkessky family's wealth comes from a slave-breeding farm in the Crimea, or rather their wealth did come from those estates until Alexei Cherkessky's Tatar cousin destroyed the farm. The Cherkessky farm raised white, blond slaves only. Blonds bring a fortune in the markets of the Mid and Near East, you see. The prince's prize male stud, Lucas, had my coloring, silver-gilt hair with light eyes, and was known to breed mostly daughters. Females are a more valuable commodity than males when you are raising expensive slaves for harems, rather than slaves for work. When Sasha saw me he knew that I was exactly the woman the prince had been seeking for several years—a perfect mate for his Lucas."

Amanda gave a little shriek of horror. "Miranda! What are you saying? People do not breed people, only animals."

"No, Mandy. There are people in this world who breed other humans for profit. Do you remember, before Jared and I were married, you were telling me the tale of a minister's daughter who was transported to the West Indies to a slave-breeding farm? I remember I pooh-poohed that tale, but the breeding of people for profit is going on right now, and for most of the last year I have been an inmate of such a hell."

Amanda's eyes grew enormous, and she paled, but she would not allow herself to faint. Her twin had been through hell, and the least Amanda could do was to listen.

Miranda paused to sip at the pale sherry in her glass, sneaking a glance at her audience. The men, she realized, had begun to suspect the drift of her tale, and Jared was looking grim. Oh God, she thought, why have I the kind of nature that forces me to tell the truth?

"Continue, Miranda." His voice startled her.

Their eyes met for a moment, and she was puzzled by what she saw there. She saw compassion. She saw tenderness and understanding. She saw love! Her voice caught in her throat and she could not speak. Crossing to her, he put a strong arm around her. "Go on, my love. Put it behind you."

And so she filled in the details of her time in St. Petersburg. At one point, Jared interrupted.

"My God! If I ever get my hands on Gillian Abbott I shall kill her!" he said fiercely.

"She is already dead, Jared. Gillian was the body in the Neva. Her hair was blond then."

She went on with the Crimean chapter of her story, her listeners becoming more spellbound with every revelation. She saw fear on their faces, and disgust, and outrage, and pity. She tried not to look too closely at any one of them, afraid that if she did, she would not be able to continue.

"I was a slave, you see, and my purpose was to breed with Lucas to produce daughters. I tried once to escape by sea, but was caught.

"Fortunately, Lucas was a kind man." Here her voice began to quiver. "I...we were put together in the breeding hut."

Jared drew a ragged breath, but his brother asked, "What the hell is a breeding hut, Miranda?"

"It is the place," Miranda said slowly and deliberately, "where the slaves chosen to be mated are sent for that purpose. It is a small, windowless building with a pallet bed. There are no amenities."

"My God!" Jared's voice was soft in her ear. Adrian and Jonathan had to look away, and Amanda and Anne were both openmouthed with shock. Miranda's lashes lowered against her pale cheeks. She forced herself on.

"I fought against what they wanted. Sasha even beat me once, but in the end I was overcome. You must all understand that I have been dishonored, and no decent man can want me now."

There was utter silence following her declaration. Weren't any of the men going to respond? She began to panic, and then plunged ahead into the rest of her narrative. She explained about the raid and Sasha's attempt to redeem himself by telling Prince Arik that she might be handsomely ransomed. Still, no one interrupted, and she finally finished. "Fortunately Kit Edmund was at the embassy that day, and his friend, Mirza Khan, ransomed me quite lavishly from the Tatars, and sent them on their way. You know the rest."

The room throbbed with the heavy silence that followed. At last Anne Bowen Dunham said in her quiet voice, "It is indeed a horrifying story that you have told us. To think that one's fellow man could act in such a cruel manner...But you are home, safe with us now. You must put it all behind you, dearest Miranda."

"Did you not comprehend what I have said, Anne? I have been used physically by another man. Under church law that makes me an adultress! No better than the bits o' muslin kept by so many fashionable gentlemen up in London. I am not fit," and here her voice broke, "I am no longer fit to be a gentleman's wife."

"You were forced," Anne cried. "The shame is not yours. Besides, no one knows what really happened to you but us, and we will never tell. It is ridiculous to call yourself an adultress." This was as angry as anyone had ever seen Anne.

Adrian Swynford came forward and knelt before his distraught sister-in-law, taking her hands in his. "Miranda, I am ashamed that any man would do to a woman what Prince Cherkessky did to you."

Then Jonathan was there, too. "You are not less in our eyes for your terrible experiences, Miranda! Your great courage has only increased your stature. It took great strength just to keep your sanity, let alone to return home to us. Why on earth would we reproach you, Miranda?"

"Oh dearest," wept Amanda. "You have suffered so terribly, and been so very brave! We must put it all behind us, and we will! Oh Miranda, we will!"

"I do not think I can eat dinner now," said Miranda, "please excuse me. I want to go to my room." She fled.

Jonathan Dunham looked hard at his brother. "If you desert her now, I will kill you myself!"

Jared did not flinch from his gaze. "I am to blame, if the truth be known. I should never have left her."

"No," said Jonathan, "you shouldn't have." Let Jared suffer a little remorse. It would be good for him.

Jared looked to Amanda. "I would like to be with my wife," he said. "You had best not hold dinner any longer." He was quickly gone, taking the stairs two at a time, and hurrying down the hallway to their apartment. Bursting into the salon, he ordered Perky, "Out!

You're dismissed for the night. I'm sure that Martin will be as glad to see his wife as I am to see mine."

"Yes, m'lord, and thank you." Perkins bobbed a smart curtsey and hurried out.

Jared crossed the salon and strode into the bedchamber.

"What do you want?" Miranda's face was streaked with tears.

"You!" he answered fiercely, and threw himself on the bed, pinning her beneath him. "I want *you!* I want my wife back!"

"Where is your pride?" she cried at him. "Does it not matter to you that another man used me?"

"Do you love me?" he demanded.

"Yes, damn you! I love you!" she cried back.

"Did you enjoy it when he took you?" He was confident of her reply, and therefore somewhat shaken when she said to him, "You never told me that a body can respond to lust as well as love. The first time it happened, my body responded all by itself and the shame almost killed me then and there."

"And afterward?"

Dear God, did he really want to know? "I learn quickly, Jared. Surely you remember that." She could not resist hurting him a little. Then she shook her head. "Afterward I closed my mind to what he was doing, and I felt nothing."

"I love you, Miranda," he said simply. "If anything, I love you more for being so brave." His lips moved to the soft skin left bare by the deep V of her neckline, playing lightly across it, teasingly darting his tongue into the valley between her breasts.

"Your wife should be above reproach," she said, a trifle breathlessly. "No mistress of Wyndsong has ever had the slightest blemish upon her reputation."

"The only scars that remain for you, Miranda, are within your own mind. We are going to begin now, madam, to eradicate those scars."

"You don't understand," she said, desperately trying to squirm away from him, but he held her fast as he pulled her up.

"Oh, yes, wildcat, I understand. You believe that because you responded to another man's touch you have somehow betrayed my honor, but that is not so. You are not like the elegant married ladies of the ton who whore to amuse themselves or sell themselves to further their husband's careers. It is preposterous of you to apologize." Getting her dress undone, he pushed it over her shoulders, and it fell into a puddle around her ankles. He undid the silk straps of her petticoat, and it slid down to join her gown. She was left standing in her lacy drawers, stockings, and garters. Carefully he undid the waist tape that held the drawers, and they fell to the floor.

He let his eyes learn all over again the long pure line of her back with its slim waistline, the soft mounds of her buttocks, the slender thighs, and long, shapely legs. God, had he ever really forgotten? She stood very still, and then suddenly she raised her arms and undid her long hair, her fingers carefully unplaiting the thick braid.

"Are you sure?" she asked him quietly. "Do not take me back out of pity, Jared. That would be a far crueler fate. I do not want your pity."

"Oh, wildcat, the person I pity is me, if you don't come back to me. Wait now, I have something for you," he said, and crossed the floor into his dressing room, re-emerging a few moments later.

He took up her hand and gently pushed a ring onto her finger. Looking down, she caught her breath. *"My wedding ring!"*

"That was the only reason Ephraim Snow was willing to believe that the body taken from the Neva was yours. He never saw the body; he believed you would never willingly part with that ring."

She stared at the ring, its tiny diamond stars winking up at her. For a moment she remembered when he had first placed it on her finger, and then she said, "I never would have parted with it willingly. I imagine it was removed while I was unconscious." The tears fell unbidden from her sea-green eyes, and she rapidly blinked them back. "Dammit! All I seem to do is cry these days." Then she looked at him. "You were quick to undress me, sir," she said, and walking boldly up to him, she loosened his white cravat, pulled it off and flung it to the floor.

"That took poor Mitchum twenty minutes to tie," he said with a mock sigh.

"Take off your coat!" she ordered him, and with a grin he complied. "Now the waistcoat!" Again he obeyed. Her fingers impatiently opened the pearl buttons of his shirt, and, palms flat, her warm hands pushed the white silk apart, smoothing over his big shoulders, and down his strong arms. Suddenly his arms came up to pull her against him.

Her breath caught as she felt the silken fur of his broad chest against her sensitive nipples. "Look at me!" His voice was demanding. "Two can play at your game, my pet." He tipped her heart-shaped face up, and his bottle-green eyes blazed down into her sea-green ones. He held her about the waist with a deceptively loose arm, and she knew if she moved an inch he would crush her against him. She felt him kick off his evening shoes *then* as he unfastened his pants, shucking them off, yanking off his tight underdrawers at the same time. His eyes never left hers. He was daring her to pull away.

Naked, he knelt, slid one garter of pink rosettes down her leg followed by a black silk stocking, and then bared the other leg. Her skin was beautiful, soft, fragrant, without blemish. Rising, he caught her to him again, and found her mouth. Her arms slid up around his neck, and she pressed her body to his.

"Oh, Jared," she whispered, pulling her head away from his, "oh, my darling, I missed you so very much!"

He swept her up and carried her to the bed. She held out her arms to him. Groaning, he joined her, drawing her into his arms to kiss her. His mouth demanded, and she eagerly responded.

His hands scalded her flesh, sliding down her back to caress her buttocks. His fingers tenderly followed the sweet curves of her body, and she moved against him with an abandon that left him breathless. He sought the globes of her breasts, and she shivered as he nuzzled against her breasts. She sought to divert him by reaching down to catch at his hardening rod with her hand.

She stroked him with knowledgeable fingers, and was rewarded by a quickening in his breathing. Miranda quickly twisted her body around, and her head moved downward, her pale-gilt hair spreading over the soft dark fur of his lower belly. She kissed the top of his throbbing manhood, and then her lips closed over him. Her tongue gently flicked round and round the head of his sex, and his body arched with pleasurable shock.

He'd never taught her *that!* For a moment he was angry, and then he realized exactly what she had been trying to tell him. He knew she wasn't a promiscuous woman. She would not seek out other men. But she was a woman, had been from the moment he had taken her virginity. In the time they had been separated she had learned from another. She had tried to warn him, and he realized he would be foolish to become prudish now. Oh no! Not now when her mouth tortured him so sweetly.

"Wildcat," he managed to gasp. "Let me move around a bit." Turning around, he tasted of her. His fingers gently parted her adorably plump lower lips, revealing the dainty, pouting, deep-coral flower of her womanhood. His tongue taunted the sensitive flesh, and she cried out sharply as lightning streaked through her. He continued to tease her, and her lips reciprocated, growing more passionately frantic as her own excitement mounted.

Finally he raised his head, muttering, "Enough of this, Miranda! I have hungered for you for over two years now!"

He swung around, and over her. His manroot was swollen enormously, and it throbbed. "Look at me, you green-eyed bitch," he commanded her softly. "Look at me!" He caught her roughly, and she gazed up at him. There was love in her eyes, love and urgent desire.

"Jared! Oh, Jared! Love me!" she sobbed, and then she guided him through the gates of passion, and he thrust home. Miranda felt unutterable joy filling her. She clung hungrily to him, wrapping her legs tightly around his body, her pelvis pushing up to meet his fierce thrusts. "Oh, my darling!" she wept. "Oh, how I love you, my dearest, dearest husband!"

He could easily have released his desire into her at that very moment, for her passionate declaration excited him beyond everything else. But he wanted to prolong their pleasure, their reunion. This was not the girl he remembered. This was a woman, a woman he had helped only a little in shaping.

It was so sweet. Miranda closed her eyes and allowed herself to float. It had never been like this, even with her beloved friend, Mirza Khan, for though he possessed her with tenderness and caring, though he had loved her, her heart had always been with Jared. And Jared loved her. Jared's body had been the first to love hers, and he had claimed her heart from the very beginning. With a flash of understanding she realized why Mirza Khan had not tried to keep her with him. Lovemaking could be perfect only if lovers loved each other wholly. Friends could pleasure one another, but that was all.

Her nails scored his back, and he laughed softly. "Still have your claws, eh, wildcat?" Relentlessly he drove her up peak after peak after peak so that her luscious body shuddered again and again and again until, sure that she was satiated with his love, he pushed her to new splendors and quickly followed her.

She awoke in the deep of night to find him sprawled on his stomach, one arm cradling her possessively. A happy little smile played at the corners of her mouth. He still loved her! Mirza Khan had told her that if Jared were any kind of man he would not hold her responsible for what had happened, and he didn't. She almost felt remorseful over the charming prince who had been her lover. *Almost*. She smiled again, remembering what she had said to Mirza Khan: "There are certain things in this world that a wife must keep to herself."

❧ Chapter 17 ❧

Miranda was feeling exhilarated. This was to be her first large social function since her return to England. It almost seemed that she'd never been away. The coming-out ball of Lady Georgeanne Hampton, eldest daughter and heiress to the Duke of Northampton, was the first truly important affair of this season. It was to be held at the duke's magnificent mansion, which was within shouting distance of the Prince Regent's London residence.

Miranda welcomed this change, for she felt strong and whole once more. She had lived quietly at Swynford Hall for several months, basking in Jared's love and the love of her family, and learning all about the small son of whose early life she had been so cruelly cheated. Whatever doubts Jared might have entertained about her suitability as a mother were obliterated forever on the day he saw them together in a chair, Tom showing Miranda a grubby treasure that he prized. Miranda, her whole face alight with her love, was wholly entranced.

How he wanted another child! But she wished to wait until she knew Tom better. Forcing little Tom to share her when she had barely returned seemed so unfair. Besides, she wanted time with her husband, too. Their third wedding anniversary was the first one they had actually celebrated together, and in general they had spent more of their marriage apart than together.

After Christmas had come the welcome news that on December 24, 1814, in the city of Ghent, Belgium, a treaty had been signed between England and America, ending the war. Come spring, they would be free to travel home.

"I want our next child born on Wyndsong," Miranda declared, and Jared agreed.

The Treaty of Ghent had been a great disappointment to Jared Dunham, and only reaffirmed his belief that politics was a fool's game. Never again, he vowed to himself, never again would he involve himself in that which he could not personally control.

Their lives had been almost destroyed by the war, and for what? None of the problems that had led to the war had been solved. The treaty merely provided the return of all captured territory to the power that had been in possession before the war.

Jared was very proud of his wife. Easily the most beautiful woman at the duke's ball, she greeted old friends warmly with the dignity of an empress. Her ball gown with its bell-shaped skirt was a deep shade of green known as "Midnight in the Glen." The neckline was low enough to have evoked a protest from him when he first saw it. It dipped down to barely cover the tops of her nipples, and in the back it was just below her shoulder blades. Laughingly she had instructed her dressmaker to add a bit of trim—a dyed-to-match swansdown— as a concession to husbandly outrage. His satisfaction had evaporated this evening when she put the dress on and he realized, to her mirth, that the swansdown only tempted the spectator to blow it aside to see what lay beneath.

The gown had no real waistline, the ankle-length skirt beginning beneath the bustline. There was a wide band of swansdown trimming the hem as well as the neckline. The little puffed sleeves were made of alternating stripes of velvet and silk gauze. Her dark green silk stockings had small gold stars embroidered upon them, as did her dark green kid slippers.

Miranda's gown was deceptively plain. It actually served as a frame for her magnificent jewels. Her necklace was of round-cut emeralds, each stone surrounded by small diamonds and separated by gold links. It lay flat, glittering against the translucent skin of her chest. There were a matching bracelet and earrings. Her right hand bore a round diamond surrounded by emeralds, and her left an emerald surrounded by diamonds, as well as her wedding ring.

Miranda did not care for the curls and ringlets of current fashion. Neither did she care for the braided chignon which she felt was unhealthy for the hair. She wore her hair just as she had worn it two years before, parted in the middle and drawn lightly over her ears so as to leave bare the lobes and her earrings, and then gently affixed in a soft chignon at the nape of her neck. This was by far the most flattering hairstyle for her heavy, pale-gold hair.

Having greeted the duke, the duchess, and the blushing Georgeanne, Miranda and Jared moved into the ballroom to be scrutinized by many old friends. Lady Cowper came forward smiling, her hands outstretched to catch at Miranda's. She kissed Lady Dunham warmly on both cheeks. "Miranda! Oh, my dear, it is miraculous to have you among us again. Welcome! Welcome back!"

"Thank you, Emily. I am quite happy to be here, especially so because this will be our last London season for some time."

"Say it is not so!"

"Emily, we are Americans. Our home is in America, and we have been away for three years, far longer than we ever anticipated. We want to go home!"

"Jared, I appeal to you!" Emily Cowper turned her beautiful face up to Jared.

He laughed. "My dear, I confess to wanting to go home myself. Wyndsong is a magnificent little kingdom, and I had just been getting to know it when I came to England. I shall be glad to be back."

Lady Cowper pouted. "It will be boring without you both."

"Now, Emily, I am quite flattered," said Miranda, "but the ton is never dull. Unpredictable, but never dull! What is this I hear about Princess Charlotte and Prince Leopold of Saxe-Coburg?"

Emily Cowper lowered her voice confidentially. "Last summer little Charley had her heart set on Prince Augustus of Russia, but as there is no chance of that she has now decided on Leopold. My dear, the boy is so poor that last year he stayed in rooms over a greengrocer's! What will actually happen one may only speculate upon."

"She is wise to avoid the Russians," Miranda said quietly. Hearing her name called, she turned to face the Duke of Whitley.

"My dear," he said, his eyes mischievously dipping to her neckline, then returning quickly to meet hers, "how good to see you again." He bowed low over her hand, his turquoise eyes openly admiring.

She colored becomingly, remembering their last meeting. Sneaking a peek at Jared, she instantly realized that Jonathan had told him of Whitley's attempted seduction! Jared's expression was quite icy.

"I thank you, Your Grace," she replied prettily.

"May I present to you Lady Belinda de Winter," said the duke.

Miranda's sea-green eyes flicked to the petite brunette in the pale-yellow silk gown who was clinging to the duke's arm. It was an appallingly awkward moment, and even Lady Cowper was somewhat taken aback by Darius Edmund's lack of tact. Miranda smiled a very small smile. "How d'ye do, Lady de Winter," she said.

Belinda de Winter looked boldly at her archrival. "Your husband was quite surprised by your survival, m'lady," she said sweetly, deliberately implying a far greater intimacy between herself and Jared than actually existed.

Emily Cowper sucked in her breath. Dariya de Lieven had been right about the de Winter girl! What would Jared say? For dearest Miranda to suffer any further after all she had been through! Miranda, however, was quite capable of defending herself.

"Jared has spent every moment since my return reassuring me of his devotion," she said as sweetly as she could, which was very sweetly. "I can only hope, Lady de Winter, that when you finally find a husband of your own he will prove as loving and as considerate as my husband is."

The Dunhams bowed to the assembled company, and strolled away. Lady Emily Cowper turned on Belinda angrily.

"I shall be watching you, miss," she said sharply. "You can be barred from Almack's if I decide it. Your behavior toward Lady Dunham was improper, to say nothing of deliberately cruel. I hope you realize that your expectations in Lord Dunham's direction are simply not valid now." Lady Cowper turned away and stalked across the room to find her friend, Princess de Lieven.

"The old cow!" Belinda sniffed.

"She must be twenty-seven if she is a day," murmured the duke, amused, "but you would not be wise to make an enemy of Emily Cowper, Belinda. Surely you do not continue to harbor hopes in Lord D's direction? He is quite devoted to his wife, and she to him."

"He was ready to propose marriage to me," Belinda said low. "If she were not here I would be his wife!"

"But she *is* here, my dear," he said quietly, "and in a few short months they will return to America. They will no longer be part of your life."

Belinda de Winter did not respond because she was busy sorting out her impressions of Miranda Dunham. She was forced to admit that the lady was an incredible beauty. She and Jared made an extraordinarily handsome couple, both tall and elegant, his dark good looks complimenting her delicate fair coloring.

For some time Belinda was overcome by bleak despair. She wanted to be Jared Dunham's wife, to be the mistress of his American manor, free of her father and brother.

The dancing could not begin until the Prince Regent and his daughter, Princess Charlotte, arrived. Clinging to Whitley's arm, Belinda made the rounds of the ballroom, and was pleased to see that none of this year's debutantes was as beautiful as she was. It was most reassuring.

In the hall below there was a sudden flurry of activity indicating a noteworthy arrival. "Ladies and gentlemen, my lords and my ladies," the majordomo announced in stentorian tones, "His Royal Highness, the Prince Regent, and Princess Charlotte."

The band struck up the appropriate tune as George, one day to be the fourth of his line, and his pretty nineteen-year-old daughter entered the ballroom. The royal couple passed between the line of bowing couples, then suddenly stopped before Miranda Dunham.

Gently the Prince Regent raised her to her feet, and smiled in his kindly way.

"My dear, we thank God that you have been restored to us."

Miranda smiled at the rotund Prince Regent. "I thank his Royal Highness for his prayers. I am relieved that the hostilities between our countries are now over."

He tipped her face up, and said, "So lovely! So very lovely!" Then, "Have you yet met my daughter, Lady Dunham?"

"No, Your Royal Highness, I have not yet had the honor," said Miranda.

The Prince Regent beamed on his only child, with whom he had only recently been reconciled. "Charlotte, my dearest, this is Lady Miranda Dunham of whom we have spoken."

Miranda curtseyed. The princess smiled. "You have had a most fortunate escape, I am told, Lady Dunham. We are pleased to finally meet you."

"Thank you, Your Highness," Miranda said.

The Prince Regent beamed at the two women, and then the royal couple moved on. The band struck up a waltz, and the Prince Regent led the blushing Lady Georgeanne Hampton onto the floor while the duke, her father, partnered Princess Charlotte. After a respectable interval the other guests joined in the dance, and the ball was officially begun. As the evening wore on, several latecomers arrived, and were duly announced.

Jared was a little annoyed to find that his wife's dance card was quickly filled, leaving only one dance left for him. On the whole, however, he found the situation satisfactory. Between Lady Cowper and the Prince Regent, Miranda's credibility was assured, and her reputation totally restored. He was not in the mood to dance with anyone else, and so he stood on the sidelines indulgently watching as she was whirled about the floor.

Suddenly Belinda de Winter was standing next to him, asking, "Are you truly happy, my lord?"

"Indeed I am, Lady de Winter."

"Oh, Jared, I love you!" she whispered.

He never even turned to look at her. "You imagine it, Belinda."

"You love me, Jared! I know you do! You were going to propose marriage. Everyone expected it! You came to tell me that your wife had returned so that I should not be embarrassed."

"I was, of course, aware of your expectation, Belinda, and that is why I did you the courtesy of personally informing you of Miranda's return."

"I mean to have you, m'lord Yankee," she said vehemently.

"Good God, Belinda, that is the sort of bad line uttered by the villain in a ha'penny street play!" He turned and looked down at her, not sure whether he was annoyed or amused. "I love my wife, my dear. If she had died, I would have married again only to give my boy a mother. I am sorry to be so brutally frank, but apparently I must be if I am to convince you."

"You lie!" she persisted.

"Belinda, you are going to make a fool of yourself if you continue, and I prefer not to be involved in even a minor scandal. Good evening, m'lady."

"Prince Alexei Cherkessky," announced the majordomo.

Jared whirled, not sure that he had heard correctly. He scanned the dancers, looking for his wife. Catching sight of her, he wove his way through the swaying couples and rudely cut in, good manners forcing the elegant guardsman whose dance it was to withdraw.

"Jared, what on earth is the matter?" She was looking puzzled.

"The Russian who kidnaped you. What was his name?"

"Alexei Cherkessky. Why?"

"He is, it seems, a guest at this ball. They have just announced his arrival."

She faltered, then laughed shakily. "I imagine I shall give him a very bad turn," she said.

His arm tightened about her, and she read the admiration in his eyes. "We don't have to stay, Miranda."

"What? And have people saying that I forced you home because I saw you talking with Lady de Winter? Never!"

"Could I not be taking you home because I want to make passionate love to you?" he demanded.

"What gentleman of breeding makes love to his own wife, sir?" she teased him. "Oh, no, m'lord! We stay. What did the petite Mistress de Winter want of you?"

"Chitchat," he lied, "and to wish us happy."

"How nice," murmured Miranda, not believing him for a minute.

Across the room Alexei Cherkessky was forcing himself not to stare. He had asked his hostess, disbelieving his eyes, and she had said, "Oh yes, Your Highness, a most beautiful woman, and a most fortunate one! She is Lady Miranda Dunham, an American. Her husband is Lord Jared Dunham, of Wyndsong Island Manor, an American holding. She was swept off her yacht almost two years ago, and lost at sea. It was believed that she had drowned, but she turned up in Istanbul several months ago.

"She was, it seems, rescued by a passing ship bound for the Turkish capital. The shock of her accident wiped her memory away, and so the captain of the vessel who rescued her brought her to his home, and made a daughter of her.

"Then one day when she was out in the bazaars with the women of the family she saw an English friend, and it triggered the return of her memory. Believe me when I tell you that she arrived home in the nick of time. Her husband was about to offer for another lady. It is a miraculous story, isn't it?"

"It certainly is," the prince murmured. "How disappointing for the young woman who nearly married Lord Dunham."

"Yes, it certainly was," and then Sophia Hampton lowered her voice, and said in a confidential tone: "The poor girl is my own godchild, Lady Belinda de Winter. Oh well, she is a pretty child, and someone else will come along."

The prince nodded, his face drawn into an expression of sympathy. "Of course, Your Grace." He scanned the room. "I am looking forward to meeting your daugher," he said. "The Tzar insisted that I come to England and enjoy myself, once I had come out of mourning."

"How tragic to lose both your wife and child at the same time," the duchess sighed. Tragic for you, but how marvelous for my Georgeanne, she thought. A handsome, wealthy Russian prince with huge estates in both the Crimea and the Baltic, who stood close to the Tzar. It would be the coup of the season, and it would be *her* coup! She was going to mark Alexei Cherkessky for her own Georgeanne tonight, and if any of the other old cows thought to snag him for their gawky daughters, they would quickly be disappointed.

"I am going to introduce you to my darling shortly, Your Highness, and I wonder if you would indulge me in just a small favor. It would be so thrilling for her if you took my little Georgeanne into supper."

"It would be my pleasure, Your Grace," murmured the prince. Damn! It was going to be easier than he had thought, snapping up a virginal English heiress for his next wife. Like a wolf contemplating a rabbit, he wondered about the size of her dowry. He also wondered if the exquisite Lady Dunham of the silver-gilt hair would betray him. Could she do so without betraying herself? That was the question. He didn't think so, and yet...It was really quite a marvelous story that they had invented to cover her absence.

Dearest Sasha had been right. The lady had told the truth about herself. Alexei Cherkessky wondered how much her husband knew of her fate. He also wondered what had happened to the brat she had been carrying. If it lived it belonged to him, and God only knew he had precious little left anymore.

It had been a terrible year. His estates in the Crimea had been utterly destroyed. He had been at the end of his resources, and the spring slave sale was to have refilled his coffers for the next year. The Tatar raid had ruined him.

Soon after the raid, his meek little bride had walked in when he was with the charming boy he had recently taken. Tatiania had viewed the sexual scene and left without a word. He had thought little of it, assuming that she had accepted the revelation with good sense.

Ear-splitting screams had roused him several hours later. The cause of the household hysteria was his wife's suicide. Tatiania Romanova had hanged herself with the sash of her silk dressing gown, killing not only herself, but her unborn infant, *his heir*.

He was financially ruined, widowed, without an heir. Because of his wife's relationship with Tzar Alexander he had been forced to mourn a full year, and the only consolation was that he had not been held responsible for Tatiania's death. No one knew what had really happened that afternoon. Their short marriage had been considered a successful one.

His elderly in-laws passed away shortly thereafter, and his luck seemed to be turning for the better at long last. They had left him all they had, modest in comparison with what he had once possessed, but it was a start. He needed a wife, but he needed a rich one, and Russia was not the place to find one. He had decided to try England first, for the English were particularly susceptible to princely titles.

Just as he was preparing to leave Russia, he had received another piece of lucky news. His prize stud, Lucas, had managed to survive the Tatar massacre! The prince intended breeding slaves again, but it would take time. This time, however, he would raise them on his Baltic estates, safely away from Tatars. The Turks, bless them, would never tire of blond women.

He had brought Lucas to England as his valet, and together they sought out blond beauties to restock his new farm. He valued the man's judgment. Alexei Cherkessky pulled himself from his thoughts at the sound of the duchess's insistent voice.

"Your Highness, may I present my daughter, Lady Georgeanne Marie."

The prince focused his glance on the lovely, elegant girl who stood before him. Never letting his eyes leave hers, he raised her hand to his lips and kissed it. Then he held it just long enough to bring a blush of color to her cheeks. "Lady Georgeanne," he said, "my heart is already ravished by your beauty. I can only hope that you will spare me a dance."

Georgeanne giggled self-consciously. "Oh, Your Highness," she said in her high, nasal voice, "all my dances are taken."

"Nonsense!" The duchess snatched her daughter's dance card from her wrist, and quickly scanned it. "Here, child, is a free dance you can spare the prince. The supper dance is available."

"And I can only hope you will allow me to escort you to supper," the prince interjected smoothly, wondering what young swain had been exchanged for him.

"Of course she will allow you to escort her to supper," said the duchess briskly, "won't you, my love?"

"Yes, Mama," came the dutiful reply as Georgeanne replaced the card on her wrist, thinking that Lord Thorpe of Thorpe Hall, the gentleman bumped to make way for the prince, wasn't very interesting anyway. She would be the envy of every girl in the room tonight, taking supper with the prince.

She liked the way he looked at her, coolly assessing her, his eyes clinging to her well-filled bodice. Still she kept her eyes modestly lowered, for she knew that men, especially the experienced ones like Prince Cherkessky, liked innocence in young girls.

"Lord Dunham!" the duchess called out as Jared and Miranda danced by. They were forced to stop. "Your Highness, may I present Lord and Lady Dunham, of whom I spoke earlier. This is Prince Cherkessky of St. Petersburg, and, of course, my daughter, Lady Georgeanne."

Jared bowed politely to Georgeanne, coldly to the prince. Miranda swept the group a graceful curtsey, every nerve raw, desperate to scream as Alexei Cherkessky took her hand and slowly kissed it.

"I have heard of your miraculous escape, m'lady."

"I escaped nothing, Your Highness," was the calm reply. "I was merely fortunate enough to be rescued from the sea."

"I meant your escape from the cold arms of Hades," he fenced with her.

"My wife was incredibly fortunate," Jared said. "I don't intend ever to let her out of my sight again. We are soon returning home to America."

"If Lady Dunham were my wife I should certainly not let her out of my sight, either," was the prince's mocking reply.

The two men locked eyes for a moment. Alexei Cherkessky wasn't surprised by the blazing hatred he saw in Jared Dunham. So Dunham did know! But he loved his wife and he would protect her. So, concluded the prince, I am safe. They won't say anything.

"I'd only wish I could kill him," Jared muttered as they danced away.

"I wonder what he's doing here," Miranda said softly.

"Emily Cowper or Dariya Lieven is sure to know. Ask them. I will find a moment to check with Palmerston to see if it is anything official, although I doubt it."

"My lord?" An elegant dandy was at his elbow. "I believe this is my dance with Lady Dunham, sir."

"Of course." He stepped aside, and Miranda was whirled away.

Actually it was Amanda, even more horrified than her sister at Alexei Cherkessky's appearance, who found out why the prince was in England. They had all arranged to have supper together, and she was bursting with information.

"His pregnant wife committed suicide," Amanda said dramatically, her cornflower-blue eyes wide. "Now what made her do that, I wonder?"

"Was there any scandal attached to it?" asked Jared.

"None that anyone's heard, but one cannot help but consider it. At any rate he is here in England looking for a new wife, and rumor has it that he's singled out Georgeanne Hampton. *And,* her parents approve!"

"My God," said Miranda, "the man is a sodomite, a murderer, and a debaucher of women. That poor, poor child! Jared, is there nothing we can do to prevent such a match? The duke and duchess cannot know of his reputation or else he wouldn't even be here. He is a devil!"

Adrian Swynford shook his head. "It is impossible, Miranda, for us to expose Cherkessky for the villain he is without exposing you. It will embarrass not only you, but my family as well. I will not do that. Amanda and I now have a daughter to consider as well as little Edward. If I were now in Northampton's position, seeking a good husband for our Arabella, I would damn well check him thoroughly—princely title or not. If the duke doesn't get stampeded by his silly wife he will delve a bit into Cherkessky's background. Georgeanne will be looked after. I'm not worried."

They were sitting at one of many little round tables that had been set up informally in the supper room to accommodate the buffet. The tables were backed by a screen of green potted palms in large yellow and white Wedgwood cachepots. Behind those benign plants Lady Belinda de Winter had heard all she needed to know.

Belinda's eyes secretly caressed the man she desired so desperately, lingering on the superb fit of his trousers. How often her eyes sought out that part of him. He was such a magnificent animal! She longed to reach out and run her fingers down the outline of his manhood, fondling him until he burst through the constrictions of his marvelous tailoring and, maddened by desire, took her there on the ballroom floor. She sighed, nearly swooning at the thought.

She shook herself. Dreaming would not bring Jared back to her. And he must come back. No one had ever denied Belinda, and no one ever would.

The following day Belinda sent a note to Prince Cherkessky, who was staying at Pulteney's Hotel, one of London's most elegant and discreet establishments. The note was quite to the point. It read:

If you are serious in your quest of Georgeanne, then I can assure your success if you will but give me a few minutes of your time.

She boldly signed her name, sealed the missive, and, handing it to her personal maid, told her to await a reply. She had no intention of being fobbed off. Not with victory so near!

❧ Chapter 18 ❧

The Prince Regent was giving a masquerade at Carleton House for two thousand guests. The occasion was the arrival of the vernal equinox—spring—and there was to be an appropriate pageant presented in the gardens. There wasn't a dressmaker of note in London who wasn't busier than she had ever been, and there were a number of up-and-coming modistes who hoped to make their reputation in one night on the masquerade costumes they were making for their wealthy clients.

The Duchess of Northampton had decided on the costumes to be worn by her daughter Georgeanne and her godchild Belinda de Winter. They would be garbed as Roman Vestal Virgins, draped in white muslin robes with wreaths of hothouse roses in their hair, yellow for Belinda, pink for Georgeanne.

The duchess could not have been more pleased with the season's progress. Her two charges were doing beautifully. Prince Alexei Cherkessky had most obviously singled out her Georgeanne. He was paying the girl most ardent court, as were several other suitable young men from good families. Georgeanne, dear child, had asked her mama's advice, and Sophia Hampton had carefully pointed out the advantages and disadvantages in all her child's suitors. It hadn't hurt that Belinda was so enthusiastic about the Russian.

"It's like a fairy tale come true, Georgy! Imagine having a prince come to carry you off to his castle. He is so distinguished, too. I find his eyes quite magnetic. I truly do! Oh, you are so lucky!"

"Russia is very far away from England," ventured Georgeanne doubtfully.

"Pooh!" came the reply. "St. Petersburg is called the Paris of the North, and the summer nights go on forever in a sunlit haze. It is all too romantic! I would simply perish if a man as experienced and as dashing as Prince Cherkessky were seriously paying me court. Think of it, darling. You will be Princess Georgeanne!"

"I will wear a diamond coronet all the time," Georgeanne giggled.

The duchess smiled indulgently. It was all going quite well. Perhaps she might plan a June or July wedding. It was going to be a triumph! Even her dear Belinda was doing much better this season. Darius Edmund, the Duke of Whitley, seemed to be quite serious in his intentions. If she ended the season sponsoring two fashionable weddings. . .she almost swooned with pure delight. Her daughter to a prince, her goddaughter to a duke. There wasn't a mother in London who had ever done *that* well. She could already hear the congratulations ringing in her ears, and she lifted her chins proudly. Then her face fell. If she did this well for Georgeanne and Belinda, what would be left for her two younger daughters, Augusta and Charlotte? Anything short of heirs to reigning houses would be terribly disappointing. She had best start looking around. With all of Algie's money, surely they could find an old but poverty-stricken title. Germany was full of them. Yes, they would look to Germany, and possibly to Italy. Algie's title might have to go to his wretched nephew, but the money was theirs!

In the meantime, one smaller problem on her horizon was getting Algie into the toga of a Roman senator to match her Roman matron. He really was so damned stubborn. After all, he would be more covered in a toga than he ordinarily was. Men!

Amanda, Lady Swynford, and her sister Miranda, Lady Dunham,

had hired an unknown but talented young seamstress to make their costumes. The girl was to live at Swynford House while she worked, and would not be released to return to her own home until the night of the masquerade. The word was already out that Lady Swynford would be coming as a medieval page boy, and her beautiful twin as a wicked witch. It was exactly what the sisters wanted everyone to think. They had decided to switch costumes. No one, not even their husbands, knew that it was Miranda who would be the page boy, and Amanda, the wicked witch.

They wondered how to make up for the differences in their heights. The difference, they decided, would be corrected by Amanda wearing four-inch clogs beneath her long robes.

"We shall both dress here at Swynford House and then we shall see if we can fool Adrian and Jared," chuckled Amanda. "If we can fool them, we can fool everyone! I don't know why Prinny insisted on everyone registering their costumes with his secretary. I don't for a moment believe that nonsense about avoiding duplication of costume. That's half the fun of a masquerade, knowing that your friend is coming as a harlequin, but being unable to tell which of the six or ten harlequins he is!"

"Use your head, dearest," said Miranda. "Prinny has had everyone register costumes with his secretary so he may know who is behind each mask. You know how he loves his little games. He will come up to one or the other and coyly guess their identity, at which point the costumed guest will be wise enough to congratulate his Royal Highness on his excellent guess."

"How can he possibly learn the identity of two thousand people?"

"Oh, he won't bother with everyone, just some of his friends," said Miranda.

"What if he comes up to one of us?"

"Giggle, nod your head, and then run in the other direction," Miranda suggested, and both young women burst out laughing with the hilarity the situation suggested.

"I don't think I can do much running in these clogs," Amanda gasped. "It's all I can do to keep my balance," and she promptly fell into a heap on the floor.

"You must practice more!" Miranda exhorted her sister. "It simply will not do if you fall on your face before the prince." They laughed helplessly.

Mary Grant, a pretty girl with a turned-up nose, was delighted to be part of the joke. She had done a beautiful job on both costumes, and had been assured of much additional work from both ladies. Miranda intended having an entirely new wardrobe to take back to Wyndsong, for she knew that she would not be seeing England again for a long time. As for Amanda, a society lady in the Prince Regent's circle needed at least two full wardrobes a year.

The witch's costume was exquisitely sensual and romantic as well. Of flowing black silk, and black gauze chiffon, it had a neckline that was scooped low and edged in black swansdown. The sleeves were full from the shoulder to the tight wrists done in bands of heavier black silk embroidered in silver thread with stars and moons. The bodice was fitted straight down to just above the hips, where it flowed out in a swirling, graceful pleat of full skirts. The hemline was edged in black swansdown and concealed Amanda's clogs. Her headdress was the typical steeple-shaped brimmed hat associated with witches, except that the brim was not as wide as usual, and soft black silk gauze flowed from the hat, making a long veil in the back and a short one in the front. Beneath the veil Amanda wore her mask, a creation of black silk and silver lace. From beneath the witch's headdress there flowed a marvelous mass of silvery gilt hair, a wig that had been made in great secrecy, matched to a small lock of Miranda's hair. Amanda wore a necklace of black onyx rounds set in silver, which lay flat on her chest above a marvelous swell of breasts.

"My God, Mandy," breathed Miranda. "You are simply splendid in that costume. There is no doubt that you will fool everyone! I would swear it was me!"

Suddenly Amanda burst into tears. "In our whole lives we have never been able to play the kinds of tricks on people that identical twins do. Now, when we can, it is to be not only a debut but a farewell performance. Oh, Miranda, I don't want you to return to America!"

"Mandy dearest, Wyndsong is my home. England is not my

home, America is. You are far more suited to life as an English noblewoman than I am. It is as if you were born for this sort of thing. You are gentle, and mannerly, and witty. You are content in this lovely, manicured land with all the silliness that attends the ton. But I, dearest, I am an American.

"Oh, I have tempered my rashness, it is true, but beneath the veneer of the lady of Wyndsong is a headstrong and brash Yankee who thinks it is ridiculous to drive around leaving calling cards to say we have been at someone's house when the woman in question knows damned well we were there because she peeked through the curtains and saw us coming up the walk. I have no patience for that sort of life, and neither has Jared.

"The majority of the ton are useless, Mandy. Those who do anything worth doing are in the minority. Jared is not satisfied to lead the life of a butterfly and neither am I."

She brushed away her sister's tears. "You are going to spoil that lovely costume that Mary has worked so hard to make. Stop now, Mandy. I will not put up with it!" She sounded so like the old, impatient Miranda that Amanda laughed. "Get dressed, Miranda! You shall make us late as usual, and then they will blame me, for I am supposed to be you!"

Miranda laughed and bade Mary help her dress. As perfect as the witch's costume was for Amanda, the page's costume was equally effective for Miranda. Mary had made the dark blue silk hose herself, and incorporated into them a close-fitting panty of the same material. "You could hardly wear white muslin drawers, madam, they would show and spoil the whole effect," was her comment when Miranda expressed reluctance. Next came a pale-blue silk shirt with a round neckline, and full sleeves with a tight wrist held together by tiny pearl buttons. Over this was a deep-blue sleeveless tabard that ended several inches above Miranda's knees. It was banded on the sides and around the neckline in silver thread, and had a lion rampant embroidered in its center both front and back. The sides of the tabard were held together by silver frogs that closed over large pink pearl buttons. Miranda's shoes were silver glacé kid with ridiculous turned-up toes, and upon her head, which was covered by a golden wig that turned under in pageboy fashion, was a lighter blue flat velvet hat with a single white egret feather. Her mask was of light blue velvet and silver lace.

Fully dressed, she turned to her sister. "Well, Mandy, will I fool them?"

"Oh, yes, Miranda! Yes! Yes! Yes!" Amanda turned around excitedly, her dark robes swirling. "This is going to be the most memorable night ever, twin! Let us go and see if we may fool our husbands!"

Miranda smiled at Mandy's childlike enthusiasm, then turned to Mary Grant. "My sister and I both thank you, Mistress Grant, for your great efforts on our behalf. The embroidery on both these costumes must have taken hours. Please remain at Swynford House tonight so you may get the first decent night's sleep that I imagine you've had in many weeks. Tomorrow my sister and I will settle our bill with you."

Mary Grant curtseyed. "Thank you, milady. I appreciate your kindness. The truth is that I have not slept in three days in order to finish your costumes on time."

"I suspected as much," came the reply. "Thank you again."

The two sisters left the sewing room, and hurried downstairs to the library, where they had arranged to meet the gentlemen. Jared had chosen to come as an American frontiersman in fringed deerskin jacket and leggings, beaded moccasins, coonskin hat, and Kentucky rifle. Somehow, he lent elegance to the rough-and-tumble costume. Adrian was garbed as an Arabian prince, in white pantaloons, and a white-and-gold-embroidered Persian coat. His enormous turban had a pigeon's blood ruby and three egret feathers in its center. His boots matched the ruby.

"Magnificent!" Lord Swynford exclaimed as the two women entered the room. "Amanda, my pet, you are an adorable page." He put an arm around her and kissed her on the cheek. Miranda giggled as Mandy would have done.

Jared Dunham voiced his approval of the costume worn by the woman he took to be his wife. "Yes, my dear, you are the perfect witch, although you do not really look too terribly wicked." His arm snaked out and pulled Amanda close, and his head dipped down to meet her mouth. Amanda's first reaction was to shriek and fight him off, but then she remembered that she was supposed to be Miranda. She was also overwhelmingly curious to know what it would be like to be kissed by this man. She quickly found out, almost swooning in his fiery embrace.

Jared Dunham chuckled wickedly, and murmured against her ear, "Don't faint, pigeon, or you'll give away the masquerade."

"Let's go," Adrian hurried them. "It would not do to arrive after Prinny's grand entrance, and that is scheduled for quarter past ten. I suspect traffic on Regent Street will be unbearable." Taking the arm of the page, he moved out into the foyer, where the footmen waited with their cloaks.

"You know?" Amanda whispered to Jared.

"From the moment you both walked into the room," he answered. "Your sister's legs are beautiful, not easily forgotten, particularly by an attentive husband."

"Then why did you kiss me?" demanded Amanda, indignant.

"Because I've always wondered what that button of a mouth tasted like. It's very sweet, pigeon. *And* because I wanted to see a spark of outrage in Miranda's eyes, which I did."

Amanda laughed. "You two deserve each other," she said. "I wonder if Wyndsong will be big enough to contain the pair of you."

"Come, Jared, Miranda," Adrian called from the foyer. "There'll be plenty of time for lovemaking after the masquerade," and Amanda chuckled, wondering if Adrian would remember that remark later, after their deception had been revealed.

Carleton House was a crush of people, but the festivities had been planned well. Regent Street from Oxford Circus to Piccadilly had been closed to all traffic but the two thousand guests. The side streets leading into Regent Street along that route had also been closed off to all but the invited, and each carriage attempting to turn into Regent Street was stopped by a guardsman who checked invitations and counted the inhabitants of the vehicle. This allowed the guests to proceed smoothly right up to the entry of Carleton House, where they left their carriages to linkboys holding lighted torches.

The invitations were checked again at the doors to Carleton House, the Prince Regent's residence, and then the guests proceeded inside, unannounced, as announcements would have spoiled the surprise of the disguises. In the main ballroom of the palace musicians played chamber music and everyone awaited the Prince Regent. He came at precisely quarter past ten, as anticipated. Passing between the lines of bowing, curtseying guests, he made playful remarks to certain guests as he went.

"Alvaney, is that you beneath that doublet? Yes, it most certainly is. Your new tailor can no more cut a doublet properly than he can a morning coat."

Good-natured laughter sounded, and Lord Alvaney capitulated gracefully, acknowledging his master's superior perception.

"Ah ha! 'Tis Lady Jersey, I'll be bound!"

"Oh, how did Your Highness know?" Lady Jersey sounded properly piqued.

"Why, madam, if you are going to try and disguise yourself to me you will have to hide that fetching beauty mark."

"Oh, sir, your eye is certainly keen!"

The Prince Regent chuckled, and passed by. Suddenly, well into the ballroom, he stopped before a beautiful gypsy and asked, "Will you do me the honor to open the ball with me, Princess de Lieven?"

Dariya de Lieven was far too intelligent to play games. She curtseyed elegantly, and said, "I am honored, Your Highness," and the band struck up the first waltz as the Prince Regent, garbed as his famous ancestor, Henry VIII, opened his masquerade by dancing across the floor with a beautiful gypsy, who was really the wife of Russia's ambassador.

After an appropriate interval the rest of the guests joined in, and the ballroom was soon filled with waltzing couples. Within the hour the masquerade was well under way with guests spilling out of the overheated ballroom into the gardens of Carleton House. In the

Gothic conservatory of the palace a buffet table was set up filling one hundred and fifty feet of the room's two-hundred-foot length. The Irish damask cloth covering the table was of one piece, woven especially for this occasion in a Tudor rose design.

At ten-foot intervals down the long table were large, round Waterford bowls. In the centers of the bowls were six-armed silver candelabra surrounded by a profusion of tall, multicolored, sweet-scented flowers. The candelabra burned cream-colored beeswax tapers. All the serving pieces were of the finest silver. Although the guests would not be invited to partake of refreshments until after midnight the food was already on the table.

The long table had been set, from the far end of the room, with the appetizers first, the fish course next to that, and so on to the end of what would be a large, sumptuous meal. At the far end were large silver and china bowls of prawns, oysters, and clams. There were smaller dishes of spiced sauces, for many of the fish were served cold. There were lobsers and crabs with bowls of hot melted herb butter. Next were platters of Dover sole, served hot, and platters of salmon *en gelée* and cold trout in herb dressing. Large lemons, whole and delicately carved, adorned all the fish platters.

There was plentiful game as well, and the Prince Regent's friends had vied with one another to see who could put the most game on his table that night. There were a dozen platters of quail and partridge, and three whole swans. Ducks had been roasted to a golden brown and baked in sauces of cherry or orange. Pigeon pâté nestled in a bed of fresh watercress. Claw-footed silver platters held the ten roasted, stuffed turkeys and smaller platters held thirty dozen *petits poulets a l'Italien*. In the center of the table rested the most enormous boar anyone remembered ever seeing. Surrounding the boar were huge sides of beef and venison, and surrounding these were legs of lamb and smoked hams studded with cloves and baked in champagne and honey.

Huge serving bowls filled with green beans, celery with bread crumbs and cheese, and cauliflower done three different ways marched toward the near end of the table. There were tiny peas done in a delicate butter sauce—a great favorite in London that season—as well as seven different potato dishes. There were the usual roasted potatoes, potatoes in sauces, and tiny puffed potatoes.

Nearing the end of the table were breads of every description, in small white loaves and long rye loaves, egg-glazed brioches and tiny crescents, soft rolls and hard rolls. Each bread was accompanied by its own small silver dish of iced butter.

Even that majestic table could hold only so much, and the desserts had been placed on a long mahogany sideboard. There were individual soufflés of mocha, raspberry, lemon, and apricot, each in its china dish. Vying for attention with all the tortes and custards were twenty varieties of iced cakes, and as many fruit tarts. Fruit tarts were a perennial favorite, as were jellies flavored with exotic liqueurs. The Prince Regent and his friends kept up a running competition to see who could contrive the most outrageous jellies. The Prince usually won.

There were cheeses and, of course, many platters of carefully arranged crisp crackers, as well as enormous footed crystal bowls of fresh fruit, including Spanish oranges, cherries arrived from France two days before and preserved in ice, green and black grapes from the hills of Southern Italy, green pears from Anjou, and that most treasured of all rare fruits, pineapples from the faraway South Sea islands. English strawberries completed the bounty.

Because of the vast number of guests, and because it was assumed that most had eaten substantial dinners, the Prince Regent's buffet table was a modest one in comparison with the usual thirty-six-course dinners he served his guests at Carleton House and at his pavilion in Brighton. A separate table set up along one wall of the Gothic conservatory held the liquid refreshments, which included iced champagne, fine wines both red and white, and Madeira and port.

Tables with silver services had been set up in the gardens, and the guests who wished to eat there or rest from the dancing came to sit in the cool evening air. Earlier, a rather silly pageant depicting sweet Spring banishing cold cruel Winter had been held. It would, decided Amanda, have been a great deal more successful if sweet Spring had not been played by the hefty Lady Jersey, who was one of Prinny's favorite ladies.

"Milady?"

Amanda looked up to see a bewigged footman. "Yes?"

"His Royal Highness would like to see you, Lady Dunham. I am to take you to him at once."

Good Lord, thought Amanda. Was Prinny planning to get amorous with Miranda? What would she say to him? She should have to admit their deception, and hope that his sense of humor was firmly established this evening. She rose and followed the footman. It was as she had suspected, for he led her deep into the darkest part of the garden. There could be no mistaking the Prince Regent's intentions toward her twin sister. She rehearsed what she would say to him, but nothing seemed to sound right. Oh Lord, what a pickle! The noise of the party was becoming fainter. At least no one would see this meeting, she thought.

Abruptly her headdress was ripped away and something stifling was thrown over her head. Viselike arms wrapped around her, but somehow Amanda managed to scream and began struggling wildly to free herself, flailing out blindly.

"Jesus, she's a fighter!" she heard a voice say. "Can't you shut her up?"

"No one can hear her down at this end of the garden, but the prince don't want no trouble. Hold on till I get the stuff."

Amanda flailed at her captors, using every ounce of her waning strength to kick out with her heavy wooden clogs. A voice howled as she made contact with shins. The two men wrestled her to the ground, and then one of them pulled the blanket from her head while the other forced a sweet-smelling linen cloth to her nose and mouth. Amanda tried not to breathe, but finally she gasped and the sweet scent burned down her throat, quickly overcoming her.

"Whew," said one of her captors, "I thought we'd never get her quieted down. The hall door's open so let's get her through it and into the coach. Then we can go back and get the gent. My advice is to cosh him on the head right off."

"You cosh him, and I'll get him here. What'll I tell him?"

"What the prince told you to tell him, you fool! That Lady Miranda Dunham would like to see him in private, and you're to lead him to her. Go on now. I'll put her into the coach, and then be waiting for you."

The festivities went on, and then at two o'clock in the morning the signal was given for the guests to unmask. Standing next to the blue page, Jared Dunham stayed the hand that reached up to remove the scrap of blue velvet and silver lace. "Did you really believe I could look at those legs of yours, wildcat, and believe them Amanda's?" His bottle-green eyes were laughing at her.

"You rogue! You knew?" She pulled her mask off. "When did you know? Did I fool you at all?"

"No. You might have if you had worn something that covered more of you," he answered.

"You knew from the beginning? You kissed Amanda deliberately?"

"She has a sweet mouth," he teased her, "but she kisses like a child."

Miranda laughed, and said, "Do you remember the first time we went to Almack's after we were married?"

"Yes," he said slowly, and then he laughed. "Do you mean, milady, that you want to go home now?"

"Yes, milord, I do. I have had enough eating, drinking, and dancing to last me a lifetime."

"As always, madam, your slightest wish is my command," and he took her arm.

"Fiddlesticks, milord, you lust after me as I lust after you!" she shot back.

"I do indeed," he chuckled.

"How are we getting home? Our carriage was sent back."

"We'll take Adrian's. The last time I looked he was playing cards with Prince de Lieven, Lord Alvaney, and Prinny. We'll send it right back."

"That's rather rich company for Adrian to play with, isn't it?" Miranda worried.

"Adrian's no fool, darling. He was winning. The moment he

begins to lose anything he can't afford he'll take his winnings and leave the table. He has such a charming, boyish way about him that nobody ever gets offended when he does it. They've all played with him at White's and Watier's often enough."

They found their way through the wide corridors of Carleton House back down to the main entry hall, and Jared ordered his brother-in-law's carriage brought around while they got their cloaks. Helping her into the coach, he ordered the driver to take them home, and then to return to wait for Adrian and Amanda. The vehicle clopped through the silent city streets while its inhabitants embraced passionately. Holding her in the crook of one arm, Jared let his other hand roam her body beneath the velvet tabard, finding the small pearl buttons of her silk shirt, opening them, and pushing through to cup a full, sweet breast. His lips moved to the softness of her neck, and she murmured restlessly, her nipples hardening against his palm. His hand moved up again to pull her feathered bonnet off. Running his fingers through her lovely hair, he whispered, "You were the most fetching page I have ever seen, wildcat. It was all I could do not to whisk you away hours earlier."

"Say it!" she commanded.

"I love you, Miranda," he replied.

"And I love you, Jared. Now can we please go home? Really home, I mean. To Wyndsong."

"Will next week suit you, milady?"

"Next week?" She sat up, shaking his arm off. "I have packing to do! It isn't like before Tom was born, Jared! Traveling with a child is next to impossible. You must take everything imaginable, for there are no shops in midocean."

"Dream Witch will be back next week from Massachusetts, wildcat. We can go anytime you're ready."

"Next week!" she cried joyfully. "I'll manage somehow." Then she thought a moment, a little smile on her face. "I wonder what Anne thinks of America. And I wonder what your father and mother think of Jon returning with a second wife, her two children, and their own two babies, Susannah and Peter!"

"Well, at least Father can't accuse Jon of being idle these two years. When you add Jon's three children by Charity, he now has seven children. We'll have to work hard to catch up with him, wildcat."

"Unless you have another wife, Jared Dunham, we will have to concede to your brother in this matter. I have given you the next lord of the manor. Now I want a daughter, and then I am finished."

"You may have your daughter, milady, but I must have two sons."

"Two? Do you remember how badly your father treated you because he didn't want you to try and rob Jon of his place as heir?"

"I am not my father. Besides, I will need the second son for the ships. If Tom is to be lord of the manor, he cannot handle the trading business as well. One son for the land, one for the sea, and a daughter we can both spoil."

"Agreed," she said solemnly. "We will begin serious work on Jason Dunham tonight," and they laughed.

"Jason, is it? I like it, milady. It has a good ring to it. I assume that since you have named both my sons I get to name our daughter?"

Her eyes clouded as she thought of Fleur. Then, knowing that he expected an answer, she said brightly, "Indeed, milord, you must name our daughter. I am very bad with female names."

He had seen the momentary lull in her high spirits, and wondered as he had more than once since her return just what secret she was keeping from him, and why.

The Swynford carriage turned into Devon Square, and pulled up before their town house.

Jared dismissed the house servants for the evening while his wife went upstairs to undress. Perky, dozing by the fire, quickly sat up as her mistress entered the room. Her jaw dropped, and she rubbed her eyes sleepily, looking hard at Miranda.

"But I thought you was to be a wicked witch, and Lady Swynford, the page," she said, confused.

"Which was just what we wanted everyone to think," said Miranda. "That's why we would allow no one but the seamstress to help us this evening. Amanda and I have always wanted to play that trick on someone, but because we don't look alike we have never done it. This masquerade gave us the perfect chance."

"Well," said Perky, "I must say you make a pretty page, milady, and that's the truth."

"Thank you, Perky, and Mandy was marvelous as the witch!"

As Perkins helped her mistress undress, Miranda spoke again. "Perky, we are going home to America in another week or two. I would like you and Martin to come with us. I know that Martin doesn't like driving a coach, but rather, aspires to the type of position that Simpson holds in this household. Wyndsong is a far different place from London, but we are going to need someone for our home. If, however, you choose to remain in England we will give you and Martin both the most complimentary references, and you will be paid for the full year; of course, through Michaelmas. You may also remain until then, in your quarters. The house, however, is being closed, and only the senior servants who have been in my husband's employ for some time will remain to serve Mr. Bramwell, who stays to care for my husband's European interests. Everyone else will be paid for the year and given a reference. We will try to place some of the servants among our friends, but time is short."

"Martin and I have often talked of asking you to let us come with you to America," said Perky, "but one thing worries us, milady."

"What is that?"

"The wild Indians."

"What?"

"The wild Indians, milady. We're mortally afraid of those savages. Martin's grandpa fought with the Redcoats in your war back almost forty years ago. He says the Indians was terrible cruel."

"There are no Indians on Wyndsong, Perky, nor are there any in the surrounding area. There haven't been for over a hundred years. It's as peaceful as the countryside around Swynford Hall. London is much more dangerous than Wyndsong."

"In that case it's just possible that we'll come with you." She paused and looked at Miranda curiously. "Is it true that all people are equal there?"

"Not really," Miranda answered honestly. "In one sense it is the same as anyplace in this world. Those with money have power. But it is different in that the opportunity for wealth and success is there for everyone. The class distinctions are not as rigid as here in England, and the people are truly freer.''

"Then our children could be better than us?''

"Yes,'' said Miranda, "it is possible.''

"I'll talk to Martin, milady,'' said Perky thoughtfully, placing her mistress's costume in the wardrobe.

"Go on to bed, Perky. It's quite late,'' Miranda said. "I'll finish.''

"If you're sure it's all right, milady,'' and when Miranda nodded, smiling, Perkins bobbed a curtsey and left the room.

Jared, wearing a green silk dressing gown, joined her several minutes after Perky had gone. He admired his wife at leisure while she bathed her face and sponged herself lightly, having had a full bath before the ball. He was at the point of suggesting a little dalliance when suddenly there was a discreet but insistent knocking on the bedroom door.

"Milord! Milord!'' Simpson sounded urgent. Miranda quickly wrapped a gown around herself and Jared answered the summons.

"What is it, Simpson?''

"Lord Swynford is downstairs, milord. He is most distraught.''

Adrian was pacing back and forth in the library. "I can't find Amanda,'' he burst out as Miranda and Jared entered the room.

"I went to look for her, the blue page, but no one had seen her, and no one had seen the witch or the frontiersman, either. I guessed you might have already left, and so I went in search of my coach. Horsely told me what you had said, that you and Amanda had switched costumes right from the beginning, and so I shouldn't be looking for the page, but the witch. I went back into Carleton House and looked everywhere. She wasn't in the ballroom, or the conservatory, or anywhere in the gardens. No one had seen her for hours. Nobody remembered her at the unmasking. I thought perhaps that she had taken ill, and gone home early without telling us so as not to spoil our fun, but her maid said she hadn't returned home at all.'' He looked at them helplessly. "Where is my wife?'' he asked them. "What has happened to my Amanda?''

Jared Dunham walked over to the grog tray and poured a full

measure of smoky Irish whiskey into a cut-glass tumbler. He handed it to Adrian, and commanded, "Drink it down. It will calm you, and we can think this out." The younger man gratefully swallowed the liquid fire, and then Jared said, "Adrian, this may seem an impertinent question, but have you and Amanda been happy lately?"

"Good Lord, yes!" was the immediate reply.

"Then did Amanda have any admirers? You know, one of those precious fools like Byron or Shelley who attach themselves to happily married women, and pay them outrageous court because they know it is safe. Sometimes those idiots begin to believe themselves, and try and make off with the lady."

"No," said Adrian, wearily shaking his head. "Before we were married she loved the attention that they paid her, but since our marriage she has had no time for such silliness. In fact on the few occasions that she has been approached by one of those gentlemen, she has sent them packing most unceremoniously."

"Was any one in particular more attentive than the others?"

"No. It has been months since anyone paid her that kind of attention."

"You are absolutely positive that she had no lover?"

Adrian looked crushed, and Miranda snapped, "She had no lover, Jared! If she had I would have known. The only secret Amanda has ever been able to keep was our secret tonight about the costumes."

"Then she has been kidnaped," Jared said flatly.

"*Kidnaped?*" Miranda paled.

"*Kidnaped?* Why would anyone kidnap Amanda?" Adrian demanded.

"Adrian, did you win much money tonight?" Jared asked abruptly.

Looking even more bewildered than he had a moment before, Adrian said, "Yes, I won more than usual. It was twenty-three thousand pounds, actually, from Prinny and the other two. What does that have to do with Amanda?"

Jared sighed and ran his long fingers through his dark hair. "It more than likely is why she was kidnaped. You were seen gambling.

I saw you myself. Like as not, someone saw you winning and has taken Amanda to be ransomed. If so, she is probably safe enough, Adrian."

Adrian was outraged. "But who would do such a thing?"

"Possibly some member of the ton who is badly in debt," Jared explained. "They will not hurt her. You must go home, Adrian, and await a message from them. When it comes, you will inform us and we will plan our course of action."

Adrian looked a trifle encouraged by his brother-in-law's confident tone. "Yes," he said. "I will go home then, and wait."

Jared and Miranda returned to their bedchamber and she asked fearfully, "Do you really believe that someone kidnaped my sister for her husband's gambling winnings?"

"I don't know, but I believe that morning will bring us some answers," he said quietly. "Come, wildcat, don't worry. Wouldn't you know if something had happened to her?"

"Yes, I would," Miranda said flatly.

"Then let us try and get some rest," he suggested.

Dawn was already beginning to stain the city skyline before either of them slept. An hour later, Miranda suddenly awoke. Jared was gone. Heedless of appearances, she walked downstairs without bothering with slippers. As she descended the stairs, a woman's voice floated up to her.

"Jared, my poor darling! I weep for you, beloved! I am so ashamed that a member of my own sex could behave in such a disgusting, low manner."

"I do not understand you, Belinda. What are you doing here, unchaperoned, at such an hour?"

"Oh, darling, I had to come! The moment I heard that your wife had eloped with Kit Edmund last night my heart went out to you. I realized how bitter you must be, but I want you to know that all women are not so despicable."

Miranda continued to the bottom of the staircase. Belinda de Winter looked quite fresh for a lady who had spent most of the night dancing with the Duke of Whitley. She was wearing a lavender taffeta Bavaria pelisse robe with two lines of lilac trimming extending from her shoulders to the ankle-length hem. Matching the gown was a high-crowned Angoulême bonnet decorated with lilac silk ribbons that tied at the side.

"Good morning, Lady de Winter," Miranda said sweetly. "What brings you to our home so early? Good news, I hope."

The color drained from Belinda's face. Slowly she turned around to face Miranda. *"You!"* she hissed. "What are you doing here?"

"No, no, my dear. *I* must ask *you* that question," Miranda toyed with her.

"He promised me," Belinda whispered. "He promised me!"

Jared moved across the large hallway to put an arm around the stricken girl. "Who promised you, Belinda?" he said gently. "And what was promised you?"

"Prince Cherkessky. He was going to take your wife back for his slave, Lucas. Then I was to marry you. You were going to ask me. You were going to ask me."

"Lucas is dead," Miranda said weakly.

"No. He survived."

Jared saw his wife fighting to retain control as the terrible memories assailed her.

"Alexei called you a cat," Belinda said. "He said you had used up all of your lives. How did you escape us? How?" She was beginning to sound hysterical, but her face was still deathly pale. "They were told to take the witch from the masquerade! The fools bungled it!" An angry light came into her blue eyes. "Or did the prince betray me? I helped him to win Georgeanne and last night he received the duke's permission to ask her to marry him. She accepted him."

"My sister and I exchanged costumes," Miranda said wearily. "The men hired to take me, took her. You must tell us where she has been taken, Lady de Winter."

Belinda de Winter raised her chin haughtily at Miranda. "You upstart American whore!" she snarled. "How dare you even speak to me?" She turned back to Jared and her voice was heavy with loathing. "Have you any idea the kind of woman you are married to, milord? She is a slave, a brood mare mounted by a stud. She has lain beneath another man, spreading herself to be fucked like an animal! I've seen him, you know. His lance is like a battering ram. She fucked him willingly. Yet you prefer her to me?

"I loved you, and I wanted to be your wife, but now I hate you! If you were a real gentleman you would prefer me to her. You are as low as your whore! Good riddance to you both!"

"Where is my sister?" Miranda demanded.

Belinda de Winter suddenly began to laugh wildly. "I won't tell you," she said slyly, childlike, and then before they realized what she was doing, she turned and darted out of the house, almost falling over the little tweeny who was scrubbing the front steps. Still laughing, her blue eyes focused on something no one else could see, Belinda de Winter ran into the street. There was a shout, the screech of wheels, a high-pitched scream, and then silence.

Lord Dunham leaped the steps to the street, and helped pull Belinda from beneath the carriage. She was dead, her skull smashed.

"She run right in front of me, she did!" babbled the terrified coachman. "You seen it, sir! She run right in front of me!"

"Yes, I saw it. It was not your fault."

"Who was she, sir? Did you know her?"

"She was Lady Belinda de Winter, and I knew her. She was not well."

"Oh Gawd!" muttered the driver. "A toff! I'll loose me license for sure, and then who'll support me wife and kids?"

Jared stood up. "It's all right. You were not to blame. As I have said, the lady was not well." He tapped his head for emphasis.

Enlightenment dawned. "Oh, I gets you, milord. The lady was crazy as a bedbug."

"Who is your master?" Jared asked.

"Lord Westerly," came the reply.

"Tell your master that you have been in an accident, but that it was not your fault. Refer him to me for corroboration. I am Lord Dunham, and that is my house."

"Thank you, milord! Thank you!"

Jared turned and walked back into his house. Simpson and two of the footmen were bringing Belinda de Winter's body inside. The Duke and Duchess of Northampton would have to be informed immediately.

Miranda stood crying inside the hall. "We'll never find Mandy now."

"Cherkessky knows," he said fiercely. "If he or any of his people have harmed the pigeon I will kill him! He cannot, of course, be allowed to announce his engagement to that innocent Georgeanne Hampton. I shall put a stop to that also."

The Duke of Northampton was having an early breakfast in the small family dining room of Northampton House when his butler came to tell him that Lord Dunham was calling on urgent business.

Making a sound of annoyance, the duke rose from his table, tossed down his napkin, and went to his library. "Good morning, Dunham. What's more important than my breakfast," he joked.

"Belinda de Winter is dead," Jared said without any preamble.

"What?"

"She was part of a plot to kidnap my wife, but the plot went awry and my sister-in-law was taken instead. Belinda, not aware of the mistake, came to my house in Devon Square this morning. When she saw Miranda her mind snapped. She ran into the street, and was run down by a carriage."

"You must be mad, Dunham! Belinda hadn't the resources for such a complicated ploy. Besides, what was she going to do with Lady Dunham?"

"She wanted to marry me, my lord, and Miranda was in her way. Her ally was Prince Alexei Cherkessky."

"My lord!" The duke's face grew red with outrage. "I must beg you to be wary of what you say. Prince Cherkessky is to marry my eldest daughter Georgeanne in July. The announcement will be in the newspapers tomorrow."

"You had best withdraw that notice, my lord," said Jared ominously, "unless, of course, you do not mind that you are matching your daughter with the man who murdered Lady Gillian Abbott, whose wealth comes from a slave-breeding farm, and who is in disfavor with the Tzar. The man kidnaps innocent women for obscene purposes, and he wants your child only for her wealth."

"You can prove these charges?" The Duke began to wonder if Lord Dunham was quite sane.

"I can prove all of it."

"Let us sit down," the Duke of Northampton sighed.

They sat themselves in two large, leather-upholstered wing chairs next to the blazing fireplace, and the duke, leaning forward, said bluntly, "I have never known you to be either rash or foolish, Lord

Dunham. You are neither an idler nor a gossip, and so I am going to listen to what you have to say. Be warned, however, that if I think you are lying to me I will have you thrown out of my house."

Lacing his fingers together, Jared began, "First, my lord of Northampton, I must have your solemn word that you will not divulge certain things that I am about to tell you. Lord Palmerston can vouch for my veracity in some of this. Will you give me your word?" The duke nodded, and Jared told his story, beginning with his secret journey to Russia. When, close to an hour later, he had finished his story, the duke was astounded and furious.

"When my wife returned home she told us—her sister, Lord Swynford and me—what had happened. You see, we could do nothing without exposing Miranda to shame and ridicule. The ton would not easily forget such a scandal, and Miranda's life would have been made unbearable as long as we remained in London. You can understand what it is like for us, knowing what Miranda has lived through and being able to do nothing. We wanted to warn you because of your child, but we could not do so."

The duke nodded. The thought that he had almost entrusted his favorite daughter to a monster shook him to his core. Finally he found his voice. "I do not understand how Belinda is involved, Dunham. Will you enlighten me, please?"

"Frankly I am not entirely sure myself. Somehow she found out what had really happened to my wife, and ingratiated herself with Cherkessky. She told us she helped him by convincing your daughter of the prince's devotion and suitability. In return he was to capture my wife again and remove her back to Russia. It was to appear as if Miranda eloped with young Edmund. I haven't even had time yet to see if he was taken, but if he too was kidnaped then I believe he is in mortal danger.

"This morning, Belinda appeared at my house babbling that she had heard the shocking news of my wife's elopement with Kit Edmund. She begged me quite prettily not to hold all womankind responsible for the despicable acts of one woman. When Miranda came down the stairs and Belinda saw her, she went completely to pieces. I believe she went quite mad. I am very sorry."

After a pause, the duke shook off his thoughts of Belinda and said, "Of course I cannot have Georgeanne marrying Cherkessky. But what am I to tell my wife? She will want a good explanation, Dunham. She has quite set her heart upon a prince for Georgeanne, and the Duke of Whitley for Belinda. What am I to tell her?" he repeated.

"My wife has told me," said Jared, "that the prince's half-brother was also his lover. I do not imagine that the leopard has changed his spots simply because he is visiting England. Tell your wife that you have discovered that the prince enjoys men for lovers as well as women. In view of this disturbing fact you cannot possibly entrust little Georgeanne to him. If your wife is still reluctant to give up the prince, tell her that his wealth was lost when his estates in the Crimea were destroyed. Tell her he is in disfavor with the Tzar. And tell her that his wealth came from raising slaves, not vegetables. Remember, my lord, you are the head of your house, not your wife."

"What will you do, Lord Dunham? How will you find sweet Lady Swynford?"

"I shall go to Prince de Lieven. He is the Tzar's ambassador, and will certainly want to avoid a scandal. He will force Prince Cherkessky to tell us where Amanda has been taken."

The two men stood and shook hands. "I cannot thank you enough, Lord Dunham. You have saved my child from a nightmare. God only knows how he would have treated her once they were back in St. Petersburg. I will arrange to have Belinda's body removed from your house as quickly as possible."

"I think it would be wise to say that Lady de Winter had come to bid my wife and me farewell, for we are soon going home to America. That should explain her being in Devon Square this morning, and avoid any scandal."

The Duke of Northampton nodded his agreement. "Indeed, we must avoid the taint of scandal for the sake of the ladies."

Jared Dunham left Northampton House and directed Martin to the residence of Prince and Princess de Lieven. They were still sleeping, but Jared convinced their butler of the urgency of the matter, and shortly both de Lievens appeared in their morning room where Jared waited. Once more the lord of Wyndsong Manor told his story, and as he spoke Prince de Lieven's face grew darker and darker, while his beautiful wife first grew pale and then began to look angry.

When Jared had finished Prince de Lieven said furiously, "It is unthinkable that Cherkessky should be allowed to get away with this! I will, of course, send for him immediately and demand the whereabouts of Lady Swynford. As for what he has done to your wife, I understand your desire to keep the matter a private one. She has a magnificent and unconquerable spirit, Lord Dunham." The Prince sighed. "This is not the first time Cherkessky has done something like this. Remember when we were in Berlin several years' ago, Dariya?"

"Yes, two girls disappeared from Baron Brandtholm's estate. He denied it, of course, but they had been seen entering his carriage. He paid the baron an indemnity—goodwill, I believe he said—and still denied taking them. Then, in St. Petersburg three years ago, there was the matter of Princess Tumanova's governess. She was the love child of the Duc de Longchamps, you know. I cannot help but wonder what happened to her."

"She died on the Tatar march from the Crimea to Istanbul," said Jared, not distressing the princess further by telling her how Mignon had died.

"How awful," exclaimed Dariya de Lieven, "and poor, poor Miranda! How very brave she has been through it all."

"Enough, darling," said Prince de Lieven. "Lord Dunham is aware of his wife's bravery. Our task now is to find young Lady Swynford before she can come to any harm. By now they have realized their error. We must stop this thing before it goes any further."

The Russian ambassador reached for the embroidered bellpull. He sent a message to Pultney's Hotel. The de Lievens and Lord Dunham sat down to wait. They were rewarded in a shorter time than they had anticipated by Prince Alexei Cherkessky's arrival.

"De Lieven," he said, entering the room, "you caught me just in time. I was on my way out."

Prince de Lieven looked coldly at Alexei Cherkessky. "I want the whereabouts of the woman you had kidnaped from the Prince Regent's masquerade last night, Cherkessky, and I want them now."

It was only then Alexei Cherkessky spotted Jared Dunham. Looking directly at the American, he smiled, and said in answer to de Lieven, "My dear Prince, I haven't the slightest idea what you mean."

A wicked smile appeared on Jared Dunham's face. "You got the wrong woman, Cherkessky. My wife and her sister exchanged costumes. The woman your men snatched was not my wife, but her sister, Lady Swynford."

"I don't believe you!" the prince said, oblivious to the de Lievens. This was now between himself and the arrogant Yankee.

"Belinda de Winter came to me this morning to commiserate with me over my loss. You can imagine her shock when my wife came downstairs. I have already been to see the Duke of Northampton. He knows everything about you. There will be no engagement to Lady Georgeanne, Cherkessky. Prince and Princess de Lieven have also been told everything. I do not believe that the princess will allow you to be received socially in any decent house in England now, will you, Dariya?"

"Most certainly not! Your conduct has been immoral and unforgivable!"

"Lady Swynford's whereabouts, Prince. What I say in my report to His Imperial Majesty, the Tzar, depends on you. You have little enough left as it is, Cherkessky. If you wish to be allowed to retain what you still own, you had best cooperate with us. I have the power to arrest you here and now, and return you to the Tzar's justice."

"Do so," came the cool reply. "You will still not have Lady Swynford back."

"How much?" inquired Jared Dunham coolly. "Your price, swine?"

The prince smiled wolfishly. "A duel, Lord Dunham. To the death. Pistols. If I win, I get your wife. If you win, you get Lady Swynford and I will get out of your lives forever. I will write down the exact whereabouts of Lady Swynford and place the paper in my pocket. It will be there for you if you win. If I win I will return Lady Swynford only in exchange for Lady Dunham."

Princess de Lieven turned to her husband. "Kristofor Andreivich! You cannot let him do such a thing!" she cried.

"I trust," said Jared, "that I have your word as a gentleman, Cherkessky, and that you will deal honestly."

"You American upstart!" snapped Alexei Cherkessky. "Do you dare instruct me on manners? My family goes back to the foundation of Russia. My ancestors were princes while yours were tillers of soil! Peasants! My word is good!"

"Done, then," replied Lord Dunham. "Since you have chosen weapons, I choose time and place. It is here and now." He turned to Prince de Lieven. "I trust, sir, that you can supply the weapons."

"Lord Dunham! Jared!" pleaded Dariya de Lieven. "You cannot endanger Miranda like this! Not after all she's been through."

"I am not endangering my wife, Dariya."

"You have agreed to turn her over to Prince Cherkessky if you lose!"

"I do not intend losing, Dariya," Jared replied coolly.

"Arrogant Yankee!" snarled Cherkessky. "I am a champion of the pistol."

"You are also a fool, Prince, to believe that you can kill me."

"Why do you say that?"

"Because my reason for winning is more powerful than yours. It is love, and love can overcome the blackest evil. Look at my wife if you desire an example of the power of love. No matter what you did to her you could not conquer her spirit. She escaped you, Cherkessky, and fought her way home to me and to our child. Is your desire to win over me *that* strong? I think not. And if not, then you will lose."

Alexei Cherkessky looked shaken. He didn't like all this talk of his dying. "Let's get on with it!" he snapped. "I have written Lady Swynford's whereabouts on this paper, and now I place it, so, in my jacket pocket. I now put the jacket on the settee for Princess de Lieven to guard."

Prince de Lieven removed a pistol case from a cabinet drawer.

Opening it, he showed it to the two combatants, who both nodded, satisfied. The pistols were primed and loaded, and de Lieven handed the weapons to the two combatants. "You will walk ten paces," he said. "Turn at my command, and commence firing. This is a duel to the death."

The two gentlemen stood back to back.

"Cock your weapons," came the command, and two clicks followed.

"One, two, three, four, five, six, seven, eight, nine..."

Alexei Cherkessky whirled and aimed at Jared Dunham's back. A shot rang out.

Jared Dunham turned slowly, gazing with surprise as Prince Cherkessky fell to the floor, dead. The Russian ambassador stared openmouthed as his wife lowered her small, still smoking pistol to her side.

"He broke his word," Dariya de Lieven said. "I knew he would. The Cherkesskys haven't told the truth in two hundred years."

"I owe you my life, Dariya."

"No, it was we who owed you, Jared. How can we ever make up to you and to Miranda what was done to her at the hands of one of our own people? Not all Russians are barbarians, Jared. Please believe that." She reached into the dead man's jacket and pulled forth the folded paper. "Let us hope he was confident enough to really write down the whereabouts of poor Lady Swynford," she said. She smiled. "Lady Swynford can be found at Green Lodge. It is the first house outside the village of Erith as you go toward Gravesend."

"I will come with you," said Kristofor de Lieven. "The prince may have the house guarded by his Russian servants, and my authority will open all doors."

At that moment they heard a commotion outside the morning-room door. It burst open to admit Miranda and a disgruntled butler.

"She insisted, Your Highness," the butler apologized.

"It is all right, Colby. This is Lady Dunham."

"Yes, Your Highness." Colby looked at the body of Alexei Cherkessky. "Shall I have that removed, Your Highness?"

"Yes. Arrange to have it buried in the parish churchyard."

"Very good, Your Highness." Colby withdrew, imperturbable as always.

"You dueled with him?" Miranda's eyes were angry. "You could have been killed!"

"I had no intention of being killed," was the cool reply.

"Well, at least you killed him before he could injure you."

"Dariya killed him."

"What?"

"He cheated. He turned on the count of nine. He was going to shoot me in the back. Dariya had her pistol and shot him. She has a wickedly keen eye, wildcat. Dariya, how is it you had that little weapon of yours available?"

Dariya de Lieven smiled. "When Colby woke us, I slipped it into my dressing-gown pocket. I had a feeling that trouble was brewing. It was simply a hunch, and I followed it. I always follow my hunches."

"And a damned good thing for you, Jared Dunham!" Miranda was furious. "What would have happened to us if you'd been killed, I would like to know!"

Dariya de Lieven began to giggle, her nerves beginning to register the strain. "If Jared had been killed you would have been turned over to Prince Cherkessky."

"What?!"

"Jared agreed on the duel. If he won he was to get Amanda back. If he lost, you were Cherkessky's prize."

"Do I mean that little to you, milord?" Miranda demanded in a dangerous voice.

"I had to offer him something worth having, wildcat," he said softly. "Are you not the greatest prize of all?" He bent and kissed her lips.

Prince de Lieven smiled to himself. What a rogue that daring Yankee was. And he handled his woman like a Frenchman, too. Admirable!

Miranda began to laugh. "You cannot wheedle me, milord," she said.

"No?" he chuckled.

"Well, perhaps a little. But dammit, don't ever do an idiot thing like that again!" She paused a moment, and then said, "In the midst of this farce, did anyone bother to find out from Cherkessky just what he has done with my sister?"

"She's being held in a house just outside the village of Erith. It's down the river toward the sea," Jared replied. "Prince de Lieven and I were on our way to get her when you arrived."

"I'm coming with you," she said.

"We can travel faster alone on horseback."

"And how do you intend to transport Amanda? You know how wretchedly she rides."

"Of course," said Dariya. "You must use one of our coaches. It really is the only sensible way, Kristofor Andreivich. It will reassure poor Lady Swynford to have the company of her sister. The poor woman must be absolutely terrified."

It would have done Amanda's spirits good to know that as the sun crept toward noon, her deliverance was at hand. Prince de Lieven's comfortable traveling coach rumbled along a secondary road that led to the village of Erith. Inside were the prince and Jared and Miranda Dunham. They had not stopped to get Adrian. There was no time.

Around them was a beautiful spring day. They passed clumps of yellow and white daffodils. The meadows were newly green. Silently watching, Miranda was painfully aware of Lucas. Lucas was alive. She was glad he had escaped. Yet his being here presented a terrible problem. How would Jared react to the man who had taken his wife? His foolhardly behavior in dueling with Prince Cherkessky was frightening. She wished Lucas no harm, but she dreaded the meeting between him and Jared.

As if reading her thoughts, Jared took her hand in his. "All we want to do is free Amanda. And young Kit Edmund, if he's there," he said.

She smiled weakly. He seemed so cool, but what would happen when he stood face to face with the handsome Greek? Would he still love her after today? *Never apologize!* She started, and looked at her fellow passengers. They were absorbed by their own thoughts. Hadn't they heard it? She certainly had! She had clearly heard Mirza

Khan's deep voice sternly admonishing her, and now she felt her courage returning. She sent him a silent thanks.

A small signpost announced that Erith was one mile away, and soon they were driving through the village, carefully looking for the house the prince had rented. "There!" said Prince de Lieven, pointing to a high stone wall. There was a shabby wooden plaque on it that read: GREEN LODGE. He leaned out of the coach window and instructed his driver. A groom jumped down from the box and, finding the gates unlocked, opened them wide for the carriage. They passed through and up the drive.

The house, a tumble-down brick affair dating back to Elizabethan times, appeared empty. Many of its diamond-paned windows were heavily overgrown with dark green ivy. The grounds were unkempt and overgrown with weeds.

Lucas heard the carriage as it came up the drive. At last, he thought, relieved, the prince has come. He was uncomfortable in this strange land, although in his few months in England he had gained a command of the language. Of course, he had learned a little English from Miranda. Miranda! How he wanted her back!

He ran to the door. The prince must be told of the error at once. The lady was not Miranda. He flung open the front door and jumped back, startled. Facing him was not Alexei Cherkessky, but an elegant gentleman who spoke to him in flawless Russian. "I speak English," Lucas said, not sure of the stranger's dialect. The gentleman nodded. "I am Kristofor Andreivich, Prince de Lieven. I am the ambassador to England from his Imperial Majesty, the Tzar. You are the serf Lucas?"

"Yes, Highness."

"Your master is dead, Lucas. I have come for Lady Amanda Swynford and young Lord Edmund. I trust they are both unharmed."

"Yes, Highness," Lucas answered slowly. Was this man telling the truth? Suddenly the door of Prince de Lieven's coach opened and a woman descended. It was she! It was Miranda!

"Little bird," he whispered, "you have returned to me!" He brushed past the prince and swept her into his arms, his great leonine head dipping to seek her lips.

Miranda twisted away from him. "Lucas! I have come for my sister. Where is Amanda?"

"No," he said. "You have returned to me. You love me. We were meant to be together. The prince gave you to me?"

"Oh, Lucas," Miranda said quietly, her heart going out to this beautiful, childlike man, "the prince did not have the right to give me to you. You must understand. You are free now, Lucas! With Prince Cherkessky dead you are free, as I am free! I am going home to America with my husband and my son, and you must make a life for yourself."

"But I do not know how to do anything but be a slave. If I am not a slave, then what am I?"

"You are a man, Lucas!"

Sadly he looked at her, and shook his head. Then Lucas turned to Prince de Lieven. "Lady Amanda is in the house. The young man also. I will take you to them, Your Highness," and without another word to Miranda he turned and went back into the house.

Miranda began to weep. He had not really understood. What was to become of him? He had spent most of his life being told what to do. He did not know how to be a man. "I hope you are in Hell, Alexei Cherkessky!" she cried. "How many lives have you ruined? Sasha! All those slaves! Lucas! Mignon! Me! If there really is a God in Heaven, you are burning in Hell, and I curse you!"

"Miranda, my dearest love," murmured Jared Dunham. "Don't, my darling. It is finally over. There is nothing more to fear, wildcat. I understand everything now. I do!"

"Miranda!" Amanda Swynford flew from the house.

The two sisters embraced, just as Prince de Lieven emerged. Kit Edmund, a bad bruise on his forehead, his harlequin costume much the worse for wear, was leaning on the prince's arm. In an exhausted voice he said, "Will someone please tell me what the hell this is all about? Prinny's parties are certainly becoming dangerous. I am safer at sea in a damned hurricane, than in the gardens at Carleton House!"

They laughed. They could not help it, and as their mirth grew it brought relief. "It's a very long story, Kit, but we'll try to explain," promised Miranda.

"I certainly hope so," replied the young Marquis of Wye in an aggrieved tone.

Prince de Lieven's coachman and two grooms had entered the house, and now they returned hustling out two protesting men. "These two did the kidnaping for Cherkessky," said Prince de Lieven. "I wonder what to do with them?"

"Let them go," said Jared. "Cherkessky's dead, and my wife and I would like this matter to remain private."

"It seems a shame just to let them go," murmured Kristofor de Lieven. "Now in Russia, we would flay them alive." The two culprits paled. "If I should ever see either of you in London," began the Russian slowly and menacingly, but the two were already running down the drive.

Suddenly Miranda said sharply, "Lucas! Where is Lucas?"

"He was in the house," replied the prince.

At that moment Amanda cried out, pointing to the river at the end of the lawn. "Look!"

They turned and looked toward the river. The great blond man was swimming downstream against the incoming tide. Riveted, they watched, horrified, as he tired and finally sank beneath the waves. His head bobbed to the surface once and then he disappeared.

"Oh, the poor creature," whispered Amanda. "The poor, poor creature!"

"No," said Miranda, the tears rolling down her beautiful face. "Be happy for him. I am, for in death, Lucas is no longer a slave." She felt Jared take her icy hand in his, and then he said, "Let us go home, wildcat."

"To Wyndsong?" she asked.

"Yes, my love," he answered. "To Wyndsong."

Epilogue

Wyndsong,
June 1815

D ream *Witch* plowed through the gentle seas, her sleek keel cutting the dark waves like a knife. Above her, bright stars silvered the night sky. Toward the southeast in the constellation Scorpius, Red Antares glowed fiery. In the west and close to setting, the star Regulus slid down the Sickle of Leo into the sea, while blue white Venus twinkled at midheaven. All was silent but for the gentle hiss of the waves, and the steady breeze that filled the ship's sails. In the bow the watchman hummed tunelessly to himself while the helmsman in the stern watched his course, thinking of the wife he hadn't seen in two years.

In the master's cabin Jared Dunham was caressing his wife's beautiful body. Naked, she lay like a nymph, her warm, silken skin vibrating beneath his skilled touch.

Miranda reveled in his passion. She pushed him back, and mounted him. Taking his face in her hands, she slowly kissed his quivering, closed eyelids, his forehead, his high sculpted cheekbones, the cleft in his chin. Her slender hands tangled in his dark hair.

Sitting up, she reached back and began to fondle him, her hand moving with slow, sensuous strokes at first, her tempo increasing as he grew hard with her touch. Watching her through half-closed eyes, he saw her half-smile of triumph. The little bitch, he thought, amused, remembering his shy bride of three years before. It was time she remembered who was the master.

He swiftly slid his hands beneath her adorable bottom and moved her forward. His fingers dug into her backside and his tongue found its home, flickering rapidly back and forth as she whimpered. Her sex grew stiff as her excitement increased, and when she thought she could bear no more he stopped and pushed her down onto her back, spreading her legs wide, teasing her further by rubbing the ruby head of his manhood against her throbbing womanhood.

"Bastard!" she hissed at him through clenched teeth, and he laughed.

"I love you, you impossible bitch," he said, "but if you try to drive me, you must accept the consequences of your own provocative actions." He turned her over and, laying his body along the length of hers, pushed her gilt hair aside and began licking the side of her neck. Miranda shivered with delight, and began to make little murmuring noises as his tongue moved across her shoulders and then followed her spine, ending with a sweep around each rounded satiny buttock.

She squirmed out from under him, and pushed him down, beginning her own taunting tongue play, around and around his tender nipples. Then suddenly her tongue began to follow the provocative line of his dark hair down his belly. Lower and lower her head moved until he pulled her back with, "Enough, you witch! The time for play is over!"

Quickly she was beneath him, and he was filling her. Slowly, slowly, he pushed into her, feeling her yield as he moved deeper and deeper inside of her. When he could go no further, he lay still for a moment. Then he felt her initiate the sweet rhythm between them, pushing her slim hips, goading him. "Ah, wildcat," he murmured against her ear, "you are ever impatient." He thrust hard and fast into her.

Miranda gave herself to him entirely as she had never given herself to anyone else. Their passion was like a comet flashing across the dark heavens, trailing gold stars to burn as brightly as their love. At last their fulfillment washed over them, leaving them helpless yet safe within the comfort of each other's arms. Exhausted, they slept, the fingers of her right hand and his left hand intertwined.

She awakened and listened to the wonderful sound of his breathing. She was safe. She was loved. She was with Jared. And tomorrow they would be home on Wyndsong.

The Dunhams and the Swynfords had stayed at Swynford Hall for four days before Miranda and Jared left for Welland Beach, where *Dream Witch* awaited them. To their delight, Martin and Perky, as well as Jared's valet, Mitchum, had decided to come with them. Jared had promised the three servants that if they didn't like America he would see them safely returned to England after a year. But he doubted that they would want to come back.

Miranda and Amanda had spent much of those four days in each other's company, joining the men only at meals and at bedtime. It would be a long while before they met again, and there was so much to talk about in the little time left. On their last day together, Amanda had run into the dining room laughing and brandishing a gazette.

"You won't believe this, twin! Darius Edmund, Belinda de Winter's suitor, is engaged to Georgeanne! How's that for a happy ending?"

Miranda smiled at her sister. It was a deep smile, a wistful smile that ached at their parting.

"Oh, Mandy," she teased, her old self again. "You always were one for happy endings!" And their husbands joined in the laughter.

Beside her, Jared stirred. "Are you awake?" he asked.

"Yes. Wyndsong is near. I smell it." She chuckled. "I remember coming home from England four years ago, and Mandy and I rose early to see the island first, but Papa was right behind us. It began as a wonderful day, and ended so tragically. Yet I sometimes wonder, if it had not ended that way, whether you and I would have married."

"It was what Cousin Tom seemed to have in mind all along," he said quietly.

"Yes, Papa was always full of plans," she sighed. "Let's get dressed, and go on deck. I want to see Wyndsong!"

"I'm afraid I will have to join you," he teased, "lest you leap overboard in an effort to get there before the ship."

Laughing, they dressed in their elegant London fashions. She refused to bind up her long hair. Her Bavaria pelisse robe was an immensely flattering shade of jade green with gold trim.

"I hope you won't mind if I leave off these magnificent clothes once we are home," he said. "I do not see myself going around Wyndsong in a morning coat, with my cravat tied in some precious fashion like 'Dormant Waterfall.' Mitchum is, I fear, going to become discouraged with me."

"We shall have to give a lot of parties, so we may wear our clothes and please Mitchum and Perky."

"I thought you hated parties," he teased. "It seems to me that I remember a girl who hated parties."

"The girl became a woman," she said.

"Indeed she did," he agreed, admiration in his voice, as he kissed her.

They went up on deck, where the watch bid them a smiling good morning. "See anything yet, Nathan?" asked Jared.

"Oh, we're right atop it, Master Jared. Fog should lift in a few minutes, and you'll see we're smack in the middle of Gardiner's Bay."

"I told you I could smell it," teased Miranda.

"Mama! Papa!" Little Tom, his cat clutched in his arms, came running forward, Perky and Martin behind him. "Are we home, Mama? Are we?"

"Almost, my darling," Miranda smiled at him, and Jared picked the boy and his cat up in his arms so the child could get a good view. "Keep watching, Tom," she said. "The mists will lift in a few minutes, and you'll see your home. Be patient."

Behind them the sun was an iridescent rainbow of color, the sea about them flat and smooth. Then suddenly a small breeze sprang up, and the fog swirled about them, the light wind catching streamers of it, and drawing it away. The sun rose full, now spreading a wash of gold and mauve, rose and scarlet onto the water. The sky turned a bright blue. Ahead of them was the lowing of cattle, the warm smell of earth. Above them a gull hunting his breakfast circled and whirled.

Then suddenly the fog was lifted away by the wind and ahead of them Wyndsong Island rose from the waters of the bay, green and beautiful.

"Look, Mama! Look, Papa!" Little Tom cried, excited. He pointed a chubby finger. "I have come home," the little boy said almost to himself. "I have come home."

Miranda reached out and tucked her hand through Jared's arm. He smiled at her over Tom's head, and while his rapt gaze rested on her beautiful face, she turned toward the island, scanning the coast to make sure that it was everything she remembered. It was. She had come home to Wyndsong.

She lightly brushed the top of Tom's head and, her voice breaking, cried, "Yes, my darling, we have come home!"

Bertrice Small

B ertrice Small, known to her friends as "Sunny" because of her cheerful disposition, is the best-selling author of *Skye O'Malley*. She owns and operates a gift shop, where, between sales, she writes her novels in longhand at a small antique desk.

Sunny lives on eastern Long Island, New York, with her husband and their young son.